Books by Jeremy Hodgson

HISTORICAL ROMANCE

Dance on the Terrace

ADVENTURES IN RESEARCH

Curing Emily

Secret in the seas

ROMANTIC AFRICAN ADVENTURES

Leap of a Lifetime

We are One

EGYPTIAN SAGA

Take me Instead

AERIAL ADVENTURES

Breathe on Me

TARIK

A Science Fiction Adventure

JEREMY HODGSON

ISBN: 978-0-7961-6878-8
e-ISBN: 978-0-7961-6879-5

Jeremy William Hodgson
Villa 99, Tamarina Golf Estate
Black River, Mauritius
90922
jwhodgson42@gmail.com

Structural evaluation by Wesley Thompson
Proofreading by the author
Cover by Nikki Meier
Typesetting and ebook by Liquid Type Publishing Services

For my brother Trevor Jolyon, a forest scientist,
his wife Hazel, and their daughters Amanda and Sally.

Interlude

No human gazed along what resembled an ancient road, paved not with stone but an interwoven mesh of huge branches with the spaces filled with vines and lined on either side with massive tree trunks and overgrown with short saplings and bushes that drooped and looked like they had given up hope of growing, or, at least, only grew when they felt excited. Branches formed a ceiling of intertwined wood and vegetation sixty metres above, letting little light through. It was deathly silent, a silence so intense it would suck in any sound, tear it to shreds, and scatter the bits out of hearing.

But there was an observer, a silipuss, or an excuse for a cat. It had to be an excuse, for it groomed itself between periods of motionless observation, but when it scratched an itchy spot, it did so carefully, with a long, razor-sharp claw on a front paw. Then, it lifted the other forepaw to rub an eyebrow. Cats do that, sitting on their back legs and grooming with the front, but they don't have a tail that reaches behind, finds an anchorage point and wraps around it with the same ease as a Spider Monkey.

It's not an excuse but a wise precaution because cats might always land on their feet, but fifty metres is a long way to fall.

But what was the silipuss observing? And why was it smiling, really smiling, not purring?

Two creatures dancing a ballet were approaching it. One remained stationary, vertical, like the silipuss, its tail and back legs anchoring it solidly. In contrast, it used two forelimbs to gather a thin cord attached to the other creature that danced, with jumps, leaps, gliding and stuttering feet from one side of the roadway to the other, steadily coming closer until the dancer passed the stationary anchor and the cord extended again until it reached its limit.

The dancer then anchored its tail. Their roles reversed; the other began to dance with graceful leaps, short runs and long jumps while the anchored dancer gathered the cord as the other approached.

As the dancing pair passed and disappeared, the silipuss finally stood, turned and vanished. A trick of light? Camouflage? Into another dimension between two trees? Who knows if it had enjoyed the joyous spectacle?

Prologue

Star History Series No: 12689. Journal of Stellar expansion. Edition 324096.

– As agreed at the Interplanetary conference on Old Earth to standardise interplanetary reporting, 2240 Old Earth date. – All dimensions, measures, and times are in Old Earth units.

The first astronomer to spot the planet around the K-type star, named Tarik after the astronomer who discovered it, did so by measuring the star's wobble. He couldn't make sense of his numbers, but he announced that Tarik had a planet and named it Tarik-1.

A thousand years passed, a tiny moment in the life of a planet, and with so many stars in the sky, Tarik received only occasional attention; however, one astronomer did look at it, and an article in *Astronomy* stated.

> The eccentricity of Tarik-1's orbit is due to the proximity of an orbital body, which we believe to be a captured comet due to its reversed orbital direction, named Tarik-1c. This eccentricity results from the perihelion of 1 and 1c occurring every eight months, so the perihelion position rotates with Tarik 1, which remains within the green belt at the perihelion and aphelion.
>
> *Life, if it exists, might be startlingly different.*

The 'Possibility of Life' column in Tarik's entry in the planet catalogue got a big green tick.

Nothing further about Tarik, but a lot more happened, for when astronomers discovered that space curved as Albert Einstein had predicted, high schools taught with models of space that resembled the paper lanterns made with multiple differently shaped curved strips interlocking each other. A team decided to investigate what happened at the intersections.

Eventually, they found that the junctions were always close to a star and that a rocket probe that flew to it could rotate as it arrived at that precise point and, with a minor acceleration in the alternate intersecting space curve, would disappear.

Whether condemned or brave is unrecorded, but the man went, and after a year's travel, he rotated his spaceship and then pressed a return button. The scientists examined his ship's photos. Nothing happened. Except that the star changed from a red giant to a G-type star, and the cosmos of stars changed entirely. It took a *super-super*-supercomputer a month to figure out that the G-type was eight hundred light years away. Travelling huge distances in only a few years of near-lightspeed boredom between intersections became possible.

When the fourth colonised planet, like the other three, became overpopulated and resource-exhausted by the descendants of Earth, the scientists on it took another look at the data collected about Tarik. It wasn't the only planet they studied. After four Exoplanets had filled with humanity, all called Earth by their inhabitants, except the original one now called Old Earth, they needed at least another two. The first, which they named New Egypt, had high UV radiation levels and low gravity, so they passed the data to Exo-Earth-Two, which had similar numbers. Exo Earth four concentrated on Tarik, whose gravity and UV level resembled theirs.

One astronomer's observations excited them; unlike the populated Exo-Earths one to four, Tarik's spectrum indicated substantial amounts of iron in the crust, and the astronomer suggested many other metals. When a multi-world mining conglomerate learnt of this and applied pressure, the scientists sent a probe to Tarik. The probe reported favourably and included photographs of three small moons, photos from space with a powerful telescope, and radar scans from the orbiting probe.

The planet had ice caps that grew and shrank simultaneously in an eight-month cycle. It was sixty-one point six per cent green between the icecaps that accounted for five to eight per cent of the surface, had one small sea of approximately twelve per cent, and an uncountable number of tiny shallow lakes in the forest.

A powerful and confusing magnetic field surrounded Tarik. A scientist who drafted a paper analysing the probes reported magnetic field data stated the only explanation for the oddly fluctuating field was that Tarik's outer shell or crust rotated slower than the core.

> As astronomers believe Tarik-1c is a nickel-iron comet captured by the Tarik system, the repeated close passage of Tarik-1c may provide sufficient drag of the magnetic crust of Tarik 1 to slow it down. It may also explain the verticality of Tarik 1's axis of rotation to the orbital plane. The planet will have only a minor seasonal variation in temperature due to its eccentric orbit.

The radar scans were confusing; the green spectrum showed chlorophyll vegetation, but the radar indicated the underlying ground was one hundred and eighty metres below the green surface. Only one scientist had the imagination to say.

> The scans are accurate if I assume the forest is a primaeval one, then a secondary one that has grown above it, and then a third. The attenuation of the scan signal indicates about fifty to sixty metres for the lowest level, sixty for the second and then fifty for the top.

He added.

> The scans reveal a remarkable lack of features. The highest ground is no more than one hundred and fifty metres above sea level, but the ice caps may be higher. With no valleys, canyons, or hills, the entire planet is a smooth ball. This unique planet, with only one sea in the south, must have rivers that drain from north of the equator to the sea, invisible under the forest canopy except in some photos. Several expansive deltas are visible along the coastlines.
>
> The scan corroborates the photographic images that show balloons in the skies and fixes the altitudes at which they float. They vary widely, and a few are incredibly high.

The first spaceships of scientists and their support crews left to colonise a future home for humanity. With memories of a failed recent expedition to another distant planet, the ten-year plan was extensive: Two hundred and fifty transport spaceships carrying twenty thousand colonists in groups of ten thousand to each of two sites, with successive spaceship departures at monthly intervals to more sites. The previous failed expedition had a secondary effect. Instead of planners from the political class who didn't accompany the expedition due to the imagined consequences of a second failure, they left the task to scientists who would. As a result, the genetically selected colonists were unobtrusively scientists.

The planners ignored non-scientific definitions of gender but insisted the captains and crews be female at birth and sterilised all male colonists to prevent babies during an eight-year between-transition journey. Still, the males could conserve a sperm sample in cryogenic storage. It brought such resistance that the organisers accepted a cryogenic semen-storage jar would accompany each group of ten thousand. Although the plans stated equal numbers of males and females, the females had to be fertile on arrival. With an eight-year journey ahead, they were all between eighteen and twenty-four.

They weren't all scientists; every ship had a carefully chosen mixture of skills, with a few administrators, some engineers, farmers and machine operators. The unpublished intention was mining and colonisation, and the financiers insisted. All were declared genetically clean of inheritable defects and diseases.

Tarik had no satellites to aid messaging between the expedition sites. Still, the first two expeditions launched powered satellites to circle the planet in polar orbit. Sporadic communication would be possible between the colony sites until more became necessary.

The first transporter spaceship matched orbits with Tarik eight years later, then slid slowly to a halt above its north pole.

Star History Series No: 22776. Journal of Stellar expansion. Edition 645956.

After contact with intelligent beings that communicate telepathically, this journal will formally adopt the commonly used verb *theel* for a telepathic message: Noun and past tense *Thelt*.

1

Gordon and Martha Furnival's twelve-year-old son Timothy was packing his shoulder bag in his room on a Saturday morning. A stranger would have judged him to be fourteen, for he was above average height and filling out, and when he looked at someone, the intelligence displayed in his forest green eyes was of a grown man.

Although bigger than the bedroom of other children in the planet's colonies, his was almost identical, with two outside horizontal log walls at right angles and a woven reed panel that separated his room from the living area, with another panel concealing the bathroom. A window in one of the log walls had a yellow gauze screen.

The decorations revealed Timothy was unlike other children. He had covered the longest of the reed panels with plant samples, some fresh, others drying or dried out, all attached with lengths of fibre stripped from vine stems, so although no other child on the planet did the same, what Timothy placed in his bag fitted harmoniously with his physique and decorations.

He carefully packed twelve wooden pegs about thirty centimetres long, tapering from a point to two centimetres in diameter before swelling to a square head in the last centimetres. Three had a hole in their heads. Timothy was an expert at making them in his dad's workshop from a hardwood tough enough to withstand hammering – he had made seven hundred and fifty in the last two years.

Timothy added three more items he had made, each from a thirty-centimetre slice of a tree branch cut three times on his dad's table saw. One lengthwise cut made a flat side and removed a third of the branch. The two other cuts along the length removed a quarter circle from the side opposite the flat. Placed against a wall, it formed a small shelf. Timothy had bored two holes in the thin section between the flat side and the missing quarter, and under the shelf was a third.

Next was a wooden mallet, too heavy for a child his age. It would have surprised an adult who saw him place it in his bag.

The rope packed with a climber's carabiners that came last suggested he would climb something.

The last item, a packet of sandwiches his mother had given him at breakfast, wrapped in green leaves and tied with strands peeled from a wiry vine, was familiar enough, although there was no water bottle. Timothy knew where to find an endless supply.

He was about to lift the bag onto his shoulder when he heard his father talking to someone on the porch. Timothy listened until he recognised the voice of Mr Arvak Dirovic, Colony Nine's administrator. Timothy knew he shouldn't interrupt, so he decided to wait and fetch a glass of his mother's mint water from the kitchen. While drinking it, he could hear them talking. Timothy adored his dad and endlessly asked him about the forest behind their home and the animals there, for his father was a research biologist. Timothy listened, as he always did when his mother or father talked.

Timothy heard Arvak say, 'Gordon, the problem's origins stem from when the first colonists landed here. I'm sure you know why we don't have even-numbered colonies.'

Then his dad replied, 'Yes, Colony Ten landed with us for security. All the even numbers landed where the odd one did.'

'No one considered that the planners chose the sites for ten thousand colonists, with expansion to four times that. They might have imagined multi-story dwellings in a distant future, but we never received machinery allowing such buildings. Twenty thousand landed here, and after the first generation of births, we number a little over forty-three thousand. While half are children living with parents, there's no problem. Those children will want houses as they mature, and we have no space.'

Timothy decided the conversation was not worth listening to and would continue, so he shouldered his bag and walked onto the veranda, 'Excuse me, Dad. Good morning, Mr Dirovic.'

'Yes, Tim.'

'I'm going to add more steps, Dad.'

'Okay, Tim, but can you answer a question first?'

'If I can.'

'What can Mr Dirovic do if colonists want more space to build houses?'

'Why is that a problem?'

Arvak replied, 'It isn't right now, Tim, but I must plan for the future, and within ten years, we'll have no space left.'

'I still don't see a problem. You can lay out a nice extension to the colony along the beach away from the river, roads draining towards the sea, drains far into the sea, trenches for water and electricity when it's needed, give the plots numbers, and then all you need do is tell whoever wants to build a house to choose a plot and do so. They can take the poles from the palisade fence for walls.'

Gordon supported Tim, 'There's your suggestion, Arvak; I was about to say the same.'

'Are you proposing we scrap the palisade fence completely?'

'We don't have one along the beach or river side of the colony. Tim will tell you we don't need one on the forest side. He wanders alone in the forest, as do Martha and I, and we have never come to any harm. If we respect them, none of the beasts will come onto our territory.'

With a young boy's earnest voice, Timothy said, 'Mr Dirovic, you must tell people they mustn't dump rubbish in the forest. That will attract giant boars and worms; they will eat people as part of the rubbish. The rubbish, all sorts, must go to a recycling centre.'

'Thanks, Tim, you can leave. How high up are you now?'

'Thirty-eight metres, Dad. Only twelve more to do.'

Timothy left, and Arvak asked. 'What's he doing?'

'Building a stairway on one of the enormous trees to reach the first forest level.'

'How long will it take him?'

'He's been doing it for two years; another three months should do. I helped him at first. He's careful; if he keeps it up, I'll help him more.'

'You have an unusually determined kid. I wish more of the boys were like him. If you're confident that's a workable solution, how can I convince the committee?'

'They're open forum meetings. Martha and I'll list the people we have met in the forest; it will be extensive. You can pack the meeting with them. I'll bet you'll have their support.'

Timothy undressed and then, nude, climbed his stairway with two safety straps from his belt snapped to the rope handrail as his dad had instructed, and when he reached the highest, he rigged his safety lines. His view over the colony and the sea never failed to inspire him, so he paused to feel the sea breeze on his face and body. It felt to him like gentle caresses as he absorbed the vista. Far out to sea, Timothy could see the snake-like head of a sea monster moving east and several slidagons on the beach until it vanished in the haze. Then he began his day's task: three steps to add.

Gordon was proud of his son and thought he would be a superb biologist. But Gordon was born on Earth Four, and although Timothy's physical development had surprised him, he had yet to learn that the first Tarik-born generation would also differ mentally.

TWENTY-FOUR YEARS AFTER PLANETFALL

Twenty-year-old Jessica Kruger, a cabin attendant working for the GravBus company, woke in the tiny overnight crew room at Colony Nine when the light filtering through the solitary glassless window's yellow-coloured screen lit the room. Jessica recognised the screen as one made by her mother's company. As temperatures on Tarik are constant at twenty-nine degrees centigrade, with only two degrees between day and night, glass is an unnecessary luxury; the screen kept the insects out, for although they didn't bite or sting, their buzzing was a nuisance. Jessica's evolution studies explained why insects had yet to evolve into ones that stung naked humans; however, they did attack clothes. The colonists soon noticed that coloured clothing attracted them and avoided wearing black, red and purple.

The GravBus crews had jammed a mixture of wood fibre and mud into gaps between the unpainted logs for the same reason. For a raging thunderstorm, the shutters outside were the standard window dressing.

The square building under the GravBus landing platform gave a false impression of the available space; most of the log-built building was cargo storage space, with a small office for the booking clerk who came there at fixed hours. The allocated crew living space was a lounge room with a door, two screened glassless windows, and a bedroom on each side. The interwoven reed internal walls, a standard in the early housing, provided sight but not sound privacy. Every time she saw the reed panels, they reminded her of her bedroom in Colony One, where her father had replaced the reeds with the composite boards made by her mother from Tarik plants.

One of the bedrooms had two bunks, a shower, and a washbasin for the pilots. The other had a low bed, shower and basin for the cabin attendant. It seemed odd to Jessica when she first visited one because she expected a shared bathroom. Still, she had learnt that the pilots were all men and equal shareholders in the company, and the cabin attendants were young women who signed three-month contracts. There was a permanent shortage of attendants, for most refused the long hours and irregular overnight stops in the kind of room she was in.

It was her tenth overnight at Colony Nine in the two months she had worked for the company after a brief training period with a skimpy manual. After the initial excitement, the job became routine and boring. She was sure the passengers saw her uniform but not her, but she had to watch for one who became agitated and nervous. During an eight-hour flight, claustrophobia in the windowless capsule could trigger panic. Once, she had ripped the safety strip off her anaesthetic ring and, after gripping the wrist of a passenger headed for the door, had gently spoken calming words and led him back to his seat before he collapsed. None of the other passengers had offered to help.

She had read most of the graffiti on the room's walls, left by the other cabin attendants, although one was new. A stick figure lying on its back and another kneeling between the spread legs of the horizontal figure clearly illustrated what was about to happen; the triangle on the head of the kneeling figure designated it as a captain and a short line as a man. However, the short line curved to indicate a flaccid penis. Jessica smiled; she thought the drawing was the work of Anova, one of the attendants she had met and talked to in the Colony One terminal between flights. Anova had said, 'Jess, this is a boring job; the only cherry on the top is luring one of the pilots into my bed during an overnight, although most of them are not much good.'

She had often thought about the graffiti. Was it the same on her mother's planet? She supposed young women always talked about sex, but her generation on Tarik was surprisingly explicit. She had also been surprised when she peeked into the pilot's room and saw no graffiti; she had thought the men's culture remarkably different.

Feeling depressed, Jessica rose, squatted in the shower and peed. She could do so in Colony Nine and three other colonies, for the water supply was generous enough for her to flush the shower. The toilet at the building's rear meant dressing and a trip outside. She had asked and learnt that the soil, mixed with beach sand, allowed rain to keep the underground water level high. At the other colonies, including hers at Colony One, the soil was cloying clay, with water rationing. Several colonies were building U-shaped catchment barrages to stop rainwater from draining into the forest.

She sat on her bed for several minutes, asking herself why she felt so tired. Her period was due in a day or two, but it never had that much effect. Was it only that she had no idea what to do with her life?

She showered, dressed in her uniform, and walked through the lounge, then continued a hundred metres along the narrow sandy road to the restaurant contracted to feed crews and supply passenger meal packs.

Run by Jorg, the fifty-five-year-old owner, cook and general handyman, supported by his buxom companion and eighteen-year-old daughter, the food was better than most, and his meals were exclusively fish, unavailable except at one other seaside colony – or vegetarian. When Jessica asked, Jorg explained.

'There's a youngster called Piotr who has worked for years with Gordon Furnival catching fish for research. He traps a lot of fish. As Gordon only takes the ones he hasn't seen, the kid has a good business selling fish. If you want to visit where he catches them, one of the children near the beach will show you.'

She had visited when a flight had arrived early one afternoon, seen the half-oval rows of poles that advanced into the sea and back, and talked to Piotr. She realised Jorg must remember him as a kid, but sunburned to a mahogany brown; he was twenty-one, armed with a fishing rod. He told her the poles protected him from slidagons and described the fish he caught.

'Most of them are brackish water fish; they don't like the river because of the massive predators there, and they don't like the sea for the same reason, so in the mixed zone, there are lots of them, Gordon reckons ten different species, although I catch mostly two that like the lures I use.' He showed her a garishly coloured lure. 'You must talk to Gordon to know more about the fish.'

Slidagons interested her; the kids told her about them and offered to show her one, but she didn't have the time the following day. However, she promised herself she would the next time she came.

When she told Jorg they had a full passenger load, he confirmed he had the twenty-nine lunch packs ready for her flight back to Colony One, then served her breakfast. She enjoyed a delicious piece of fried fish with various vegetables that differed from those at her colony. She recognised them as Tarik vegetables but with a much saltier taste.

While eating, she thought of Colony Nine. She liked it. The people were friendly and relaxed, with no signs of pressure or tension. With only a few anachronistic pieces of the palisade on the forest side and the wide-open vista of the beach and sea, there was a feeling of liberty she had never experienced at home. With another month to end her contract, she wondered if she should refuse to renew it and try moving to Colony Nine.

Her initial idea of studying hydrology, stimulated by the water shortage at home, now seemed pointless.

The pilots arrived for breakfast as she finished and joined her at her table, but she stood. 'I must load the lunch packs; I'll see you at the bus.'

Jorg's daughter Juliana carried half the packs as they walked to the bus.

'Juliana, last time you said you were trying to decide what to do after school. Have you decided?'

'Yes, Jess. I talked to Dad and Mum. I'll stay and one day run the restaurant. I'll have to find a man to join me, and I'll have a child or two before I take over.'

'Will finding a man be a problem?'

'Not if I have a business that suits him. Men aren't interested if a girl has nothing, so I can be choosy and find one to work with me.'

'Lucky you. We seem hugely different from our parents; Mother said it was the other way around on Earth Four. I have no idea what I want, certainly not my mother's business in Colony One. I would enjoy living here, but Binky Deepenhout is already running my mother's subsidiary here, and she's only twenty-three.'

'Binky's great. I see her often; she told me she strips naked when fetching plants from the forest.'

'Why would she do that?'

'She says that clothes catch on plants, and she feels free and safe in the nude.'

Hugely different may be an understatement. It's more like an evolutionary mutation.

'Keep looking, Jess. You'll decide one day.'

2

A kilometre from Jessica, now twenty-two, Timothy had woken simultaneously in his parent's log house. He didn't leave his bed; he lay thinking, for he would hear his parents when they rose and his mother when she made breakfast, which she had done all his life. He had time to spare. The room he woke in had been his room from age two, although the bizarre decorations came after his twelfth birthday. He had created a mural on the windowless log wall. At the bottom, he had fixed a collection of dried plants collected from the forest at ground level. At each side and in the centre, a grey panel resembling tree bark represented three massive trees supporting a tangled mess of stems and vines for the first floor. It then repeated for the upper floor, but above it, a mass of greenery shot with violent reds, greens, and yellows terminated in a blue sky that spread onto the ceiling. A carefully painted label on a wooden plaque stating, 'Unknown Territory' hung at the top.

In each of the three sections, a plaque listed animals he had seen at that level; the top one had:

Darters,
Raptors.

The middle section had:

Tarizards,
Squirrels,

Neurotic Pigs,
Silipusses,
Scorpalons,
Worms-hard shell.

The lowest section had:

Giant boars,
Worms-no shell,
Terragons,
Megalons-female,
TeeGulls and EssGulls,
River Monsters.

The other log wall had two small windows and a heteroclite collection of items. The most notable were two dried skins, the first of a tarizard, the Tarik equivalent of a lizard half a metre long. Dried and spread out, it showed the feet with opposed claws and another pair on the prehensile tail. Tim had painted the inside of its gaping mouth to resemble the colours when it was alive. Red, purple and black, like a flower.

The second skin was a squirrel, at least remarkably like one, except the head turned sideways revealed a wicked row of teeth, the fur was short bristles, like a hedgehog, and the feet had opposing claws plus on the front feet a single forward-pointing claw.

The other items were equally odd: The skull of a pig with tusks, then an unusual, curved jawbone packed with small, hooked teeth. Occupying the full height of the wall was a pair of pincers from what could only be a massive crab. On the bathroom screen wall, an enormous poster showing signs of age from stains and tattered edges displayed a picture of a green planet against a black background scattered with stars, and underneath, the words:

Tarik needs you. Call 10785648395 for information.

A week earlier, Timothy had received an invitation to visit the university in Colony One, following an application made a month earlier when he received notification of a first-class biology degree award. He had naturally discussed it at breakfast with his parents, for his father had mentored him throughout his four years of remote study.

'Dad, I have an invitation to interviews at the university, but I'm now reluctant to attend. I can't explain why, but I would rather stay in the forest and continue my research.'

'Tim, that's a natural reaction; attending the interviews isn't a commitment. However, I'll add to that. I said before that you're still young; earning a teaching post at the university and completing a thesis for a doctorate will take only three to four more years. You may feel that you don't need status; no one in the forest has any status besides species, size, and sex. However, if you intend to participate in the life of a colony, status plays an important part in how easy life will be. A doctorate in biology, especially Tarik's biology, is an award that will allow you to speak out, and if managed correctly, people will consult with you. The decision is yours, but attend the interviews.'

Martha asked, 'Tim, is there a girl here?'

'No, mum, as I'm fertile, I stay away from them. I haven't met one who interests me, and none of them has shown any interest; the girls aren't interested in men.'

'Yes, I've noticed that, and the reverse. As a sociologist, I think that's a danger sign.'

'Okay, Dad, I'll confirm the appointment.'

He made a booking and carefully chose his seat.

Timid Tim, as his schoolmates called him, was discreet to an extreme, for he had secrets to hide. He never jumped off a cliff unless he had assessed a minimal chance of a broken leg. He planned. The cliff is a good example; a friend might leap with excitement into the water, Timothy would seek the spot on the clifftop where no protruding branch would skewer him from below, and no rock hidden below the surface would drive his foot above his knee. Nevertheless, his friends noticed Timothy's projects had an uncanny success rate.

His seat decision, after analysis, was based on four criteria. The first was that the two rear seats had the highest survival rate in the case of a crash, and he knew the probability of an event was significant.

The second was that the two missing seats from the last row of four were where a toilet stood, the only refuge for a passenger. For thousands of years, sailors had prized the availability of a port in a storm, and Timothy, known as a boy who loved roaming, must have inherited a sailor's gene. However, thinking of the toilet as a haven in a storm required a stretch of imagination.

The third was because the GravBus had its wings at the back. It gave him a warm feeling to think he sat above the wing, although he knew they were small and only functioned as stabilisers at high altitudes and speeds. The MagLev lift engines underneath in the centre raised the GravBus vertically to operating heights; the thrust engine at the rear was small.

The fourth was for pleasure. Timothy knew cabin attendants didn't spend much of their lives on a GravBus; they might not die, but the stress usually led to a resignation. He had learnt they were young women, for a GravBus was one of the few ways a woman could see a part of the planet. Only, of course, if the captain illegally allowed a cabin attendant to look out the cockpit windows, for there were no other openings. The GravBus used inertial navigation as there were no GPS satellites.

If nothing else, on an eight-hour flight, having someone to talk to rather than trying to nap in an uncomfortable, non-reclining seat was worth much.

Timothy packed his shoulder bag carefully; few people would have considered the items he placed into it as usual. Flat in the bottom was a circular piece of charred material, then he added a sheathed, lethal-looking knife with a thirty-centimetre blade and a tiny roll of heavy fishing line beside it. A flint-and-roller lighter without fuel followed, then his razor, an odd-looking short piece of knife with a thick back on a hand-length handle. The only clothing was a second jockstrap and one pair of socks; he intended to wash his clothes and socks each night. The next item was a club, a ball with a polished handle, unlike any other club. Finally, something extremely odd. Four shiny and sharp hooked claws wrapped in leather. The heaviest item he placed on top was a copy of the thesis he had written for his degree.

After breakfast, Timothy said goodbye to his parents, shouldered his pack and left for the GravBus terminal.

Jessica cleaned the GravBus cabin, crossed the seatbelts, took the trash bag downstairs, and brought up the lunch packs. She marked seat numbers on them, for each passenger had selected his meal from a list – most had chosen the fish, and only two were vegetarian. While doing so, Jessica heard the crew loading freight in the hold between the Maglev vertical lift engines. She fetched her holdall, placed it in a locker, checked the water bottle count, and waited by the door for the passengers to arrive.

Jessica didn't know the GravBus company was unlike anything on Earth Four; it operated on an as-needed principle, an amalgam between charter flights and a country bus service. Because the communications via satellite were slow, the company scheduled a trip once sufficient passengers applied to travel from one colony to another. Before departure from one of the planet's three home terminals, a board indicated the scheduled departures to attract unplanned passengers. The clerk at each colony it would visit wrote the destination, date, and departure time on a similar board. Each GravBus returned to its home terminal after stops at up to three colonies.

The first passenger was a young man she thought looked different from other men she had met. He said his name was Furnival. His intense green eyes captured her attention – *the same green as the forest.* Then she felt uncomfortable. *They're looking; I think they can see inside me.*

She broke eye contact and saw his face: *no softness, rugged, almost computer-drawn from flat planes, older than me, and oddly attractive.*

She looked on her list and said, 'Seat twenty-six, Mr Furnival. That's the aisle seat in the last row. Put your bag under your legs.'

She dutifully smiled at him and returned to greet another passenger, remembering that Timothy's dad must be the biologist researching fish.

Jessica was sure she would spend the flight sitting on the jump seat beside the entry door. Twenty passengers had come from Colony Eleven to the west; they had stopped to collect them the previous day. She thought it unlikely that one of the six from Colony Nine would not show. She was right.

Timothy was disappointed, and the woman sitting beside him, twenty years older, opened a folder of documents and began reading. He leaned back as far as he could and closed his eyes.

Three hours after departure, Jessica's seat, uncomfortable at best, had heightened her depression and was applying pressure that felt like a full bladder. The toilet was vacant, so she walked down the narrow aisle to it and entered. As she came out, she looked at Timothy in the seat opposite the toilet. He had awakened from his light sleep when she locked the toilet door. When he saw she wasn't in her seat, he knew she was in the toilet. He turned to watch her when he heard the door unlock.

Those green eyes are looking at me again.

'Miss, will you tell me your name?'

'Jessica Kruger, I know you're Timothy from the passenger list.'

'Tim, please. Can you talk a moment?'

He's very polite. 'Only a moment. Standing here, I'm blocking the access to the toilet.'

Timothy sensed unhappiness but grinned, 'That's part of my plan; you'll have to sit on my lap so a passenger can pass.'

He's different; Colony One men don't say things like that.

'I'd squash you, Tim.'

'I doubt it, but it would be an experience worth having. How long have you worked on GravBusses?'

'Two months. And before you ask, I studied ecology for two years and then dropped out. This job is a filler. Are you Colony Nine?'

'Yes, I'm visiting the university for interviews. I applied for a job as a lecturer,' he smiled, 'but now I might have another reason to come to Colony One.'

Jessica liked his smile. *It's not lascivious; it's Colony Nine friendly.*

'Then I must tell you I intend to move to Colony Nine.'

Jessica saw the change in his expression and felt triumphant. *That blocked him.*

Surprised, Tim asked, 'Why?'

Jessica frowned. 'Because I'm unhappy in Colony One, I can't decide what I want to do, and Colony Nine is great. I feel free there, and the people are friendly and nice, relaxed.'

'That's nice to hear. What will you do there?'

Jessica smiled, 'Fish with Piotr. I've never fished. I know he catches fish for your dad's research.'

'That's worth doing. It's fun, especially if you catch a big one, but it's boring when you have a long wait between bites.'

A passenger stood and approached them, clearly bent on reaching the toilet.

'Tim, move your legs away; I'll squeeze in to let him pass.'

Timothy did and found an attractive backside in his face. He reached up to her waist and pulled. The last word he had spoken was fresh in his mind as he said, 'Jess, sit before you asphyxiate me, or I bite your bum.'

She did, shocked. *Tim's legs are like wooden poles.*

'There, you didn't squash me.'

'No, but my seat by the door is far more comfortable. Let me up.'

Timothy lifted her into the aisle where she stood. *He's more powerful than he seems.*

'I must return to my seat, Tim.'

'Okay, Jess.'

As she turned and walked away along the narrow aisle, Timothy watched: *Blue-grey blouse and skirt, slim, pear-shaped, nice hips, good shoulders, intelligent, lovely face; No bra under that blouse. I liked her blue eyes, and she sensed my query.*

The woman in the seat next to him said, 'Young man, thank you.'

'Excuse me, Ma'am, what for?'

'I haven't heard a conversation like that since I left Earth Four. It has given me hope for the future. I wish you luck, but this generation of girls doesn't know how to flirt. They're incapable of playing the greatest game of all.'

'Ma'am, may I ask your profession?'

'I'm a historian. Do you know what game I'm referring to?'

'Yes, ma'am, I'm a biologist, and I know that every animal plays the same game in different ways.'

'I'm surprised; what's your name?'

'Timothy Furnival.'

She smiled, 'Gordon's son? Then I understand how you know. I'll try and sleep again.'

Timothy returned to somnolence.

Jessica didn't; she sat trying to understand her feelings, made no progress, and the depression returned. She decided to forget Tim, although he intrigued her.

The GravBus landed gently on the platform at Colony One, and after Jessica opened the door and stepped out of the way, the passengers filed out. Timothy stepped to one side to allow the historian to pass him, and as she did, she smiled slyly at him and said, 'Good luck.'

Jessica stood by the door waiting for the pilots to leave when Timothy exited and stopped. 'Jess, apart from a short interlude, it was a boring trip. I'll stay at the university for a week or ten days. Can we meet one evening for a chat?'

'Why, Tim. So you can bite my bum?'

Timothy laughed, 'Jess, it's too nice for me to do that. I have two reasons. Apart from a name on paper, you're the only person I know here. And I like you.'

'Tim, we're understaffed, and I fly most days and often spend nights away. It might be fun, but I can't make a date as my flight schedule changes daily. I must also decide what to do with my life and whether to sign on for another three months with the company. So no. If you don't come to Colony One, and I move to Nine, we'll meet; if you come here, you can find me at the weaving factory; my mother runs it. So let's put it off until at least one of us decides.'

'Jess, my phone works here; I won't mind a last-minute call; I'll likely be reading in my room as I have nothing else to do. Take my number, and if you have an evening free, call me, and we'll meet in a quiet restaurant.'

'Don't you want a nightclub and music? There are two.'

'No, Jess, I don't like crowds; I want to talk to you.'

'No promises, Tim; where's your phone?'

He took it from a pocket, and she took hers from her bag, placed it on his and pressed a button. Her phone beeped. 'Don't expect me to call, Tim; I'm usually too tired when the bus returns. All I want to do is sleep.'

'Okay, I'll live with my memories of you on my lap until we meet again. Bye, Jess.'

'Bye, Tim.'

He might forget, but I won't; he's the only man who's ever suggested something as rude as biting my bum.

3

Six days later, Jessica woke as the first light filtered through the yellow gauze curtains covering her bedroom window. *I've had those curtains since I can remember; it's about time I changed them.*

Still dissatisfied and her menses over, she didn't know why she felt so lethargic. *It's like being in a room with many identical doors and no labels, and I don't know which one to open. I tried the one that led to ecology and then returned. Without knowing what's behind the doors, I can't choose.* Her bedroom, in a small house near the colony's barricade, was where she grew up. The walls were either the two-centimetre panels made by her mother or a thinner panel lining on the outer log walls. They were off-white, the closest to white her mother could achieve with a natural bleaching agent. The items stuck on the walls, added in chronological order, showed the interests of a growing girl: the early childish sketches that became steadily more sophisticated, the homemade doll and its clothes, the hand-carved hockey sticks, the faded rosettes awarded for sporting achievements, hockey and netball. Life had been interesting; she attended school, played with friends, and helped her mother, who was starting a business as a weaver of cloth and ropes. Although she called him 'Dad' from the day she learnt to talk, Jessica discovered after several years that he was her mother's companion and that she, like all the children, didn't know their fathers, so one of the perennial discussions on possibilities always started when a girl in a group asked, 'Do you think I look like Mister Johnson.'

She knew the sperm bank inseminated volunteer women without revealing the sperm donor name, and the genetic centre that housed the sperm bank sterilised boys over sixteen, so 'Who is my biological dad?' was a permanent question in children's minds. Jessica hadn't failed to notice the man referred to was always one from the upper hierarchies, so she avoided asking that question.

She loved her dad and was sure he adored her. She admired how he helped her mother find fibrous plants for spinning and weaving and how he had bred hybrid plants for food, using the seed the colonists brought from Earth Four and forest plants he selected to give high crop yields of different but edible produce. As the colony had doubled since its founding, the colonists had cleared all the ground around the small dry lake up to the massive trees, and her father's farmland had grown steadily.

Her dissatisfaction began when she finished high school and registered for a degree in evolutionary studies. She had thought lack of exercise was the cause of her discontent. While at school, she had a gym class twice a week. Although the children of all sexes changed in the same spacious room, the naked boys ignored the nude girls, although Jessica thought the girls looked more often. At the university, she had no obligatory gym sessions, and she decided to return to the twice-a-week regime; the changing room atmosphere was identical to her school gym, but it hadn't helped, and her attendance had tailed off to once or twice a month.

While still in bed, she thought, as she had done for two months, *is it the evolutionary studies work I didn't like? Did I make a mistake by dropping out?*

But this time, she added, *or did it start with that first experience of sex?*

She had forgotten the first and had difficulty remembering Ivan-the-second but remembered she had agreed to sex because all the girls at school said they were doing it or had already done it. She also recalled that the experience gave her no pleasure; she had thought Ivan was inept and had never repeated the pointless activity. Something not difficult to avoid at university, for she noted that the young men concentrated on their studies and took little or no interest in girls other than as colleagues who could help with a document. *Was that where my dissatisfaction started?*

There's no point in dwelling on it, although I wish I had enjoyed it. I have a job.

She rose and took a shower with the limited water supply, the colonists' usual wet, soapy cloth wipe, and then a quick rinse. She wore a light blue-grey blouse, a darker blue-grey skirt, black shoes, and five-centimetre heels. For several months, the water shortage for showers had bothered her to the point where she had wondered if she should study hydrology and try to improve the colony's water usage.

She made her bed, two sheets with no other cover, lifted a homemade teddy bear wearing swimming goggles from the floor, placed it between the sheets on the pillow, and spoke. 'There, Goggles, you can look after my room while I'm gone.' Jessica had followed the routine for years, and although

Goggles rarely slept with her, he was there for comfort; she had made him when she had tried, unsuccessfully, to swim in the small school pool and had never tried again as the school emptied the pool to conserve water. His presence had helped, and when she bought her first phone after leaving school, she named the AI in her cellphone Goggles.

Jessica joined her parents in the kitchen, 'Good morning, Mum, good morning, Dad. I'll be back later. I have a flight out, lunch, and then the return.'

After a light fruit breakfast, Jessica slipped on her anaesthetic ring, picked up her bag, and left for the walk to the school and university campus in the colony's centre. The walk had become longer while she grew, winding between vegetable plots and houses, but so had her legs, and it still took half an hour. She had followed the same route for years and had met everyone who lived or worked within hailing distance, so people in the fields or outside the tiny houses waved or called out, 'Hi Jessica' as she passed. When she recognised Hooben Ramgoolam, whom everyone called Ram, she frowned, and when he called a greeting, she replied, 'Hello, Ram, why are you digging in the Pringles farm?'

Ram stopped digging and leant on his spade. 'Because they've left, Jessica, and I've leased his land.'

'Left? Where to?'

'He said northwest of here but didn't say how far. He found a job that he said pays well.'

'That's strange; the GravBus doesn't fly northwest. Did he take his family?'

'His wife and the two boys, too.'

'Won't they miss school?'

'I asked, and he said something strange, "They'll learn more and grow up as men working with me."'

'How old are they? I haven't seen them for some time.'

'I was a guest at the eldest's fifteenth birthday two weeks ago; the other is about two years younger.'

'I suppose we'll see him again one day. I must run. Bye Ram.'

'Bye, Jessica.'

I wonder what Mr Pringle meant when he said that. He must have been unhappy like me, and now he's gone. He might have left with his family to avoid the sterilisation of his son.

The GravBus terminus was next to the campus, and as she walked, she thought of Timothy. She couldn't understand why he kept popping up in her thoughts. *I'll be back early; maybe I'll feel energetic enough to call him.*

Arriving at the terminus, she had things to do. The pre-departure routine differed from Colony Nine only because the meals for all the GravBus departures that day were already in storage boxes at the terminal. She checked the passenger manifest. With only twenty-six seats available, it took only a few minutes. She hardly looked at the names; the meal type and seat number mattered. Each had a specified meal type, and she had to collect the correct meals from the supplier's storage boxes. Each box contained one meal type. She had to mark the lunch pack with a seat number, store them in the bus, and check for neatly crossed belts on the seats, ready for the passengers.

The GravBus returned with Jessica at four pm. At four thirty, after the passengers and crew left, she cleaned the cabin; when she closed the GravBus door and stood looking over the colony at the forest, her depression returned. Standing on the Gravbus platform, the highest point in the colony, she could see the entire panorama except where the Gravbus blocked her view. The surrounding palisade, twenty metres high, seemed insignificant against the background of the forest that soared a hundred and fifty metres into the sky. She turned slowly, saw the packed houses and narrow passages between them, and observed the surges of people moving in both directions. Further away, near the palisade, she could see her home in the corner of a green vegetable patch. When she faced east, alight from the setting sun, the intense bright green of the forest overwhelmed her and brought the thought – *the same colour as Tim's eyes.*

Her thoughts turned inwards. *Should I call Tim?*

She took her phone from her bag and spoke to it. 'Goggles, call Timothy.' *He's probably forgotten me.*

Timothy woke that same day in the University guest lodge. As a qualified biologist who had applied to the university for a teaching post, his status merited a university lodging. Like Jessica, he was unhappy but for distinct reasons. He didn't like Colony One, the university, or the attitude of the academic staff. If asked why, he might have said Colony One gave him a touch of claustrophobia, for there were no limitless open views.

Although conceived in Colony One, his parents had moved to Colony Nine before he was born, for his father, a biologist, believed the sea was the cradle of Tarik's evolution and Colony

Nine was on the seashore.

He had grown up without feeling claustrophobic because his parents had allowed him to roam the forest from the age of ten, and the colony, with a palisade only on the inland side, had expanded along the seashore as the population grew, and after he turned twelve had steadily removed the barrier using the logs for housing.

There was no other reason he could pin down when he had thought about his feelings. Like all the others, Colony One was roughly oval, surrounded by the one-hundred-and-fifty-metre-tall mass of vegetation. He knew all the colonies, except the seaside ones, were similar. Now visible as the colonists had cleared the brush and shorter trees before them, the most impressive trees were the massive fifty-metre-high base trees five to eight metres in diameter, with the upper levels shrouded in vegetation. Further expansion was an enormous task as the planned heavy machinery had never arrived. Forty thousand citizens packed the area, not in multi-level apartment blocks, but in tiny wooden houses that reminded him of the Medieval cities of Old Earth he had seen in pictures. Surrounding this were the farmlands. Timothy thought the University, now crammed in the centre, might bring on claustrophobia.

Timothy never mentioned his sensory problems because he knew others would not understand. The smells bothered him; used to the natural odours of the forest, the smells generated by packed humanity disgusted him.

He could also sense the swirl of thoughts and feelings of packed crowds; he preferred solitude or no more than one or two people generating thoughts that confused him.

It was one of the reasons he never returned to the gym after fourteen. The other was the fear of an erection when he saw the naked girls in the changing room. He consoled himself with the thought that he had enough exercise in the forest and only realised years later that it was far more than enough.

He felt the people made it worse. He sensed many negative thoughts and feelings; Colony Nine was happy, possibly because it had spread. However, Colony One seemed desperate, with people, including the university teaching staff, holding on to the past to avoid facing the future.

A future he was unsure would come.

On arrival in Colony One, the university had handed him a document labelled 'University Rules of Conduct', and one of the rules warned against going beyond the barrier wall alone. Yet, he had been doing so for twelve years. It also said women required a permit to do so, something he had never imagined possible. It generated an odd feeling that teaching biology was unimportant and there were more important things to do to ensure the colonists' survival. He did wonder if it was due to the poster in his bedroom that stated, 'Tarik needs you.'

He had interviewed three professors that day, and not one had asked to see his thesis. From their questions, he was sure they hadn't read more than the summary. After lunch at the canteen, he visited the library to study the 'Life of Known Worlds' catalogue in the university electronic library, searching for something with six legs that resembled the beast he called a 'Giant boar'. There were hundreds of six-legged entries, but he whittled it down to ninety-five by refining the search using estimated size. He was reading number forty-three when his phone buzzed.

He took it from his pocket, saw it was Jess, and whispered, 'Puss, tell her to wait two minutes and why.' Then he stood, shouldered his bag, and left the library.

'Hello Jess, you've just saved my sanity.'

'Why.'

'I hope you've called to accept dinner with me. I'll tell you then.'

He's dangling a carrot, and I'm the donkey. He wants me to meet him!

'Okay, Tim, I can make it at six thirty. Ask for the "Forest Barbecue".'

'Bye, Jess, don't dress up; I've only the clothes I'm wearing. See you there.'

Jessica hurried home to shower and change; with a half-hour walk each way, she had only minutes to shower.

4

Timothy arrived ten minutes early at the restaurant to look around and choose a table. Erected on a raised plinth of mud bricks and rammed clay, which Timothy estimated at half a metre high and fifteen metres by ten, the building covered only five of the fifteen metres; one side was open, and a thin reed sunroof covered the rest where tables and chairs waited for the evening patrons. The kitchen and a bar with stools filled the log building, and as Timothy approached, he saw two brick barbecues with rotating spits. He deviated to check what was grilling and found only Earth Four chickens and pigs, the kind the colonists had brought to Tarik. To Timothy, the name 'Forest Barbecue' on a banner above the building was a lie.

When Timothy mounted the steps to the dining area, he saw a long table between the kitchen and the patrons' tables on which two women were placing plates of various salads. A quick inspection revealed the salads, if not pure Tarik, were at least hybrids. The notice beside it didn't surprise Timothy.

Welcome: One Price, one person, one meal, eat all you want buffet.

'Good evening, I'm Gershwin. Can I help?'

'Good evening. I have a guest for dinner, and we'd like a quiet table for two.'

'Then I'll put you on an outside corner. Follow me...

'When you want drinks, wave. Eat when you want to.'

Timothy sat and looked around. Still nearly empty, he was sure the clients in view were from the university.

Timothy and Jessica saw each other when she was fifty metres away. He watched and admired her free striding walk. *She must walk often*. He stood as she arrived.

Jessica watched him as she approached. *He's looking again. I'll ask why.*

As she slipped into a chair and he sat, she said, 'I felt like a biological sample moments ago. What did you see.'

Timothy grinned, 'Sorry Jess, I can't help it. I think you're beautiful, but the way you walk entranced me.'

Unusually flattering but ambiguous. 'So what weird or injured animal do I walk like?'

His unexpected reply stumped her.

'One like Jessica, who can't control a body that wants to walk free and possess the world around her.'

That confirms it. There's no man in Colony One like him. What do I say?

Sensing she needed a pause, Timothy asked, 'What would you like to drink?'

Relieved, she replied, 'They have a Tarik root beer; Gershwin is the brewer. Non-alcoholic. Try it, and I'll have one, too.'

Timothy waved, then ordered.

Jessica avoided his earlier remark and asked, 'Now, tell me how I saved your sanity.'

Her expression of authority without a 'please', 'if you don't mind' or 'can you' was not unusual; men, being sterile, had lost one of the factors that gave them power over women and free of the necessity for a man to have children, the women had become far more authoritative. Furthermore, the GravBus company prized cabin attendants who could deal firmly with fractious passengers. Timothy had noted the metallic band on her middle finger during their first trip; an extended argument with a claustrophobe who wanted to exit the GravBus at high altitude was the last thing the crew wished to deal with.

Timothy had experienced such behaviour and knew it was not rudeness, so he complied.

'If you studied ecology, you must have looked at the "Life of Known Worlds" catalogue. I was searching through it for something that resembled our native giant boar. After filtering, I had ninety-five entries to read. I was reading number forty-three and was feeling like a boar when you phoned. Much longer, and I would have grunted.'

Jessica laughed; their beers came. Timothy tasted his and said it was good, then Jessica asked, 'Will you tell me why you were studying that?'

'I will if you insist, but I'd rather you told me why you called me.'

'It's silly, Tim. I can't explain it.'

'Then don't explain, just tell me, and I'll guess.'

He'll guess wrong, but how wrong will be interesting.

She told him about looking at the colony from the Gravbus landing and how the green of the trees reminded her of Tim's eyes. Then added. 'I don't know why, but that's when I called.'

Timothy thought momentarily, then asked, 'Jess, can you look into my eyes without turning away?'

'Why, Tim?'

'So I can check something to help me guess.'

'Okay.'

Timothy held her gaze for two minutes; he could sense her indecision, depression, confusion, and then fear, so he *thelt* each feeling slowly. To him, it was a mental caress, like hugging a child physically – *Calm…Relax …Lovely…Delightful… Brilliant…Relax ….*

Jessica, her eyes fixed on his, first thought they were even greener. Then she thought, *they're looking inside me again, not at me*; she wanted to turn away but forced herself to keep her gaze fixed on his eyes. *I wonder what they can see inside me.* Tendrils of fear raised a thought. *I hope he can't learn that I pee in the shower.*

Timothy sensed her effort not to break off, so he repeated his *thelt* feeling chain.

Jessica's fear vanished, and then, wonderingly, she thought, *He thinks I'm marvellous.* Then she relaxed, and a feeling of languor invaded her as Timothy smiled and spoke. 'Let's eat, Jess. I'll tell you my guess while we eat.'

'Okay, if you answer one question. Were you hypnotising me?'

'No, Jess, not even trying. I've never hypnotised anyone.'

They moved to the buffet, and Jessica noted that Timothy didn't serve himself any barbecued meat. 'Tim, are you vegetarian?'

'No, Jess. But I'm not used to Earth Four chicken and pork. I find it tasteless. These vegetables are Tarik grown, and I like them.'

'But the chicken and pork are the only meat we have.'

'Yes, here, but you know we have fish in Colony Nine. There are also food animals in the forest.'

'You must tell me about them. If you've loaded your plate, let's eat. I want to hear your guess.'

After the first three mouthfuls, Tim put down his utensils and said, 'Your walk gave me my first clue, Jess. You want to run and jump; you're full of energy that you're fighting to keep from bursting out. You didn't call me because my eyes are green, although that might have reminded you, but when you were up there on the GravBus platform, you felt hemmed in by the palisade and remembered Colony Nine, where we aren't enclosed. I know girls in this colony need permits to enter the forest; have you been into it?'

He continued eating.

'Yes, Tim. Years ago, permits for women were unnecessary, as there were no children, and my parents had permits because my father collects live plants for hybridisation or cultivation. My mother collects vines for their fibres. I've been with them in the forest since I was two. I know all the plants and vines they collect.'

Fantastic! I need to know more.

'Only on the ground level?'

'I don't know anyone who climbs up; I often wish I could; it would make vine collecting much easier.'

'Explain that, please.'

'You'd laugh if you saw us. When there's a tree with several vines growing up it, they curl around the tree, and we must unwind them to extract long fibres for ropes. The vines also cross over each other, so Mum, Dad, and I take a vine each and walk round and round the tree, pulling our vines down and winding inside or outside the other as we cross. It's like the Maypole country dances we saw in school history lessons.

'If I could climb up and cut the vines up high, we could pull them down easily.'

'Have you seen any of the animals?'

'No, we stayed close to the barrier when I was little, and then I was in school and didn't accompany my parents except on weekends or holidays. Dad told us he had seen a giant boar once and a monster worm. He said he ran away.'

'That's sensible; they don't bother with people that run away.'

'So what's your guess?'

Tim finished his last mouthful.

'You can't decide on your future because you haven't learnt what's outside this closed microcosm, and you're confused by conflicting information. You don't believe it's dangerous in the forest, yet the authorities say it is. You like the vistas of my colony, yet here you're locked into a life imported from Earth Four and feel the wrongness.'

'What's the wrongness?'

'We should be a true pioneer society, with virtually no administration, yet we aren't. We pay administrators to make rules we feel are wrong.'

'So what should I do?'

'Move to Colony Nine until you decide; my Mum would welcome you, and then you would have alternatives.'

'I suppose I could once my contract ends. How about you, Tim?'

'I've two more days of interviews; then I'm returning home. I must tell you two things: first, I don't feel I can live here, and second, I'm doing biological research, so if you're in colony nine, I'll bug you for a fish dinner at Jorg's place when I'm not in the forest.'

He's friendly and different but not so different from the others. He thinks I'm lovely but isn't interested in girls – like the others.

'Tim, I have a flight tomorrow, and I must sleep. Thanks for dinner, and I hope we'll meet again.'

Two days later, Jessica joined her parents for breakfast.

'Dad, Mum, I won't be back tonight. I have an overnight in Colony Nine.'

'How far is Colony Nine? You seem to visit there frequently.'

'Not that often. I looked it up, Dad. It's a little over six thousand kilometres, an eight-to nine-hour flight.'

'Jess,' asked her mother, 'have you met any interesting people?'

'I told you, Mum, during the flight, everyone snoozes or reads, and when we arrive, I'm too busy to make friends. On the last flight from Colony Nine, I met a guy who talked to me. He took me to dinner two nights ago. I might meet him again one day.'

Tim said he might bite my bum. Why can't I forget that?

After eating some fruit, she packed her overnight bag. She had done it many times and knew what she needed; although all the flights to the nearer colonies were out and a return in the day, half her flights had an overnight stop before returning, and a few had two or more.

The GravBus terminus was next to the campus, and as she walked, she thought of her job; Jessica had to renew her contract in two weeks or look for a different job. She had naturally talked to the other attendants before and after signing her contract. They had told her that only a few renewed and that after a GravBus crashed, most of the attendants didn't continue. Some had complained that the pilots sometimes expected sex, using a visit to the cockpit to look out the window as bait. Fortunately, her pilots hadn't asked, and after the first time looking over the endless unchanging green surface of Tarik from a high altitude, she had no desire to view it again.

Arriving at the terminus, Jessica completed the pre-departure chores, and then the captain and co-pilot arrived and entered the cockpit. Jessica opened a fruit juice and sipped it while waiting for the passengers. The attendant for the following GravBus in the row stopped to say hello. 'Hi Jess, I hear you have an admirer.'

'That's news to me; where did you hear that?'

'Anova told me a passenger called to ask if you were on today's flight.'

'How would she know?'

'She's sleeping with the booking clerk and says he's pretty good.'

Maybe Tim is on the flight; how could I have missed his name?

'I'll check to see if there's anyone I know on the list. Have a good flight, Savannah.'

Tim's name is here. Seat twenty-five, he must have planned his return flight because of me.

It pushed her depression back. Then she moved the passenger from the seat next to Tim forward two rows. *We can at least talk.*

Timothy rose according to his planned schedule; he had to shower and dress, visit the canteen for breakfast, and pack his small rucksack; there were no clothes; he had lived naked in the forest as a child and had accepted a jockstrap at puberty. He remembered that first time.

His father gave it to him when he left the house one day.

'Tim, your mother found your clothes below the tree with your ladder. What do you wear up there?'

'Nothing, Dad. Clothes catch on stuff.'

'Then here's a jockstrap; I think it'll fit and stop your equipment catching on *stuff*.'

During breakfast, he reflected on the meeting he had attended the previous evening.

Gregor Popov, one of the geneticists at the university, had contacted Timothy and invited him to dinner because Timothy's father had messaged him about Tim's arrival. Timothy had accepted. When he reached Gregor's house, he discovered he wasn't the only invitee; there were two other scientists, one a plant geneticist and the other a specialist in evolutionary genetics.

Gregor introduced them and said, 'We meet regularly to discuss our research, and I thought you might find it interesting to join our meeting; if the university employs you, it's the kind of meeting you'll frequently have.'

'What's the topic?'

'It varies, but we're currently discussing which genetic strains in the colonists will likely die out.'

Timothy listened and found it weird that people could dispassionately discuss a problem that would affect the colony's future and do no more than blame the original colony planners without proposing solutions.

He asked, 'If I understand correctly, you say the planners selected colonists for jobs that should exist but don't because the ships carrying the heavy equipment never arrived, and now there are men who cannot do the work they qualified for.'

Gregor replied. 'Exactly, and with only manual labour in the fields as an alternative, we have never imagined crime levels and an inexistent police force.'

'We don't have that problem in Colony Nine. We have no palisade between the colony and the forest, and I guess the people you refer to have found things to do there.'

The specialist in evolutionary genetics, startled and incredulous, said, 'You don't have a barrier?'

'We did once, but our men dismantled it to build houses. Once the colony expanded along the seashore, they didn't extend it. My dad convinced the administration that there was no danger and they had better things to do.'

'What do you mean, no danger? What about those massive beasts in there?'

'They have a survival instinct very different from ours; they avoid us and never attack unless challenged, so they're no danger to the prudent.'

'Including women and children?'

'Very much so; I've roamed the forest alone since I turned ten.'

Gregor, the geneticist, remarked, 'Convincing this administration to allow that is impossible now. We must wait to see if the genetic makeup of the next generation is the same.'

It reminded Timothy of something his father had said, so he said nothing, for his father had said, 'I suspect.'

The last reason for his dissatisfaction was a reaction to his university interview questions the previous day. He had sensed a lack of interest in the biology of Tarik and enslavement to the dogma of the Earth Four textbooks. He decided. *I shall discuss this with Dad.*

The GravBus terminal was next door for his flight home. Timothy shouldered his pack and left.

5

Jessica recognised Timothy as he approached and smiled; 'This is a welcome surprise, Tim. Yours is the rear seat beside the wall. Put your bag under your legs.'

'Thanks, Jess. Who's next to me?'

'I hope it will be me; I've planned it that way.'

'Touché. I booked this flight because you're on it.'

He's not only polite; he's honest.

The captain ordered the door closed. Jessica complied, checked the passengers' safety belts, and then came to sit beside Timothy.

An observant passenger might think they were a remarkable pair, but on Tarik, due to gene selection, the children had similar characteristics; both were shorter than their genes would have dictated on Exo Earth Four, although they were still growing. Timothy was a metre eighty-eight, and she a metre eighty-two. Tarik's slightly higher gravity caused them to grow slightly slower, making their bones more robust. Timothy's pale green loose-fitting shirt and trousers hid unusual muscular development. Jessica had small breasts, one of the genetic criteria for selecting the women to hyperjump on the voyage to Tarik. High gee forces can play havoc with chest muscles. Timothy had light gold hair with green eyes, Jessica was red-tinted platinum with blue eyes, and both had hair to their ears and no further. With water rationed, men often shaved their heads, and women cut their hair short. Her skin was pale, and his light tan, either genetic inheritance, sunshine, or both. The incidence of red or reddish hair, a genetic variation coupled with sun-sensitive skin, was high amongst the colonists.

They chatted continuously for the first half of the flight.

Jessica began by asking an innocuous question.

'Are you returning home?'

'Yes, Jess. The way I feel, I won't be coming to Colony One.'

'Why?'

'You know, Jess, you told me last week. My colony is a much nicer place to live, but mostly because of the attitude of the professors who interviewed me.'

'What did they say?'

'It's not what they said, it's what they didn't say. They were uninterested in Tarik's biology, and I felt sure they'd never seen Tarik's animals except in photos and only knew what they'd heard from other colonists.'

'That sounds familiar, Tim; I've completed two years of evolution studies. As we know little of Tarik's evolution, everything was the history of the other Earths. I decided to change courses as what I learnt seemed unnecessary, so I'm considering hydrology. I'm still young enough to change at twenty. I took a short contract with the GravBus company to see part of the planet while I decided.'

'Have you decided?'

'No, Tim, and I wish I knew why. Have you ever played "What is My Future?"'

'The game where you have to pick a fortune teller card off one of six piles when you throw a six with the dice?'

'Yes.'

'No, never. I've always wanted to study Tarik's biology. Why do you ask?'

'Because I feel I should choose a card, but without any idea what it will say, I'm scared. Are you still sure of what you want to do?'

'Yes and no, Jess, the biology, yes, but teaching, no, I've tried for weeks to figure it out. I touched on it during our dinner, but after the last two days of interviews, I'm beginning to see a picture. It's a generational problem. Our parents came here as adults and brought Earth-Four knowledge, attitudes and motivations. After landing, they had no choice but to be pioneers and build a new life on Tarik, but they've done so from the base they brought with them. The colonies are duplicates of their life on Earth Four, but that life evolved on an overcrowded planet. The Tarik-born children feel the restricted life in the colonies is frustrating and want something different, but we have yet to work out what Tarik wants us to do.'

'That's a funny way to say it, like Tarik will tell us, but you're the first person to tell me that; I don't feel so alone. I guess that's why Binky Deepenhout strips naked when she collects forest plants.'

'I didn't know she did. Good for her. Will you renew your contract?'

'I might do if I can't decide to do something else. The company pays well, and getting the job is easy because most girls fear the forest. All I've seen so far is green treetops and colonies like my one, yours excepted.'

'I don't understand why you say girls fear the forest; they don't in my colony. Binky is a good example. I must ask her if she strips to feel part of the forest; she may not be the only one.'

'The girls in six of the seven colonies I've visited are fearful due to the colony's leaders, yours excepted. I'm sure they think that women who can bear children need protection as they're the key to survival, so they try to frighten us. The older women do visit the forest. It may be what you said, Earth Four attitudes.'

'I know what you feel about your ecology studies. At my interviews, I suspected I knew far more than the academics interviewing me. Like you, I'm unsure. I like teaching and research, but I doubt the professors will allow me to deviate from the current course material. Spending three or four years repeating the same lectures about biology on Earth Four to students whose only interest is to pass an exam and receive a certificate turns me off. I'll discuss it with my parents, who are scientists.'

Jessica's mind made the connection. 'Your name's Furnival. Is your mother Martha?'

Surprised, Timothy asked, 'Yes, do you know her?'

'It would be surprising if I didn't; I reckon every woman on the planet knows her name.'

'Because of the Martha Furnival test for fertility?'

'Yes. Now I must serve lunch; you can tell me how your mother discovered it when I return.'

After distributing the lunch packs, she returned to sit with him, and they ate slowly and wasted nothing, a social trait due to scarcity. Then Jessica ordered. 'Now tell me about your mother.'

'Mum was Martha Gerontsky. She was in the first shuttle to land on Tarik. She told me about it and what she did. There were two hundred and fifty others, but Mum, a sociologist, had a commission from the expedition planners. She had a report to write for them that she would send with the third expedition spaceship when it returned. She had no designated tasks after landing, only orders to observe the colonists' behaviour for three months.

'She said they landed as planned beside the small lake that's now the centre of Colony One, surrounded by an area that indicated the lake had once been far more extensive. A narrow, bare beach revealed the extent of the lake in the wet season, and then the vegetation, some low bushes and then young trees grew denser and taller with increasing distance from the lake until they blended with the primaeval trees.

'The area is much bigger now that people have cleared and cut the young trees. The big ones are a massive task to remove.

'She told me she walked around, observed and noted that the planners had done well, for the wooden buildings appeared where planned, the scientists set up their laboratories, and the farmers began turning soil for crops.

'And then Colony Two grew on the lake's opposite side. That was unplanned; she said it should have been on the opposite side of the planet. For thirty days, the four shuttles brought equipment and people daily. Then, instead of building their houses around the central buildings in serried rows, the colonists constructed log cabins between the two colonies. Within another month, it became one colony with two administrations and the university between them.'

'That's new to me, although it's like that, except the administrations have merged. Did your mum say why?'

'Yes, she said it was typical political behaviour. When the day finally came to land, the two leaders were too scared and had no one to blame for failure, so they changed the plan to be close to each other. The colonists felt that between the first buildings to house the administrators was safer, and the scientists wanted to be central. The same happened at all the sites, so we have odd-numbered colonies and no even ones.

'As a result, they screwed up the plans, and now your colony has a problem, although mine doesn't.'

'I guess she's correct, and you'll have to explain why it screwed up the plans, but continue with your mother.'

'Well, Mum learnt she had no job when she finished her report, although she had another report to write after a year. She composed it, but no ships came after that first year, and she couldn't send it. The colony didn't need a sociologist. She decided to be a schoolteacher, for she worked out the skewed demographics. Most of the women had visited the sperm bank centre and were pregnant by then, and a massive birth bubble was due in nine months.

'She had time to study the planet's creatures and teach behaviour. She dispatched her report on time; the summary is interesting, but the reams of statistics are not.'

'What's the summary say?'

'Is your phone on?'

'No, there's no signal outside a colony or inside a GravBus. During my training, the instructor said I must tell worried passengers that the shell they're in is a composite that contains an iron-alloy powder to deflect the MagLev generator's magnetic field around us. It also deflects all radio signals, so the pilots are in front of the shell in the nose where their radio can receive.'

'I have Mum's report on mine, and you can read it.'

Jessica did.

Although relationships developed on board the expedition spaceships with sterilised males, no children were born. Nudity on board lost its social stigma, as it does on such voyages in a closed, constant-temperature community, with body paint replacing clothes at social activities. Total nudity became common. Strangely, with the knowledge that no male was fertile, the sex drive of women diminished. It appears that knowing they could not father a child had the same effect on males; courting and aggressive interactions between men and women became rare, although transactional sexual activity reduced but did not cease. In the three months since landing, eighty-one per cent of the women have applied for randomly selected insemination from gene-matched spermatozoa without revealing the source. As, before departure, the genes of all colonists were clear of genetic defects, the population of Tarik should be healthy.

Although the plans required the first spaceship to settle two colonies, the fear of the unknown and comfort in numbers led to one settlement of twenty thousand; the other expeditions that arrived did the same.

The people have agreed to sterilise all male children reaching the age of sixteen after collecting a sperm sample, a practice that may ensure the overpopulation of Tarik does not occur.

A side effect is the almost total disappearance of gender-related crimes, punished if they occur by banishment from the colonies, for they refuse to support anti-social members. Inevitably, isolation leads to a quick death.

Note: The above is a personal observation; no statistical data from Earth Four is available for comparison, and the cause may not be male sterilisation but the genetic selection criteria of the colonists. A study comparing a similar genetic sample on Earth Four might assist in future colony selections.

'Well, that explains a lot, although, to me, she has one bit wrong. You must still tell me how she discovered the fertility test. But I must leak.' She stood and entered the toilet.

Timothy gave her sufficient time and then stood and shouldered his small backpack, a strange thing to do when visiting the toilet, but it never left his side. He stepped into the aisle to block other passengers from reaching the toilet and waited for Jessica.

He heard two sounds simultaneously – the clack of the lock as Jessica unlocked the toilet door and a high-pitched whistle. Timothy reacted instantly as the toilet door folded inwards. He stepped forward, pushed Jessica in, said, 'Sit on the floor,' then closed and locked the door before sitting himself and pulling a bewildered Jessica down beside him.

She protested, 'Wha...'

She didn't finish her question because of a terrifying explosion, and the toilet spun and tumbled. The light failed. Timothy had braced his legs against the commode, and when he felt Jessica, weightless, floating from the floor, he pulled her down and held her. Fifteen seconds later, the tumbling stopped, and the weak red emergency light above the mirror came on, leaving only the sound of air hissing as it leaked through cracks in the door hinges. Timothy reached out, grabbed the entire pack of paper towels and quickly spread them over the leaks where air pressure held them. Ten seconds later, he had only one minor hissing leak to find.

As he blocked that, at first bewildered, Jessica began to feel terrified and opened her mouth to speak. Timothy whispered,

'Don't talk, don't move, breathe slowly.' It terrified her further, so she said nothing, shut her eyes and buried her face in his chest. With a knot in his stomach, Timothy clutched Jessica for comfort as he sensed the GravBus's sickly swaying and swooping that slowed its fall. *Some wings remain – Wait.* He focused intently on his paper towels to shut out his fear. When they blew off the door as the leak reversed – *four thousand metres* – he whispered urgently, 'Feet against the commode, back straight against the wall, arms against the basin, brace yourself, and don't make a sound.'

Timothy held his breath as he felt the GravBus plunge into the leafy forest canopy with an explosion of shrieking and banging sounds, jolting and jerking; he knew the upper forest contained fifty metres of cushioning material and sensed the impact was violent but angled. His heart raced, and he silently prayed the GravBus would miss a massive tree trunk and that the cracking and screeching ear-shattering noise was from breaking branches, not a disintegrating GravBus. It didn't hit a tree before striking the upper forest floor. Then he thought the wings, or a part of them, tore off as a loud screeching sound and sudden deceleration forced him and Jess against the commode until the GravBus broke through to fall nearly sixty metres to the middle-level floor, fortunately carrying with it a massive bundle of interwoven roots and branches that cushioned the final impact.

Silence fell, and then Timothy breathed again and strained his ears.

6

Half an hour later, Timothy spoke, 'Jess, it's left. Let's leave this toilet. Fortunately, it's the right way up, and we haven't drowned in shit.'

'What's gone?'

'The megalon that hit us.'

Trying to avoid the situation, Jessica asked an irrelevant question. 'I've seen them in the sky; what are they like?'

'I'll tell you later; we've more important things to do now.'

He cracked the door open, and then it jammed.

'Jess, change places with me; I want to remove the lid from the toilet.'

When he wrenched the cover sideways, he ripped off one of the hinges and then had to manoeuvre the seat into a position where he could break the other. He couldn't see what he was doing in the weak red light; the hinge was in shadow. It seemed impossible until Jessica said, 'I can't wear these shoes with heels; they might help. I think there's a spike inside the heel.'

The shoe worked as a fulcrum, although the heel broke off as the seat snapped loose. Then Timothy wedged the rounded seat end into the door crack and levered. It opened with a tormented squeal five centimetres more, and then, with Jessica holding her other shoe between the seat cover and the wall, Timothy forced it further centimetre by centimetre until, after three more tries, the door sprang open with an agonised shriek.

'Let me look first, Jess.'

Beyond three rows of seats, including his row, there was no GravBus.

Timothy stepped forward for a better view. In the second last row, three men, still strapped in, were dead; blood and something gooey had run from their nostrils – *explosive decompression. The toilet saved us.* The unbuckled seatbelts of the fourth seat signalled the occupant had flown on alone. The row ahead of that had one body, a small woman. Timothy thought her mass was insufficient to break the seat belt, but the other seats had unbuckled belts. Beyond that row of seats, the missing front part of the GravBus allowed a view of the forest's middle terrace, silent and dimly lit with struggling plants between massive tree trunks scattered ahead of him until a hundred metres ahead, he could see no further.

His thought was odd. *We're in the shit, but we're alive and at least I'm home.*

While Timothy silently absorbed the view, his heartbeat slowed, and adrenaline dropped while he thought about what to do next. Then Jessica reminded Timothy of her presence. 'Tim, how about letting me out?'

He backed to the toilet, 'Sorry, Jess. Are you okay? We have work to do.'

As she came out, he put his arm around her, and when she saw the gloomy forest and the bodies, she began to tremble but clamped her jaw shut and put her hand over her mouth. Timothy held her tight for two minutes until the trembling stopped, and she again buried her face in his shoulder. Another minute passed, and then she surprised him, muffled by his shoulder, 'This isn't in the GravBus training manual. How long must we wait for rescue?'

'The emergency beacon was in the cockpit; now it's somewhere else or in a megalon's stomach. It doesn't matter because we're five times further away from a colony than a drone's range. So, rescue is impossible.'

He released her, and she looked again at the remaining seats and the bodies.

'I'm supposed to look after the passengers, but only we are alive, and I've no idea what to do. Do you know?'

'Yes, Jess.'

'So we won't die?'

Timothy hesitated. *She needs reassurance.*

'Jess, I don't understand why you might think that; we've been lucky and have landed in the safest place on the planet.'

'Tim, are you alright? Have you hit your head on something?'

'Not that I remember.'

'If you hit your head, you might not remember. But explain why it's safe.'

'Jess, do you think the colony is safe? Can you walk around at any time in any place without fear?'

'You know you can't, but I avoid those places and any people that I feel are dangerous.'

'There are only a few animals to avoid here, and none will attack you if you move away. It's far safer than the colony.'

'Right, I accept that you think that, but what about food? I can't see much to eat.'

'Jess, I've lived in the forest for years and know the rules for survival. I can teach you. Like all the animals here, as a male, I must look out for myself and any females or children, human or otherwise. If I fail, I might die, but you won't. You're a female; the animals here are intelligent and will bring you food.'

There are two things I don't understand in what he said.

'Tim, that's the weirdest thing I ever heard. I should check your head. I suppose you'll say they talk.'

At least with lots to think about, she's fighting her fear by being aggressive.

'At least one species does; they're telepathic. I'm a poor telepath, but I'm improving and managing with one species; I'm sure there are others, but I haven't had the chance to talk to them. Approaching them is difficult; they flee. You'll learn it's true, Jess, but it won't be easy. Survival never is. I'll take you to my home, but it will take planning and time. But first, we must dispose of these bodies before they begin to rot.'

'How?'

'We search them for anything useful; then I'll find a hole in the terrace floor in front of us and tip them through it. It's fifty metres to the ground.'

'I've never touched a dead body.'

'Jess, there will be many things you've never done before. I can walk away in the next five minutes and travel eight to ten kilometres each day. I must stay for you, but if you don't do your share, we won't survive.'

'Why? The men I know would walk away.'

Would they? I must ask later. 'It's the forest rules. If you don't believe me, put it down to the need to help each other, or something might kill us. That's another rule. Help each other.'

He didn't say because he wanted to; his rules might be a better reason, but I know he's staying. 'Okay, I'll try.' *I must; I don't have a choice. But I'll sort out this telepathy stuff.*

'Tim, we're short a word. "*Think*" is something in your head; what's a telepathic message?'

It must be shock. Jess jumps from one thing to another!

'Jess, now you're having fantasies.'

'No, just practical. How about *theel*?'

'I guess that would do, we think to ourselves and *theel* a telepathic message.'

'Okay, the past tense and noun are *thelt*.'

Funny, I never thought of giving a name to a telepathic message. For some reason, theel *seems right.*

'Right, do we have the survival pack, and how much food do we have?'

'We have eight remaining; they're in a locker behind our seats. The safety kit is in the one next to the wall.'

'Wonderful; it gives us four days before I must hunt. Now I'll fetch the rope from the survival stuff; there's usually a hundred and twenty metres. You search the bodies; don't look at their faces. Remove belts from the men if they have them. Do the front-row person first. If there's any ID, keep it. Put anything you find on our seats.'

The manual doesn't mention what to do with dead passengers. I guess the company doesn't want to mention crashes.

His detailed instructions steadied her while Tim found the rope, tied a double loop Spanish bowline on one end with deft movements, removed his shoes, stepped through the loops, and tied the rope around his waist. He measured ten metres with his arms and tied that point to one of the aisle-seat supports.

Jessica could only think he knew what he was doing as he stepped into what she thought of as the jungle. Tim sensed her feelings, which overlayed the fear and insecurity generated by the unknown. *She's great. For her, this must be like landing on another planet.*

'Jess, feed the rope out so it doesn't catch on something; pull it back if it becomes too loose.'

'It's too thin to hold you; it'll break.'

'The fibre is the strongest known, and the load rating is twelve tons.'

She watched him move slowly, gracefully jumping, arms spread for balance, from one place to another, then fluidly squatting to poke the floor with a stick. He didn't move far; the rope would have stopped him, but on his fourth attempt to find a hole, he called, 'I've found one here.' She saw him clear some debris with a broken stick, then rise smoothly.

'Jess, pull back the rope slowly.'

'Okay, that's enough. Can you tie a loop where I must tie it to the seat?'

She did. 'Now pull in the rope as I return.' Tim returned in graceful, connected leaps; his feet hardly touched the floor below him. She had to pull in the rope rapidly.

'Tim, you seem terrified of falling, are you?'

'Yes, Jess, I am. If you lose your balance or step on a weak bit of floor, the fifty-metre fall will kill you. Ten will cause severe damage. If you had a rope under your armpits, a ten-metre fall would tear your arms off. I had ten metres of rope but less than eight after leaving the bus, and I tied it under my backside between my legs. Falling would have hurt, but I could climb back. Once I had moved two or three metres more, it would not have hurt much. A four-metre fall is only massive bruising.'

'But what if you want to travel much further?'

'Then I'll wrap the rope around a branch near you as a friction brake, so if I fall and you hold the rope tight, I wouldn't fall far. When I'm alone, I take the other end and control my safety.

'I'll tie the rope where you marked it.'

Jessica turned to the passenger in the first row and searched the corpse's pockets; she found a purse, and as Timothy reached her, she said, 'There's only a purse.'

Timothy sprung the safety belt catch and tied the other end of the rope around the woman's chest. 'I could carry her, but the weight might unbalance me; I'll pull her to the hole. Put her purse on our seats.'

An hour later, they had disposed of the bodies. 'Jess, please help me remove all the seat cushion covers and disconnect the safety belts; they have snap connectors.'

'What will you do with them?'

'The padding might make a mattress, but the covering material is worth having. It's megalon's hide. Belts are useful.'

Surprised, she asked, 'What's special about megalon's hide?'

'It's almost impenetrable, water and airtight, very soft and flexible; I'll make clothes that don't tear.'

It left her puzzled, but she removed the cushions from their covers.

'Even our seats?'

'No, I'll release the seat frame snap catches from the floor; we'll move ours against the wall to sit on and pile the others across the open end as a barrier.'

As they finished, Jessica asked, 'Tim, are you setting up a camp here? When are we leaving?'

'Jess, our departure depends on you. I hope it will be no more than a month, but it might be longer.'

'But I'm ready now!'

I'm sure she isn't, but I should check.

Timothy stripped off his shirt, 'Jess, I need to assess your strength. There's a mirror in the toilet; join me, and we'll compare.' Wearing only his jockstrap, Timothy waited for Jessica, who, thinking it was like being in the gym, removed her blouse and skirt. Then Timothy said, 'Now, come into the toilet; we'll stand beside each other.'

She followed him, and he said, 'Now look carefully at me in the mirror and yourself.'

She doesn't have enough muscle to climb a rope.

7

Standing in front of the toilet mirror, Jessica looked first at Timothy. She hadn't *looked* at him except for his face until that moment. It only took a few seconds to recognise a body sculpted by exercise; she saw muscles she had never known existed. His shoulders were broad, his waist narrow, and his biceps and triceps well developed. *His boobs are as big as mine, except the nipples are much smaller.*

Then she looked down; his legs were similarly muscled. *That's how he can gracefully jump from branch to branch and why they were so hard to sit on.* She then examined herself.

I'm skinny. I can't see muscles; my arms and legs are matchsticks compared to Tim's. My hips and waist seem okay, but I have no tummy muscles.

'Tim, can I feel your bum?'

Strange request. 'Okay, Jess.'

She did, then reached behind her and squeezed. *My backside is a ball of fat, and his bum is hard muscle.*

'Tim, I can see and feel the difference. I've seen naked young men at the gym, but none had muscles like yours. How and why do you have that body?'

'Like you, I was born on this planet, in Colony Nine, but from age ten, I've roamed the forest, and from age twelve, the middle terrace where we are. The upper deck is dangerous; the darters, flying creatures with spear beaks, attack anything that moves, and the lower terrace is darker with massive dinosaur-like beasts, which the colonies defend against, although I've never seen or heard of an attack. I told you, we're fifty metres up. I can leave a rope dangling to the ground, rappel down, and climb it in a hurry if needed. I have strap-on claws in my bag; I can run up a tree trunk like a cat. Exercise for hours every day builds the muscles, sculpts the body, perfects our sense of balance and timing, and improves our reaction time.'

'So, must I look like you before we can travel?'

'Not quite, Jess. We'll stay here until I feel you won't be in danger when we travel. I'll carry the backpack and equipment, but I can't route-find and watch you simultaneously; I must feel confident you're unlikely to fall or hurt yourself. But there's a reward at the end: when you can dance effortlessly through the forest, you'll love it. It's a glorious feeling.

'We have three thousand kilometres to travel; I said I can do ten a day, but we'll be lucky to do five at first, so five hundred full travelling days. With rivers to cross, we'll make it in six hundred days. An extra thirty is nothing.'

'You look like Tarzan; how can I look like you in a month?'

'Who's Tarzan?'

'A fictional hero raised in a jungle by apes – tailless giant monkeys. The author who created Tarzan was one of the earliest eco-enviro-aware people on Old Earth, but no one listened to his messages.'

'Was he alone?'

'Who? Tarzan or the author?'

'Tarzan.'

'At first, but when he grew up, he rescued a woman called Jane, and she became his wife and lived in the jungle with him.'

'Did he swing from tree to tree on a vine?'

'I think so. Raised by apes, Tarzan must have done.'

Timothy had an idea: *Will a new name help to change her view of the forest?*

'If you don't expect me to do the impossible, I'll be Tarzan, and you can be Jane.'

'You must say, "Me Tarzan, you Jane."'

'Why?'

'Because that's what he said in the story.'

'Okay' – *Crazy, but it might help; otherwise, we'll die.* 'Me Tarzan, you Jane.'

'Why is swinging from vine to vine impossible?'

'Because they hang straight down. Monkeys jump from one to another, but swinging is impossible unless someone pre-arranges the vines.'

'How do you know?'

'I tried.'

Jane laughed; *he's human. He might look like Tarzan, but I don't think he's the kind of macho male in the book.* Then she stepped from the toilet and fell to her knees as the GravBus shuddered and settled.

Jessica's reaction was to lie flat. Timothy grabbed the side of the toilet doorframe and held on.

'*What's happening, Tim!* Is the GravBus about to fall?'

It became stationary again after cracking, crunching noises, and a final, drawn-out symphonic groan.

'No, we're on a thick pile of vegetation that was once the upper forest floor. The hole in the upper floor is about fifty metres behind us. The vegetation is drying; the moisture is squeezing out, so the GravBus will settle.'

'So there's no danger?'

'No, the floor supported the GravBus; it won't fall through.'

She remembered to call him Tarzan. 'Okay, Tarzan, I'll stand.'

She did, and Tarzan came from the toilet, put his arm around her and said, 'You have guts, Jane; I'll show you the basic exercises you must do. After a week or two, I'll show you others.'

He dropped to the GravBus floor and did fifty press-ups in rapid succession. On the rise, he lifted his hands, clapped them, and then caught himself on the fall.

'You need arm muscles to climb a rope. Press-ups build triceps and shoulders. I'll rig a chin-up bar for the others. Now, this is a squat.'

Smoothly, his arms stretched horizontally forward; he dropped until his bum lightly touched the floor, his feet underneath flat, and then stood in a single effortless fluid movement.

'Sit-ups are for tummy muscles.' He lay on his back, legs flat on the floor, put his hands behind his head, and did ten sit-ups that ended with an elbow beside his knees.

'We'll die on the trip unless you can do these exercises without thought and effort. So do them several times a day. Count how many squats and press-ups you do each day and sleep each night exhausted. You'll feel yourself weakening for six to eight days; then, you'll feel a daily improvement.'

'Why will we die if I fall?'

'Not you, Jane, me. A one-hundred-metre rope will connect us. We each must rely on the other if one of us falls. If I do and you don't have the strength to help, I might die if I cut myself free, and you don't know the way to my home. If you fall, I can haul you up, but we'll have to wait days for any bruising to wear off.

'Anyway, we can't leave now because there is equipment I must make. I'll work on it and hunt for food while you build your body.'

'What food?'

'Squirrels, and fruits. I'll need some bottles to collect water; what do we have?'

'Five or six one-and-a-half litre ones in a locker. The empty ones were in the forward trash can. But will I look like you?'

'Not for a year or two, but you're much lighter than me and will be lighter still; in a month, you should have enough muscle for your weight. Take care of the bottles; we won't need them once we move. There's water everywhere except in a GravBus. What did you find on the bodies?'

'Wallets, two pens, and three lighters.'

'Thank God for the Boy Explorers.'

'Why?'

'Because of a myth that a man with a lighter can scare off dangerous animals. It may have existed since man discovered fire. I'm guilty; I have one in my bag. Rubbing sticks together is demanding work.

'I'll check the toilet. If the tank leaks or I can open the discharge valve, we can use it as it won't fill up.'

'Tarzan, you haven't dressed.'

'I won't; this is all I wear up here. Clothes catch on things and can unbalance you and cause a painful or terminal fall.'

'Like Binky does?'

'Yes, as you're staying on the GravBus, you can wear your blouse, but a skirt will hamper your exercise.'

'Can you cut my blouse shorter, just below my boobs?'

'Let me fetch my knife.'

'Tarzan, I'm covered in sweat. How do we wash or shower?'

'I should have thought of that; there's a Cascade Creeper on the tree trunk nearest us. There'll be an axe in the safety bag; there always is. Tomorrow, I'll cut branches and lay a walkway and a shower platform so we can shower. Use one or two water bottles tonight and wipe yourself down.'

'Why is there always an axe in the safety box? I asked when I saw it, but no one could tell me why it was there; they said nothing can cut through a GravBus shell,' then she added ruefully, 'although they were wrong.'

Tarzan replied, 'I saw a picture of one of the first-ever hot-air balloons in a history book, and it had an axe strapped to the basket. It was necessary to cut cords when it landed. Knowing how slavishly humans can follow a tradition, I expect someone has ordered an axe placed in every flying machine since.'

'Shouldn't it be on the wall where it's easy to reach?'

'Jane, it would make passengers uncomfortable; imagine if, on a cross-water flight, the crew boarded wearing swimming goggles and flippers!'

She laughed a strained laugh and changed the subject.

'What's a Cascade Creeper?'

'I'll show you tomorrow. I'll cut off my shirt sleeves tonight, and you can use one as a cloth to wipe yourself down. Let me know when, and I'll wipe your back.'

'Then I'll do yours.'

Fifteen minutes later, they lay down to sleep. 'Jane, you can pack the cushion insides to make a bed and a pillow.'

Jane did. She found a comfortable position on the GravBus

floor, thought she would be happier if Tarzan were closer, and then thought, *my bed at home is better.* That led to thinking of her parents and how far away they were.

'Tarzan, do you miss your parents?'

'I haven't had a moment to think about them; I might in a few days. I've spent up to two months away from them, so their absence hasn't registered. Do you miss yours?'

'It's strange, I don't when I'm away for two or three nights, but now that I know I won't see them for two years, I keep thinking of them and what they will feel when I don't return. I wish I could tell them I'm alive.'

Tarzan moved closer to her. 'Jane, I'll be here with you constantly; I expect you'll sometimes wish I were elsewhere. I can't say it will work, but you can try something.'

'What?'

'Where will your parents be right now?'

'They aren't expecting me home; Mum will be in the kitchen preparing some food. Dad will be with her. They'll only start worrying tomorrow night.'

'Then we'll try to reassure them tomorrow night. My parents must know by now that the GravBus didn't arrive and must be worried. I'll try to reassure my mother.'

'How?'

'They must be in our lounge. I'll *theel* a picture of our house from my tree, then change it to the lounge with my parents in it. Dad may be holding Mum. I'll then *theel* a feeling of happiness and a picture of Tarik moving around the sun.'

'Will they receive that?'

'No, but they might feel sure I'm alive and returning.'

'Then do it.'

Gordon and Martha Furnival had waited in vain for the GravBus's arrival at the Colony Nine station and returned to the house when the clerk said the GravBus must have crashed.

Martha had collapsed on the couch, and Gordon sat beside her and put his arm around her as she moaned. 'He can't have died!'

'Martha, it's a possibility we can't rule out, but I can say that if he's alive, he's the only man I know who can, one day in the future, walk down the steps of the tree behind the house.'

Martha started remembering Timothy as a child, then a teenager, and finally, as he had left for the interviews, and as she did so, her confidence that he would return grew.

'Martha, look at me.'

She did, and Gordon saw a misty look in her eyes that frightened him; then she said, 'He's far away but alive and will return.'

8

Jane patiently waited while Tarzan thought of his parents, and when he turned to look at her and said, 'I hope that message reached them,' it highlighted her enormous separation from her parents. It wasn't only the distance; it seemed much more significant because of the time.

'Tarzan. I'm scared of feeling alone. Can you put your arm around me?'

I need a diversion to take her mind to something else.

'Of course, Jane. Did Tarzan and Jane have sex?'

'There was no sign of it in the book, but back then, I think writing or talking about sex was taboo.'

'When was back then?'

'Over a thousand years ago, just after exploiting Old Earth's resources had become a crazy objective. They ran out of most of them about two hundred years later. We learnt about it in the history of ecology studies.'

'That reminds me, you said the men you know would walk away. Did you mean that?'

'Yes, I've been trying to work it out for two years; I think it's like your mother said. Because men are sterile and don't know which child is theirs, most men don't care about children; the women must raise them with the help of the community. You know about the permits in Colony One. I think the authorities won't allow a woman with a child to enter the forest in case of an accident that leaves her child an orphan. We don't have the luxury of grandparents to care for an orphan. Since we arrived, there hasn't been a traditional marriage as described in history books, the "until death us do part" kind. So, the couples that do form only last if each feels the other is doing an equal share, for they don't have a biological child, which was once the reason to work out any problems and continue. The man or the woman walks away.'

'That's interesting. Although I know of one marriage, that of my parents.'

'Then they're unusual. Did it happen in colony One or Nine?'

'I never asked. Do you think the lack of marriage is good or bad?'

'I'm not sure; our teachers told us that a legally binding tie is unpopular because it leads to violence between couples. Even if it's better without such ties, men should know the children they father. The teachers said every child has a DNA test after birth on Earth-Four, so the father knows for sure. Your mother might have a better answer. I think that bit she said about male sterility preventing overpopulation might be wrong.'

'In what way?'

Jane appeared reluctant to discuss it, 'Well, your mother wrote that before you were born; she might write something different today.'

'Jane, please explain what has happened; I can't imagine what you mean.'

'There was the baby boom your mother talked about, but since then, births have dropped to near zero as the women have aged.'

'But what about our generation?'

'We learnt in college that on Earth Four, girls had babies

from fifteen onwards, usually unintended, but the intentional births began at eighteen. I haven't heard of any eighteen-year-old girls having a baby, although they can volunteer for insemination. I don't think we'll see babies again until our generation of women approaches thirty, and even then, I wonder if many of us will want babies. The sterilisation program might cause us to die out, and that's one of the reasons the colony administrators try to keep girls out of danger.'

'Don't you want a child?'

'Not right now; I want to do something worthwhile first. I will one day.'

'Okay, when we reach my home, we can ask my Mum. Put your head on my shoulder and make yourself comfortable with the cushions. Good night, Jane.'

'Good night, Tarzan.'

Strangely, the change of names has made her forget how precarious things are.

Jane opened her eyes to complete darkness. So black that she thought, *am I dead*? Then she heard the noise; *I remember that. It woke me.*

She whispered, 'Tarzan, are you awake?'

He whispered a reply, 'Yes.'

'What's that noise.'

'Giant boars, it sounds as if there are three. They're eating the corpses.'

'How horrible. We should have buried the bodies.'

'The boars would have dug them up; this is the cleaning service at work. Ignore them; they'll leave soon. Try to sleep.'

'Then put your arm around me again.'

Physical exhaustion and the comfort of his arm brought sleep.

Tarzan lay thinking as the morning light slowly strengthened. He didn't wake Jane; her exercise had more effect than nervous exhaustion, so she slept soundly.

Eventually, he stood, stepped silently to the emergency bag, removed the axe, carefully tied a piece of fishline he took from his bag through a hole in the handle, strapped on his trouser belt above his jockstrap, and tied the line to it, rigged the rope and left to look for suitable branches and roots. He stayed within sight and hearing.

Jessica, not Jane, had dreamt Goggles was beside her; in the first moments of awakening, she reached out for Goggles, found he wasn't there and opened her eyes. She sat up bewildered, saw the piled-up seats, and remembered; panic growing, she looked wildly for Tim, then leapt to her feet. The pain in her tortured muscles reminded her. *I'm Jane. Tarzan must be here.* 'Tarzan, where are you?'

Relief flooded her when she heard his reply, 'Here.' Then she saw him fifty metres away, waving the axe. Feeling foolish, she waved, then fetched a water bottle and took a long drink before beginning tentative stretching exercises. *I must work out the kinks first – Damn the agony!*

'Jane, come and look.'

She continued her press-ups until she couldn't do another, sat back on her knees and then groaned as she stood. In front of the remaining GravBus, a short walkway of branches tied in place with green vines led to the nearby tree, where a wider area made a small platform.

Tarzan stood on the platform. 'Come.'

Barefoot, she walked tentatively along the walkway to join him as he held out a hand. 'This is the Cascade Creeper. It grows around tree trunks and receives water from the upper levels. These leaves that resemble conical cups collect rainwater on the upper level, although it's usually nightly condensation. When they've filled, they tip over, and the water pours into cups below. It doesn't rain here, or under us unless the storm above is furious, and when it is, everything drips. The plant is watering its roots and the roots of the others below it.

'You can shower; one leaf contains about a litre of water. I brought a piece of soap from the toilet.'

'Thanks, that was thoughtful. I didn't know you meant this plant; my mother calls it the "Water Lily".'

Surprised, he exclaimed, 'You know it?'

'Yes, we use this one for the water in the cups because it's rainwater and pure. Once I can explore with you, I'll tell you which ones I recognise. We'll need one I know that gives soap.'

'There are several; if I see one, I'll bring it to you.'

'The one I use has spiky leaves.'

'That's a good one, but rare up here; it's more common below.'

'Does the toothbrush plant grow up here?'

'It does, but it's also rare. When I see one, I cut at least a dozen sticks. The mint taste is great to chew. If we run out, I can drop and find some below.'

'Then cut me some, too; I must brush my teeth.'

'I'll bring you some toothbrush sticks from my bag. Stand here, and you can tip one of these leaves so the water falls on you. By tomorrow, water will have cascaded down to fill it again. Between us, we can use eight each day, but we must fill our drinking bottles first, although I can take them to another plant.'

That's welcome news; she knows more than I expected about Tarik plants.

When she finished her ablutions, she called, 'Can I return alone?'

'Of course, just step carefully.'

'I feel much better now, but I'll be sweaty again later.'

'If you keep the shower to two cones, you can wash twice, at lunch and before sleep.

'We'll eat a lunch box soon. We'll share one after a third of the day and another after two-thirds. We must eat frequent small snack meals; we can't carry much food.'

Sitting side by side on the seats, now with their backs to the sidewall, Jane opened the first lunch box. 'Tarzan, I think we'd better eat one each. I don't think these will last four days. This citrus fruit will, but not the rest. We can eat two each today and tomorrow. If we save the fruit for the third day, we can make the eight last three days.'

'Okay, I can hunt sooner.'

'Tarzan, what do those horrid creatures that eat dead people look like; you called them giant boars.'

'They're like a giant pig, about four metres long and over a metre and a half high. I think they're a mutation, for they have six legs. They're too heavy for both upper levels and stay on the ground. The middle legs are just supporting stumps, and the main legs don't have knees; they may be in the feet. I've seen them from above and when I was on the ground level. They eat anything fresh that's died; rotten meat they leave for the worms.

'Their eyes are huge for the dim light, and they use their tusks to plough the ground. They dig up bulbs and roots to eat. They do sometimes damage the trees if they're hungry.'

'That sounds impossible.'

'They use the tusks to dig the soft wood from the tree, making vee-shaped gorges. If they dig out all the vees around a single tree, it might die before it recovers, which it will do if the pig only cleans out two or three.'

'What vees, and why only might die?'

'Millions of years ago, when the planet cooled, it was an almost smooth ball. It started raining once it was cool enough. Without deep valleys or basins to drain the water, the planet became covered in water that accumulated in the small lakes we see in the forest today. At first, the water was a vast surging mass moving east to west from the effect of our sun. It ground away at the surface, building up mud until the planet's surface was smooth, soaking and muddy, with free water only in the lakes and our sea. Then the ice caps froze, taking up much of the water, vegetation began, and the land became swamps.'

'Do you mean it was like the whole planet was a shallow sea at first?'

'That's a better description than mine.'

'Fine, but those lakes, where are they now?'

'There are still millions, but plants that evolved grew higher towards the sunlight, first reeds and then trees, but the trees are very different.'

'How?'

'Growing in mud, they needed support and evolved with long surface roots that became buttresses to support the trees, and eventually, the successful ones needed more ground area, so some killed off others, and the first-tier forest grew spaced out as we find it today.'

'But when I've looked at the first tier, the trees don't have buttresses.'

'They do. If you see a tree stump in the forest, you can see them. It's a small tree in the middle with five or six dense buttresses and soft, spongy wood wedges between them. They're the vees that the boars sometimes dig out. The trees gained an advantage in the swamp, but it handicapped the height they could grow to, as the ground and root structure can't support the mass of a tree more than sixty metres high.'

'I know nothing about trees, but the plants my mother collects die if the roots are underwater and can't breathe air.'

'The trees would, too. Dad believes we'll learn they can feed oxygen into their roots. Some species do that. Others have roots that grow up above the water.

'As they kept other trees out of the forest, they could branch sideways to maximise light, and eventually, this created the first level floor from intertwined branches that also helped them from falling over. The branches below fell off. Then, after several million years or more, that floor became filled with vegetation, a fertile ground for a second round of vegetation and trees. Those trees must be a mutation; they added their roots to the floor, and Dad believes they work with the ground-rooted trees to keep them alive, for the primaeval trees no longer receive enough sunlight. Sometimes, a branch and a root join. Eventually, they built the second floor. It also squashed the lower-level trees shorter into the massive ones we see today. The top level will develop for millions of years. Currently, it's a jungle open to the skies.'

'That's quite a story; what proof is there?'

'Very little, that's why we must research, but I can tell you something I know.

'It's hard to believe, but these aren't individual trees; it's one forest with a planet-wide network run by fungi that connects them. The injured tree will receive what it needs from the others around it until it recovers. If it's an outlier on the edge of a lake or river, it might not receive enough support and die.'

'What's the boar's role in the ecology?'

She still thinks of ecology. That's good.

'To oxygenate the soil and assist in the breakdown of the vegetation and aid conversion of dead animals that fall on the ground, they're the gardeners, helped by the giant worms.'

'Well, I don't want to meet either.'

'If you walk away, they're harmless. They won't attack anything that moves away, although the first time I met one, it terrified me.'

I'm sure one would terrify me, too.

Jane showered again before the light faded. Exhausted by the exercise and fearing a fall, she returned on all fours.

The dim light faded as the moon set, and Tarzan lay beside her.

'Can I try to reassure my parents now?'

'When you were on the GravBus platform, could you see your house?'

'Only just.'

'Can you picture the kitchen in your mind, with them in it? Try to remember a scene you've seen before. Think of the first picture, your house, block out everything else, then move to a second picture, zoom in on your mother, and think what I did, feel happy, and picture Tarik moving around the sun.'

...

'I feel happier now. Maybe Mum felt it.'

9

Tarzan woke as always, silent, unmoving, his senses alert. Jane was breathing steadily, so he remained motionless and thought, *I never imagined I would sleep with a woman beside me for many years.* Then Jane's breathing changed as sleep took flight, and her body adjusted to a new rhythm, checking its condition.

When she woke, her first words were, 'I don't think I can stand.'

'Why?'

'I ache everywhere.'

'I can't help; it will wear off if you stretch slowly.'

'I know. When I overdid the exercises in the colony gym, it was the same, but the masseur helped.'

'We don't have any oil, and I've never massaged anyone.'

'There's the skin cream in the shower and a bottle in the woman passenger's handbag. Either should work. If I tell you what to do, can you try?'

'I'll probably hurt you.'

'Just do as I say.

...

'Where do I start?'

'Use two fingers, find what feels like a ridge on my back by pressing gently near a shoulder, and use some cream...

'Higher.'

'There's a hard ridge here.'

'Yes, that's one. Now try to ooze the top end up and the bottom down…

'Oww, too hard!'

'I warned you.'

'I know, please continue, I'll grit my teeth.'

Better, he's learning, 'Yes, that's nice, more…

'Now that one's just an ache. Find another and continue…

'That's much better; do the other shoulder. Now I know about the Cascade Creeper; what about the megalons?'

'What do you know about the megalons?'

'All I know is that they float around in the sky, and our colony has missile defences against them.'

'I know more; my dad has been researching the fauna and flora for twenty years. What you see floating in the sky is a hydrogen-filled ovoid that the beast can fill or vent as it wishes to choose an altitude and allow the wind to carry it while it looks for something to eat.'

'And the two tails that hang down?'

'Only one; the other is a neck. The tail has a massive ball at the end. That's the beast's hydrogen factory; it doesn't float, so it hangs. The ball is also a pressurised hydrogen store.

'The neck is like a tentacle, highly flexible, and the end has four eyes and a toothed mouth. Two eyes are on the top of the head so it can see forward with the head hanging down. The two others looking down are like telescopes; they can make out details from thousands of metres up. As the bag is hard to manoeuvre, the neck allows it to reach quite far.'

Jane had more instructions. 'Okay, for my shoulders, now do the small of my back. Careful at my waist; the sit-ups have made it hurt.'

'Okay, I'll start gently; tell me when to press harder.'

'But why do we need defences against megalons?'

'Because, if it decides that a human is a source of iron, remember we have haemoglobin in our blood, it can deflate and flatten its neck to steer with as it falls. It can build up a lot of speed because the ovoid becomes a streamlined sausage. It swoops, grabbing and swallowing the prey, and then its momentum allows a climb while it refills the gas chamber with hydrogen. Our defences would shoot an explosive dart into the megalon to explode the hydrogen bag. The bag's skin is incredibly resistant to damage and is non-porous. Hunting the megalon is illegal; we don't want to antagonise them. One interesting thing about them is that they must understand our defences; they've never attacked a colony.'

'Are there lots of them? Whenever I've looked at the sky, I see no more than two.'

'The forest area of Tarik is about six hundred million square kilometres. If the area you're looking at is a kilometre square, and you can see one, the megalon population, including females, must be over a billion.'

The enormity of the number left Jane without a reply, so she asked, 'How does it sense metal?'

'Dad thinks it drifts around looking but also senses changes in the planet's magnetic field. You must have learnt that it's a powerful field. Do you know the GravBus doesn't have a mythical anti-gravity unit?'

'Yes, it uses magnets to overcome gravity.'

'Well, Dad thinks that the GravBus disturbs the magnetic field, and the megalons can sense this.'

'But there aren't many GravBus accidents. Why were we hit?'

'Our pilots screwed up. The GravBus, the smaller GravEx, and the cargo-carrying GravLifter can rise, descend, and travel horizontally much faster than the megalon hydrogen bag, except at the end of the megalon's near-supersonic dive. The megalons all float around in a narrow altitude band, between three and four thousand metres, high enough to deflate and reach a high speed before they swoop and grab their prey, but not so high that they can't identify their prey. The GravBus pilots check that the sky above is clear, then climb quickly above this altitude before the megalons can deflate and gather speed. Up there, the GravBus pilots think they're safe. Still, occasionally, a megalon isn't looking for food, just travelling from one spot to another, looking for somewhere less crowded. They rise to high altitudes where stronger winds blow in different directions. The pilots should keep their eyes out for one they will pass under within range. I guess our pilots didn't and never knew what hit them. They might have been eating lunch and not keeping a lookout.'

'Why didn't it eat us?'

'It should have done. The bulk of the metal is under the middle of the GravBus, but trying to control a supersonic dive onto a moving target is difficult. It swooped down at an angle and snapped at the GravBus when it could. Lucky for us. Once we fell through the upper floor, we were out of reach of one floating above us.'

'What do they eat, except GravBusses and us?'

'Jane, I'm confident they don't try to eat us; the metal of the GravBus, particularly the MagLev units, attracts them. We're consequential damage.

'I'll tell you more about them later; we have two years for me to do so.

'Come, we have things to do. Put the cream back in the toilet for the next time you want a massage.'

Jane put the cream away, then cleared a space and began her exercise regime with press-ups as Tarzan selected a seat cover from the pile on one side and carefully cut the sewed seam threads to lay it out flat. When Jane struggled to do the twelfth press-up, she said, 'Tarzan, I can't do as many press-ups as yesterday.'

'That's good, Jane, do the squats, then sit down and rest.'

'What are you doing?'

'Cutting up a seat cover, I'll make you a bikini bottom with a belt. With a breast strap, that's all you'll wear.'

'Why?'

'Because you can see or feel any insect that lands on your body. Wearing clothes, apart from cloth catching on things, you won't know an insect is there until it thrusts its sting through your clothes into you. They can't pierce this hide.'

'But I learnt the insects don't sting us because they haven't evolved to do that.'

'Quite right, but they sting clothes because they can't sense what's under them.'

'How can you make clothes without a pattern?'

'I'll make the bikini too large and trim it like I did when I made my last loincloth.'

Jane took her panties off and said, 'Use these; women aren't the same shape as men.' She handed them over.

'Jane put them on again and then turn round. I don't think they are wide enough to protect your bum when sitting, so I must see how much more to allow. She did, shivering when she felt Tarzan measuring with his fingers. Then, when he said,

'About two fingers wider on each side,' she took them off and watched while Tarzan marked the piece of thin, tough hide to match. Then she asked, 'Will it have frills or tassels?'

She's thinking about what it looks like!

'Why would I add those? For the look?'

'Not to look nice. But tassels are supposed to flap around and discourage annoying insects.'

She's right, and I'm wrong. She does have a sensible reason.

'Okay, how do I do that?'

'If you make the front and back much higher and let the top bits fold down over the belt like the pictures I've seen of loin-cloths, you can slit those bits to make tassels.'

'Okay, I'll try.' He moved the panties down fifteen centimetres and asked, 'Will a fifteen-centimetre piece be long enough? Too long, and you'll sit on it.'

'That looks about right.'

'I might have made the back too wide across your bum for sitting on; it might still need trimming.'

Tarzan handed back her panties, and she put them on. 'If the hide's so strong, how do you cut it?'

'I have a chisel and a mallet in my bag.'

He searched in his bag and found them.

'That's a funny mallet, just a ball on a handle.'

'It's not for cutting leather, although the ball is as hard as iron. It's a seed, and I had to burn a hole using a metal door pin with a red-hot end. When you're ready for it, say in three weeks, I'll show you how to throw it.'

'Why three weeks?'

He held the mallet towards her, 'Tell me if you could throw this.'

She took it and almost dropped it. 'It's heavy.'

'A kilo; it should feel much lighter in three weeks. But when I make one for you, it'll be lighter. I'll fetch an anvil.'

With a short length of tree branch between his knees, Tarzan spread the hide and then tapped and cut his way around the markings using his stubby knife on an extended handle. 'There, Jane, try that on. It's higher than your panties and has ties like a bikini on the top sides; then, I'll make a belt and thread it around the top and fold down the flaps that I'll split.'

'When I've finished, you'll find them better than your panties; the hide will protect your skin when you sit on rough surfaces. It should fit tightly so an insect can't crawl inside, and it won't catch onto something. If it rubs anywhere, tell me where to trim it.'

'What else will you make?'

'A breast strap and a pair of sandals, simple ones, just a piece of hide and thongs to tie them in place. They'll last at least two years. And then, for me, a loincloth and belt to hang my knife and things.'

He thinks we'll still be alive two years from now; that's encouraging.

'Can you put a fringe or tassels on the breast strap?'

'I'll put shorter ones. If they annoy you, I can cut them off.'

'What do I do with our clothes?'

'Before we leave, we'll find a use for them.'

'How will you make the belts?'

'That's easy, the seatbelts and their catch. The belt inside the bulky padding tube and the catch are like a man's trouser belt, but they'll hold tons. One seat will make one belt. Those you took from the male passengers are good for holding up a protruding belly, not much more. Are you hungry?'

'Yes, I'll fetch the last lunch packs; then we'll have only the fruit left.'

As they lay down on the GravBus floor that night, Jane asked, 'Tarzan, where does the light come from in the middle of the night? I woke last night and could see the toilet door.'

'I switch that light on so you can see the toilet if you need it at night.'

Jane sounded sarcastic, 'Tarzan, thank you for your courtesy, but I asked where the light you switch on comes from.'

With a grin, he replied, 'Sometimes, Jane, it's one, two or all three moons, but when they're down, the forest lights itself. There are luminous plants that give different coloured light, mostly blue-purple or slightly reddish and others that appear yellow. I'll point to one now; you can look when it's darker.'

He stood, and she followed with a groan. 'I should have re-membered standing is agony!'

'Over there, at the foot of the tree on your left, there's a patch, and I can just see the glow.'

'I can, too; that's the yellow shade. What and why, please?'

'That one has a lovely flower that opens some nights and only lasts one night. It's a tiny flower. If you investigate it with a magnifying glass, it has a tiny glowing sun in the middle, and the petals are narrow stalks with even smaller stars on the ends. The luminescence results from a chemical process that accelerates its death, rotting as you watch. The light attracts insects that brush against the interior and then carry pollen to flowers on other plants. I've seen the results when a patch of the floor hundreds of metres across glows and lights up the for-est as much as when all three moons are up, but with a lovely yellow light. I call them star lilies.'

'That must be lovely to see. I hope we'll see it during our trip.'

'I'm sure we will.'

'Are the flowers or the plant edible?'

'Not for us. There is a creature that adores the lilies, but I'll tell you about the worm another time; we may never see one. Let's sleep. If I see other luminous flowers during our journey, I'll point them out.'

10

Jane woke but didn't open her eyes. *I know I'm Jane today; I ache.* She listened for a while, trying to separate the sounds she could hear. The background was a low-intensity rustling. *I think that must be the leaves on the upper level.* The absence of sound seemed to cloy, like a greasy, dense fog, then it split, and the *tok-tok* sound she heard came through the gap. *That's something far away.* The sound-deadening fog returned, and she heard much closer noises – those of scurrying tiny feet. *A squirrel is trying to find food.*

Then she heard slow, rhythmic breathing. *That's Tarzan beside me.*

She opened her eyes, the light too dim for her eyes to focus, her world a blur of shadows. *It may be moonlight; it's like opening my eyes underwater.* Then she thought.

Tarzan breathes slowly. Can I do the same?

She tried to match her breathing with his; she breathed in when he did and then out simultaneously, but before he breathed again, she felt her body rebel and couldn't wait.

I must ask how he can breathe with such gaps.

She stopped trying, relaxed, shut her eyes, slept and woke again. *It's daylight that's coming now.*

His whisper startled her. 'Jane?'

'Yes, how did you know I was awake?'

'I was listening to your breathing. It had hiccups.'

'Oh, I listened to yours earlier; you breathe slowly while asleep. I tried to slow my breathing, but I couldn't.'

'You'll notice an improvement as you become fitter. Six months from now, you'll tell me I breathe too fast.'

'Okay, before the megalon rudely interrupted us, you were about to tell me about your mother's discovery.'

'If ever I learn to speak megalonese and meet that megalon, I'll tell him he's rude. I must tell you about Dad, too.'

'If it delays the agony of my exercises, I welcome it.'

'I told you that my mum realised she would not have a job as a sociologist. She began searching for a scientist who could teach her about the planet and its inhabitants so she could earn a living as a schoolteacher. She discarded twelve of the first thirteen she approached.

'As she was thirty-two years old, the five scientists younger than her showed no interest, and the seven others she discarded because they were secretive about what they had learnt and abrupt in their speech; she realised carving a reputation on Tarik would be a cut-throat business. The thirteenth she found refreshingly different. He liked her; his name is Gordon Furnival, and he became my dad.'

Jane showed interest in more detail, 'How did that happen?'

'Mum told me she met him in the canteen; he's a biologist, one of the scientists on her passenger list, and like the previous twelve, she had sat down in front of him at the midday meal and introduced herself.'

'I like your mum already; she's a no-nonsense woman like my mum. So, what did he say?'

'"Martha, you know my name, so either you have a proposition or a question. Which is it?"'

'I like him too. What did your mum answer?'

'She asked, "Which would you prefer?"'

'Great answer. It puts the responsibility back on your dad. Let me guess he said something like – "I would welcome either, but despite the behaviour of our female colleagues, I suspect it's more likely to be a question."'

'Spot on, Jane; she told me she asked, "What is your approach to research?"'

'Then he asked her to be more specific, and she asked, "Do you look for precise causal relationships, X causes Y, or do you investigate relationships where many factors may or may not participate?"'

'He told her it was the latter, then asked, "Why did you ask me?"'

'She told him she wanted a biologist to tell her about the planet so that she could tutor children. Dad told me when I was fourteen that he liked her direct approach, so he replied, "Come with me tomorrow into the forest. I have some plants to look at."'

'And how did they decide to marry?'

'That's what Dad told me when I asked him about the fungus. He answered, "On every planet humanity has visited, they're the first complex life to evolve. They're symbiotic; under the harsh conditions that the first lifeforms experience, their existence and survival depend on cooperative behaviour between themselves and other life that has developed. No one knows why or whether the other lifeforms would have evolved without them."

'He said my mum asked the same question as me while they

collected fungus specimens shortly after they met, and then she said it was time to make the proposition mentioned in the canteen – because his hands were gentle when he handled the fungus.'

'And what was her proposition?'

'She first asked him to kiss her, then said, "I want a child, but I want my child to have a father. Will you share my life until our child has grown up?"'

'So, she proposed to him? That's marvellous.'

'Yes, except he didn't say yes; he told her to apply for insemination with his name as the prospective partner, and when notified of a suitable match, they should make love and then decide.'

'That's unusual; why did he make marriage depend on sexual compatibility? Although the history books mention that was the case on the other planets, I've never heard it mentioned on Tarik.'

'Mum said it was because he believed having sex was something they should want to do frequently for the rest of their lives. But Dad said something to me privately. He said he wanted to believe that I was genetically his child.'

'I'm sure I'll like your folks.'

'They moved to Colony Nine after marriage, for it was close to the sea, and Dad believes the planet's evolution began in the ocean.

'I was born there.'

Binky was also born there; I thought she might be a mutation. Tarzan might be an evolutionary mutation, too.

'Tarzan, you must continue your story tomorrow. I need to stretch and exercise.'

'Fine, Jane, start stretching carefully, be progressive, don't push too hard.'

'I ache all over. I'm tender, but it doesn't hurt like yesterday.'

'Your body has learnt what you're asking and is adapting. A massage might be good for you.'

'Okay, you're good at it. Your hands are strong – shoulders, calves, and waistline. Don't poke too hard.'

'Or too long, Jane. We'll be out of food today, so I must hunt.'

'That's enough massage, Tarzan. I want to try my new clothes, and then if you fill the toilet washbasin and fetch me some soap plant, I'll wash them before exercising.'

'I'll be wearing mine; you can wash them when I return.'

...

'You look good wearing that loincloth, Tarzan. Have you worn one of megalon's hide before?'

'Yes, and you look good too, like a woman who belongs in the forest. How are the sandals?'

'I can hardly feel them; they're great. Why don't you have any?'

'My feet have hardened naturally, but I've made a pair as a safety measure if we cross rivers. Feet slip easily, but megalon's hide doesn't.'

'I can't swim. I tried in a small pool and sank like a rock.'

'I can, but I won't. Some monsters that eat anything live in the rivers and the sea. We'll find a place to cross on a fallen tree.'

'Why did you bring that knife?'

'It's always in my bag or on my hip; it has no metal parts.

The blade is a carbon-fibre reinforced ceramic with a diamond edge. I'll hunt for a tree squirrel. Watch how I prepare the mallet. You'll do it when you learn to throw it.'

Tarzan carefully wound six metres of fishline from his bag around the polished handle, ensuring that each wind stayed beside the next until he pushed the line into a cut near the end of the grip, then coiled the last metre of the line and pressed it into another.

'Now, watch. I'll tie the line-end to my belt and put the mallet into the pouch head down to grab the handle easily. When I pull it out like this,' he pulled it out slowly so she could see, 'the line comes from the second groove and gives me enough to lift the mallet behind my head. I throw, but before the mallet leaves my hand, I give a gentle tug to release the winding line, and the mallet flies out with the line sliding off the handle so I can recover it if it falls through the floor. I also attach my knife to my belt. One middle terrace rule is to tie everything permanently to prevent it from falling, including yourself.'

'How far can you throw?'

'Five metres, hard and accurately, up to ten with less accuracy. I'll show you. Can you see the pale patch on that tree?'

'Yes.'

'Then stand there and watch; don't blink.'

A peculiar thing to say. 'Okay.'

She just caught the explosion of movement as his hand seized the club's handle, rose behind his head in a wide swing, then snapped forward, and the club shot silently to the tree to hit the centre of the pale patch with a solid-sounding thud.

'That's what you must learn to do. Don't worry if it takes months; it took me two years, although I was still a child.'

I hope I can.

'Okay, I understand, but how do you stay safe without me holding one end of the rope? You don't have a tail like a monkey.'

'I hold it, but it limits me to half...Jane, say that again.'

'You don't have a tail like a monkey.'

'I think I love you.'

No man has ever said that to me!

'Why?'

'You've just given me a brilliant idea and taught me a lesson.'

'What?'

'We must have tails. And you have brilliant ideas.'

'That's a good thought, but where will the tail come from?'

'There are two snap carabiners in the safety box. They're there for rappelling. I'll use some rope, and we can have a tail each. With a carabiner on the tail end, we wrap it around a branch and snap the link on the rope. I've been worried about travelling with you because you're a beginner, but now it'll be much safer.

'Let me find some fruit, and then I'll make tails.'

She had to prevent thinking aloud: *you could use the tail you already have.*

'Jane, if you can control my safety for my first traverse, I can double my first leg.'

'Okay, what do I do?'

Tarzan passed the rope around a branch on the floor ahead of her, tied the end to his belt, and then passed her the coil of rope after tying the other end to another branch. 'Feed the rope over the branch ahead as I travel so it stays loose, about three to four metres free. If I fall, you must hold it and keep it tight. It will be easy as it won't slip around the branch. You can release it when I signal, and I'll pull it to me.'

He was back half an hour later with several different fruits and began the tails after they ate.

After Jane had her evening shower, she thought, *I guess my muscles have woken up; I can almost feel them eating up my fat, and I'm not as tired as yesterday.*

She lay down feeling a strange satisfaction.

Tarzan, the tails finished, lay down beside her. 'Sleep, Jane, and if you want another massage tomorrow morning, say so.'

11

Jane woke and turned to look at Tarzan. He was lying on his side facing away from her.

I never imagined sleeping with a man, especially one like Tarzan, but it seems natural as if I've always done so.

His words startled her, 'Jane, you seem to be thinking happiness.'

'I haven't moved yet, so I haven't felt any pain. I suppose I am. Will you tell me about your mother?'

'Okay.' He rolled onto his back so he could see her.

'Mum became a schoolteacher, but in the mornings only, the afternoons she spent with Dad in the forest. After I was born, she took me to school too, initially to sleep with other babies in the school creche, then to play with them. In the afternoons, Mum carried me in a sling, sometimes in front and more often on her back or hip, to collect fungi, for Mum became the fungi specialist. As she learnt more from Dad, instead of just keeping him company, she became a research team member. Mum photographed the fungi she collected, wrote copious notes about them, and made startling observations.

'One was when she noticed another species was always present after sighting one species many times. Mum experimented; she removed one of the two species, one plant at a time and the other began to die within two days. She proved they were symbiotes.'

'But what about the fertility mushroom?'

'That was a complete accident. Mum told me I was two, in a sling on her back, and she wanted to pee. She backed to a tree, spread her legs, bent forward, pulled her panties to one side and did so. Crouching is risky, where innumerable creepy crawlies scramble amongst the debris. She couldn't help but notice she had peed on a mushroom listed in her catalogue and was amazed to see it pop open to shed spores.'

'Okay, and then?'

'She told my dad, and he said, "Do it again."

'She did, every day for a month, on a fresh mushroom each time and then presented her results to Dad. She peed on Fungus forty-three in her catalogue, and the mushroom shed spores five times, and the five times were on adjoining days. She asked him, "Does the fungus have a fertility cycle?"

'And he replied, "Maybe it's responding to yours; do it again and take your temperature each day."

'Of course, that wasn't the end of it. The insemination centres became involved and did tests with many female volunteers. It took six months before they declared the test more dependable than the temperature check because women forgot to take their temperature or did so at differing times, and hormone analysis is laborious and expensive. I think it amusing that with all the available technology, the insemination centre won't waste sperm on a woman who doesn't pee on a mushroom to prove she's fertile.'

Jane laughed, 'For us, it's a serious matter, but I can understand you thinking it's amusing. So is your mum now a researcher or a schoolteacher?'

'Full-time teacher, but since she arranged the distribution of her book on Tarik's fungi, she also has another job.'

'Explain, please.'

'The book has pictures of each fungus she has identified with copious notes, and though it's a scientific document, my dad made sure everyone could understand it.

'A quarter of a million people landed on Tarik, half were women, and a year later, about a hundred and fifty thousand children arrived. Not only did that mean education, but it also meant food, and since then, people have been visiting the forest to scavenge in steadily increasing numbers. If the graph on my mother's wall is right, the visits are accelerating.'

'What's the graph show?'

'The messages she receives from colonies asking about fungi. They come when someone eats a poisonous or hallucinatory mushroom; they see it in the *Mushroom Book* and then ask what to do. She must receive at least one question a week.'

'So, she knows the antidotes?'

'She told me there are very few, but there's a successful palliative treatment for many.

'Let's rise, Jane. I must hunt.'

'I'll peel some fruit, then begin my exercises.'

Jane watched Tarzan leave, his new tail hanging over his left shoulder. He passed the rope around a branch and tied the end to his belt. She took the coil of rope to feed out as she had done the last time as he leapt forward onto a prominent root. A hundred metres later, she saw him attach his tail to a branch, then she released the line, and he stood reeling in the rope to start again for another fifty to sixty metres. She returned to her exercises, which included chin-ups to a bar across the toilet entrance.

An hour later, Tarzan returned with a backpack full of fruit and two squirrels hanging from his belt by their tails. He pulled the rope back and coiled it carefully. 'Jane, this is our lifeline; we must take care of it.

'The tail works well, but it cuts into my shoulder. It needs padding.'

'Use the tubes we took off the safety belts.'

'My love grows in admiration.'

He's doing it again; I never expected to hear that.

'Don't exaggerate, Tarzan. With the padding, it will look like a real tail. You'll soon think like a monkey, and I don't believe they knew what love was. Which reminds me, I need to know what other beasts I might meet.'

'Maybe monkeys didn't love, Jane, but I'll always be a man with a tail, and we're experts on love.'

Jane grinned, 'So far, from my two experiences, I don't think men are experts. More like bumbling idiots who don't know what to do with a tail!'

Tarzan ignored her comment as he undid the thin vines supporting the squirrels from his belt.

'Do we eat those raw?'

'It's possible. I've eaten raw meat, but we can cook squirrels.'

'How?'

'The way humans cooked after eating an animal that had died in a fire. The meat tasted good, and one more intelligent than the others decided to repeat it. They must have burnt their fingers until they stuck the meat on a stick and held it over the flames. That's what we'll do.

'I'll find some dry wood, fire-starting stuff, and two skewers. But I must teach you how to weave a wood collecting basket.'

'Why not use a cushion cover?'

'Everything we carry weighs us down and makes our travelling slower and riskier. Watch me; the basket is crude, useless when it's dry, so we'll make a new one whenever we must collect wood or fruit.'

He re-tied the rope, then danced across to a nearby tree with vines growing on it, used his knife to cut some down, and cut two whip-like stems that rose from the floor while returning. Then he sat with Jane and showed her how to make two loops with the stems and weave the vines between them, splitting a vine into threads to tie the sticks.

As he finished, she remarked, 'That looks easy. Can you bring me some vine and sticks? Then, while you're looking for firewood, I can try to make one.'

If I don't, she might risk her life trying to fetch some. She's not strong enough yet to climb back if she falls.

He fetched what she needed and left with the basket.

He was back in ten minutes with sufficient firewood in the basket. Jane was tying the last knot in her basket.

'Tarzan, that was fun; if you fetch me a pile of vines and thin stems, I think I can make better ones; at least I can try. Where did you find the dry wood? Everything here seems damp.'

'I find a hole, reach in, and check for dead wood; there's usually some.'

'Is there nothing in the hole that might bite or sting your hand?'

'Yes, there is, but I have gloves. I should have shown you. Here, look in the basket.'

She looked, reached in and removed a bundle of what resembled cloth. She pulled it open, 'I thought it was cloth, but it looks like a fine net, with a sticky transparent glue in the holes. What is it?'

'Because it's not in the "Life of the Known Worlds" catalogue, it has no name. The closest thing I found in the catalogue that does the same thing is a spider that weaves a web to catch prey. It seems that between worlds, there's more commonality in behaviour and techniques for survival than the creatures that use them. You're holding a net, but the fibres signal to the glue to make it shrink. The insect that makes it spreads the net where a ray of sunshine comes through the floor above, and if something touches it, the glue shrinks. I spent hours poking sticks into these nets, and the net curled up around the stick within seconds. One day, I touched the net with my finger, and within a minute, it covered my hand in what felt like a skintight glove. So, if I look for firewood, I find two nets, stick my hands in, and then I have gloves. So far, nothing in the hole has stung or bitten me. Either they can't penetrate the net, or they're afraid of the glue. It takes a strong pull to peel the net off.'

He smiled, 'You either didn't notice or didn't want to ask. That's why I have no hair on the back of my hands; the net pulls it out. We could sell it for women to use as a depilatory.'

'Ouch, I could try it on my legs! It might be better than wax. What does the spider look like?'

'I've never seen one except as a dark shadow. The spiders are nocturnal and build their nets during the night. Later in the day, you can see the webs curled around something, waiting for the spider to check after nightfall. At a guess, they have ten legs or more so they can move in any direction without rotating, with sensors on each leg as it's dark, and it must be about the size of your hand, for the net is big, and I've seen some large prey bags. I call it a *Decaspider*.'

'What eats them?'

'The squirrels. When two or three moons are above, the light is strong enough for the squirrels to see them.'

Tarzan fetched a piece of dried skin from his bag. 'This is terragon skin.'

'It's not very big.'

'We don't need a big fire, just a little one in the centre, and we push the sticks in when they burn. Our scientists believe the terragon's predecessors evolved when the planet was much hotter, there were volcanoes everywhere, and fires were common. The skin contains a high concentration of iron, especially a thin layer on the outside, and inside, it's spongy and filled with water; the terragon circulates the water to keep it cool. Our skin allows water to evaporate to cool us. So, I first wet the inside of the terragon skin.'

He walked to their shower and tipped water from a leaf cone.

'Now, I'll lay it where it will be like a shallow plate, then start a fire.'

He arranged ten short sticks radiating from the centre point of the skin, put a handful of moss and woodchips on the centre, and then placed a strip of bark across them.

'What's that?'

'Some trees have an elevated level of complex, volatile hydrocarbons under their bark. That layer is what the tree is converting into new growth. I slice off a piece, and it will catch alight easily. The sparks from a lighter with no fuel are enough. I call it the Firetree. The core wood is hard, dense, and incredibly strong.'

'If we didn't have lighters, would you rub sticks together?'

'I would have to, but I've never tried, although I read about making a fire drill.'

Jane fetched a lighter, and Tarzan said, 'Now light the bark.'

Jane was amazed at how it burst into flame. 'Now, we let it burn while we clean the squirrels and poke a stick into them. We must put the fire out with water once we've finished with it. The terragon skin can eventually burn as the water dries out, but you saw how well the bark burns; we don't want the forest burning around us. Dad says fires are inevitable but must die out quickly here. He doesn't know why. I think it's because there's little dry wood.'

Tarzan ran his knife down the underside of a squirrel, used his fingers to scoop out the entrails, cut off the head, sharpened a stick that he pushed down the neck, and said, 'Here's the knife, you do yours.'

She took the knife, still attached to him with a line, and repeated what he did. He was impressed. 'You did that well, Jane.'

'Mum was squeamish; I did many chickens.'

They sat opposite each other, holding their sticks and rotating them to grill the squirrels. Jane thought. *Seven days ago, I was depressed, then terrified two days later. Now, I'm happier than I've been for years. Is it Tarzan or the forest?*

'How much longer?'

'Until the skin peels off easily, check by pushing it with a twig, then we eat it off the stick.'

'I've never eaten a squirrel; they don't have them in the colony.'

'They're not ground-level creatures; they live in the upper levels.'

'Tell me about them.'

'The squirrels don't yet have a scientific name, but one of the early arrivals reported them as tree squirrels, and the name stuck. They eat mostly seeds and fresh shoots and have front teeth to gnaw holes in which to live. They don't hibernate; I haven't encountered anything on this planet that does, although they may slow down in the drier and hotter season. The form of their feet repeats through other species: two toes with claws on each side and one forward. They evolved to live in the forest, which I'm sure came first on the developmental ladder. The forward claw is razor sharp; they can use it like a knife. When I killed my first one, I attached the forward claw to a stick and used it as a knife, as I didn't have one. The sideways toes and claws evolved to assist them in clinging onto branches; they can run on the underneath of a thin branch.'

'Why do they do that?'

'I'll tell you later. The squirrels live on this level because their feet aren't suitable for the ground, but they steal from the level above when a darter looks the other way.

'Mine looks done; check yours with a stick.'

'It does peel back.'

'Then keep pushing around the neck until you can grab the skin and pull it down to its tail. Then take a bite and tell me what you think.'

'It's delicious, but it needs salt and maybe herbs.'

'Jane, if you criticise the chef, you do the cooking the next time.'

'That might be fun. What fruit did you bring?'

'Open the bag and look. The two with the soft outer skins are sweet. Peel the fruits; they have tiny seeds in thick, firm flesh, and you can eat both. Do so together because the seeds have the flavour. We must finish them in the morning, for they'll be soggy tomorrow night. The other I call milk nuts; there are four of them because they keep in their hard shells. I'll collect as many as I can find. Pass me one, and I'll break it open with the axe.'

Tarzan split a nut into two with a deft axe blow and handed a half to Jane. 'The white interior is a fibrous white paste; I think it tastes like milk.'

Jane tried both fruits, 'They're super, and you're right, the white stuff is like milk, somewhere between almond and soya. However, we should eat other stuff; how do we cook vegetables? Push them into the ashes?'

'That's one way. Until we find some terragon skin to make a cooking bag, we must use a megalon's hide seat cover. We can boil water that way. There's stuff to eat. I'll show you what I learnt when I saw what the animals ate.'

'Tarzan, if I recognise anything, I'll tell you –I want to wash my pants and breast-band, so if you can fill the basin and find some soap plants, I'll wash yours, too.'

It meant half a day working naked; it became a habit, but Tarzan never tired of watching her doing the exercises. He could see the muscle definition improving and the strength flowing into them.

'Tarzan, why do you watch me when I'm exercising?'

'I'm checking whether you're doing them properly.'

Why do I feel disappointed? 'Is that all?'

'I'm also judging how well you're doing; I can see the muscles growing. Besides, you look more beautiful every day.'

I should have expected that. Tarzan says things that men never do.

As the light faded, they slept. Exhausted, Jane slept well; Tarzan was happy and did too.

12

With Jane sleeping tight against him, Tarzan could sense when she began to wake; her skin warmed ever so slightly, her breathing changed, and a leg jerked. Then he sat up, and Jane said, 'This is the best time of the day.'

'Because you don't need to move?'

'No, not that; it's becoming easier every day. I ache, but it's like a pleasure, a reward for doing the job right; it's a funny feeling as if my arms and legs want to exercise.'

'Jane, that's a sign of dopamine addiction. You must avoid it.'

'What do I do?'

'Listen to your body now. Count the repetitions of your exercises, find the number that becomes painful, and stop at that count. Even if you feel you can do more, don't; that's the dopamine acting. Only do each exercise a maximum of four times a day. You must find a balance where your body is building without overstraining it. The dopamine can hide the damage it causes, which will take a long time to repair.'

'Okay, but I like the mornings because we talk. You said you would tell me about the forest and the animals.'

She's improving rapidly, forgetting our situation and her fears. The change in a week is fantastic; maybe the names helped, and she now sees herself as the fictional Jane. Perhaps I'm changing, too; Tarzan doesn't want to lecture students.

'I'll tell you about the forest because you need to know before we travel, but the animals can wait until we meet them.'

'Was the rain always like it is now? At Colony One, we have short and violent thunderstorms in the afternoons, but only occasionally. We receive more water than we want when it rains. That's why I thought of hydrology – how to mitigate the irregular thunderstorm effects.'

'At Colony Nine, it's much the same. I've heard that the colonies close to the poles in the temperate regions have different weather; their storms are milder and last longer, but the rain still comes in storms. We're lucky because we dug drainage ditches to the sea that's not far away, although our sandy soil absorbs the rainfall unless it's torrential.

'The foliage above this forest level protects us, except when the storm passes directly overhead. A storm caught me once. It can be dangerous if branches break and fly around.

'I hope we won't experience one.'

'Why does it come in violent storms?'

'The first reason is that Tarik is a smooth ball; no mountain ranges or high hills exist. The winds are steady and undisturbed. At the equator, they're constant from east to west. It's the reason that temperatures vary so little. At the equator, it cools to twenty-eight at night and builds to thirty during the day. The average temperature drops the further north or south you are, but the variation is still two or three degrees.'

'But what about the dry and wet seasons?'

'Two degrees cooler in winter, but diurnal variation is still two degrees. The moisture content builds from the day's sunshine, convection creates thunderclouds, and the thunderstorms are small, violent, and randomly distributed. Most of the water in the Cascade Creepers is condensation at night, except when a storm breaks over us.

'I've visited the upper level; there are masses of unusual flowers, many plants with roots that wave in the air, and others that grow on the floor. It's beautiful and dangerous, so I didn't stay long.'

'Okay, that's the trees, but what about the lakes?'

'I'll tell you when we see one; there are several kinds. Many have disappeared as the trees invaded them, but the remaining ones may be drying and becoming shallower. I've seen some mostly filled with reeds; the trees will eventually invade and absorb them. They grow a little and shrink again with the seasons.'

'What about the rivers?'

'I'll tell you when we must cross one.'

'Okay, continue with our part of the forest; what is there to eat or use?'

'We're lucky, Jane. The plants up here don't have high iron levels like those on the ground, so they're tasty. There are three that have leaves we can eat raw, but we must boil the others. Then, there are three vine species with roots on the ground; I'll show them to you when I see them. You might recognise them, and others that I don't. They taste good boiled, and one of them is essential because it has a high salt level. There are also mushrooms; my mother is an expert on the ground-level ones, but I avoid them because I'm not sure which are poisonous on this level.

'Then we have the practical plants, you know about the Cascade Creeper, and the basket vines and willows; there are also the soap plants, the one we use as wipes, and one with berries we can press for oil.'

'But we only have squirrels for protein?'

'That, a kind of pig, and the lazy lizard I call the tarizard. The tarizards spend most of the day motionless at our level, so they're easy to kill but hard to spot with their camouflage.

'I'll tell you about them when we see one. Let's start work. I need a fruit basket, and we need more soap plants. I'll keep the silipuss as a surprise.'

'Tarzan, I shall spend all day wondering about the silipuss; that's a fantastic name.'

'It's a fantastic creature.'

Jane followed instructions; she took rest periods between push-ups, squats, and other exercises Tarzan had shown her. She made baskets. When Tarzan returned after an extended foraging and hunting trip, he asked, 'Why all the baskets?'

'I'm experimenting; look at this one. I've made it with an angular weave. If you can bring me longer pieces of vine, it will be even better and quicker to make. I'll try a denser weave tomorrow; it might last two or three days.'

'But when we travel, we can't carry them.'

'No, but I could make a small one like your mallet holster to collect nuts or fruit. If I can produce one with a softer vine, I could stuff the basket and make a pillow.

'Let me do the fire and prepare that squirrel. I must learn.'

'Okay, I'll fill the water bottles.'

When Jane lay down that night, she sighed, 'I enjoyed today, having something to do, not just exercise. Tomorrow morning, you must tell me about the silipuss.'

Jane woke, stretched, rose and visited the toilet as the first dim light allowed her to orient herself. Tarzan felt her move as she disturbed the airflow, and the hair on his face riffled. Like any wild animal attuned to the sounds around him, he heard the rustle of wind in the leaves, the scratch of an insect, and the flop and trickle of a Cascade Creeper cone emptying its liquid load into one below it. The pad-pad-pad of her bare feet was enough to wake him, but only his eyes opened. Tarzan watched; he knew she thought he had built the seat barrier to deter any wildlife from entering their sleeping area when it was to stop her from stepping inadvertently off the platform. As she moved silently, a drifting shadow in the gloom, he thought, *I need not worry; her coordination is superb.*

As she lay down again, she whispered, 'If I woke you, would you tell me about the silipuss?'

'I told you about me; tell me about your mother.'

'No, Tarzan, you leave me alone here when you hunt. If an animal comes, I won't know what it is or what to do, so tell me about the beasts that might attack me.'

'There's only one during the day; if you stay still, it will ignore you. The other is nocturnal, and I'll be here.'

'If you don't tell me about the daytime one, I'll waste all my exercise time looking for it.'

'Okay. I knew about the silipuss as some people had mentioned them. When I first visited the middle-level forest before I met them, they watched me often because sometimes I thought an animal the size of a medium dog was looking at me. Still, it always disappeared behind a tree when I looked towards it. The funny thing is I was sure they weren't dangerous, just discreet. When I saw one, I thought, "That thing is watching me again." There's been one watching us every day, different ones.'

'So how did you meet one?'

'I was just fourteen and beginning to roam. Before that, I climbed up the tree with steps and hooks that I pegged to it with wooden pins, then just looked around a small area. Most of the time, I crawled; I didn't stand and jump. By fourteen, I was growing and had worked out how to use a rope for safety, so I was traversing further and further from my base tree. I had marked every tree I reached, pointing the way home. Then, one day, I had just finished a traverse. Without a tail, I had to sit on a branch while I coiled the rope and prepared for another traverse. When I stood to start, I heard what sounded like a scrap I couldn't see, lots of thrashing around and grunting, twenty or thirty metres away behind a tree. So, I decided to look.'

'And there was a silipuss. What was it fighting?'

'A neurotic pig.'

'Tarzan, this sounds like a fantasy tale.'

'It's not. The neurotic pig is another animal, like the silipuss, named by the first person who saw it. The neurotic pig is usually confused, never knows whether it will attack or run, and hates anything that moves. It has two tusks sticking up from the lower jaw with a row of grinding teeth, and the upper jaw is a bone plate. Its eyes look sideways, so it waggles its head as it scans around it. It's vegetarian and has the Tarik signature feet, but its claws are so large and powerful that a pig can hang underneath the floor despite its mass and travel upside down. The first guy to see one said it looked like a pig but was neurotic. I don't think it's neurotic, just that it has a terrible inferiority complex.'

'That sounds like more fantasy.'

'No, Jane, just logic. If you were half blind, had teeth only in your lower jaw, and knew you were good to eat, how would you react if you saw something odd?'

'Okay, I'll give you that one. Where's the advantage of walking upside down?'

'Work that out yourself, Jane; look up at the third-level floor, imagine that turned over so the bottom was on top and ask which floor, ours or the imaginary one, would be easier to travel over fast.'

Jane looked, thought, frowned, and then smiled. 'Our floor has dead wood, leaves, and hundreds of shoots and small saplings growing on it. We must work our way around or through them; up there, it's clear, nothing grows down, and the pig can travel in a straight line.'

'Exactly, and the pig, like the squirrel, can escape by dropping upside down, except the neurotic beasts often attack; I believe they do that if there's no hole to drop through. They're vegetarian but can seriously damage a tree with their tusks, as they like to rip off chunks of bark and eat the soft underside. This forest is alive, Jane; it's an ecosystem. If the pigs do too much damage, the trees call on the silipuss to eat them. The silipuss eats tarizards and squirrels, but a pig is a feast for several.'

'When I rounded the tree, I saw a silipuss with a leg in a pig's mouth, trying to scratch its eyes and avoid the tusks.'

'What did you do?'

'My dad gave me my knife as a fourteenth birthday present, that's why I can remember the date, and the first thing I did with it was to carve one of the bigger shoots into a spear. They're dead straight and hard, but the diamond on the knife can cut anything. It was a bit shorter than my height. I had it slung over my back, so I removed it and tried to find a place to stick it into the pig. It was difficult as they were moving in their struggle, but when I shouted, "*Stand still*", it frightened them, and they did for a second, and I thrust the spear through the pig.'

'So, you killed it?'

'Maybe. It fell on its knees, and the silipuss finished it with a swipe of its cutting claw, so I suspect I only injured it, perhaps mortally.'

Jane tried to imagine a fourteen-year-old boy with a wooden spear becoming involved in a fight with two wild animals. Those boys she had known would have run home. Then Jane felt an odd affection for him. *He makes me feel safe.*

'What happened then?'

'It was interesting; the puss cleaned out the entrails, and before he finished, three others arrived, and they began cutting bits off the pig. I wanted a bit for myself, so I stepped forward. They let me reach it, and I cut off a steak. I used the diamond knife, and I'm sure one of them had watched and *thelt* something like, "Nice claw."'

'So then?'

'I just sat down by the tree and watched. Others came and took a piece of meat, and the first four sat with me and chewed their bits, so I did, too. It was the first time I ate raw pig; it was tasty. The injured puss was the last to leave after nothing remained. I was sure he said thanks, so I thought him a "Glad to have helped."'

'So, have you seen him since?'

'Unless I see one with scars on his leg, I wouldn't know, but now you won't believe what I say. All the silipusses, whether they've seen me or not, all over the planet know about me and what I did. I'm an honorary silipuss everywhere. If they see me wherever I am, they come and say hello.'

'What do they call us?'

'*Thing.* For the two years before I met them, when I sensed one was watching, I thought, "That thing is watching me again." They must have caught the thought and now use it as their name for us. They *theel – Hello Thing.*'

'Why haven't I seen one?'

'They're in the shadows, Jane, trying to assess you; maybe you'll see one when they're satisfied you won't scream.'

'What do they look like?'

'Twenty kilos of muscle, with a prehensile tail they can use to hold onto a branch. That allows them to stand on their back legs and use the claws of their forefeet. They're dark grey, with darker multi-shaded green stripes, so you can't see them in the shadows. The heads are like round balls, and the widely spaced eyes look forward, giving them excellent binocular vision for judging how far it is to the next branch. Their ears are small, with thick hairs that are more like thin, flexible bones and stick out sideways. The mouth is wide, it curves around, and they can open it wide like a smile. Their teeth are a mix that suits a carnivore that eats insects and occasionally meat.'

Jane was silent while she reviewed what she had learnt, then asked, 'Is that the only time you were close to one?'

'No, I had one live with me for three weeks about two years ago, during a holiday.'

'Then tell me.'

'I had returned from a hunt with two squirrels; one should have been enough, but the first one was small, so I tried for another, and the second was huge. I had sat down to clean them when a puss appeared and sat opposite me. It looked hungry and a bit underfed, and then I noticed swollen teats and a drip of milk. I imagined two little kittens, and the puss said I was right.'

'How?'

'I just sensed I was right. So, I offered the big squirrel to it. I'm sure it said, "*Wait.*" Then, it disappeared and came back some minutes later with two kittens in its mouth. I gave the small squirrel to the kittens and the big one to the mother, then stood up and thought, "*Hunt*", and returned with another for myself.

'The mother left the kittens with me when she hunted and regained her condition rapidly.'

'Thanks, Tarzan. I feel more confident knowing about them and the pig. We should shower, then you can hunt while I exercise.'

'I must renew the vines binding our shower platform first; they've dried, and if I don't, they'll loosen, the branches will move, and we might slip and fall.'

'Okay, after I shower, please. Then I'll start with pull-ups.'

Tarzan left to collect vines and returned ten minutes later with a bundle over his shoulder. Jane, still naked after her shower, was pulling herself up to the bar and counting, 'Twelve, thirteen, fourteen...'

As Tarzan finished his work on the platform an hour later, he looked at Jane. 'What are you doing?'

'I've done a complete cycle of the exercises; now I'm stretching. I've found these yoga positions in between cycles keep the stiffness away.

'I'll do another cycle soon, then make baskets while I rest.'

'Great idea, Jane. I'll hunt.'

13

Naked, Jane was exercising when she noticed movement not far away. Distracted, she stopped doing press-ups to look. Seventy metres away, what seemed like an oversized Earth chicken slowly approached her. It appeared to have attracted the attention of something else. To one side, half hidden behind a tree, a shadow moved. She thought it was watching, but the chicken-like figure either didn't see it or ignored it. Alarmed, she could only hope it didn't attack. As the small animal neared, she could tell it was quite different from a chicken, although it did walk on two legs, picking its way slowly towards her, sometimes shuffling sideways on a branch or root until it could step forward to another. It had no wings but two delicate arms.

She estimated it was a metre high and could make out its head; its face resembled the pictures she had seen of Chinese dogs in the evolutionary handbook, with big, soft green eyes and a snub nose. Its feet were a bigger version of the squirrels' feet, and the hands the same but smaller. It was visibly male.

Jane sat so she would be at the same height and waited until it reached her. She was surprised when it plumped down before her, carefully looked at her, and said – *Mama.*

It hadn't opened its mouth, but she knew what it said!

Is this telepathy? And I understood?

Jane understood the next feeling – *Hunger.*

I wonder what it eats. I hope it's fruit.

She reached to the side, pulled the fruit basket to her, and removed one of the soft fruits. She could see the boy was excited when she gave him the fruit. She watched while he used his front claws to peel the fruit deftly, then surprised when he offered half to her and sensed – *We share.*

She took it and tried a *theel* – *Thank you.* She finished her half first and removed a milk nut from the bag. The boy looked and then turned away. She wondered if he disliked the fruit or didn't know what it was. The axe was beside her with the basket-weaving plants, so she cracked the nut in two, offered him half, and tried to *theel* – *We share.*

After a good sniff, he dipped a claw into the milky inner and then licked his claw. Jane heard – *Good, Good,* and the boy tucked in, scooping out the milky fibre.

Still seated, Jane watched the little creature cleaning the last dregs from the milk nut half with the claw on his hand when Tarzan returned from his daily scavenging with a branch that he laid to one side. Her visitor immediately jumped into Jane's lap and faced Tarzan.

'Jane, what have you found?'

'I didn't; he found me. I think he's a child, and I heard him say "Mama."'

'That must be a *thelt*, a telepathic message. You have breasts, so you're a mother. I'll try to ask him something – *We Share. Lost?*

The reply was simple but surprisingly loud – *Warm, happy.*

Surprised, Jane said, 'I understood what he said.'

'He's intelligent, Jane, and you have a child to look after, or at least he's decided you'll look after him. Forest rules, Jane, we must care for him.'

'Then you'd better double the fruit collection and fetch lots of milk nuts; he adores them. Will he stay, Tarzan? Something was watching him as he came here.'

'How big, Jane?'

'I could see only a part of a shadow, maybe about his size.'

'I'll guess that's a silipuss. But I expect a parent is looking for him. I'll try to broadcast a message.'

'How will you do that?'

'I'll *theel* an image of you and the child and say – *We Share, lost child.*'

'I heard that. To whom?'

'I hope a silipuss will pick it up and retransmit.'

'Okay, why did you bring that branch?'

'It'll take some time, Jane, but I'll carve that while you exercise. Although I expect I must collect milk nuts for a while.'

'Carve what?'

'Rope levers, I'll show you when you're strong enough to climb trees. I found this branch; it broke off a Firetree, and as I told you, the centre is a superb hard-wearing wood.'

'I can wait for you to show me, but what are they for?'

'The rope we have is too thin for our hands to grip. To climb it, we would have to wrap it around our hands, and that's painful. Also, if it's wet and slides from our fingers, it can burn away the skin on them. Rope levers are like having wooden fingers that we can't feel.'

'Then I'm in favour. Carve away!'

The child seemed tired after eating the milk nut and fell asleep. Jane lifted him from her lap and laid him to sleep on his stomach. He wriggled a bit, then fell asleep again. She and Tarzan ate some of the fruit he had brought, then he made another foray for milk nuts, and she exercised.

Later, with Tarzan watching, she broke open another nut and gave their visitor a half nut and an empty shell of water. When they settled down for the night, he snuggled between them.

'Tarzan, I was initially worried, but he's toilet trained. He left the GravBus to pee.'

When they woke in the morning, the little one was still asleep. Tarzan asked, 'Jane, after your mother, tell me about Jessica.'

'That sounds odd, but it's accurate. I don't feel like Jessica any longer.

'I can't recall much before I was five or six. I can picture my room, Mum, and Dad, but I don't remember school before I was seven or eight. I learnt to read when I was young, and Dad told me stories about the plants he grew. He was good at making them up.'

'Can you remember one?'

'Yes, quite clearly, the story of the "Lonely Seed".

'It was about a plant that shed its seeds and didn't mind when a little animal ate all the grains but one. It felt happy to feed the animal. But one tiny seed was all alone when the wind blew it into a space between branches, and then it began to grow. The story continued with the seed's problems, like drought and different insects as it struggled to grow, and how it made friends with another plant, and they helped each other.'

'It sounds like your dad believes in evolution and symbiotic plants.'

'Possibly, but I told you he's a practical and straightforward man; he would say that it's not a belief; it's what he's seen.'

'That's the best kind of belief. Knowing, not guessing. Please continue.'

'Those stories had a lasting effect on me; at primary school, my favourite subject was nature studies, although the teacher knew little about Tarik. I found myself trying to replace all the plants the teacher spoke about with those my mother used and those my father grew. I found it fascinating.'

'Jane, I did say something two days ago, although it seems like months, that between worlds, there's more commonality in behaviour and techniques for survival than the creatures that use them. I was talking about the *Decaspider*, but it applies equally to the plant kingdom. To survive, they must combat drought and predators on any planet and will use a selection of the same techniques and behaviours.'

'I remember you saying that. Once I started on that road, it seemed natural that evolution and ecology became my subjects. I was like all the girls in my age group; we played with dolls when we were young but grew out of that quickly once we understood about sex and the insemination centres; our interests were group sports like netball and hockey. Looking back at that period, I can't remember many girls interested in art or dancing, although, in the later teens, we danced in groups and sang. I'm a terrible singer. None of the girls was overly interested in boys; we all had things to do to help our parents once we were free of the day's studies. It must have something to do with survival.

'Then I started studying at the university, and it took two

years to learn that, like in school, all the course material comes from the other Earths. There was nothing about Tarik. That's when I began to think of a more practical subject.'

The child woke, and Jane gave it another half milk nut and one of water; then she reached for the basket weaving material and began making a basket. The boy first retreated, then as the basket grew, he came closer and watched, interested. Jane knew he couldn't understand her words, but she began talking as she started on the sides and showed him what she was doing. 'See, I'm folding up the bottom radial strips and holding them in place with this vine fibre; then I'll wind it around again....'

Tarzan came over as she finished the basket. 'Is it ready, Jane? I need to hunt. I heard you talking. Have you taught Happy to make baskets?'

'That's a good name. I don't think he can without hands like ours, but he was interested.'

'Then make a little basket for him and show him what to do with it. Put some leaves in it.'

She did – and then thought. *Well, Happy is sleeping. I can exercise.*

Two hours later, Tarzan returned. The boy woke, and Jane gave him another half-nut of milk and one of water.

He had almost finished when he stopped and looked towards where he had first appeared.

'Jane, I sense a parent is coming.' – *We share.*

Thank you. We share.

Jane estimated the figure appearing from the gloom was as tall as Tarzan but much slimmer. She recognised its walk and how it shuffled occasionally along a branch. When it finally reached them, she saw a face that resembled the child's, with the same green eyes, and that it was male.

It seemed to have a silent conversation with the boy, who showed signs of sheepishness, so Jane thought it was a rebuke, but when the child exhibited his basket to its father, the father showed interest and smiled – *like us. We share.*

Then, the child held out a hand that his father took and led him off the platform. As they walked away, Happy carrying his basket, Jane and Tarzan heard – *thank you, we share.*

As they disappeared between the trees, Jane said, 'You never told me about that species, Tarzan, and I miss Happy already. I didn't know what having a child to look after was like. Mothers should have a baby lending system for girls without sisters and brothers.'

'I doubt they would lend their children, Jane, but I have never met that species on Tarik before, although I think Dad must have met one from the description he gave. He called it a *TerraKid*. I'll have to think about what makes us capable of telepathic communication, but I'm sure we'll both improve until we don't need to talk much. We have a long way to travel and will meet that species again.'

'And they'll know who we are?'

'Yes, like the silipusses, and I suspect the megalons, terragons, and others, too.'

'Tarzan, you sound psychotic; I'm beginning to wonder about your sanity.'

'Jane, you know the humans on the planet are prisoners;

there's no way we can leave, and no one will come and fetch us.'

'Yes. At school, we learnt the megalons ate the shuttles that we used to reach the surface from the transport ships. And then, all the incoming transports had no shuttles to unload their colonists. Instead, they had heavy machinery. They turned back, and we never received that equipment or more colonists.'

'Did you learn how it happened?'

'No, just that it did.'

'The leaders lined up the shuttles in rows, eight at each colony, far from the centre, and out of missile range, ready for the next incoming transport. The megalons ate none of the shuttles in the first year, but then a megalon ate one. That megalon must have thought it tasty, for he told his mates and the following day, different megalons ate all the remaining shuttles worldwide. Tell me how that could happen.'

Jane's reply was expressive, a meek, 'Oh.'

Then she asked, 'So a *thelt* travels further than a spoken message?'

'From my limited experience, I would say a little. It can be a private message, a whisper that no one else hears if you can see the other person, like Happy and his dad, or a broadcast that anyone in range receives. But if it's not for them, those receivers send it on, and the message can travel much further.'

14

For six more days, Jane exercised diligently, and Tarzan collected firewood, fruit, and squirrels. Every morning, they explored each other's thoughts and memories.

'Jane, do you have dreams or ideas about what you want your life to be?'

Jane hesitated, 'I must think about that...

'Tarzan, sometimes I'm sure you understand how I feel before I tell you, and the last time you massaged me, I thought you felt where I ached before I told you. Is that a dream?'

'I don't think so. There are some things I can tell you.'

Put your arm under my head.

'Tarzan, I just thought, "Put your arm under my head," and you did. Did you hear me think it?'

'No, Jane, but it's an example of what I'll say. I sensed you wanted to be closer to me and wanted comfort, so I put my arm under your head; I couldn't put it anywhere else unless I lifted you. I believe that all life, whether it can talk with words or not, can project feelings as a form of speech. We, the word speakers, use "body language" to describe it, but depending on the individual's species and age, I think there's more than just a physical display. Sometimes, it may result from learning or training; I read an article about "How your dog trains you." It explained that a dog owner learnt what certain of the dog's body language displays meant, and later, the dog needed to only display a part, like a sad look, for the owner to understand it was hungry. But that doesn't explain everything. I have read about experts who claim we have gestures and postures that are common between people and that they can interpret them, like folding your arms, crossing your legs, or scratching your nose or head. But it doesn't explain why they're common or how someone who isn't an expert can sense the same thing.'

'Continue, this is interesting.'

'If a sender can project feelings like radio waves, they can provide a structure the receiver needs to fill in. I know that if I look into a person's eyes and think, "Tell me about you," it may make the person feel uncomfortable, and I sense something.'

'Like you did when we first met.'

'I'm surprised you remember, but yes.'

'What did you sense?'

'It upset you a little, but you liked me.'

'I guess that's right. Have you always done it?'

'I can't remember doing so when I was young, but if you watch babies who can't talk, I think they do, so maybe it's something we lose as we grow older.'

'What have you seen while watching babies that can't talk?'

'Have you seen a baby smiling in its first week or two?'

'Yes, although it's not a smile, it's a grimace because they've swallowed air, and it hurts.'

'Only at first, it takes only a few days for the baby to learn that if it wants a hug, the smile will work, so what was a natural reaction to an air bubble has two meanings and the fascinating thing is that the mother is never wrong, she knows the difference, and yet it's not something visible to a stranger. The baby can project the feeling of happiness or agony, and the mother senses it.'

'Then why haven't you lost it?'

'I reckon first the forest and then the silipusses combined to keep the ability alive. The pusses can project more than just a feeling; they can project a picture we can interpret, which we have always been good at.'

'Tarzan, you're complicating your description. Explain.'

'Say I want to tell a hunting partner, "Stick your spear into the side of the beast." I must say it: he must know and understand the words and hear them over bellowing and screaming. If I send him a simple picture, the stick figure of a man with a spear plunging it into the beast, he will understand immediately and do it, a limited but far more effective communication than words. Hundreds of thousands of years ago, when those two returned to their cave with their kill, one of the men might have painted the scene from his head on the cave wall, and the others in the cave would have understood the meaning.

'Present-day humans can't project those images, but we like pictures and know which ones have a message. Projecting such a message or feeling is as good as projecting a picture. On Tarik, something stirs up the genes and our ability. Projecting such a feeling is a *thelt.*'

'Jane, you can tell me tomorrow about your dreams.'

'I will.' – *Put your arm around me.*

Tarzan slept as he usually did in the forest like anyone asleep in familiar surroundings, yet the slightest unusual sound, smell or light change would trigger a sense and wake him; his confidence that his senses would filter out the moonlight, the rustle of leaves, and the changing smell of the night air, allowed his deep sleep.

Jane didn't; she slept with the question, 'What are my dreams?' so she tossed and turned several times. An hour before dawn, she woke and lay thinking. When she heard Tarzan's breathing change, she thought, *He said breathing has hiccups when you wake.*

'Tarzan, are you awake?'

'Yes.'

'I've thought about your question and my dreams. There are two answers, one before the GravBus crash and the other after. Before, I was too young to have formed any firm opinions. I think taking the GravBus contract was a sign of dissatisfaction. The idea of hydrology had simmered for a while. I felt useless and wanted to do something worthwhile with results I could measure and see. That ended with a life-changing experience in a toilet.'

Tarzan laughed, 'A marvellous description, Jane. For us both. But what about your social life and personal likes and dislikes?'

'I didn't have much social life; none of the girls did. We spent most of our time helping our parents. From what I read about the planet we came from, life for us is hugely different, and I can't say much without being able to compare. I can't remember girls discussing what food they liked; it must be the same for boys: we ate what was available and still do. As for people, there's little competition; if we're competing, it's with the planet, not each other.

'I suppose we all expect that one day we'll have one or two children, but as men cannot give us children, we feel it necessary to reach a point where we can provide for ourselves and a child before visiting the insemination centre.'

'So, you don't expect to marry or have a man in your life.'

'That's what's so odd; we all do. The young women feel as I do that men may not be necessary to make us pregnant, but we want a close and loving relationship to fill our environment to raise a child like Mum and Dad. I'll add that my personal feeling is that I would like a man to marry me as a mark of his love and commitment to my children and me. It doesn't need to be a formal or legal ceremony, just something special between us.

'Do you think I'm odd?'

'No, Jane, unless being more normal than most women is odd, I believe what you feel is genetic memory. But thanks for telling me.'

'Can you explain what you mean?'

'I could try, but it would be a biologist's explanation, and you'll probably accuse me of being a macho misogynist.'

'I promise not to. Although I might think so.'

'Okay, all sexual creatures have pre- and post-mating behaviour that falls somewhere between two extremes; these are where the female eats the male after fertilisation, and the opposite end where the male receives the fertilised egg and manages the pregnancy and birth.'

'Tarzan, do those extremes exist? If they do, it's fantastic.'

'Several insect species on the known planets eat the male after mating. On the other end, I know of two. On Old Earth, there is a fish called a hippocampus, although it's often called a seahorse. There is also a long, thin fish, Syngnathinae, which they call a pipefish, which does the same thing. A similar species exists on Exo Earth Three.'

'Okay, I'll believe that. Where do we fit?'

'Somewhere between the extremes, where monogamy exists

in three groups. Most humans fall into one of these three: until birth, the child reaches adulthood, or life ends. Although a small percentage may not, all three groups are "perhaps until".'

'That's not very encouraging. But what does that have to do with me not being odd?'

'The males of the monogamous group stay around to share the task of raising children. In most egg-laying species, they must, or the species would die out because the female can't feed herself and incubate the eggs. The males share the task, bring her food, and then help feed the babies.

'When proto-humans began to walk upright, the skeletal structure changed, and the females gave birth to babies that needed extensive care for months. She needed the help of a male. That continued for hundreds of thousands of years. That's your genetic memory and why you want the same thing, although the advanced and complex social systems on the overpopulated Earths have relieved men of the necessity to help women by taking on that responsibility: creches, schools, orphanages, social and medical services, government support and handouts. It's men who have benefitted the most, not women. In our pioneer society without the trappings of Earth Four civilisation that never arrived, men must learn to take on that role again. Hence, the way you feel is biologically correct.'

'And the Tarik animals?'

'I can only tell you about those I know; they're pre-monogamous, like humans when we lived in groups where all participated in the responsibility. But on Tarik, the group includes every intelligent being on the planet, and they have standard rules of behaviour. I don't know why, but I'm determined to learn the cause.

'But now, let's work. I must find some food.'

15

Jane began her exercise regime, and five minutes later, Tarzan stepped into the forest to search for food. He returned in forty minutes with an overflowing basket of fruit and plants that Jane examined.

'Tarzan, if you don't let me search for food, you must take orders.'

'Why?'

'This plant you've brought, are we eating the leaves?'

'Yes, boiled, they're good.'

'Well, if you had dug up the roots, which are bulbs, we would have delicious roasted apples.'

'Then I'll look the next time I see them; only once I'm sure I won't have to scrape you off the forest floor will I approve of you leaving here.'

'Then look for another plant; the leaves are the same shape and size but have longitudinal yellow stripes. Don't bother with the leaves, but the bulbs are like onions.'

Tarzan grinned, 'Anything else, Jane? Some ice cream, perhaps?'

I'll show him. 'If you can find the onion plant and a bunch of purple and yellow orchid flowers, I'll make your ice cream.'

I deserved that.

'Well, we have no ice cream tonight, but I have a squirrel and some onion bulbs.'

'That's great, and that reminds me. There's a plant that looks like the onion one, but the leaves aren't smooth; they're very wrinkled around the edges. The bulbs are like garlic when they're dry. When you're looking, don't just look; crumple a bit of leaf in your fingers and smell it. Bring me some leaves and bulbs to check if there's a strong smell. There are several herbs to make a roast much tastier.'

'I will Jane, I'm sure you can do better than my camp cooking. But now I want to carve the rope levers.'

He fetched a piece of roughly shaped wood and began carving while Jane watched. She watched his hands moving unhurriedly yet with strength, forcing his knife to shave precise strips from the wood. *He's like a skilled sculptor who can sense the grain of the wood. I would enjoy having him carve me if I were a piece of wood.*

She appreciated how carefully he carved a slot. *He would have to start with a new piece of wood if he messed up that bit.*

'There, Jane. A rope lever.'

'It's a handle with a small paddle with a half slot on one end and a lump on the other. How's it used.'

'I'll hold this piece of rope vertically; it's so thin that gripping it with your hands is risky; they can slip and burn you. I could climb by wrapping the rope around my hand, but I accidentally discovered this when a stick with a broken side branch tangled in my rope.

'Hold the handle and slide the slot over the rope. It's wide enough if the handle points upwards; then, pull the handle down, and it grips the rope. The lump helps your hand from slipping if it's sweaty.'

Jane did and exclaimed, 'That's cool!'

'I'll do three more when I have a moment; I'll fetch firewood now.'

As they lay down that night, Jane reminded him.

'Now it's your turn to talk about your dreams, Tarzan.'

'Jane, you haven't said anything about your post-crash ambitions.'

'I won't; I have only one, to finish this exercise program and begin travelling with you. Ask again in six months, and I'll have an idea. But you can tell me yours.'

'I'll continue from where I left off.

'With a laboratory to check for poisonous content, Mum had an extensive list of edible plants and fruit, and I grew up spending long hours with my parents in the forest, eating berries and fruit, chewing on leaves and leaf stems, and drinking the rainwater that filtered down the vines from the upper levels. We saw an occasional odd beast that never attacked when we tiptoed away. Overall, Jane, the forest was friendly; I was happier there than with the kids in the colony.

'After my seventh birthday, I spent more time listening in the corner of Mum's classroom than playing in the junior school.

'At ten, I wanted to look at the first forest level. Dad helped me at first to build a stairway, but it took me over two years. My parents watched me but didn't intervene.

'Dad gave me an axe, a knife, and a rope. He then spent hours with me practising knots and taught me about safety.

'From then on, the middle tier was my hunting ground. I didn't think about what I wanted to study. I signed up for

Biology and Botany; the courses were remote. My father was my teacher, and I didn't need to live in Colony One, but I almost failed. I didn't like the subjects because, as you said, everything in the course came from another planet.'

'But you passed?'

'Yes, Dad fixed my problem. He said what I've repeated to you, "Timothy, they may not be the same plants or life forms, but the forces of evolution, survival, and the techniques adopted are the same. For every plant or lifeform in the course material, think of a Tarik equivalent that would fit, and you'll find they do. At the end of your studies, you'll have a Tarik course on biology. If you modify the course material like that, you might earn a place at the university as a lecturer."'

'I did what he said. Dad was my proofreader, so I took the GravBus to Colony One and met you on the flight.'

'And now, Tarzan?'

'I'm changing too, Jane; lecturing is no longer important. I'm unsure, but I'll tell you once I know.'

After two weeks, Tarzan said, 'You're looking good, Jane. Your body has used the fat and soft tissue; exercise will build extra muscle.'

'I think you're growing too, especially your arms. My progress seems unusual; do you have an explanation why?'

'Compared with what it would be if you were eating our so-called civilised foods, it is. The squirrels are high in protein, but it's the planet's protein, high in iron compounds like most plants and animals. We'll both improve at a surprising rate. Although I developed earlier, my time in the trees was never continuous; we're both in a gym, exercising twelve hours a day. We're also alone; you don't need to fight off the bacteria and viruses propagating between people. You'll never be sick.'

'Is that why you stare lasciviously at my naked body?'

'You stare at me too, but I'm checking on your health and progress, trying to decide when to begin new exercises.'

'Oh, that's a letdown; I thought you were thinking about sex with me.'

'Do you make love often?'

'I don't think I ever have; made love, that is. I've had sex twice. Like most girls over fifteen, I've tried. The first time was a failure, the second a washout. Now that you men are all sterile, somehow, it's not the same thing. Sex has lost something. In the history books I read, keeping men away from young girls was an imperative operation with laws and taboos. They've vanished because we girls can't fall pregnant. The men have lost interest as they can't propagate their genes. There are always some men who want to try it and others who treat it as another form of masturbation or a pleasant way to pass the time. For girls, it's either better than masturbation or relief from boredom – something that girls restricted to a colony feel a lot more than men – or often in return for a favour or company, what your mother called transactional sex in her summary.

'So, Tarzan, I don't understand what the books call love or making love, and none of my friends could tell me anything more.

'In the meantime, we can both enjoy looking. But I must be practical; I have nothing for my menses due now.'

'That's why I said to keep our clothes: Cut and fold pads and wash them. They should fit snugly in your megalon's hide bikini.'

'Okay, now what was that about my health? Is it about vitamins and things?'

'I'm no expert, Jane; we both have everything we need, even though our food has little sunshine and variety. I suspect the squirrels have all the various vitamins and minerals, and although the fruits don't see much sun, they're on vines that hang down from above; they have their leaves in the sunshine, so the fruits have vitamin C.'

Later that morning, Tarzan made her exercises more challenging. She was fluidly pulling herself up to the bar until her breasts touched it, and when she stopped, he said, 'Jane, watch me.'

He gripped the bar with one hand, lifted himself to his nipples, and then continued the movement, changing the hand position until his waist was on the bar.

'Why must I do that?'

'If you need to climb a rope, there are two ways: With one, you lift yourself with both arms with the cord wrapped around a leg. You can lock it with your feet while you slide your hands up for the next pull. It's like those caterpillars we see that move the back-end forwards, and the middle rises in a hump, then they move the front forward. The other way is hand over hand; it's like walking up the rope with your arms only; your legs are just security. It's much faster. Sometimes, speed is everything if you need to avoid a predator. You can climb hand over hand if you can pull up with one arm as I did. Alternate the arm you use for the pull-up.

'The sit-ups have built your tummy muscles; I can see them.

You must strengthen your back muscles. I'll bring you a log. Hold it across your shoulders, lie on your tummy, hook your legs under a seat, and try to raise your head as far up as possible.'

'Finally, I think you're ready for some balance exercises. I'll bring you a beam. I'll have to find one first.'

He brought the beam, a four-metre branch length; it rocked slightly from side to side when he laid it down. 'There, Jane, try walking along it.'

She stepped onto it and stood precariously, trying to balance when the beam moved. Eventually picking up courage, she took two steps and fell off. Annoyed, she said, 'Show me how you can do it.'

He stepped onto it and stood without moving.

'How can you do that?'

'Look at my feet, Jane.'

'They're wobbling just a little.'

'Like you were waving your arms around and overcompensating. My body has learnt what to do. You have enough strength now – practice; it will come.' Then he walked casually the length of the branch and back. 'You should manage that in two weeks.'

That night, as Jane lay down, she could feel the ache in her upper body. She had done single-arm pull-ups with each arm until she could do no more.

16

Jane woke and could still feel the exercise's after-effects. 'Tarzan, is there still some cream left?'

'Yes, do you want another massage?'

'Only my shoulders and arms.'

'Okay, I'll fetch it.'

'Jane, I guess as your parents didn't marry officially, Kruger is your mother's name.'

'Yes, and she told me once her mother was Jessica Kruger, so she named me after my grandmother. I suppose my grandmother never married.

'Do some more between my neck and shoulders...

'That's fine, Tarzan. I feel much better. Hunt, I'll stretch, then exercise.'

Tarzan gathered his hunting gear and left after eating yesterday's fruit with Jane, who fed out his safety rope and then stood watching him. Once he had disappeared in the distance, she began her exercise regime with press-ups. After following the press-ups with squats, she fetched the wooden log that she used to weigh her feet while she did sit-ups. Once it had felt heavy, but little more than a one-and-a-half-metre branch four to five centimetres in diameter, it now felt much lighter, but it was still enough when jammed under the side seats to hold her heels from lifting.

Jane did a variation of Tarzan's exercise. As she sat up with her hands behind her head, instead of the right elbow to the right knee, she touched the right elbow to the left knee and, on the following sit-up, the left elbow to the right knee. It forced a twist of her body that she hoped would help build her back muscles.

With her feet under the log facing the sidewall, with each sit-up, she looked alternately at the toilet door or the gap in the seat barrier fence as she counted aloud.

'Twelve, thirteen, fourteen ... thirty-one, thirty-two.' *What's that?*

She had seen movement between the seats at the limit of what she could see in the gloom.

With a niggle of fear of the unknown, she thought. *I'll see better standing.*

She bent forward to grasp and remove the log over her ankles and used it as a support to stand, then stood gazing over the seat barrier into the distance between the trees. Nothing stirred.

Two minutes later, about to sit again, she caught a flicker of movement to the left of the line where she looked.

A shadow moved, but it was not in the same place. *Are there two?*

She waited, leaning on her stout support, motionless apart from her eyes moving from side to side.

...

It's there; a beast is coming. I mustn't move, and it will ignore me.

The shadow to the left flickered again, and as Jane turned her head slowly to look, another shadow moved to her right. The tendril and her tension grew.

There's more than one, at least three.

The first beast resolved from a moving shape, and at fifty metres, Jane thought. *That one fits Tarzan's description of a neurotic pig. I mustn't move, but I'll hide in the toilet if it attacks.*

Her fear and tension faded once she had a backup plan, and Jane, still motionless, watched as the pig approached, only her eyes switching to either side.

Those other shadows are closer. I think they're following but hiding from the pig.

Jane smiled as the pig approached; she thought it amusing as it waggled its head from side to side to see where to walk, and six metres from the GravBus, tensing for a jump into the toilet, the pig changed direction to avoid the GravBus, and when she lost sight of it, she relaxed.

The pig reversed its direction, and when Jane turned to look for the other shadows, her movement was enough for the pig to catch sight of her three metres away as it passed the gap and immediately wheeled and charged.

Jane didn't have the time to enter the toilet, but instinct and the schoolgirl hockey player took control. The log rose as the pig came through the gap, and she swung as hard as she could, smashing the pig on the side of its head with a resounding thump that broke the log.

It collapsed, and Jane, standing with only the stump of her weapon in her hand, froze as she had yet to work out the next step.

Before she had fully understood that the pig was either dead or unconscious, in a blur of movement, something she had never seen appeared from behind the seat barrier and fell on the pig with slashing claws.

Mesmerised, Jane didn't move, and then the beast backed

away, sat and stared at her – *Hello, mother.*

She had no idea why she didn't feel frightened. *It seems friendly, and it thinks I'm a mother. It might be a silipuss, but whatever it is, it's handsome.*

Then, two more appeared silently without warning and sat beside the first. Perplexed, Jane felt she had to do something but didn't know what to do. Then, one of the three, followed by the two others, turned to look where the pig had first appeared.

Oh no, more trouble.

Relieved when she saw Tarzan, Jane relaxed until he was close enough to call, 'I see you have some friends.' He *thelt* – *Hello, Kitties, We Share.*

Tarzan saw the dead pig when he heard their reply – *We share.* Surprised, he asked, 'Jane, where'd the pig come from?'

'It attacked me, so I knocked it flat, and the first of these three killed it.'

Tarzan arrived, removed his knife from his waist sheath, and said, 'Then it's your kill. Take this and cut a chunk off a backside for us, and then tell the silipusses they can have it; that's what they're waiting for.'

Bemused, Jane cut off a thick rump steak and asked, 'How do I tell them?'

'Make a gesture, like pushing it to them and think "We Share."'

The cats leapt forward.

'I'm surprised they waited, Tarzan.'

'Those are the rules, Jane; you knocked it down, you have the first pick, but they waited because they can see you're female.'

Suddenly, the three cats stopped carving up the pig and stepped back as a fourth silipuss approached. Puzzled, Jane asked, 'Why did they stop?'

'Because that one's a female, look at her teats; she has kittens, so she has the right to some of the pig. Use my knife again, turn the pig over, cut off the other haunch and a back leg, and then give it to her. Try to *theel* "We Share" when you do.'

Concentrating on the task, Jane did so, and the female took the haunch in her mouth and walked away. Wonderingly, Jane whispered, 'I felt a kind of thank you.'

'A *thelt*, Jane, she did say thanks. Now come here and watch the others finish off the rest.'

When the pig became a collection of bones that the cats dropped through a hole in the floor, Tarzan urged, 'Jane, try and *theel*, send them a message, just the feeling that we're pleased to share.'

'I have.'

'They received it and replied with the same feeling. You're now an honorary silipuss, but more than that, a citizen of Tarik.'

'I must think about that. I feel good, but I need a new log for exercise.'

Tarzan laughed, 'Jane, you're marvellous.'

I'm glad he thinks so.

'I'll find you a log, but we mustn't let the pig steak spoil.'

They cooked their slab of pig. They took turns holding the skewer over the flames while the other pushed roots and bulbs into the ashes. Tarzan brought two leathery leaves to use as plates and cut the slab of pig into two after Jane, who had repeatedly bitten off a corner 'to check', declared it ready. Tarzan passed Jane his knife to cut their food into bite-sized chunks they could skewer with a pointed piece of wood. 'Can you carve us forks, Tarzan?'

'I can try simple ones with two or three tines if I find suitable wood.'

...

'That was a meal fit for royalty, Jane. We should sleep; we'll lose the moonlight in a few minutes.'

The night's darkness was less dense than usual, for later, the middle-sized moon rose. But Tarzan, with his arm around Jane, didn't wake. Nor did she, but she thought the day was breaking when she awoke early. But Tarzan continued to breathe steadily, so she waited, then dozed until he moved.

'Jane, I can tell you're awake; tell me about your mother.'

'The expedition planners selected my mother, Joanne Kruger, because she's qualified as a textile scientist. I look like a younger version of her.'

Tarzan interrupted, 'Jane, you must explain; what is a textile scientist?'

'It wasn't a science once. Mum told me making cloth began on Old Earth thousands of years ago. People found plant and animal sources of fibres, like cotton, wool, silk and other plants, and learnt how to extract the fibres, spin them into threads, and then weave them into cloth.

'It became a science when synthetic fibres came into production, and woven cloths became reinforcement in composite structures.

'So, the planners thought someone who knew the science

was necessary, but Mum found they were wrong when she arrived here because there's no manufacturing of artificial fibres. She decided to find natural fibres.'

'She's a brave woman.'

'She is and is also authoritative. I suppose that on Exo-Earth Four, a scientist had to be if they wanted to progress. Do you think I am?'

'Brave but no more authoritative than other women. I'm not much of a judge as I have little experience of women your age, and I accepted the authority of older ones long ago.'

So I'm not too bossy. 'For weeks, Mum asked any man entering the forest to scavenge or collect firewood if she could accompany them, sometimes more than once, until she found my father, Rashan Samoon. Mother told me they weren't married, but that's normal.'

'What's he like?'

'He's a farmer, or should I say Agricultural Scientist. He's soft. Mild-mannered, speaks quietly, is never upset, and is always gentle. He's tall and slim, with light brown hair. Do you know there was a lottery amongst the farmers to allocate the plots for growing things?'

'Yes, where's his plot?'

'He drew one of the plots nearest the centre and then exchanged it with a man who drew one close to the palisade.'

'Why?'

'He told me that even then, he believed Tarik plants would produce more food than imported seed, and near the trees was the right place to be.

'Mum joined him on his third or fourth trip to find edible plants, and they stayed together.'

'How did he know they were edible?'

'He didn't. Mum cooked a part of what they collected, then took the cooked and fresh parts to the chemists, and they ate those the chemists found weren't toxic – to check the taste. Dad soon had twenty or thirty plants that tasted reasonable, but most needed cooking to remove the iron in them. And he was right; once he planted them, they grew well.'

'So, you recognise those plants?'

'Of course, but they were ground-level plants and might not exist here. Once we travel, I might find some.'

'And your mother found plants with fibres?'

'Yes, Mum said she chose Dad because he's dependable, someone she can lean on, and who helps with her business. He has a colony permit to grow and collect them. I sense they adore each other; that could be love.'

'He's a brave man.'

'I think so too, but he says he's not. He joins others who hunt and forage and once told me that if he hears a suspicious noise, he doesn't investigate but runs immediately.'

'Running is the most ancient survival strategy; all animals and insects do it, including me. So that's not fear. What does your mother do with the fibres she found?'

'She studied the clothing industry. I learnt that the vines give her different fibres; the right ones give long and high tensile threads, and she spins and weaves them. Dad's a practical man, and he made rollers for her that crushed the vines, her spinning wheels, and weaving machines. They're all made with wood, which he collects when he gathers vines.

'After soaking for ages in water, some of the plants become a soggy mess that they spread out to coagulate then dry to make paper, although it's more like the papyrus I've read about. Mother experimented with plant saps and binders and can produce boards about two centimetres thick for boxes and furniture. She has five women helping her now.

'Mum makes several woven cloths and some ropes and strings. Some are strong, and others are soft.'

'Binky Deepenhout does, too.'

'My mother trained her, and her business is a subsidiary.'

'Was it your mother who decided to have a child?'

'No, she told me that she hadn't dared to ask Dad because he might refuse and leave her. It was Dad who suggested it about eighteen months after they met. Dad had bought the plot next to his for my mum's business and built a small house in a corner, and when they moved in, he told her he wanted to be a father.'

'Nice guy.'

'He is. Now, let's begin the day's work. I'll finish my story tomorrow.'

17

Jane woke when the light was sufficient to rise and padded to the toilet. Tarzan watched her. She returned for a shower, and two minutes later, she shook the excess water from her hair. Tarzan stood with a superbly fit animal's continuous, lithe, effortless movement.

'Jane, every time you do that, it reminds me of a wild animal coming from the river.'

'What? Shaking my head to dry my hair?'

'Yes.'

'Well, if you haven't noticed, I'm a wild animal walking naked in the jungle. Were you asleep, or did you wait for me?'

'I waited.'

'How did you know I needed to pee?'

'You felt uncomfortable. Why did you ask?'

'Because sometimes I sense you want the toilet in the morning, and I wait for you. How does that work?'

'We're two naked animals, sleeping beside each other and touching. We feel each other's basic rhythms.' Tarzan grinned, 'Now I want to feel something else.'

'What?'

'Do you remember the first day you squeezed my backside?'

'Yes, it was rock hard, and mine was jelly.'

'Well, I want to squeeze yours.'

That's unusual. Does Tarzan want sex? 'Fairs fair – you can.'

Jane had checked her bum regularly to judge her progress and knew it was now solid muscle, but when Tarzan ran his hand over her backside and gave a gentle squeeze to one of the lobes, she couldn't help a shiver. *That was a feeling I never expected to feel. Did he like doing that?*

'Well?'

'Jane, I think you've reached the exercise plateau.'

Damn. I was expecting something else, at least 'Nice Bum'. 'What's that mean?'

'You've lost all the fat, and your muscles are strong enough for your body weight. From now on, continuous exercise will build strength, and you'll gain that by travelling. But we must check. I'll climb a tree to rig a rope, and you can climb it.'

Though her more intimate thoughts would return often, the thrilling news drove them away. 'Okay, although I'm keen to travel, I'll be sorry to leave our home.'

'We'll make a nest of branches every night; you'll soon become used to it. We still have preparations to complete and traversing practice, so I reckon it will take three to five days.'

'I'll make pegs and finish the last rope lever so we can carry two each.'

Armed with fifteen carved wooden pegs in loops around a waist belt and his mallet, Tarzan tied the rope to Jane's belt, then placed the coil of rope on her left shoulder and clipped her tail to a branch with a carabiner. He passed the other end around a branch and tied it to his belt.

'Jane, our safety while we travel depends on us managing our safety lines correctly and identically. We must know what the other will do.

'For the first traverse, I'll be the leader tied to the rope; you'll be the anchor. You do the same as you've done when you fed the rope to me whenever I left for food. When I stop and tie my tail, you can take the rope from around the braking branch and secure it to your waist. I'll untie my end from my waist and pass it around a suitable branch for braking and signal. I'll wind it in as you come to me, then feed it out as you advance as the next leader.'

'Okay, let's try.'

She had done it many times, but anticipation built for her first foray from the GravBus as she fed the rope out to Tarzan, who jumped, hopped and danced away from her until he stopped. She saw him attach his tail as he had always done and signal. After she recovered the rope around the braking branch and tied it to her belt, she signalled, and he pulled it tight.

She released her tail; it thrilled him to see how lightly she jumped and leapt. Still breathing normally, she reached him. 'That was super!'

'Okay, now it's your turn to lead. Keep looking for a signal. I don't want to pull the rope and unbalance you to stop you from traversing too far. Then you do the same as the anchor, and I'll come to you.'

He let her jump and leap for fifty metres, raised an arm and *thelt – Stop*. She stopped, anchored her tail, pulled in the remaining rope, set a brake, signalled, and he joined her.

'That was perfect, Jane. And this tree is good for climbing.'

'I heard you say "stop".'

'There must be a silipuss around here.'

'Why do you think that?'

'I didn't say stop, just *thelt* it. You couldn't hear me, but you felt it. A silipuss could have caught it and sent the thought to you.'

'Tarzan, are you pulling my leg again or having another fantasy thought?'

'No, Jane. I'm glad they're around. Stay there with your tail attached. I'll anchor myself at the tree, and then you can join me.'

'That was your first lesson, Jane; we *never* take any risks. Attach your tail. Tie it and give me the carabiner.'

Tarzan waited and said, 'Only now that you're attached will I release the rope. I'll strap on my claws.' He took them from the bag at his belt and strapped one to the inside of each foot below the ankle and one to each wrist. The claw, with a loop to his little finger, settled in the palm of his hand. 'Tarzan, let me look at those.'

'The foot one is simple, Jane, just above the ankle on the inside of my leg, with a strap under my heel and around my leg. They're very sharp at the end, careful of the point. The hand ones are flexible. If I bend down my little finger, the pad that supports it folds down, but my weight hangs on my wrist when climbing. I need the carabiner.' He passed the coil of rope under a branch and gave it to her. 'Now hold it and feed it to me as I climb.'

He disconnected his tail, removed the carabiner, lifted his right foot, placed the inside against the tree with a slight push, and pressed down; the claw dug into the tree. He slapped his left hand as high up as possible, straightened his right leg and slapped his right hand against the tree, 'There, I've stuck my claws into the tree. Give me about two metres of slack and maintain that.'

Jane did.

'I'll climb four metres and hammer in a peg.' He clambered

like a cat, hammered in a peg, hooked on a carabiner with the rope passing through it, scrambled up four metres more to repeat the peg and carabiner process, then said, 'Now Jane, let me down. I must collect the first carabiner.'

Eight minutes later, he reached the upper floor, crossed over a branch, descended for the last carabiner and climbed up again.

Five minutes later, Jane had the rope attached to her belt, and Tarzan held it with a branch as a brake; the other end of the rope hung from a bough to which Tarzan had secured it.

'Okay, Jane, climb up the fixed rope. Use hand over hand; I'll keep your safety line tight. Using the levers, you mustn't let the lever flip up; if it does, you slide down.'

Jane hooked on the first lever, did a one-armed pull-up, and slid the next lever into place with her free hand.

She climbed up without a pause and looked down as she reached the top, then stopped breathing as her tummy clenched. Her grip tightened as she forced herself to relax. Tarzan sensed it. 'Jane, are you okay?'

After three deep breaths, she replied, 'I didn't appreciate how high this is until I looked down. It scared me until I remembered you were holding a safety rope. I'm okay now.'

'Great. Now you know why I'm terrified of falling. We're as high as the twelfth floor of the housing blocks you've seen in photos. Don't slide down the rope; you need a megalon's hide sleeve for sliding. Let yourself down, then do the two-arm climb, and practice it four or five times until the coordination between hands and legs seems right.'

'Why if I can climb hand over hand?'

'You might need to carry a weight or be tired, so it's important.'

Jane descended. *The height did scare her; she's being extra careful.*

'Jane, you don't need to remove the levers to descend. Lift the handle of the lower one and slide it down, then push the handle down to lock it, and then the other one. There are twice as many steps, but it's as fast and much safer.'

Jane practised the two-handed climb three times, then Tarzan said, 'You're far better than I expected. We can travel. Tomorrow, we prepare, and then we leave. Let's return to the nest.'

They returned to the GravBus, and when they arrived, Jane asked, 'Where did you find the claws?'

'The first ones I made from a neurotic pig, but though they worked for my weight then, they were too small when I grew. I thought of a ground boar, but their claws have worn, so my dad helped me make them from titanium, so they're non-magnetic. I know where to source natural ones, but they're beyond my reach.'

'Where?'

'If we see a river monster during our trip, you'll see its teeth.'

'As long as it's from a distance. Meanwhile, I'll wash our clothes.'

'And I'll see if I can extract a pin from a toilet door hinge. I lost the one I had; then I can make you a mallet.'

Moments later, Jane heard hammering from the toilet. 'Tarzan, what are you doing?'

'The hinge pin is too small, but the sliding door latch has a good one. I'm trying to break it out.'

The hammering continued, and then a scrunch or two later, Tarzan came from the toilet, proudly carrying the door latch, to find Jane sitting on the floor of the GravBus, drawing with a burnt piece of stick from their fireplace.

'What are you drawing?'

'You said we must be safe and always tied to something; all the tying and untying might be dangerous. We could make a mistake if we're tired or the rope is wet, and like you, after seeing how high we are, I'm terrified of falling. I'm trying to work out how to be the brake yet remain tied to each other permanently.'

'I don't think it's possible. Have you found a solution?'

'I think so. I'll draw it for you.'

Jane used a cushion to rub her scribblings from the floor. 'Now, this is me.' She drew a side-view stick figure with a tail tied behind it. 'Now, this is you.' She drew another and chuckled, 'I'll add a tail, so we know it's you.'

'Jane, I'm sure it's longer than that!'

'Okay, I'll flatter you.' She lengthened it.

'Now, here's a branch in front of me.' She drew a circle at the feet of the first figure. 'Now, the rope tied to both waists.'

The line descended from her figure's waist, down before the branch, then up and over the branch to his figure's waist.

'But where's the brake?'

'I'll reach over and under the branch, grab your rope, and pull up a loop. Then I'll have the same control as before.' She rubbed out some of the upcoming rope and drew her description.

Tarzan studied her drawing silently for a minute. 'That's brilliant and ingenious; it'll make traversing faster and safer. I love you, Jane.'

He's repeated it. I must ask him to say what he means.

'Do you mean me or my brain, Tarzan? You only say things like that when I have an idea.'

'You. I think you're adorable; you've grown more beautiful every day, but when you have flashes of genius, you seem like a goddess, and my heart beats faster in admiration.'

I asked, but I didn't expect that answer. 'Then why haven't you tried to kiss me?'

'I want to, but we're a wonderful working partnership that I won't ruin, so I'll wait until you tell me you want to kiss me.'

'Okay, that's fair, but I won't want to kiss a bear.'

'What bear?'

'Your beard has grown for a month; in another, insects will nest in it.'

'Then I'll shave.'

'With the sword that you call a knife?'

'No, I'll use the chisel I used to cut the megalon's hide. It's also my razor. There's a mirror in the toilet.'

'Are we taking the mirror with us?'

Puzzled, Tarzan replied, 'No, why would you think so?'

'I didn't, only to emphasise there won't be one in another month, and I'll have to shave you. Let me practice now. I saw how my dad shaved, although most men have beards.'

'Okay, Jane, but please be careful; it has a diamond edge. Leave me with both ears. Have you any soapy water left in the soap cup?'

'Enough, sit here and rest your head against the seat.'

...

'You're doing well for a first-timer; you can leave my moustache.'

'I don't like your moustache; it's raggedy, so it's coming off.'

'Can you at least leave my nose?'

Jane lathered soap over his upper lip.

'I saw how my dad does it; he grabs his nose and pulls it up like this.'

'Doan pill mi node so hiy.'

Jane grinned, 'There, you don't look like a bear any longer. In fact,' she leaned forward and kissed him, 'you look kissable.'

Tarzan stood, put his arms around her, and kissed her enthusiastically.

'That's enough for now, Tarzan. Tomorrow, we travel; we need to sleep.'

I've changed. I've never wanted to kiss a man, but for some reason, I liked it.

When they lay down to sleep side by side, as usual, Jane cuddled, and Tarzan lay thinking about the kiss and then relaxed. His sense of smell, always on the alert, warned him. Something, somewhere, filled the air with an elusive odour. He tried to remember all the flowers and plants he had smelt but couldn't pin it down. He turned his head towards the forest; the smell faded slightly. He shifted to look at Jane beside him on her back, eyes closed and breathing regularly. The scent seemed more pervading but mixed with Jane's usual smell. Using his arm and hand furthest from Jane, he stirred the air and concentrated.

Could Jane's pheromones be different if she's ovulating? I must sniff every night; that might be why she kissed me.

18

'Tarzan, that was our last night on the GravBus. I've packed my few things. What about our phones.'

'Leave them; they're flat, useless and extra weight.' *Besides, we have something better.*

'Tarzan, I'll put them in a locker; they'll be happy together.'

'Okay, Jane.' *Sometimes, she says some unusual things.*

Sorry, Goggles, I can't take you with me. Sleep well. But I'll put you in a safe place.

...

'Right, Mister Guide, tell me how you know our course without a beacon.'

'Before we left, I checked as I always do. We had six-thousand-four-hundred kilometres to travel, and the course followed was east to west at an angle to the equator of thirty-two degrees towards the south. The first rays of the morning sun through any hole in the upper floor will tell us where the east is. There's a plant here with long, spiky leaves; the iron content is high, and the leaves align with the north-south magnetic field, but it can't tell us which is north. That we have from the rising sun. It's not unusual behaviour for a plant; I read about a palm tree called the traveller's compass on Old Earth that aligned itself north-south to maximise the sunlight it received. So, with the east behind us, we use the compass plant to angle about thirty degrees to the left.'

'But we may be far out when we've travelled three thousand kilometres!'

'We could be, but we'll err on both sides of the line and shouldn't be too far out at the end. It's more likely rivers and other difficulties will throw us off course, but we may hear a Cargo Drone or find another sign to give us an idea. Finally, we must reach the sea, and as my colony is between the seashore and a river, I'm sure we'll find it. When we're close, a silipuss will help with directions.'

'I won't ask how they can help. Do Cargo Drones fly low down?'

'Only when loaded; they don't have pilots and are too fast for the megalons. They don't have the backup systems of a GravBus, so when something fails, they crash.

'I kept some cold food from last night; we'll eat it and start moving as soon as it's light enough to be safe. I'll kill one squirrel a day because we can't carry more, and we'll pick fruits when we see some. I hope we find fruit to eat at midday. We stop every afternoon well before dark as soon as we see a Cascade Creeper. You cook what we've collected, and I'll build a nest to sleep on, just a collection of branches. If you feel thirsty, say so, and we'll stop and drink when we find a creeper; dehydration will make travelling dangerous. We're in no hurry. We'll travel faster as we become used to the routine.

'Jane, strap on the axe holster.'

'Why?'

'Because you have no weapons until I can give you the mallet. When I do, you can keep it on the other side for balance if you wish. I have my knife.'

'Okay, Tarzan, let's eat. I want to travel.'

As they began eating, Tarzan spoke, 'I said I'd tell you about the animals as we met them, but there's one I must warn you about. Don't approach an odd-looking pile of leaves; they will be about half a metre high and have a roof made from big leaves to guard against rain. It might look like a giant mushroom. Approach means no closer than ten metres; call me if you see one.'

'What is it?'

'It's the egg stack of a beast that I call the scorpalon. A scorpion is the closest species in the "Life of the Known Worlds" catalogue. It's about the same mass as me, crawls on six legs with Tarik-type feet, has a long fat tail, and has two big crab-like pincers. It lays its eggs in layers between leaves, puts the lid on it, and hides in a burrow under the debris to guard it until the eggs hatch. The silipusses love the eggs but can't fight the scorpalon. The tarizard waits for the eggs to hatch and then gobbles the hatchlings.'

'Is it poisonous?'

'No, but the pincers are powerful. Once it seizes something, the pressure grows slowly until the two sides meet.'

Worried, Jane asked, 'Won't you be looking out for them?'

'Of course, but we'll be doing hundred-metre traverses. I can't see the details clearly when you're a hundred metres ahead of me.'

'Then I'll be careful. How do you know about the scorpalon?'

'I passed too close to the first egg pile I saw, and one shot forward from under the leaves and grabbed my leg. I used the axe to smash its mouth and eyes, then buried the axe in its head, but had a problem removing the pincer from my leg.'

'Why?'

'It has unique pincer actuators, although some Tarik insects might use the same method. The upper and lower jaws extend behind the hinge, where there's a hydraulic jack; the muscle in front of the hinge closes the jaws, but then the beast pumps up the jack to raise the pressure of the jaws. Killing the beast relaxes the muscles but doesn't empty the pressure chamber. One day, I'll dissect a pincer to determine how it works. Eventually, I made a hole in the right place and used my knife to puncture the reservoir. It took ten days for the bruises to vanish.'

'Are there many of these horrors?'

'No, and if you stay away, they ignore you.'

'So how do the silipusses steal the eggs?'

'Five or six of them play tag with the beast, jumping out of the way when it attacks and slowly leading it far enough away until others can rush in and collect the eggs. The eggs stick to the leaves, so they grab a leaf stem, then run for it.'

'That would be exciting to watch. I'll be careful.'

'I saw a group of four young males once; they behaved just like a group of teenage boys, teasing the scorpalon and waiting for a chance to ram a claw into an eye. One of them was stupid, stabbed an eye, and *thelt – Got him* instead of leaping away. The scorpalon pincers seized him. One of the others managed to pierce the other eye, but it was too late to save the one in the pincers; I could see he had a crushed pelvis. I thought it best to let the pincers break his spine for a quick death, so I left.'

They were slow, as Tarzan had said. For Jane, it was the first time she had travelled two hundred metres from the GravBus. She didn't look back. *I can't; that's now the past.*

They managed eight one-hundred-metre traverses each hour. Tarzan was delighted. *Jane's moving well, and the tails are superb. That's over six kilometres daily, but we'll have delays.* They did stop. The first time Tarzan spotted some fruit, they ate. The second time, he killed a squirrel, then finally, after six hours of travel, Tarzan said, 'There, Jane, beside the Cascade Creeper on that tree is a good place for a nest.'

'Why do you call it a nest? I can't lay an egg.'

'It's a word used for anything that's a haven, and it suits. Make a wood collecting basket, and I'll begin laying branches.'

Forty minutes later, he tied the last branch in place and covered the small platform in stalks with huge, lush leaves. Jane had finished the basket and cleaned the squirrel. 'I'll take the basket and fetch some wood.'

When he returned, she had wetted the fire skin and stuffed the squirrel with garlic cloves.

'Where did you find the garlic?'

'I looked around and found a plant by the next tree; there were two bulbs.'

Worried, he asked, 'But I had the rope. Were you untied?'

'No, I used three belts to lengthen my tail and crawled.'

'Smart, Jane.' *I must learn to have confidence in her ability.*

'You must show me how to find those webs for gloves, then I can collect wood too.'

'Okay, if I see one tomorrow.'

Tarzan watched as Jane lit the fire and roasted the squirrel, and then they ate.

'Tarzan, how did I do today?'

'Better than expected; you're marvellous. Let's shower and sleep.'

Standing beside the Cascade creeper, Tarzan tilted a cone above Jane, and the water dribbled onto Jane's hair. As he did so, she stuck her fingers into their soap cone and ran them over and through her hair. Tarzan took a washcloth from its peg in the tree, wetted it, and Jane wiped her soapy fingers on it, then returned to her hair, ears, face and neck, while Tarzan used the cloth to wipe her body from her neck to her feet. Then she took the cloth and wiped it between her legs. He poured more water from cones over her hair, and she used her hands to wipe the soap from her skin. Then, they changed places. Being taller, Tarzan had to control the cones while Jane wiped him down.

They stood while most of the water drained and dried, then lay side by side. Jane snuggled. 'You smell clean, Tarzan.'

'That's the best smell.'

'Maybe, but bring me some flowers; I might use them for perfume, but they would look pretty. Good night, Tarzan.'

After Jane slept, Tarzan sniffed quietly. *It's been three days, and the smell is still there.*

Three days later, they had developed a rhythm and were averaging six kilometres a day when Tarzan spotted a root he had been looking for and stopped beside it. She then caught up to him.

'Jane, we must stop here. I need to cut a piece from this root. I'll stay anchored; you look for a Cascade Creeper.'

She skipped to the first tree, and he watched as she inspected the trees. With a hundred metres of rope, she had many to choose from. When she returned, she said, 'That last one has a plant and a good place for a nest. There's also fruit hanging from a vine, but it's too high to reach. Why do you want to cut the root?'

'Seeds from the Firetree that sprout on the upper terraces drop their tap root straight down if they survive long enough. Finding one is lucky. I once cut a piece out for a bow, and two months later, the two ends had reconnected.'

'That's fantastic.'

'It's a superb wood for making a bow. I've carried one for years. There are lots of arrows; look at the growth on the floor. It'll take me a few days to cut and shape a bow, and you can practice with the mallet. When I've finished the bow and had some practice, you can carry the mallet.'

'But where does the bowstring come from?'

'I had one from a neurotic pig sinew, but if I can work some threads from a safety belt and plait them, it will be even stronger.'

'Okay, tell me what I must do.'

'First, I'll build a nest while you make a basket, then we'll collect firewood together. I'll show you the glove nets and hunt a squirrel for tonight. When we return, you can do the camp and dinner, and I'll start working on the tap root. The axe will have difficulty; I must chop at it slowly with the knife.'

'When you have time, can you carve me a stick with a hook so I can reach fruit high up?'

'That's a great idea; I'll watch for a suitable branch with a hook. It'll be my next project.'

''Night, Jane.'

'Goodnight, Tarzan. That was a good day.'

'It was.'

He sniffed again, and the odd odour had disappeared; Jane smelt as she always had.

The following morning began with the comfortable routine: wake, drink, toilet, wash, fruit and cold meat if there was any, and then tooth cleaning. However, the routine then changed.

'Jane, let me set up a target for mallet throwing practice.'

Tarzan tied on and reached a tree about ten metres away in a dozen leaps. He carved a small patch of bark, leaving the white pith visible, then paced five metres along a branch and flattened four stakes growing from the floor before returning.

'Now, Jane, let me tie the holster around your waist. You saw what I did when I demonstrated: I'll hold the rope to your waist while you step over to the tree, then tie it. Throw the mallet when ready, return to the tree while winding up the line, and return to do it again. If you fall, it will be less than three metres, and you can climb back. It's practise, practise, and more practice until your arm hurts. I'll check on you while I carve, and if I see anything, I'll give you a tip.'

He watched, looking up at intervals. He saw Jane adjust her position on the branch several times until she settled on one. He then kept looking as she found a comfortable hand height for the forward throw, sensed how to let the handle slide smoothly from her hand, and called only once, 'Jane, don't try to hit too hard; accuracy first, and then you can increase the force. Point your index finger at the target when you throw.'

He marvelled when she continued for three hours with only a short break for a drink. *I was much younger, but Jane is far better than I was then.*

'Tarzan, my arm is aching. It will worsen if I do more.'

'Okay, Jane, we'll find fruit. Then you can try throwing with your left hand when we return.'

'Why? And can you?'

'Because if you hurt your right arm one day, you'll still be able to hunt with your left and won't starve. I can, although not as good.'

'Okay, I'll make a fruit basket. How's your carving progressing?'

'I might finish one end today. I must be careful and carve slowly; if I cut too far, I'll ruin it and must start again. I had to make three the first time before learning how to make one that works.'

...

'Okay, Jane, let's hunt. Please give me the mallet; you take the fruit basket. I might hit a squirrel for tonight.'

Half an hour later, Jane saw him change direction during a lead crossing, leap forward several paces, and throw. She was sure he had hit a squirrel, for he jumped to the tree ahead of him, picked up something and tied it to his belt.

Forty-five minutes later, Jane reached the nest, anchored, and gathered the rope while Tarzan returned.

'We make a good team, Jane; we have a fat squirrel and enough fruit for tonight and breakfast.'

'If you hold the rope, Tarzan, I'll fetch the firewood for later and then practise with my left hand.'

Tarzan watched her left-handed practice. 'Jane, when throwing with a non-dominant hand, you must teach your arm to throw – I had to. Accept that you won't have the same force for months, but if you teach accuracy, the force will come. Try throwing gently.'

...

'Jane, come. That's enough practice for today; we must eat and sleep.'

19

When Tarzan opened his eyes, he felt uncomfortable, a pervading, heavy, ominous feeling. It took several minutes for him to decide the cause.

'Jane, wake up; I'm sure we're about to have a thunderstorm.'

Jane's eyelids fluttered, reluctant to face the day. 'How do you know?'

'A feeling of heaviness, the humidity is sky high, and there's electricity in the air. Come on, sit up, and look at the Moon Lily to our left.'

...

'It's lovely, but shouldn't it have closed after the moon set?'

'It should, but the static electricity is keeping it open. I've seen that once before. If you stick a finger into it, it will shock you, and it'll close.'

'So, what do we do?'

'It'll be miserable while it rains. The rain is cool but warm enough to curl up near a tree trunk and wait it out, but we'll make a tent. I'll cut three pegs, hammer them into the tree trunk, and then rig three ropes to the floor at an angle. We'll collect big leaves and tie them to the ropes with vines.'

'Then, let's start; I don't fancy a three-hour shower.'

Two hours later, Jane was tying a last leaf in place when Tarzan said, 'I think it's not far off. The air is thick and charged. It will be a massive thunderstorm if it doesn't begin raining soon. I'll put our stuff in the tent and tie it down; the floor might flex, and holes appear.'

Thirty minutes later, the lightning began. They couldn't see it but recognised the sudden stroboscopic light flashes that lit up the middle terrace. Tarzan counted until they heard a clap of thunder. 'About ten kilometres away. It might miss us.'

'All that work making the tent for nothing.'

'Good practice, Jane; the next time, we'll be faster.'

The lightning frequency grew, the intense flashes and the ear-piercing cracks making them jump every time, and with them, the thunder, until the forest reverberated to a continuous drum roll from a heavenly band. Tarzan had to shout, 'It's massive, and it's sure to hit us.'

Then Tarzan heard it. The sound of heavy rain, not the pitter-patter of a shower but a roaring crescendo that resembled a rocky river flood, 'Jane, into the tent, quick, the deluge is coming.'

As Tarzan crawled in after Jane, his left foot received a dousing. The noise became painful, not just the thunder and the crack of lightning but the constant din of the rain on leaves. Speech became impossible, and they sat in the middle of the tent with their arms around each other. Jane scraped some moss from the tree trunk and blocked her ears.

Then Tarzan did the same.

The tent sagged.

The enormous rainfall flooded the upper level, but the upper floor was not waterproof. In the tent, despite the moss, Jane and Tarzan heard the waterfalls that developed as water found a way through, then washed a channel clear of debris and poured down until they were under an enormous waterfall with thousands of cascades. Although sheltered by the branches that joined the tree above their tent, they didn't escape, as the falling streams drummed on the tent before splashing to the floor. One cascade soon wore a hole on one side of the tent near the tree. They moved to the other side.

The terrifying sound of branches breaking spurred Tarzan. He picked up Jane, stepped to the tree inside the tent, and stood beside her so they both had their backs against the tree. It was like showering as the water running down the trunk poured over them. The sound changed to a different thunder, the upper floor collapsing.

The rain stopped as suddenly as it started, and they could hear the storm moving away.

Tarzan pulled the moss from his ears. 'Don't move, Jane. I must look.'

He pushed and pulled at the leaf roof until he had a peephole.

Jane, who had cleared the moss in her ears, whispered. 'What can you see?'

'Good and bad, Jane. The floor we're on is still standing. It's the one above that collapsed. About eight metres from us, a massive pile of vegetation came down, and above is a gaping hole with the sky above.'

'Then we're okay?'

'Yes, but there must be a hundred darters in that pile; some injured, others dead, but the remainder will want to escape and return upstairs. We're lucky the tent hides us. We don't dare move from it until the darters have left. We might manage to defend against one or two, but more than that, they will hurt us badly.

'Sit. We'll eat some of the fruit from last night.'

They took turns peeking through the leaves each hour and compared notes.

After the first hour, Tarzan remarked, 'The darters that can fly have worked out the escape route; they climb on top of the pile and fly up.'

'I can see several injured darters,' Jane contributed an hour later, 'one is trying to climb a vine with one leg and his beak. Four are climbing vines, and two more I can see are trying to force their way out of the brush pile.'

Another hour later: 'There are still three struggling to climb and another pushing its way out.'

'Jane, I think they'll have left or died by dark, but not before, so we must stay here until tomorrow.'

'What do darters taste like?'

'I have never seen anything eating one, so darters may not be edible.'

'We have a squirrel; can we light a fire?'

'No, Jane, everything is too wet; I can't search for dry wood.'

'Damn. So tell me about the darters.'

'They don't see well in the dark.'

'How do you know that?'

'Now and then, one tries to escape a predator and dives through the upper floor. I've seen three on this level; they walk. One had a broken leg, and two others climbed up vines and searched for a hole to return to the upper level; their feet, like the other creatures, have evolved with opposed claws to cling to vines. The injured one died where it lay.'

'Why do they have four wings?'

'Two are large to support its main body; then there's a long neck and the head. That beak you've seen has a sharp point and can be as big as this.' He indicated about a hand and half a forearm. 'The head is too heavy, so it has the two extra small wings behind the eyes; they don't flap much; they're used as a glider and steering to keep the head up, so the darter can't slow down without the head dropping, the mouth is underneath the beak about half a hand width back.'

'Why do they have that long neck?'

'They eat the dozens of small creatures that infest the foliage on the upper terrace. With their neck, they can spear through the foliage to reach them. I believe that one day we'll find that the darters and the megalons had a common ancestor millions of years ago, and it had a long neck and four wings.'

Jane woke and wondered. The light that seeped into the forest, she imagined, was water leaking into a sinking boat where she lay. Jane tried to convince herself it was the same as every morning since the GravBus crash, but it wasn't. She felt the light was alive, not sliding slowly but quivering, poking holes to pass through, twisting and wriggling its way through every available passage, bursting with joy when it found its way through, lighting the forest around her with twinkling lights. *It can't be different; it must be me, but what?*

She lay unmoving, watching the shadows move, and thought. *The forest loves me, and I adore it.*

I forgot. I'm in our tent. The light must be from the hole in the upper floor.

Tarzan opened his eyes. *That smell is back.*

When Tarzan sat up, Jane rose with happiness in her heart. It overflowed, and he felt it, too.

Many days would pass with nothing happening except a sameness to the day before. For a journey that would take years, it was inevitable. However, occupied with survival, the days were never dull, and the routine was comforting to both, for if they survived yesterday, they would endure an identical day.

Sometimes, though, something happened, often minor, as it did on day fifty-four of their travels.

Jane found a stick.

Leading a traverse and looking for a suitable place to stop and anchor, she saw a root on the mid-level floor that re-minded her of a hockey stick. She anchored beside it, and when Tarzan joined her, she reeled in the line and asked, 'Is that root suitable for a fruit hook?'

'After I chop it out, strip it, and then carve it a bit, it should be.'

'Then I'll chop it out and carry it until we stop. Show me where to cut.'

'We'll find a place for a nest with a Cascade Creeper; I must finish carving my bow before I can start on your stick.'

Tarzan carved and hunted a squirrel, Jane practised throwing the mallet, wove collecting baskets, and gathered fruit and fire-wood. Finally, as the day ended and the light began to fade, Jane asked, 'How's the bow coming along?'

'I've finished it, except for a little polishing tomorrow; I'll make some arrows and try to make a string.'

'If you show me what you want, I can try to extract filaments from a belt.'

'Okay, I'll show you, let's sleep.'

The following morning began with their usual comfortable ablution routine. Tarzan first, and then, while Jane followed, he removed a belt from his bag and started working on it. He said when she dressed, 'I've cut three filaments just behind the buckle and carved you six toothpicks from a tough wood. If you work at a filament carefully, it will come loose. I've tried, and you must extract the filaments from under one cross-strand at a time. Once you've removed one filament, the next two should be easier.'

'If I plait them together, will the bowstring be long enough?'

'I hope so; I'll cut two strips of megalon's hide that will loop around the bow ends, and the string will attach to them. They will be the adjustment. You do the filaments, and I'll polish the bow, cut the megalon strips, and then make some arrows.'

Sitting silently and carefully picking at filaments in the safety belt, Jane sensed when Tarzan stood, rigged the rope, and stepped away from the nest. She watched as he traversed slowly beside a row of trees, checking thin shoots and saw him kneel and cut five before he returned.

'What kind are those?'

'Ones I've used before. The plants grow slowly in the poor light, making the wood strong and hard. The only leaves are at the top; the first grow strong stalks to hold the leaves far from the stem, and the higher leaves are shorter. The assembly looks like a pale flower.'

'Is that important?'

'Very, I read about arrows; they're fletched at the back, which means they have little wings to make them fly straight. They used bird feathers, but I've not seen a bird with feathers on Tarik. I have nothing for fletching, so I invented a different method.'

'What method?'

'Continue picking; I'll show you when I finish one.'

...

'There, Jane.' He handed her an arrow.

'It's straight and pointed, and the point is sharp. It doesn't have wings, but these three spikes are a hand width before the notched end. Do they work as wings?'

'Not like that, Jane, but after many experiments, I found that if I scrape the spikes thinner towards the ends on the notched side, I can bend them towards the notched end with a finger until they match. Now let's push that end into a spider web, and you'll see the result.'

'That's fantastic. The web has forced the spikes back into a curve and filled the space between them and the shaft. They look like little wings. How long do they last?'

'Only one use, then I must make another unless I'm lucky and can fix it with another web. I carry three arrows; I can make more when I lose one. Have you finished the first filament?'

'Almost, but it's easier to do the other two simultaneously. Another half hour should do.'

'Okay, Jane, tell me when you finish.'

...

'The filaments are free.'

'Shall I cut them?'

'No, I'll plait them first while the ends are still in the snap fitting. Then, you can cut the plait after I tie a loop around each end. Are you ready for it?'

'Nearly. I have four arrows and one end loop; I'll finish cutting the second one.'

An hour later, the bowstring was ready, and Tarzan tied it to the megalon's hide bottom loop, stood the bow on a branch, placed a leather loop on the high end, and said, 'Jane, I'll press down to bend the bow. Can you pass the string through the loop once I say so and tie the string?'

'Do you want it tight?'

'As tight as you can, please.'

Tarzan released the pressure when she knotted the string, and the bow, held by the string, remained bent. 'Thanks, the string's holding; let me try to pull it.'

With a piece of hide as a finger guard, Tarzan lifted the bow and, with a straight left arm, hauled the bowstring back to his mouth with the right. Jane could see the power in his bulging biceps.

'It seems weaker than my last one.'

'You're a lot stronger.'

'I'll shorten the hide loops.'

After adjusting them, he said, 'I have a scrap arrow that I kept for a distance test. I'll try.'

He notched the arrow without fletching, pulled and released. Side by side, they watched the arrow fly out of sight, wobbling as it flew.

'Is that further than before?'

'I guess about twice. However, accuracy will be the same, so fifty metres will be the maximum and about fifteen to twenty an optimum. Let's hunt and collect fruit. I must practise with the bow before I can hand over the mallet.'

'Could you carve me a mallet to practise with?'

'I could, but we don't have any line, and you would lose it very quickly.'

'Wasn't there some in the GravBus emergency kit?'

'There might be a fishline in those that do ocean crossings, but there was none in ours.

'I'll use a piece of a belt so I can hang the bow over my shoulder.'

Days later, Jane found some hard round nuts about the size of her hand. She collected them, and whenever they stopped, she practised throwing them. Jane managed three throws per nut before losing them, but there were always more nuts. She carried three with her in a woven pouch at her belt.

Tarzan carved her fruit hook, like a hockey stick, but with a narrower hook extending slightly backwards from a bulbous end. Jane waggled it in the air. 'It's familiar, but can't you thin down the knob at the end? It's too heavy.'

'I'll take some off, but too thin, and the hook will break off. Those vines are hard to pull down, just a little. It'll take a few minutes.'

...

'Let me hang it over your shoulder, Jane; I think it's too long and will hinder your movement...

'I must make it shorter.'

20

The day after Tarzan finished the fruit hook, with Jane tied on and holding the rope coil, she said as he was about to begin the first traverse, 'We're beginning to look like Christmas trees decorated with mallets, pouches, knives, a bow and a fruit hook.'

'That's about all we can carry. But we're okay so far.'

Two days later, Jane spotted a hanging vine. 'Tarzan, there's fruit up there; I'll try my hook.'

'Don't jump; you might twist an ankle when landing while looking up. I'll keep holding your safety line.'

Her first try tore a small vine free, bringing others into reach. The second try did the same, and Jane exclaimed, 'It's coming, one more pull...'

The vine broke from the upper floor, loaded with hanging fruit, and swung down like a pendulum. Jane wrapped her hands around her head and twisted away as the vine and fruit swept past her, but she couldn't avoid two ripe grapefruit-sized balls that hit her arms and back, burst open and splattered her with their purple mushy contents.

'*Owww!* That hurt, but we have lots of fruit.'

'And I have a purple monster as a partner; we should have brought the mirror so you could see yourself. Before the insects decide you're a banquet, leave the fruit and shower under the Cascade Creeper on that tree there. Anchor your tail, and I'll pull back the rope, then join you and help to scrub it off. We'll come and fetch the fruit afterwards.'

Jane scraped fruit off her arms and face, then with a grin, she flicked it at Tarzan, who retaliated; gobs of purple pulp became the ammunition in a laughing fight that ended when no fruit remained on either of them. They scrubbed each other clean, and then Tarzan said, 'Jane, I'll make a nest here, and we'll feast. We can travel tomorrow and carry a fruit each.'

It happened after four months of travelling. Tarzan stood with his tail attached behind him, controlling the rope, as Jane demonstrated her ballerina skills while progressing in their chosen direction, avoiding rotten wood with a single glance and a too-thin branch with another, careful not to place a foot where she hadn't checked first. Sometimes, she jumped onto a protruding branch, pausing momentarily to confirm the next step.

She's good, lighter than me, but chooses a route that will carry my weight.

Suddenly, her rhythm changed. After jumping onto a slightly higher branch, she switched direction. With a flex of her leg muscles and a shift of mass, she faced a tree five metres ahead. Without a pause in her movement, Tarzan saw her hand scoop a nut from her pouch. She swung it up with a continuous, curving motion until, hurled with force, it left her hand, and she followed it.

At the tree, she bent and picked up something he couldn't identify at that distance. *It's probably a squirrel.* It brought a rush of pride. *She's not simply good; she's superb. It's time to give her the mallet.*

She arrived and proudly showed him a tarizard, 'It's not very big, but it's enough to eat.'

'Quite enough, Jane and a young tarizard is a delicacy.'

'Tell me about them.'

'I will when we eat it tonight.'

As Tarzan cleaned the tarizard that evening with Jane watching, he said, 'It's not dangerous but hard to see. Although I told you tarizards freeze waiting for an insect to fly or crawl in range, they can suddenly move fast. The silipusses ignore the small ones; they're too fast, so sticking a front claw into it is almost impossible; they only try for the big ones that grow as long as my forearm.'

'Do they have a long and sticky tongue?'

'No, they open their mouths wide and jump forward. The inside of their mouths is coloured like a flower to attract insects. Sometimes, it basks with its mouth gaping. You can look the next time we kill one. If a young tarizard comes within range, it will eat that too.'

'If they jump, how do they stay on the tree?'

'Look at the tail on this one.'

'It has a pair of claws.'

'That's its anchor, like our carabiner. Watching one that loses its grip with its feet is funny; it hangs from its tail and must wriggle around until it can grip something or take the risk of dropping.'

'What else do they eat?'

'Although any insect, flying or crawling, is prey, the big ones reach a massive size from binging on the recently hatched young of egg-laying species, such as the scorpalon. If I see a tarizard the length of my forearm, I watch for a scorpalon.'

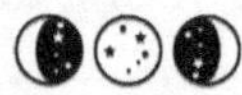

Jane woke early, without moving. On her back beside a still sleeping Tarzan, she looked at the underside of the upper-level floor above them, watching the pitch black of the night already mixing with the grey oozing through the ceiling above. The sun rose slowly, and suddenly, Jane saw hundreds of tiny holes light up with incoming rays.

It must have rained heavily here; water has washed clean holes.

As the sun rose higher, she saw small white flowers glowing in the morning rays on the ceiling. *I have never noticed those flowers before. Where did they come from?*

She watched until the ceiling seemed covered with them, then watched them fade.

They must open at night and close in the morning. Thank you, Forest, for showing me your beauty. I like you.

We like you too.

Jane gave Tarzan a prod. 'Wake up lazy.'

'I'm awake; I was watching the moss flowers.'

'The little white ones?'

'Yes, each is a small patch of tiny flowers; it makes a lovely sight at dawn when enough light comes through the floor above.'

'They're beautiful. I thought a "Thank You" to the forest and told it I liked it. It told me it likes me too.'

'Sometimes, Jane, I sense the same.'

'How far have we travelled this last month?'

'Now that you're an expert hunter, our pace has upped.

During this sixth month, I reckon we've averaged eight kilometres a day, and it's still climbing, but our monthly average is about to begin dropping.'

'Why?'

'We haven't had to cross any rivers. As we approach the sea, even a thousand kilometres away, all the little streams flowing to the sea converge. Soon, we'll come to a river and finding a place to cross will take time and may cost us a major diversion from our route.'

Tarzan had overestimated how far they had travelled, for they didn't come to a river for two more months, but eventually, as he had predicted, they did.

Three hours after leaving their last nest, Tarzan called a halt. 'Jane, it seems wetter; there's a river ahead. That's both good and unwelcome news.'

'It does seem wetter; I almost slipped on the last traverse. Why good and bad?'

'Good because it proves we're well south, bad because every river is a challenge to cross, and if there's a river, it will become even wetter. The water evaporates from the river, condensing on each side. We'll shorten our distance to ten metres each until we can see what's ahead. Move slowly, and be careful where you put your feet. You move first.'

Jane moved away, and Tarzan fed the line out until she stopped, attached her tail, and stood ready to reel him in.

Forty-three slow traverses later, they stood on two branches, peering through leaves at a river.

'Tarzan, you promised. Tell me about the rivers.'

'Because the planet is so flat, no raging rivers have carved canyons; the rivers are slow moving and shallow. That's a problem for us; they can be broad. In the drier season, they narrow significantly and leave a wide, bare area on either side. I'm not sure if they're growing broader, but in the wet season, they reach the trees and even flow between them.

'Dad says that's when the fish lay their eggs under the trees and hatch the next wet season.'

'So, there are fish so far from the sea?'

'All sorts, Jane. The littlest ones eat what floats down the river, insect larvae and insects, and then it's a chain of predatory fish with gaping jaws and teeth.'

'Do the fish have flippers?'

'No, from the smallest to the biggest, they all have two tails, one above the other, that they wave from side to side out of sync; one left and the other right. They can travel fast. And with their mouths full of teeth, they catch anything they can reach.'

'I know there are slidagons in the sea; are there any in the rivers?'

'No, they need salt water to float. There are some amphibians; some are massive. If one sleeps in the open, I'll point it out to you, although they don't like sunlight.'

'Jane, we can't cross here; it's too wide, the flow is too fast, and there's too much water. We must travel upriver.'

'How far?'

'We should be nearing the end of the wettest season, so we could wait for the flow to drop, but I hope it will be worth travelling upriver. If tributaries exist, the flow will reduce with each one until we find a crossing. It might take days.'

'It'll be slow traversing upriver in the wet trees.'

'We won't. We'll traverse away from the river until it's dry, then head upriver for a day or two, and when it feels right, we'll return to the river for a look.'

They had to return to the river five times, then ten days later, Tarzan said, 'We must have missed a split, and this is a tributary. I think there's something upriver that will allow us to cross over.'

'What suggests that?'

'Look at the water.'

'It's clean; the river was muddy before.'

'That's it, and when a river is clean, something is filtering the mud. A mass of vegetation may be blocking it. We'll continue upriver.'

A kilometre later, they found the dam. A solid mass of interlocked trees and branches packed with broken reeds. 'Tarzan, it was worth coming for the view.'

'You mean of the megalons?'

'Yes, there must be a hundred or more in the lake, eating the lake plants.'

'Different dynamics are competing with the trees. Look at the colour of the lake water; it's a reddish brown. I first thought it was because the water that flowed through the forest had collected the iron. Then, I learnt that megalons are the only beasts big enough to knock over a tree and increase the size of the lake area. The trees around the lake must have been high in iron as the megalons ate them.

'The megalons are cleaning out the vegetation that, left alone, would turn the lake into a mass of reeds, and the trees would eventually take over. If that happened all over the planet, rivers would stop running, our forests would stand in the water year-round, and the trees would die because the roots had insufficient oxygen. The megalon females are part of the ecosystem that keeps the forest alive. They keep a strip on each side of the rivers free of vegetation and clear the plants from shallow lakes. They've done us a favour; the barrage of old trees wouldn't have grown so big without the reeds they have uprooted.'

'How heavy are the megalons?'

'We don't know. Dad did some calculations; he reckons the biggest males would be two hundred tons with no allowance for gas-filled bones. Allowing for hydrogen gas about a hundred or a bit more. In comparison, the trunk of a base-tier tree may be a thousand tons, although most will be half to three-quarters of that.'

'The giant trees can't be the only tree species here; what are the others?'

'There will be others in the far north and south; one day, I want to visit and look, but I expect either a mutation of these big ones or a distinct species. There aren't many species here because the planet has insignificant variation except the north-south temperature gradient, and the more recently evolved species are all on the upper level; the only ancient one I know of on this level is the one with the inflammable bark.'

'Are they useful? Apart from being superb firelighters.'

'My colony found a dozen clumps around the open space we occupied, so we used the cores for the barrier and building cabins and the outsides as firewood. The terragons adore eating young trees before they become too hard inside.'

'Okay, how do we cross?'

'It's about a hundred metres. We'll drop down, tie ten metres of rope between us, and then scramble across: it'll be a mixture of push-through and climb-over. Let's start from the tree closest to the barrage.'

'Jane, this is how we descend. I'll throw the rope over a branch so both ends are on the ground, slide down with a sleeve, and brake with my claws. You can then pull up one end and tie it to your belt. Stay anchored with your tail until you're tied, and I'm ready; then, I'll lower you down.'

'Okay, but how do we climb a tree on the other side?'

'Unless I can persuade a megalon to give us a lift for the first bit, I'll do what I showed you when you first climbed a rope, but we'll do something different because we can climb together. When I put in the second peg, climb up and join me, bringing the first carabiner with you. Then we'll climb the rest the same way; I'll climb and peg on, then you join me; you'll soon be out of reach of anything dangerous. Let's eat the fruit we collected while I make the pegs. We mustn't hang around down there.'

They dropped to the ground to make the precarious trip across the barrage of logs and brush. It was more complicated than expected. The branches and reeds at the bottom of the barrage had packed tight from the weight above them and the water pressure, but those they had to scramble over were loose, and every step meant assessing a branch to check it would support them. Jane, who weighed less, managed to move faster, but the rope to Tarzan held her back. He sometimes had to try two or three branches before taking a step forward.

Then, more than halfway across, Jane slipped and fell, grazing her thigh as a log twisted, and her leg fell into a gap until she sat on something painful and cried out, '*Shit!*'

Tarzan called, 'Are you okay?'

'Nothing serious, but I may be stuck.'

Conscious of the risk, Tarzan was careful as he worked his way to her. 'Can I pull you up?'

'I think so; I'll push on a branch with my other foot to widen the gap.'

Tarzan found a solid footing, then bent down and wrapped his arms around Jane under her arms. 'Ready?'

'Yes.'

With a smooth pull, he raised Jane until she could stand. Then she looked down at her leg, 'Only a graze; let's leave this nightmare.'

Their hundred and ninety kilograms, concentrated at one spot for minutes, had depressed the reed and timber dam below them, and the water level rose. Water flowing around the barrier at the end they aimed to reach had eroded the soil holding it, and the extra pressure broke the dam loose. Tarzan and Jane watched in dismay as the end swung rapidly downstream. His reaction to *theel – Kitty, help* was automatic.

'What do we do now?'

'We're now on a raft. Move to the end; I hope it will hit the bank downstream somewhere.'

<h1 align="center">21</h1>

Sitting at the front of the slowly moving raft, Jane leaned against a branch and called, 'Tarzan, I like this. We could lie back and relax during a gentle cruise to the sea.'

'A two- or three-month cruise, Jane. Our bones might arrive there, but we would never see the sea.'

'Why?'

'First, we either die of thirst or risk drinking river water. If we don't catch dysentery or constipation from the mud, we risk a monster attack when we fetch the water.

'Second, we'll die of hunger; we might eat raw fish, but catching them without a monster eating us is unlikely.

'Lastly, this raft will slowly fall apart now that water pressure isn't compacting it, and then the monsters will have us for lunch.'

'That doesn't sound encouraging.'

'It's not, but be patient and keep your eyes out for a change in the river.'

...

'Tarzan, the river must bend; I can see trees straight ahead.'

'I can see them. It might be a sharp bend with a deep pool, a steep bank and a sandbar reaching into the river.'

...

'Jane, there's a sandbar; you're the lightest; move as far forward as you can without leaning over the water, then if you think it possible, jump when the water is only a few centime-tres deep. Then, run up the beach and downstream, pulling the rope, and find a tree to anchor it. I'll loop it here, and the raft will move to the shore.'

The manoeuvre worked, and when Tarzan jumped ashore and looked up, he saw Jane lying on her back beside the anchor tree. He ran.

As instructed, Jane had run to the tree and then around it. The rope to the moving raft had tightened before she could com-plete a full turn around the tree, so she leaned back to lock it with the rope around three-quarters of the tree. The rope ten-sion from the mass of floating timber and reeds was enormous, but the rope didn't slip until the raft hit the beach; then it did, and the rope pulled Jane like a skier, her feet building a heap of broken branches for the seconds it took for Tarzan to release his end and jump. She felt the pain when a jagged branch ripped a gash in her calf, and then, as the tension dropped, she fell on her back with her legs under a heap of vegetation.

'What happened?'

She told him. And added, 'I can feel my calf has a cut.'

Feverishly, Tarzan threw off the brush until he could see her leg. 'There's a cut about fifteen centimetres long, bleeding. Can you sit up?'

Jane did. Then he said, 'I'm holding the sides closed. Can you reach it and hold it closed while I find something to bind it?'

The scrabbling sound of a silipuss descending the tree, followed by it coming to them and looking at Jane's wound, distracted her for a second. – *Hello Kitty, hurt.*

'Jane, the puss *thelt* I should fetch a *Decaspider* web. Keep holding the gash closed, and I'll find one.'

He dashed away, and the puss sat beside her. Ten long minutes later, Tarzan returned with a web strung between twigs that he had broken free and a branch of large green leaves. 'This will be tricky; let me stick it underneath and hold it with a leaf so my hand doesn't stick. Then you can remove your hands, and I'll pull the web over the cut.'

...

'I can't see the cut. Is it working?'

'It is. The cut is closing, and the bleeding has stopped. I'll have to cut away the excess web and stick more leaves on it.'

Jane lay back again. 'Can we stay here?'

'No, the amphibian river monsters come ashore at night; if one comes here, we don't have a chance. I'll have to carry you away before dark. We'll be okay deeper into the forest.'

'Ask Kitty.'

'Where is he?'

'He was here until you brought the web.'

Tarzan looked and saw the puss on the beach by the water; then it returned, so he tried to *theel* a picture of a nest in the trees.

The reply was – *Wait,* so he fetched a pile of leaves to make Jane comfortable. The puss looked at the wound again, then at the scrape on her thigh, and disappeared. Two minutes later, it returned with a cone of water hanging from its mouth, propped it against her leg and used a claw to pick up the offcut pieces of the web and drop them in the water.

'Tarzan, what's he doing?'

'He wants me to mix the web with the water and put the mixture on your graze. It's odd, but I'll do it.'

'Does the *Decaspider* eat all its prey in one night?'

'No, sometimes it takes two or three days.'

'Then the web must have a chemical compound that stops decay, an antiseptic, antibiotic or both. We'll see, but I feel much happier; Tarik is fantastic.'

Jane slept. She woke suddenly from a dream. In it, a megalon stood guard before her in a suit of armour with a spiked helmet on its head, complete with a banner blowing in the wind. The banner was black, with a green-filled circle in the middle.

'Tarzan, is the megalon here?'

'What megalon?'

'I dreamed one was coming to guard us. Maybe Kitty told me.'

'It's not here yet. I'll fetch some water and fruit, and then we must move.'

When he returned, Jane said, 'We don't need to move; the megalon's nearly here.'

They watched while a female megalon lumbered along the beach, lay between them and the water, and then turned its head to look at them. They both sensed – *We share,* and replied.

They slept with the sleep that comes with a feeling of safety, with the silipuss on the tree side and the megalon beside the river, but Tarzan woke after several hours. One moon was up, and in the pale light reflected off the water, he saw a massive shadow heaving and humping up the beach. He was about to wake Jane when the megalon raised its head and swung around to the shadow, and he heard a crunching sound before the megalon swung its head back and returned to sleep. Tarzan slept, too.

As the sun rose to reveal the massive lifeless bulk of a river monster on the beach, another silipuss arrived, cut off a steak from the dead beast and left with a *thelt – We Share.* Jane counted the cats that came. Tarzan cut off two steaks. 'If the cats can eat it, so can we.'

'I've counted a hundred.'

That afternoon, Tarzan hammered pegs into the tree for them to climb and left the rope hanging down each side of a massive branch after building a nest.

'Jane, can you stand?'

'Help me up, and I'll try.'

She stood and said, 'Only bones remain, but I'd like to see them. My leg is stiff, but it's not painful.'

Tarzan supported her as she limped to the skeleton. 'There, Jane. It has short legs, two tails, and a horn on its nose, about the length of my arm.'

'Yes, with two tusks in the upper jaw at the front. It must weigh two tons. It discourages swimming. Are there other kinds?'

'I have high-speed photos of a similar one with a wide mouth and hooked teeth. My dad lent me his camera, and I took the photos at a river near my home. The hooked teeth face backwards. Once it seizes something, it can't spit it out.'

'How do you know?'

'I took a photo when one hit a giant boar that was too big to swallow. It thrashed around, trying to kill it or break off a piece. I thought it would die of asphyxiation, then another monster seized the other half of the boar, and with both thrashing around, the two monsters broke the boar in half.'

'Let's climb, Jane. I'll haul you up.'

Five days later, Jane said, 'That net is a superb dressing; I can travel now. I might be slow, but the exercise will help.'

'I've been thinking about that net. I think it must recognise us as prey. We eat only Tarik food. Our skin and blood must contain a Tarik balance of compounds. Maybe the insects will soon attack us.'

'Okay, I'll tell you immediately if one stings me.'

They travelled downriver for a hundred metres before Tarzan stopped. 'I'm being stupid, Jane; we mustn't return to our original course; we should take a direct line from here as we still have the main river to cross.'

'Okay, but what's the plant on the next tree? It has some funny-shaped fruit.'

Tarzan looked. 'Well spotted, that's edible. I call it a "Supernova". Let's collect some.'

Four minutes later, Jane asked, 'Why haven't we seen this before?'

'I've only seen it on trees beside a river. It has no roots in the ground. Some orchid-type plants live in trees and collect all they need from the moisture and dust in the air. This creeper is like them, but it requires the continuously damp side of a tree to survive. It has a fascinating method of spreading its seed.'

'Please, tell.'

'The centre of the flower is a hard ball containing the edible seeds, and the flower petals have a surface covered in fine hooks. When the flower petals unfold to form the star, squirrels come to eat the seeds, and the petals attach themselves to the squirrel. If the squirrel can't reach the ball, the flower breaks off the plant, including the seed pod, and remains stuck on the squirrel, which wanders until the flower dies. But before that, the seed pod explodes like a supernova, and the seeds shoot out everywhere. Be careful of the flower's petals; they can cause a rash if you rip them off. I'll cut the ball out with my knife, then we break it open with the mallet and eat the seeds. Let me open one for you.'

...

'What do you think?'

'Not too sweet, there's a tart taste, a bit citrus-like; I'd guess they receive lots of sunshine and are high in citrus acid and vitamin C. Collect the balls and make the nest before we eat them.'

As they lay down that night, Tarzan smelt it again – a month since the previous time.

The previous day was long; they had eaten only the "Supernova" seeds, there was no refrigerator full of food, and they carried none.

'Jane, stay here. I'll hunt.'

'Okay, wait a bit; I'll make a fruit basket. Then, while you're away, a wood-collecting one.'

Tarzan controlled her safety line as she stepped off the nest with the rope snapped on her tail and fetched some vines and a few willows on her way back. *She's built a lot of muscle and looks good now, especially without her breast strap.*

Jane sat down and began weaving, and minutes later, Tarzan left. Jane started to make the deeper and more voluminous design they had agreed suited the wood collection. She was halfway through when she felt something was watching her, so she looked up.

A silipuss was sitting before her. *I didn't hear it come.*

She tried a *theel – Hello Kitty.*

Five metres away, the silipuss watching her replied – *Hello, mother.*

She was surprised at how she understood the greeting so clearly – *You are welcome.*

We Share.

Tarzan was lucky, carrying his bow at the ready with an arrow notched on the string because he thought the game might be more prolific near the river. Within ten minutes, he spotted a neurotic pig that immediately charged. He shot his first arrow at twelve metres with enough time for a second, but the first found its mark. The pig took six more steps and fell forward onto the shaft that appeared out of its back. The diamond knife finished the job.

He quickly cut two generous steaks from the rear haunches, put them in the bag, and then had a thought that another piece would last until morning for breakfast, so he cut off another. A silipuss drifted silently between two trees as he stood and joined him – *Hello thing.*

It is for you. We share.

Tarzan prepared his rope for the return, and two more cats arrived before he departed. As he left, he felt – *Thank you. We share.*

Once Jane came into sight, Tarzan saw she had a visitor. Jane was surprised. First, when she felt he was close, then when Kitty *thelt,* – *the male comes.* She replied – *I know.*

The silipuss smiled as Tarzan danced the last two steps. 'Hi,

Jane, I see you have a visitor.'

'Yes, this is Kitty. Do you have enough to share?'

'I think she told me to bring an extra piece.'

He passed the basket to Jane. She took a steak from it and offered it to Kitty, who accepted it delicately, then turned to walk, put the steak between her teeth, and leapt gracefully away.

'Tarzan, did she say thanks?'

'Yes, I felt it too. Do you know why Kitty came to see you?'

'No, but I'll guess that she knew you had killed a pig. And was sure I would share as she and I are females.'

'Like I told you when you killed a pig.'

'Not only that, Tarzan, I knew you were close before I saw you. Do we have a connection, or was Kitty telling me?'

'We'll learn. Tarik is your home, as it is mine. I have sensed where you were for the last week or two. I'll fetch the firewood; I'll also find garlic. Cut the skin off the steaks; we'll wrap and roast them in their fat.'

Jane decided that the opportunity to eat roasted vegetables was too good to ignore. Although healthy, their routine diet of fruit and squirrel had begun to pall.

'Are we leaving after eating?'

'We should rest, Jane; tomorrow morning is fine.'

'Okay. Then we can cook up a feast. I have lots of veggies.'

'Where did you find those roots and bulbs?'

'On the beach, after crossing the river. The megalon females had dug up everything, and they're messy eaters; they left a lot of root scraps lying around. I picked them up and stuck them in my belt. Didn't you notice?'

'You have so much stuff hanging from your belt that it would be difficult.'

22

A week later, Jane asked when Tarzan had caught up. 'Before you do the lead, stand still and tell me if you feel a stronger breeze. I'm sure I felt mild gusts.'

'I think so, Jane.' He tilted his head back and sniffed, his mouth opening and closing. 'It smells fresher, too.'

'How can you smell that? I didn't.'

'We're living with no artificial smells, Jane, and we're constantly alert for dangers. Our brain normally uses every sense it can, and those senses are developing. I told you that I was not fond of crowds because I had confused thoughts, but another reason is that the smells confused my brain; it didn't know what was safe or dangerous in a colony. I must rely on my eyes and ears, and even my ears become confused with sounds they've never heard. The smells are familiar here. Like every other sense, it doesn't come to our notice if it's not dangerous. By purposely raising my head, sniffing, and using my mouth to pump air through my nose, I told my brain to smell everything, even the innocuous ones. All the animals do it, and I imitated them as a kid. I found it marvellous. If you practise, you'll smell all sorts of things you never noticed; some aren't pleasant, but others are delightful.'

'So what does that fresh smell mean?'

'Somewhere up ahead, there's a lake or a dried-up lake; the trees are open to it, and the air is blowing in and along our route.'

'Does that mean a deviation?'

'Yes, but until we reach it, I can't decide if right or left is best; we'll shorten to fifty metres each.'

Three kilometres later, Jane said, 'I can see the light.'

'Ten-metre ropes, slowly.'

Jane whispered, 'What's the cracking and crunching sound?'

'I've heard it once before: megalon females are eating trees. Take the lead and look.'

'That's a wonderful sight. What are those megalons doing?'

'What I told you, Jane, they're eating the small trees in the clearing to keep it clear. The soil is red, and the iron level is high, so the trees must have high concentrations. I'm sure those are young Firetrees they're eating.'

They stood and watched for several minutes, and then Jane said, 'That one on the other side uprooted an entire tree in one pull!'

'That gives you an idea of how powerful they are, but don't forget, the ground is soft, the centre is still soft mud.'

One of the megalons stopped chewing, turned to face the west, raised her neck straight, and waved it from side to side. 'What's that one to the right looking at? And what's she doing.'

'I can only hope, Jane, I think she's sensed a male and is looking for him; the eyes on her nose are better than on the top of her head; they're the ones they use to identify their food, or she's sending out *thelts* saying "Hello Man."'

'Why hope?'

'I've never seen a megalon mating.'

'Where is he?'

'He may be far away and high up; let's find a place to sit, eat a fruit and watch.'

'She's not eating.'

'That's a common characteristic of many species before mating; her body doesn't want to waste energy on digestion.'

'She's becoming excited if the faster waggle of her neck and head means anything.'

'Then the male must be close; wait.'

The male came over the western treetops at an incredible speed in a dive towards the female; they heard the whistle of his passage followed by a roar as he passed them and almost touched the ground before swooping up towards the open sky in what appeared an impossible curve then kept climbing.

'Wow. That was amazing! The ball on his tail missed the ground by a metre. Where's he going?'

'Up.'

'I can see that … he's looping! He's on his back; oh wow, he's rolled.'

'Watch, Jane; this will be spectacular.'

'Now he's somersaulting. And rolling again. If he continues, he'll crash.'

'He's pumping hydrogen; his gas bag is growing.'

'Then he'd better hurry; how many more rolls and somersaults will he try.'

'As many as he can, Jane. I've never seen it before, but this must be the megalon equivalent of a male mating display; he's showing off to the female like a man strutting around and flexing his muscles.'

'Well, she should be impressed, I am, and he has enough height left for a last roll.'

With a final display of his gymnastic ability, the megalon stopped only a metre above the ground, facing the female, and they stared into each other's eyes. His ball and fore tentacles held him from drifting away.

'What's he doing now?'

'Probably asking permission with a *thelt.*'

'Tarzan, he's more likely saying "Turn around Babe so I can give it to you."'

'Not Tarik beasts, Jane, the little I've seen, the animals have a ritual, but it's not macho. It would be like kicking a football if she gave him a swipe with her head. He's in a precarious situation, like a man with his pants around his ankles.'

Jane gasped. 'She's turning, she must have said yes!'

The female turned, and the male pulled himself forward with his tentacles up and onto her back as she moved her tail to one side. 'His penis is extending. Now that I can see them together, I realise how much bigger the males are. The females couldn't eat a GravBus.'

They watched the mating, and a minute later, the male began to inflate and lift.

'That didn't take long.'

'For most animals, their defences are down during mating; they keep it short but intense.'

Jane turned to him, and he saw her flushed face as she said, 'Well, that was lovely to watch. I hope she has a beautiful baby. It gave me a funny feeling.'

Tarzan guessed. 'Did it suggest having sex?'

'Yes, and you're the only male around.'

Shit, I'd better confess. 'Jane, I must tell you, I may be the only man on the planet who is fertile. I was in the forest for my sixteenth birthday, and everyone had forgotten when I returned.'

'Tarzan, that's super; suddenly, you seem different. I'm tingling. If I could be sure I'm not fertile, I would ask you to make love to me now.'

'Are you sure that's not what you said other girls do? Thanking a man for something?'

'Well, if it is, women are hard-wired to feel like that; it's because I want to.'

'Then wait until you're not fertile, and I'll relieve your genetic desire if you still feel that way, but there's something else I must say.'

'What?'

'Dad warned me; he knows I'm not sterile, and that's a serious problem.'

'Please, explain.'

'I don't know my genetic father.'

'How does that matter?'

'Do you know yours?'

'No, of course not; only the insemination records know that…

'Oh.'

'You understand?'

'Yes, we could be stepbrother and sister.'

'So, we mustn't let it happen until we can ask the insemination centre to check our DNA.'

'What are the chances?'

'Of being stepbrother and sister?'

'Yes.'

'Theoretically very low, just under one in ten thousand, but not zero, and if Dad is right, significant.'

'Right about what?'

'He thinks the program that does the matching is biased towards gene pairs with high probabilities of intelligent and scientific children, either on purpose or, he jokes, as an unexpected consequence of suppressing matches that might produce politicians.'

'Why does he think that?'

'Count the percentage of children who attend University; it's unusual, and there are no courses in politics or the arts.'

'Excuse the language. That we may be related is *shit news!*'

'Jane, does that tell me something special?'

'Yes, it does. Do you know that our generation condones sex between siblings? Step or twins.'

'No, I didn't. Does it happen?'

'Of course, often. When the man is sterile, the reason for the ban has disappeared, and as the woman will receive insemination by a stranger's sperm, sex between step-siblings is acceptable. If they have grown up together, they might have a more lasting bond, as twins do, than two unrelated persons. But you're different; sex is impossible unless I know I'm infertile.'

'I meant a different special, Jane.'

'I'll admit that when I said that, I was thinking of having a baby with you.'

'Then, when we've checked our DNA, and it's okay, you can decide. I've never thought of having a child, but in the last month, I'll admit the idea has popped up.'

'Tarzan, kiss me, but don't stir me up too much.'

'Goodnight, Tarzan. Put your arm around me, and let's sleep.'

'Goodnight, Jane.'

Tarzan was sure Jane had not dreamt of megalons when her first question the following morning was, 'I've seen pictures of your mother's fertility mushroom, grey with four big black spots and a kind of lace around the outside. Do they grow up here?'

'They do; I've seen them, usually in small groups close to a tree trunk, but only in shadows on the north or south side; they don't like light. Down below where it's darker, they grow anywhere.'

'If I find one and show it to you, how do I know it's the same?'

'I can't tell you; they may look the same but not be. You'll have to pee on them for a month or two like my mother did to confirm that.'

Their speed had increased further, raising the risk of an accident. 'More haste, less speed' is an adage that applies everywhere and to everyone. Tarzan had almost reached the limit of his lead traverse, with Jane tail-anchored a hundred metres behind, when he glanced momentarily at the next root to step on and then looked up for a suitable place to stop and anchor. The root, rotten at one end, bent down as he stepped on it, and his foot slipped towards the decayed end. Unbalanced and moving forward, his reaction was immediate; Tarzan lifted the unsupported foot to fall forward. It wasn't the first time it had happened, and his body instinctively knew that spreadeagled on the floor, the scratches and scrapes were far less debilitating than a broken leg, but this time, as his foot rose, so did the root that trapped his foot as he landed, severely twisting his foot.

Jane couldn't see what happened, but when Tarzan fell, she pulled the rope to him tight, looped it through her belt, and with pauses between jumps and leaps to keep it tensioned, she arrived in less than a minute.

Spreadeagled, he was trying to wriggle himself back towards

his trapped foot when Jane arrived.

Worried, she snapped, 'What have you done?'

'There's a root trapping my right foot. Can you look and see how to extract it?'

'Is it hurt?'

'It's excruciating. It might have sprained, but I don't think it's broken.'

Jane secured their tails, then squatted beside his foot to look. 'Your foot has jammed between two roots; how did that happen?'

'One of them moved down and unbalanced me; maybe you can push it down.'

Jane tried one root, then the other, 'Yes, this one is bendy. Let me move to a better position, and I'll try to push it down with my foot.'

'That hurt Jane.'

'Sorry, it moves, but not far enough to remove your foot, but I could push a lever in when it's down. I'll try to find a branch.'

Controlling the safety rope herself, she had a radius of fifty metres to search and returned with a branch minutes later. 'This one is okay, fresh from a recent storm. I'll try again.'

She pressed the offending root down until she could work the branch between the two roots and next to his foot, then pressed the branch down. 'Don't scream; it's nearly there.' She leant forward, put a knee on the lever, gripped his ankle with her free hand and said, 'Now.'

She put everything into it, then pulled his foot free. Tarzan, his teeth clenched, grunted.

'Okay, I'll feel your ankle and foot; this may hurt.'

...

'It did, Jane, but it doesn't feel broken.'

'No, when I wobbled it, there was no looseness. Now stay there. I'll build a nest you can rest in for a few days.'

'Thanks, Jane.'

Jane selected a tree with a Cascade Creeper and, two hours later, had a small nest just big enough for them to sleep on. Then, a silipuss arrived and looked at Tarzan – *Hurt?*

Tarzan pointed to his ankle – *Pain.*

The puss leapt away, and before Jane had added another two branches, it returned, dragging a long stem with thick leaves – *Soothing.*

Thank you.

'Jane, can you wrap these leaves around my foot?'

'I'll make it look like a gift-wrapped present. Hold still. I'll try not to hurt you.'

...

'There, how does that feel?'

'The leaves do something. The pain isn't so sharp.'

'Then, when you can, tell me. I'll release your tail and hold the rope while you crawl to our nest.'

Jane expanded the nest, collected fruit, and spent nine days caring for Tarzan, whom she undressed to wash on the first evening and left naked the whole time. She washed his loin-cloth and hung it from a peg hammered into the tree. She collected fruits but didn't kill any squirrels; each day, a silipuss brought one for her.

Tarzan watched what she did, and each day, his admiration grew. They had little time for talking, for Jane had fruit and firewood to collect, his foot to dress twice a day, and water to collect to wash him – a row of cones carrying water, supported by branches, needed filling daily for drinking and washing.

Tarzan slept and thought. He thought of his parents and his childhood, Colony Nine and Colony One. But much of his thoughts were about Happy, the young child who had trusted Jane and him, Happy's father, who had shown interest in a basket and had liked him and Jane, the silipusses that helped, and the megalons who seemed so human. And he thought about Jane and knew he wanted to stay with her for the rest of his life.

Jane had similar thoughts and began a secret campaign. She kept looking for the fertility mushroom, and whenever she found one, she peed on it. Jane had a short three-sided stick and cut a notch on one edge daily. If she had seen a mushroom, one of the other edges had a notch; one indicated fertile, the other infertile.

On the sixth day, Tarzan said, 'Jane, I think I can try walking. Help me stand.'

'My ankle is stiff and aches like a bruise, but it will be okay if I exercise a little daily.'

On the ninth day, he could do twenty squats without pain and said, 'Let's travel together to collect fruit, and if it's okay, we can leave tomorrow.'

23

Twenty days after crossing the tributary river, ten of convalescence, Tarzan said as Jane caught up. 'The floor is damper. We must be approaching the first river again.'

'So short ropes?'

'Yes.'

Ten minutes later, Jane said, 'It's much smaller now. But still too wide to cross.'

'Then we head upriver again, like the last time, but we'll do shorter steps between looking. A tree across the river is possible; the water is about fifty metres wide.'

Twenty traverses later, Tarzan remarked, 'There's a tree, but it hasn't fallen yet.'

'Will it?' Jane asked.

'As the drier season is coming, I doubt it will fall before the next rainy season unless a megalon pushes it over.'

'Do they do that?'

'Yes, it's their role in Tarik's ecology. The roots look like the water washed them free on one side, and the upper branches hold it to the forest; we can look. It might take a few days, but I can use the axe and cut them.'

'Why is the river eating the roots when it never did before? Is the river growing wider?'

'No, rivers meander, wander, and change direction when they flow across flat surfaces, and Tarik is primarily flat. Some unimportant things, like a dead animal or a stuck floating branch, can create an eddy that eats away at one bank and begins a bend in the river; on the opposite side, a mudflat starts to build. You would have learnt about this mechanism if you had studied hydrology. After hundreds of years, the river reaches a tree and eats away at its roots, but there's already another tree growing on the other side.'

'I understand that, but cutting the upper branches doesn't guarantee it will fall. We should continue and look for another place, but if you can tell a megalon to push it over, that would be best. Look at the ground; they must have been here recently.'

'Let's look at chopping first.'

After a thorough investigation, Tarzan pronounced his diagnosis.

'It's possible, Jane.'

'I don't think that tree is pulling hard, so you could chop the branches, and nothing would happen, but if it did suddenly break loose, with all that brush suddenly moving, it could sweep you in with it or injure you. Let's try upriver; Losing you isn't an option, although I'm now a good nurse.'

Tarzan grinned at her. 'You are. Can you create a mental picture of a megalon pushing the tree into the river?'

'Yes, why?'

'We know that megalons can communicate. It won't take long to experiment. I can't talk to them, but we can ask for help.'

'From whom?'

'Kitty.'

'I don't understand why I approve of such a crazy idea, but I do. What do we do?'

'First, we'll ask for help and wait to see if a cat comes.'

'Then first move back or forward to where we can have an unobstructed view. If a megalon pushed it over with us here, it would take us with it.'

Tarzan selected some broken branches as they stepped slowly away. When he picked up the third one, Jane asked, 'What are those for?'

'Climbing pegs – this is a good place. I'll call for help, and while we're waiting, I'll carve.'

'Do I call too?'

'I think so; you might have a better connection to the females.'

They both *thelt* – *Kitty, help!*

After carving three pegs, he said, 'We'll call again, Jane.'

After eight pegs, Jane said, 'It's incredible, but they're coming. I have a good feeling.'

'Me too.'

At ten pegs, a silipuss drifted towards them from a gap between two trees, followed half a minute later by two others.

Jane *thelt* – *Your coming has made us happy.*

We share.

'Jane, turn and look at the tree and *theel* your picture, and I will too.'

Thirty seconds later, they both felt a reply – *Wait*. The cats vanished into the shadows.

Two hours later, when he finished the pegs, they collected fruit. While eating in front of the river view, Jane said, 'I can feel something, like a rumbling. It's from upriver.'

Another hour and Tarzan exclaimed, 'There's a megalon!'

A minute later, Jane added, 'And two others. It's the most wonderful thing I could imagine; we're in a wonderland.'

'Yes, Jane, I've felt that for years, but I'm still learning how wonderful. If the tree falls across the river, we won't have much time to cross; the river will free the roots, and the flow's force will take it downstream. Throw the ropes down, and I'll put on my claws.'

The three megalon females arrived, and the biggest leant against the tree; Jane could hear the upper branches tearing free, but then it leant no further while the megalon stepped back, and the other two joined her. With their massive heads as high up as they could reach to increase the leverage, they pushed. The tree slowly leant further with a creaking, groaning, and shriek of roots tearing from the soil until once past the balance point, it fell with increasing speed until, with a thunderous crash that Jane thought would be audible for kilometres, it fell with the upper branches on the far bank's bare beach.

Kitty, thank you.

We share.

'Jane, let's drop.'

'Don't we wait for them to leave?'

'After pushing over a tree for us, they won't harm us, and their presence brings security.'

He launched himself down the trunk, the rope whistling through the megalon's hide tube clutched in his hands, fell forty metres, and then his foot claws dragged him to a halt as he reached the ground. Jane didn't hesitate and dropped. Tarzan controlled her fall and, as she touched the soil, removed the rope from his waist and pulled it down, then tied her on again at eight metres. 'Run!'

The first part was easy; after ducking around the megalons, Tarzan had a five-metre climb onto the tree trunk, helped by roots, and he pulled Jane up once on top, then they jogged along the tree trunk to the crown of branches on the opposite side of the river. They struggled to push through the foliage onto the clear ground. As soon as Jane was through, Tarzan said, 'That tree, Jane,' and they ran. He pulled a peg from his belt and began to climb.

Twenty minutes later, they were both sitting on the tree's lowest branch, looking back at the river as Tarzan coiled the rope, and Jane said, 'The megalons are on their way back.'

'Let's say thank you to all our friends.'

We thank all our friends for their help.

'That was a long day, Jane; let's pick fruit for tonight, then make a nest.'

That makes me happy.

'Did you *theel* you're happy, Jane?'

'Yes, it's a better way to send a feeling than words.'

Tarzan saw Jane remove her clothes and lay down in the nest, so he did as well.

'We'll be okay for rivers for a while. There may be a few streams, but they should be easy; if the water is shallow, there are no monsters, only little fish.'

'That's a shame.'

'What is?'

'That there are no more rivers. I liked meeting the megalons. Tell me about them.'

'We've seen their mating; I'll start with their birth. The females don't have a ball on their tails, so they can't float in the air; they remain on the ground. However, they don't sink in water. Although the mass of a female is enormous, its body must have a lot of gas-filled space, for its footprints are shallow.

'When she has a baby, it's sexless, has a short tail and neck, six legs, and a voracious appetite. I've seen them frequently. After it grows to a critical size and lies down to sleep, the mother covers it with a pile of brushwood, and then it metamorphoses as a caterpillar does to a butterfly. What comes out is either a male or a female; Dad thinks it might be due to the temperature in the brushwood pile. The females grow, and the males migrate – joining up in herds to visit the places where vegetation with metals is abundant. Sometimes, they eat iron-rich sand that collects at a river bend. Colony Nine is near a river where they do that. Once they've made enough hydrogen, they float into the sky.'

'And never come down?'

'They come down but only touch the ground lightly, if at all. The rear four legs wither once they fly, and the front ones become two tentacles attached at the base of the neck to anchor themselves. They use them when feeding. With that long neck, they can descend to a vegetation patch of high iron content plants, clear a large circle without moving, and then float up again.

'Dad says that massive beasts like them usually remain in one area. Randomly drifting around Tarik disperses their DNA to avoid inbreeding.'

'You haven't explained where the hydrogen comes from.'

'We don't know. Dad and I have different theories. We can only guess until we can take a megalon apart to find out. It may be both.'

'What theories?'

'Dad thinks the chemical factory in the megalon can make nitric acid from the nitrogen in the plants it eats and use the potassium and iron from other plants to release the hydrogen.

'I theorise their digestive systems are like the methane gas generators at the colonies, their digestive bacteria giving off methane as they digest. If the beast has the correct organic catalysts, the methane will combine with water and produce hydrogen.

'So maybe acids and metal from the digestive system in the balloon pass down through the tail to the factory, and extra hydrogen flows up it, but the base hydrogen production takes place in the ovoid balloon.'

'Are the females dangerous?'

'No, they eat plants. The main prey of the males are the raptors.

'The females congregate in herds in areas with high iron levels. When they have a baby, they can use their head on its tentacle-like neck as a giant club to kill. A female has no predators, and even the terragon stays away from them, although I have another idea why.'

'What's a terragon?'

'Have you ever seen photos or ThreeDVids of Old Earth's dinosaurs?'

'Yes.'

'This planet, I reckon, is ninety million years younger than Old Earth. The terragon looks very much like a Velociraptor. The only defence is a missile. Although I've never heard of one attacking a human unless the person attacked first.'

Jane shivered. Then they slept.

A month later, Jane asked, 'Tarzan, are you sure you're on the right course? I've been watching the compass plants, and you seem to vary.'

'You're right, Jane. The silipusses know where I live because I met them there, so they know where we're heading. If we err off course for one reason or another, they send me a feeling, left or right more. When we're on track, it just feels good.'

'So, if I'm lost, they can tell me how to find you?'

'Yes, just ask.'

'That makes me feel I belong here.'

The feeling of belonging pushed other senses into the background until one day...

Jane passed Tarzan with a wide grin, travelling fast, and called, 'I'm flying; it's a wonderful feeling.'

He yelled before she left shouting range, *'Don't think of your feelings; look where you're going!'*

She did, but concentrated on the terrace floor and where she would land next. She noticed the heap of leaves with a roof and tried to change direction only seconds too late, for from under a mass of leaves and vegetation to one side, a scorpalon erupted in an attack, and as she stopped, one of the claws gripped her right leg above the ankle. She fell on her left side, away from another waving claw.

Her reaction was immediate, her hand reaching for the axe at her hip, and as the scorpalon, its beak-like mouth clicking in anticipation or anger, continued the attack, she lifted it and, remembering what Tarzan had said, chose the moment to smash the axe into its mouth. It gave her a second to strike two more blows, destroying its eyes, before the other claw could grab hold. Without sight, the scorpalon began waving the free pincer in circles while the one gripping her leg tightened.

Tarzan had seen her fall and the flurry of leaves as the scorpalon attacked. He covered the sixty metres to Jane in seven seconds, his only safety being the line to Jane running through his left hand.

Tarzan had assessed the situation when he was still airborne before landing beside Jane, so as he touched down, he took an arrow from his quiver, bent and thrust it through one of the damaged eyes, searching with repeated stabs for the beast's brain. When the animal began to convulse, lashing around, he jumped with both feet on the pincer arm to stop it from throwing Jane around. The convulsions died down to repeated tremors as the beast died, then fell still.

'Jane, I'll release the pincers; lie still.'

'I can't move, hurry; I think the blood flow to my foot has ceased.'

Tarzan jammed the point of his knife into a joint at the back of the claw, worked it sideways, then turned it, boring a hole as bits of the hard shell broke away. Once big enough, he took another arrow, forced it into the aperture, and thrust it further. A spurt of dark red liquid shot from around the shaft, and Jane sighed. 'It has relaxed.'

Tarzan pulled the arrow out and then the pincers apart. More of the liquid gushed out.

'Is that blood?'

'No, it's water with a high iron concentration. I want to research this mechanism. I theorise the pressure generated is osmotic, as water in the bloodstream passes through a membrane to dilute the high iron concentration.'

'Then do it later; I'm about to start screaming from pins and needles as blood flows into my foot.'

'Let me massage your leg; you'll have a serious bruise.'

'Oww, careful.'

'I'm trying, Jane, but some pain is good. Grit your teeth.'

'We have company.'

'I felt them.'

'There are three silipusses; they can have the eggs.' Jane *thelt*
– *We share.*

Thank you.

Tarzan continued gently massaging Jane's leg as they watched the three cats dismantling the nest leaf by leaf and licking the eggs from the leaves as they removed each one. Then, a fourth silipuss arrived.

'It's a mother.'

'I can see that.'

Instead of joining the feast with the others, she came straight to Jane and looked at her leg. Tarzan took his hands away then Jane *thelt* – *Pain.*

The silipuss turned and bounded away, and Tarzan continued his massage. 'How does it feel now?'

'The pins and needles are dying away, but standing and walking will be agony.'

Then the silipuss arrived, pulling a long stem with a dozen broad leaves and dumping it beside them – *soothing.* Then, it joined the feast with the others.

'Tarzan, wrap the leaves around my leg where it pinched. It looks the same as the one the silipuss brought for your foot.'

'It is. Here, can you hold this leaf in place?'

With three leaves around her leg, Jane ordered, 'Fetch a vine and tie them; it feels better already.'

They sat watching the cats, and every hour, Tarzan changed

the leaves around Jane's leg. Each time, Jane said she felt better. The silipusses finally reached the last layer of the nest, and one brought two leaves covered in the eggs to them – *We share.*

Thank you.

As they left, Jane *thelt* – *Comfortable, thank you.*

'Let's eat the eggs, Jane, then we'll see if you can stand.'

'These eggs taste nice, a fishy taste.'

'They do; I think the cats consider them a delicacy.'

After licking their leaves clean, Tarzan asked, 'Can you stand?'

'Help me, and I'll try.'

Tarzan helped her stand on one leg; then she tried to put some weight on the other.

'It's painful. I don't think I can walk. I'll collapse.'

'Then don't. Sit again.'

Down again, she asked, 'What shall we do?'

'There's a tree about twenty metres ahead with a Cascade Creeper. I'll look at it. If it's a good place, I'll make a nest, and you can crawl there. If not, I'll look behind us; I remember passing a Cascade Creeper about fifty metres back.'

Tarzan took the axe from Jane, advanced, and then returned to say it wasn't a good place for a nest. The other tree was, and he built one there.

'Now, can you crawl onto my back if I'm on all fours?'

'I'm sure I can. But if you hold me, I can hop.'

'I can carry you, but I might slip or lose my balance on the floor, and your hopping will be as bad. I can carry your weight safely on all fours.'

Astride a crawling Tarzan, Jane asked, 'Do you think I can add riding a wild beast to my CV?'

She still has odd ideas. I hope she continues to have them.

Tarzan chuckled, 'No, at least *not yet.*'

Jane wondered. *Is he thinking what I am?*

'Rest. I'll fetch more soothing leaves, some fruit and firewood. Then we can sleep. I'll hunt tomorrow, and we'll leave when you're capable. It should be less than a week.'

24

A month later, as Jane reached Tarzan after the first half of her traverse, she asked, 'What's that smell?'

'I wish I could say. I've smelt something similar, although this is far stronger. It's a phosphate-nitrate smell. Let's shorten our ropes by half until we know where it comes from.'

An hour later, Tarzan stopped again. 'Jane, I feel bad about this direction.'

'Me too. It's not about the smell, which is terrible, but something else, and I can hear screeching.'

'That sounds to me like darters, but many of them. I've never seen them in large numbers.'

'What can we do?'

'Either return or over there,' he indicated a right-angle turn, 'we may be able to travel around it.'

'I don't want to return, so traverse that way slowly.'

After eight hundred metres of short stages, Jane said, 'I feel much better now, although the smell and screeching haven't changed.'

'Me too. I think something didn't want us in that area. Maybe a silipuss was telling us. We can turn more towards our track, then another turn after a kilometre more. We'll keep the ropes at fifty metres.'

Nine traverses later, Jane said, 'The noise is louder and growing.'

'I'm sure it is. The light is stronger in that direction; we'll move slowly towards it.'

...

'Jane, the forest appears to end at that tree over there. Let's look around it.'

Jane joined him at the tree three minutes later and secured her tail while Tarzan coiled up the rope and said, 'I'll take a peek.'

Tarzan rounded the tree, secured his tail, and stood with his back to the trunk, looking between a mass of foliage at the ground fifty metres below because there was no floor, only some massive branches with upward-growing stems and leaves. 'Jane, come and look; it's fantastic and worth seeing.'

She released her tail and quickly came around the tree. The sight filled her mind with questions; hurriedly, she bent, threw her tail's end around a branch, snapped the carabiner, and stepped forward to look between the leaves.

After months of traversing where she leant forward while standing with her tail behind her, providing support, she did the same thing. She had leant too far to recover her balance when she realised her tail was slipping. She tried to regain her position, windmilling her arms as she thought, *Tarzan, I'm sorry.* Seconds later, she began to fall.

Tarzan sensed her thoughts and reacted instantaneously. He launched towards her, his right arm stretched ahead to grab a leg, but his tail brought him up short, and he didn't reach her, almost crying out in desperation.

A moment later, he felt her tail glide over his hand and desperately grabbed at it; his thumb and forefinger closed around it, but the rope continued to slide through the tube wrapping.

After crunching up the tube, the carabiner slapped into the

palm of his hand, and instinctively, his hand closed around it like a vice. He pulled; it came five centimetres before the tail was tight to Jane's waist, and she continued to fall, not vertically downwards but in an arc that ended with her swinging head down, four metres below.

Jane, overloaded with adrenaline, disoriented, didn't know what had stopped her fall, and then she felt herself rising as she swung from side to side. *Tarzan!*

The five centimetres had given enough slack to absorb the shock, then with his muscles knotted and straining, Tarzan hauled her up with his right arm until he could wrap her tail around his left wrist, and then he pulled again. Jane's legs appeared first, then her hips and she jack-knifed so she was lying across the branch. Tarzan gasped, 'Stand or crawl, Jane, and come to me.'

She crawled, then stood, and Tarzan stood and wrapped her in his arms. The adrenaline withdrawal took effect, and she began trembling, 'Tarzan, I...'

'Don't talk, Jane, we'll discuss it later. Just relax.'

When finally she stopped trembling, he released her and said, 'Now, attach your tail securely; I'm holding the rope at your waist.'

Still feeling weak, she did, then tugged at it to ensure the carabiner held.

'Now we can look.'

'Tarzan, you said it was fantastic; what are we looking at?'

'It's a lake, a kilometre long when it's full, and half that wide. This area must be high in soluble iron. The lake water and the mud around it have that reddish colour. As the drier season comes, the lake shrinks. There must be a hundred thousand darters nesting there around the water's edge; you can see the old nests on the dry side strips; they're piles of mud with a cup on top.'

'Yes, but many are flattened.'

'They might fall apart when dry. The lake's centre is clear of nesting darters because it's too deep; I think it will fill with nests as the lake dries, and the darters will return after it refills the next rainy season.'

'If those are females sitting on eggs, then all the flying ones must be males bringing food. I can see what the closest ones are doing. Like you said, they're egg-laying, and the males must help. They fly wonderfully, landing on the side of the nest and holding on with their clawed toes.'

'That's the advantage of their canard wings; the front ones can lift them at the last second.'

'They could do that with wings at the back pushing down.'

'That's where the principal mass is; they must slow that down or knock over the nest; pushing down is the reverse of what they need. In the planetology catalogue, I saw pictures of birds with nests like these, but they had long legs and could stand over the nest and sit. The darters need short legs to live on the upper terrace, so this is a marvellous adaptation.'

Suddenly, three hundred metres to their left, a flock of darters took off in unison.

'Tarzan, why have those taken flight?'

'There must be a predator.'

'There's a terragon in the trees; I saw it.'

'It might be hunting darters. We'll watch.'

The terragon appeared and began a run towards the nests, and the darters coalesced into an attack. Before the darters reached it, the terragon turned and sprinted back to the trees.

'Well, that explains what flattened the dry nests.'

'Then, Jane, hundreds of attacks, successful or not, have occurred this season. Look, there's another. There may be dozens of terragons in the trees.'

The second terragon did what the first did, and then, with increasing frequency, terragons appeared from the trees at separate places and repeated the identical manoeuvre.

Tarzan exclaimed, 'There's a pattern; I think what they're doing is drawing the attention of the darters. That's cooperative behaviour; when most of the darters are on that side, the real attack will come from the opposite side of the lake.'

'I can't see any there.'

'They'll hide until the right moment. Showing themselves would ruin the efforts of the terragons. Wait.'

'I can see eggs in the nearest nests to us; the females must have left to help the males scare off the terragons.'

'Then it won't be long before we see something there. Keep watching.'

Jane whispered urgently, 'Tarzan, look in the forest near the vacated nests. I can see movement between the trees, but it's not big terragons.'

'They look like *TerraKids*; maybe they're young terragons.'

'I can see two; they're standing on two legs but aren't males. Apart from that and size, they look like Happy.'

Suddenly, the female *TerraKids* broke from the trees and ran to the now unguarded nests.

'There are dozens, and they're taking the eggs.'

'Yes, when they have two, they run back.'

'Some have three and carry the third in their mouth.'

It took less than two minutes, a calm fell, the terragons and *TerraKids* vanished, and the darters returned to their nests.

'The show's over, Jane; we'll find a Cascade Creeper and eat our fruit.'

Ideally situated for a shower, the first Cascade Creeper, only fifty metres away, had a solid floor area by the tree where they settled and ate.

Later, Jane spoke. 'Tarzan, something is watching us.'

'I sensed it two minutes ago; I think it's a *TerraKid*. I'll say hello.'

Friend.

The reply felt powerful – *We share.*

'It's okay, Jane, we'll ignore him unless he comes to meet us.'

'I heard too.'

'Yes, it was easy to understand. Either we're improving, or this species communicates better than the cats. After that fascinating display, I have only two questions: do the *TerraKids* live up here, and what do they do with the eggs? They could have eaten them when they stole them and didn't.'

'Your Dad thinks they live up here because of their feet, and if that's one watching us, that's further proof; I think it may be like Happy's dad. I agree they live up here, but there aren't many. I have no idea what they do with the eggs.'

'The *TerraKid* is moving towards us, Jane.'

As the *TerraKid* approached, Tarzan stood, and then Jane. Tarzan saw how its feet gripped the branches; Jane saw something else. *It's a male who can be proud of that bit.*

It stopped at five metres, and they examined each other. Tarzan saw a head shaped like a dog with a flattened face, with expressive and intelligent eyes but small ears like the silipusses. He remembered Happy and his father. They looked silently at each other for a minute, and then Tarzan felt its eyes looking directly into his and met them. A picture of a *TerraKid* female holding two eggs built in his mind, like a video transition that fades from one image to another; he saw the female offer an egg to a male, and the male ate it. The female then ate the second, and as the male displayed an erection, she turned her back, and he serviced her. Then, the picture faded.

Tarzan had a reply. He *thelt* – *We share. Thank you.*

The *TerraKid* left, and Tarzan asked.

'Did you see his pictures?'

'Yes, that was a mating ritual; he answered our question about what they do with the eggs.'

'More than that, Jane, I'm sure now they evolved in the forest. Once the females have reared babies, they descend and grow into terragons, participating in the mating process we observed, protecting their species. I'm also sure there are far fewer males, and we'll only find *TerraKids* in areas with high iron content and nearby lakes where the darters nest. They might have been far more widespread before the forest covered most of the land. The terragon females must range over large areas for the food quantity they need and only join each other in the breeding season near a darter lake.'

'Okay, why did you *theel we share*?'

'Because our rituals may differ, but we're fundamentally similar. We saw the cooperative behaviour in attracting the darters from their nests, so I conclude they're social. And I have another theory: We know the female *TerraKids* offer an egg to a male, and if he accepts, they eat one themselves. I think it's more than a ritual and gift. The eggs stimulate the equivalent of our hormone system, she becomes fertile, and he inseminates her.'

'And the third egg?'

'A guess: She offers it to another male, and he also inseminates her. She has twins; one will be male. So, the number of males born depends on a random selection of females who collect three eggs.'

'Do they lay eggs?'

'Doubtful, without sufficient males to feed them, they would need to leave the nest, and that's inefficient. I suggest they give birth to live young, then keep them in a collective nursery; the cooperation level indicates that's likely. The males will function as guardians and protectors of the young, so a male came to fetch Happy.

'We still have much to learn. But now, we'll discuss your fall.'

'Tarzan, I know what I did wrong. I'm glad you saved me, and I promise I'll never do it again.'

'Don't promise me; you can easily break promises to others. Promise yourself and the baby you'll one day have. Always ensure your safety.

'It's too late to travel far; we can traverse slowly around the lake, hunt a squirrel, find some fruit, and a place for the night.'

'Okay, learning about the *TerraKids* mating practice has made me feel even more a part of the forest.'

That afternoon, before the light faded, Jane foraged and returned with four different fruits and bunches of three berry species. Tarzan watched as she laid down two thick, leathery leaves, peeled the fruits, cut them into pieces, laid them carefully on the leaf plates and then decorated them with berries.

'That looks like a gourmet meal, Jane. What's the occasion?'

'I'll tell you later when we sleep. Let's prepare for tomorrow. I want to wash our clothes; they'll dry overnight.'

Tarzan checked the rope, metre by metre, and coiled it for the morning. Jane cut and carried a massive bundle of foliage to lay in the nest, hung their washed minimalist clothes on pegs hammered into the tree, and then they lazily ate the fruit and lay down, naked, on the bed as they had done many times.

Tarzan.

Yes, Jane.

Did you hear me?

Clearly.

He sensed her turn towards him, so he turned to her, her lips five centimetres from his as she looked into his eyes, she whispered. 'I don't know why; it's a new feeling. I want you to make love to me. I'm not fertile, so we can't make a baby.'

He whispered back, 'I feel the same. I do, too.' Then, they leaned forward, and their lips met.

He wanted to caress her, caress every curve, and feel her skin against his; she did, too. They sensed each other's intentions – but they didn't last.

After their lips met, Jane felt a ripple of ecstasy flow from her lips to her toes and then back again, stopping as fire exploded in her breasts when Tarzan cupped one. Her hand moved involuntarily to his crotch, and she gripped his member, already a rigid pole. She threw an arm and leg over him, then rolled with him in her arms onto her back, grasping tightly and in a mutual frenzy, guided him as he entered, then locked her arms and legs around him as waves of ecstasy rocked her from head to foot.

He felt the waves and her reaction, then grew further – *Now, my love. Now.*

Yes, my love. Yesss!

...

Jane whispered, 'Are you still hungry after our wedding feast? Is that why you're licking my neck?'

'Is that what it was?'

'Yes, it was the best I could do.'

'It was fantastic; I'll remember it all our lives. It's not hunger; it's just that I want to show you how much I love you.'

'I know how much. I still have you, and it's growing. You can show me, and I'll show you.' – *Slowly and gently.*

Yes, Jane.

...

Good night, my love.

25

A month later, less than ten metres into the first of the day's traverses, Tarzan stopped and called, 'Pull me back.' Jane did as he joined her.

'What's that noise?'

'Darters, they're disturbed by something. A raptor might be hunting, and they're hiding under the vegetation. If that noise comes closer, we're in trouble and must duck around the tree. If we knew where it was going, we might avoid it.'

'What's a raptor, and why is it dangerous?'

'Not to us; it's a huge four-winged beast that soars over the forest. During the day, it preys on darters; at night, it might roost, but it might sleep while soaring.'

'How big?'

'I haven't measured one, Jane, but the biggest I've seen had a wingspan close to twenty metres.

'That's enormous. But why's it a danger?'

'Because it's the principal megalon prey. That means a megalon might dive down and hit it, and if that happens any-where near us, we might have a chunk of the floor above us come down as it did with the GravBus and the darters with it. They're the danger.'

'Stand against the tree, Jane; tell me if you think that racket is approaching.'

Their backs to the tree, close to each other, Jane said, 'I'm sure it's closing on us from behind.'

'Slightly to our left, Jane, follow me around the tree to the right.'

They had shuffled four metres, a quarter of the way around the tree when something massive hit the upper floor, and with a resounding crash, a section of it broke loose and fell.

'Jane! Return quickly!'

Jane did; tied to Tarzan, she could move only three metres before he had to follow, and as the rope tightened, she turned to look back and saw the sky through the hole in the floor ten metres behind them. Then, two darters flew through from above. One went directly away from them, the other to one side, and Tarzan watched it. Almost blind in the poor light, it flew into a tree and dropped. Jane saw a third darter arrive, and Tarzan, who had turned to look at the second, was turning back when his movement attracted the terrified darter that launched itself straight at him. Jane saw the danger, grabbed her fruit stick above her shoulder and broke the vegetable fibre binding as she wrenched it off her back and yelled.

Tarzan! Drop!

Although she thought she said it, Tarzan later insisted he received a *thelt* so powerful that he reacted and dropped microseconds later. The darter, at full speed, its neck and heavy head with the lethal beak aimed straight at his chest, had almost reached him as he fell, but Jane swung the stick with the muscle and nerve memories still in her spinal column after years of hockey. The stick fractured, and the dead darter shot ten metres before falling to the deck.

Tarzan had not seen her swing but heard the thud and saw the darter land. 'Jane, what happened?'

'That was a third one, and it aimed at you. I scored a goal with the darter as the ball.'

'Thanks, Jane; what else can I say.'

He wasn't expecting the answer. 'Just say you love me.'

'I love you, Jane.'

She laid down beside him. 'Bugger the darters,' and *thelt* – *Kiss me.*

'We may still be in danger.'

'Then it'll be a double thrill.'

Tarzan and Jane were travelling fast thirteen months after the GravBus crash. He reckoned that without foraging, they could travel between eight and nine kilometres a day and both hunt while travelling, although often without finding something to eat. Jane had just completed a hundred-metre lead. Tarzan was two-thirds through the follow when he sensed something was wrong but continued and then surprised Jane, who was controlling his safety and gathering the rope into a hole in the floor. When he reached her, he stopped instead of continuing to do a new lead. 'Jane, listen.'

Motionless, they stood together, 'What is it?' she asked.

'I think it's a GravBus thrust engine that's stuttering. Can you confirm where the sound is coming from?'

She pointed. 'There, where we've come from. Just to that side.'

'If nothing else, that proves we must be on the right course for somewhere. Tell me if it's becoming louder.'

'I'm sure it is.'

'Me too. I think it's in trouble; the pilot might be trying to reach a lake to the left of our direction, up ahead.'

'Why?'

'Because the GravBus is low, and the noise is abnormal. Remember the darter's lake; there's usually a clear beach; the pilot could land to repair it. Come, we'll try to stay in his direction.'

Tarzan set off as fast as he could, and Jane launched herself after him as soon as he stopped. Each time one passed the other, the one waiting said, 'More left', 'more right,' or 'straight on.'

Finally, the stuttering caught up with them; Tarzan reckoned it passed low down, overhead and slowly, then five minutes and two double traverses later, Tarzan saw daylight through a tree ahead. He reached it, stopped, and reeled in Jane until she joined him; they rounded the tree, and from the branch, between the leaves, they could see a pond with a bare beach.

'Water's low,' remarked Jane.

'And that's a GravEx, a private executive GravBus. The pilot's cautious; he's checking it out before landing. I'll tie a double loop on one rope end, throw the rope over the branch, equal each side, and tie it to the branch. I'll strap on my claws.'

It took him half a minute. Jane asked, 'Why not wait until we see who leaves it?'

'There's either a megalon, a terragon, or both on the way. The crew and passengers must exit and run. I'll tell them. The GravEx will land here; it's the widest part.'

He swung himself over the branch and, with the twin ropes running through his hands in a megalon's hide tube, dropped forty metres, then, bracing his legs against the tree, his claws caused two furrows as he braked to a halt, turned, and began to run to the GravEx that had just landed. As he reached it, he looked up.

There was a growing dot in the sky.

Forty seconds, ten to return, count. The door had an emergency release; Tarzan hit it hard, the door swung open, and he leapt in. In the first three seconds, he saw a locker with an emergency logo on the front and a young woman cowering in one of the four seats.

He yelled, '*Everybody out and run, megalon!*'

Thirty-five.

He snapped open the emergency locker, pulled out the bag, swung it onto his shoulder and turned. The girl shrunk back against the wall. '*Come!*'

Twenty-eight.

She didn't move; she just looked dumbly at him. *Shit.* He stepped forward, snapped open her safety belt, picked her up, threw her over the other shoulder, and jumped out.

Twenty-two.

He began running, and she started to struggle. 'I'll drop you; the megalon can have you unless you stay calm.'

She stopped struggling. *Sixteen.*

He reached the tree. *Eleven seconds.*

Without releasing the girl, he lifted the rope with the double loop end, fed her legs into the loops, stood her up, knotted the rope around her chest and said, '*Hold On!*' Jane began to haul up the rope. He attached the other one to his belt, then instead of climbing, he turned to look.

Three.

A terragon appeared on the other side of the GravEx, but it heard the whistle as the megalon levelled out, so it stopped.

Two, One.

Zero!

The megalon came over the treetops at terrifying speed, dropped further, and then its mouth gaped open and engulfed the GravEx, the enormous crunching sound echoing around the clearing. Then, the megalon began to climb using its momentum.

Jane had pulled the girl twelve metres up the tree and then had tied off the rope to rest, so the girl saw everything that happened and froze, petrified when she noticed the terragon begin moving towards her and Tarzan.

Tarzan didn't move, and she wondered why. He had decided to find out something. He could be up the tree beyond the terragon's reach in five seconds, so he stood calmly watching it approach, then concentrated on a *theel – I mean you no harm; I am of this forest. We share.* It seemed to Tarzan that a chorus of a thousand voices from around the clearing *thelt* the same feeling.

I mean you no harm; I am of this forest. We share.

The terragon stopped; it looked confused, then returned to the trees it came from. Tarzan climbed like a four-legged spider; Jane reeled in the safety rope. As he passed the girl still swinging, he said, 'Another minute, and we'll haul you up.'

As Jane helped her onto the branch and laid her against the tree trunk, the girl burst into tears.

'Let her cry, Tarzan, and maybe she'll sleep; she's young, I would guess about nineteen.'

'Then I'll make a nest nearby, and we can take the girl there. If we take her with us, we must do the same as I did with you.'

'Then make a good nest; we can't leave her alone. We'll need an exercise area, a pull-up bar, and a creeper on a nearby tree. Preferably two trees with water lilies; one was just enough for two.'

Tarzan found a suitable place to make the nest, just a small area to start with so they could take her to the interior. Tarzan carried her, and Jane managed the safety rope. He laid her down; she didn't speak, and a few minutes later, exhausted by her terror, she curled up and slept.

'Tarzan, will we give her a name, as we gave each other?'

'I think we should; it worked for you. Do you have an idea?'

'First, why was she the only passenger in a GravEx?'

'At a guess, she's the daughter of a wealthy, important guy, and he arranged to bring her to him. I was returning in the academic holidays about a year ago when I met you; she might be doing the same.'

'Then she's a rich kid, and rich kids have nannies who read them fairy stories. A name from a fairy story.'

'That's something my education missed; my parents are scientists. Have you an idea?'

'There was a story about a girl who followed a rabbit down a hole under a tree and fell into another world. If only I could remember her name.'

'What was in the story?'

'Oh, there was a Queen that looked like a playing card and a cat with a smile full of teeth.'

'Like a silipuss?'

'Sort of, Alice asked it which direction to take – That's it, her name was Alice.'

Interested, Tarzan asked, 'What did the cat reply?'

'"That depends on where you want to go."'

'Logical. I thought fairy stories were fantasies.'

'They are, but not in everything. To work, they must feel real. Alice sounds like a good name to make her think she's elsewhere. I hope it will make her forget she's a rich kid; those I've known are a pain.'

'She looks like you did a year ago. Although shorter with the same hair – and grey eyes.'

'Her nose turns up.'

Tarzan laughed, 'Jane, there isn't another woman on Tarik as beautiful as you. You can be generous. I'll fetch more wood and vines and expand the nest.'

'And I'll hunt a tarizard or tree squirrel.'

26

Two hours later, the girl woke. 'Hello Alice, welcome back. I'm Jane, and that hunk over there is Tarzan.'

Alice's voice trembled, 'What are you?'

'Once we were people like you, but we've adapted to Tarik, or you could say Tarik has changed us, so we're different.'

'I can see that; you have tails and green eyes.'

Jane laughed. 'Handy things tails, I'll make one for you, but my eyes are blue, and yours are grey.'

Curiosity stifled the trembling. 'The tails aren't real?'

Tarzan heard as he came to them, 'No, Alice, although we both wish they were. Living here would be easier if we had tails like most residents, so we've done our best.'

Feeling much better, Alice said, 'I'm not Alice; I'm Elisabeth.'

Jane answered, 'Do you know a classic story called Alice in Wonderland?'

'The children's fantasy?'

'Yes, well, you were Elisabeth this morning, but you've fallen through a hole in a tree, and now you're in Wonderland; just think of yourself as Alice until you can leave here.'

'Is there a cat that smiles?'

'Hundreds, lovely smiles, I'm sure you'll meet a few.'

Tarzan thought. *It's amazing what a name can do. I hope Alice won't cause problems.*

'Tarzan, are my eyes still blue?'

He turned to look, 'A greeny blue, Jane. With so much green around us, the reflected light is green.'

From the first day, Jane had difficulty with Alice being with them; Tarzan sensed it but wisely decided to remain on one side, showing no particular concern for Alice.

Alice felt she was the odd one out. She didn't miss the signs of the close rapport between Tarzan and Jane and felt jealous, which made her moody. Tarzan didn't try to teach Alice as he had taught Jane, who could do as well as a teacher, if not better than he could, for Jane had suffered the pain of the same program. He remained distant while observing Alice's training, but Jane did report what she thought about Alice's progress. Once Jane had established an exercise routine for Alice, including pull-ups on a bar erected by Tarzan, the first bit of information came while Jane massaged her after the first exercise day. Jane asked Alice her age and why she was on the GravEx.

'I'll be twenty in two months; I finished my first year of university in Colony One five days ago, and my dad, the administrator of Colony Thirteen on the other side of the sea, arranged the flight home. I was supposed to spend a night at a colony halfway.'

'Do you want to return to university?'

'I did, but it seems that might be impossible.'

'Well, not for a year; that's how long it will take us to reach Tarzan's colony, but you'll still be young enough. What are you studying?'

'My parents are administrators and managers, so I studied business admin, but it didn't attract me. Math and Science do, but what?'

'I know how difficult that decision is. I studied ecology for two years and decided to take a three-month break and then switch to hydrology.'

'Why?'

'The history part of ecology was fascinating, but the ecology of Tarik is nothing like the course material. Hydrology might be more useful as there's so much surface water. But I won't return. I now know more about the ecology of Tarik than any other person except Tarzan.'

'How did you meet him?'

'I was the cabin attendant on a GravBus that crashed. Tarzan had applied for a lecturer's job at Colony One University and was returning home to Colony Nine. We were the only two survivors, and Tarzan knew the way to his home. After more than a year of travelling, we belong in the forest with the people of Tarik.'

'What people?'

'You'll meet them, the silipusses, the terragons, *TerraKids*, and the megalons. And other species I haven't met.'

'Can they talk?'

'Telepathically, with each other and with us, we call a telepathic message a *thelt*. I hope you'll learn too. You may know what to study in a year.'

'I've watched you and Tarzan. He handed you his knife, passing it behind his back without asking, and you took it. Did you ask him with a telepathic message?'

'I must have done. I need only picture Tarzan's knife in my mind; then he knows I need it.'

'That sounds incredible. I must do more press-ups and pullups so we can begin moving.'

When Tarzan opened the emergency bag he had taken from

the GravEx, he was delighted and said to Jane, 'There's a reel of fishing line in here, enough for two more mallets with a lot left over.'

'That confirms what Alice said.'

'What did she say?'

'I came to tell you she's almost twenty. She was on her way home to her parents.'

'How does fishing line confirm what she said?'

'Her father is the administrator of Colony Thirteen on the other side of the sea. You said emergency kits have a fishing line when the flight is over the sea.'

'I did. Will Alice study further?'

'She said she hoped to but couldn't decide what. She's not attracted to administration and management like her parents.'

'I'm not surprised. The scientists who do the sperm bank gene matching may have selective criteria.'

'Your dad's idea?'

'Yes, I had an inkling of this at a meeting in Colony One. There is a crime problem, and they said the criminals were those the planners selected for heavy machine operation and don't have jobs as we never received the heavy machinery.'

'What does that have to do with genetics?'

'The geneticist said they couldn't solve the problem and had to wait to see the results of the next generation. As if they select children with specific DNA patterns.'

'That's a moral crime.'

'I agree, Jane, but it's more than a crime; it's fiddling with natural selection and survival of the genome, but we need proof to say something.'

Two days later, Jane became annoyed. Alice was not following the exercise regime, although the first two days were satisfactory. As she tired, Alice slacked off and made only a token effort on the third day.

'Alice, why aren't you doing the exercises I told you were necessary?'

'I don't want to.'

Upset, Jane spoke sharply, 'It's not whether you want to; all that matters is that unless you build enough muscle, we aren't leaving. Don't you want to return home?'

'I hardly see my parents from one day to the next. They're so busy they might not miss me. I have no reason to return home. I told you I didn't like my studies and didn't know what else I might like to do. I'll exercise, but it hurts.'

'It's supposed to hurt. That tells your body to build muscles.'

'Well, I don't like it.'

Jane thought about what Alice said for several hours – and then spoke to Tarzan when they foraged for food.

'Tarzan, I'm leaving tomorrow, and I hope you'll come too.'

Shocked, he asked, 'Why Jane?'

'Because Alice refuses to exercise. She's typical of other girls I've known from wealthy families: spoilt and lazy. She's never had to work, has no idea what she wants, and is too lazy to do anything about it.'

'Doesn't she want to return to see her parents?'

'I asked; she suggested they might not notice she's absent.'

'If we leave her, she'll die.'

'If we stay, we will. You said the cats would feed a woman

alone; she won't die. I don't have to look after her, so you have a choice: look after her or me, but it can't be both.'

'Can I talk to her before a final decision? I love you, so I'll leave with you if she doesn't exercise.

'Talk to her, but it won't help.'

'What about leaving but returning after a few days to check how she's doing?'

That might make it easy for him; he wants to stick to the forest rules.

'I'll agree to that on condition that I decide to return, not you.'

Tarzan delayed his foraging trip for an hour and watched Alice. He could see she made little effort, taking long pauses between each press-up, but he waited until she stopped and sat before he said, 'Alice, I want to talk to you.'

'If it's about the exercises, I've already told Jane.'

'She told me, but now I'll tell you something. If you don't exercise properly, we're not taking you anywhere, and we both want to reach home as soon as possible to see our families again. So if you're not exercising as Jane asked, we'll leave.'

'And let me starve?'

'You won't starve. The silipusses will bring you food. The pusses will know as they're telepathic. We'll leave you with the emergency bag from your GravEx, so you have a rope, axe and lighters. You have the clothes, mallet and tail I made for you. We'll take ours, so you can take your time exercising and then travel when you're ready.'

As Jane expected, Alice behaved as she had for years, for she thought. *They saved me from the GravEx; they won't leave me now.*

'Then leave, and let me do it my way; I won't wake every morning in agony.'

'Okay, Alice, remember two things: don't move if you see what looks like a pig with tusks; it will then ignore you. And never approach closer than ten metres to a pile of leaves that look like a giant mushroom.'

Tarzan and Jane prepared their equipment for departure, collected some fruit for Alice, and then slept. When Alice woke the following day, they had left.

27

Alice relaxed without the usual morning activity as Tarzan and Jane prepared for the day's foray for food and firewood, showering, breakfast, making baskets, and checking equipment.

The silence eventually deepened, and she thought, *I'm alone. I've always heard people, my nanny, the cook, my parents – even people outside my house.*

She rose, looked at the shower tree ten metres away, and thought. *I can shower later. I'll eat first.*

After eating two soft fruits she liked, which tasted like apples, with no one to talk to and nothing to do, the pull-up bar drew her attention. *I must exercise, but I'll only do a little.*

She did pull-ups, but after a rest, with nothing else to do, she did press-ups. By midday, she had done all the exercises but had not reached the pain limit.

Sweaty and thirsty, she looked at the shower tree and decided, *I must drink. Jane or Tarzan held my arm before, shall I crawl?*

The thought brought a memory of Tarzan and Jane using the rope. She fetched it from the bag, tied one end to a branch at the nest, tied her tail to her belt, put the rope coil over a shoulder, and crawled towards the shower tree on all fours. After two metres, the branch she had gripped with her right arm bent downwards, she toppled to the right and managed to avoid falling over with a considerable effort, but the branch her elbow pressed on to save herself scratched her arm. Trembling, she righted herself and rested until ready. Thirst made her continue.

Shaking with the effort, she drank thirstily when she finally reached the shower tree and tied the rope to a branch. After an hour and two litres of water, she snapped her tail carabiner to the rope and showered.

She had forgotten to bring a piece of soap plant and a toothbrush stick. Until then, she hadn't thought of soap or teeth. That was when she realised that no one would bring either item or the piece of skirt she used as a washcloth.

She used her hands and fingers.

Ready to return, she remembered Jane always brought two cascade cones with her and returned with full ones for drinking water, and she had forgotten to bring one. The ten metres to the nest to fetch one seemed like a kilometre, so she laid down carefully and, reaching as low as possible, pulled a cone from the creeper. *I can't use the water in this one to shower.* The kilometre was no shorter, so she looped her tail around the rope and through her belt twice. Less than a metre from it, she crawled slowly back to the nest, holding one edge of the water-filled cone between her teeth.

Exhausted, she placed the cone carefully where Jane placed the water cones and slept. Her last thought was. *Maybe I'm stupid. It's much harder living alone.*

Alice's second day was a repeat of the first: fruit, exercise, and the shower, except the rope in place gave her confidence for her trip to the shower. She remembered the toothbrush stick and found that Jane had left six, so she took one, the cone of soap, her skirt cloth, and a water cone, and reached the shower tree without incident. She left them all at the shower tree except the cone of water. There was another difference. The loneliness grew as she returned from the shower earlier, so she did more exercises to drive away her thoughts and a new worry. *I'll run out of food tomorrow.*

When Alice woke on the morning of her third solitary day, a squirrel lay beside the two remaining fruits. *Jane was right; a silipuss must have brought it. I have a lighter, but how do I make a fire? I never learnt.*

She ate the fruit, exercised, washed, and, by early afternoon, felt hungry. She crawled again towards the shower without looping her tail so tightly to the rope. It gave her enough distance to break a large green leaf from a plant and collect several sticks that she thought might burn. On return, she fetched the axe and used it as a knife to cut open the squirrel and, with grimaces of disgust, chopped off its head and removed the entrails, dropping them through the hole in the floor that Jane had used. She felt proud to have done it.

Though she found some dry leaves and moss, the wood was too wet to burn, and she gave up. *I'll starve. I wonder what raw squirrel tastes like.*

She used the axe to cut the squirrel into chunks and then tried to remove the skin from them. It was hard to remove without cooking, but she stripped one piece with her teeth, then shut her eyes and bit into it. *It's not bad, but I hope the sili-*

puss brings fruit tomorrow. She ate as much as possible, slowly chewing.

Tarzan and Jane had travelled for two days, but slowly, after Tarzan said, 'We'll take it easy, Jane. If we decide to return, there's no point in hurrying.'

'Okay, we'll explore for six days within fifteen kilometres of Alice. If I don't feel it's worth returning, we'll head for your home.'

On the third day, Jane said, 'Make a nest here as a base, and we'll look around. I'll hunt and collect firewood and fruit. I'll also ask how Alice is doing.'

When she returned, Tarzan was finishing the nest, so they ate. Jane said, 'Alice is fine; the silipusses brought her food. They say she ate a squirrel, and I'm surprised – she's exercising. Tomorrow, we can explore north of here.'

There was fruit in the morning, but Alice had never seen milk nuts. There were three. After an examination and shaking one to her ear, she placed it on the nest floor and used the axe to smack it. Her despairing cry as the nut rolled off the nest and fell through the floor was audible a hundred metres away.

After carefully fixing the second one where it wouldn't move, she cracked it open and ate. She still felt hungry but decided to keep the one remaining for later. The lost milk nut and her failure to light a fire brought depression, and the loneliness built into despair and brought a thought forward. *I can survive, but what for? Living alone isn't what I want. I wish Tarzan and Jane would return, but they must be far away. I'm an idiot; I might as well die.*

She drove the thought away with furious exercise, and then, after another shower and milk nut, she slept with the idea. *It doesn't hurt so much, but another massage from Jane would be nice.*

It rained during the night. The thunder woke Alice, and when the rain started, she retreated to the tree and sat with her back to it. The rain didn't last long and wasn't excessively heavy, for she was on the storm's fringe, but she didn't know that. Thoroughly miserable and drenched when the rain stopped, she lay on the soaking floor and tried to sleep. She did eventually when the thunder died.

Day five began poorly; there was fruit and another squirrel, but now that she believed she could survive, the loneliness grew, and the question of her future gnawed at every thought. With it, the motivation to exercise dropped, though it was less painful. *What's the point? I'm not going anywhere. I would tell them how stupid I've been if Jane or Tarzan returned. I didn't know how much I needed them.*

Before she slept, she had an odd thought. *If a silipuss comes, I can ask it to tell Jane that I'm sorry.*

After exploring to the north and finding nothing unusual, Tarzan and Jane had left to explore to the south, making a wide loop that day. Travelling slowly, when they saw the scorpalon egg stack far away, they approached it but stayed a safe distance away. Moments after they stopped, a silipuss drifted from the shadows – *We share.*

Hello Kitty. We Share.

When a second silipuss silently joined the first, Jane asked, 'Do they expect us to do something about the scorpalon?'

'I think they do; I'll find a branch and throw it at the egg stack. The scorpalon might attack it.'

It took Tarzan two minutes to find a branch, and when he rejoined Jane, two more silipusses had appeared. 'That's a massive piece of timber. Can you throw it that far?'

'I hope so. Stand back; I'll try.'

The branch hit the egg stack, scattering the leaves. The scorpalon burst from the floor in an explosion of residue, and its claws locked onto the branch. The cats shot forward and, seconds later, pierced its eyes with their forward claws. It was over in seconds, except that it was still alive. Jane, who had the axe, ran forward and buried it in the scorpalon's head. *That's for the last time.* It thrashed around as it died.

We Share.

Thank you. We Share.

They sat with their friends and licked eggs off the leaves until there was nothing left, and then Jane *thelt* a picture of Alice.

'Tarzan, Alice is still exercising; the silipusses say she's sad. She may be learning.'

When Alice saw the fresh fruit in the morning, she remembered her thoughts about asking a silipuss, so she wondered. *Tarzan said the silipusses are telepathic; can I call one?*

She picked up one of the fruits, stared fixedly at it and thought. *Thank you for this fruit. Please come.*

She was slowly eating the second of two fruits, desperate and discouraged, when she saw something approaching the nest. Her heartbeat in overdrive, she froze. *Is that a pig with tusks?* As it came closer, she saw something in its mouth. *Is that a silipuss?*

The puss came to the nest carrying a squirrel and laid it before her, then sat back and *thelt – We share.*

Alice didn't understand, but she was sure the silipuss had come because she called; gratitude and affection flooded her. *The puss is my friend*, and she thought of Tarzan and Jane. *Please come.*

The silipuss left, and Alice, feeling euphoric, convinced that Tarzan and Jane would now return, began to exercise again. *It's been six days; they must be far away. I'll have to wait for their return.*

After another day of exploration to the south, Tarzan and Jane returned to their nest laden with fruit and a squirrel, made a fire, grilled the squirrel, and then showered.

About to lay down, a silipuss arrived – *We Share.*

A picture in Jane's mind showed Alice, but a feeling grew.

'Tarzan, Alice wants us back. I sense she asked a silipuss to tell us.'

'So, do we return?'

'Yes, I'm sure she's learnt that she can survive without us, but it's not worth living without friends. And she's exercising.'

'Ok, it should take us two days.'

Alice exercised and ate fruit and raw squirrel for two days.

Although she had decided it might take six days for Jane and Tarzan to return, doubts crept in by the end of the second day, and despair lurked in the shadows of her mind. Sitting on the nest after her evening shower, using the last dregs of the soap she had used sparingly, she peeled a soft fruit with nails that she noted were now long and might break off. *Cutting them with the axe won't be easy. I must try it after I eat.*

She tried to jam the axe on the floor to cut her nails. It kept falling over; she felt desperate when she heard Jane's voice. 'Ask Tarzan to lend you his razor, Alice. It's much easier.'

Jane saw Alice rise smoothly and smiled. *It worked.* Alice turned, saw Jane only two metres away, took three steps and threw herself at Jane, who put her arms around her as Alice hugged her so tightly Jane couldn't breathe.

'Jane, I hoped and prayed you would come; I asked a silipuss to tell you. Where's Tarzan?'

'Here, Alice.' He came from behind and hugged them both.

'Alice, can you stop trying to squeeze the life out of me?'

'Sorry Jane, I'm so glad to see you that I can't help it.'

'We missed you too, but let's begin our work and make a fire. We have two squirrels to grill.'

'I've eaten them raw, but a grilled one will be heaven.'

When they lay down to sleep that night, all three were naked. Alice had washed their clothes, for Jane had brought several water cones and soap plants. Lying between Jane and Tarzan, Alice felt a happiness she had never known.

28

It was already late when Jane and Tarzan left to hunt the following day. Jane had made two baskets and gave Alice soap plants to crush and fill their soap cup, plus new toothbrush sticks. She then cut Alice's hair and nails after a shower. 'There, Alice, now you look lovely.'

'Do I really?'

'Ask Tarzan.'

Alice turned to ask him, but he said, 'You're beautiful, Alice; with more exercise, you'll be stunning.'

Wonderingly, Alice replied, 'No one has ever said that to me. I love you both.'

Tarzan purposely left his bag in view on the platform to reassure Alice they would return from their hunt. She began her exercises. Jane had remembered and told her, 'You've done well, Alice. You must now build muscle, not destroy it. Stop an exercise as soon as it's painful, don't push past the pain barrier, and then do a different exercise, and do the cycle only four times a day.'

An hour later, after they had killed two squirrels, Jane said, 'I'm surprised by the change in her, but we must make sure she doesn't feel left out. I must persuade her that if she works hard, she will be a part of our partnership, a trio, not a pair. But I won't tell her that unless you agree.'

'Including sex?'

'She's either with us or not. With us means we share every-thing if she wants to participate.'

'Would that spoil our bond? I've just accustomed myself to the idea we'll be together forever.'

'As long as you treat us as equals, it won't be a problem.'

'If I err, Jane, you must tell me.'

Jane picked her moment when Tarzan was out foraging. 'Alice, I want to talk to you about Tarik and its people. Stop ex-ercising and eat some fruit with me.'

Alice sighed as she stopped. 'A break in this routine is better than an orgasm. What do you want to tell me?'

'I told you the people can all talk to each other. Not only that, but they also live by a set of rules. They don't say "Good morning." When you understand their telepathic messages, you'll hear them say, "We Share." That feeling is the overriding rule for survival on Tarik; it means they don't attack each other. There are other rules of conduct, but "We Share" means they will share the bounty of Tarik freely and will help anyone who asks for help, whatever species is asking. They do not fight within or between species. Tarzan and I consider ourselves part of this culture. Females and children don't need to ask; whatever their species, they will re-ceive help if they're in trouble or hungry.'

'I know that's true, for the pusses helped me, although when you say it, it sounds fantastic.'

'It is. I'm telling you this because before we reach Tarzan's colony, you'll have to decide whether to return to your colony or continue exploring the forest with Tarzan and me. If you de-cide to stay with us, I want you to know that "We Share" means we share everything between us.'

'Does that include sex?'

'If you want to share, it does.'

'I must think about it.'

'Of course.'

After two weeks of exercise, Alice did pull-ups while Jane collected firewood and met Tarzan fifty metres away from the nest. She stopped him and said, 'I want to make love tonight.'

'Okay, Jane, I know it's safe.'

'How do you know that?'

'From your smell, Jane. When you ovulate, I can smell a change in your body's odour. Now it's normal.'

'I stink?'

'No, it's a sweetness; I guess as a male, it attracts me. I said we could smell far more when no confusing artificial smells exist. All sexual animals produce a pheromone during ovulation, and many males can smell it from kilometres away.'

'Is that how the male megalon found the female?'

'It's most likely, Jane, he arrived from downwind.'

'So I've been peeing on a mushroom for nothing?'

'For a cross-check, Jane, but now Alice is here, I might become confused, so keep checking. What about Alice?'

'I'll tell her; we've nothing to hide. She wants to join us; she's working hard at her exercises.'

'Alice, tonight you must stay to one side of the nest. Tarzan and I want to love each other.'

'You mean, have sex?'

'Yes, although much more than that. Have you tried it?'

'Once, Jane, two years ago. I thought it was pointless, and I didn't experience what the other girls call an orgasm, although I've since learnt how to masturbate.'

'Then you won't be shocked.'

'Why do you do it?'

'Because I love him, it's fantastic; we join mentally as well as physically, and it's good practice for making a baby, although we must avoid it when I'm fertile.'

'But he's sterile like all men.'

'Not Tarzan.'

'Oh..., *that's great!* But how do you know you're not fertile?'

'Do you know about the mushroom test?'

'Of course, I learnt about it at school.'

'That mushroom grows up here; I'll show you. I pee on it, and when it opens, I know I'm fertile, and then, after it doesn't, sex is safe until my menses.

'You'll be with us for a year, and I'll make love with Tarzan frequently, but we must work together in harmony, and if one day you know you'll join us, you can make love with us as a full partner.'

'Do you intend to have a baby?'

'We do, and if you join us, our babies will play and grow up together in the forest.'

When they lay on the leafy bed, both Tarzan and Jane were naked, and Alice felt odd, although she had no breastband. It seemed fitting that she removed her only piece of clothing and lay on the side of the bed, but she faced the couple, curious after what Jane had said. Lifting herself on her elbow, she could see the caresses and their eyes locked to each other but could hear nothing, and their lips didn't move except for kisses and small smiles. *They don't need to talk.*

Alice thought them beautiful. *I'm really in Wonderland.* When, after what seemed ages, Jane straddled him and guided his entry, Alice's hand strayed to between her thighs. She sensed the mounting tension between the two, heard their rapid breathing, and anticipated the finale, which took much longer than expected. Finally, she saw Jane shuddering in Tarzan's enveloping embrace, and then she felt the lightning of her orgasm and lay back, exhausted.

Tarzan, did you feel Alice's climax?

Yes, ours might have been so strong because she climaxed with us.

Once she can theel like us, I'll ask if she wants to participate.

Do you like that idea?

We will be stronger as a trio, and our babies can play together.

She's asleep now, do you want to sleep?

No, a slow and gentle loving....

Due to Alice's renewed energy and determination, she reached the milestones in her exercise development faster than Jane did. 'Okay, Alice, now that you can do the two-arm pull-up, I'll make the exercise more strenuous. If you have an injured arm, you must do it with one arm, so watch me.'

Jane gripped the bar and rose with one smooth pull until she had the bar below her waist. Balanced on her straight arm and hand, she said. 'That's all we need to begin travelling, but one day, you'll manage to do this.' She leant forward until horizontal, balanced on her arm with her legs together. 'Dancing through the forest isn't only strength; balance is critical.'

After three weeks, Jane told Tarzan, 'Alice is ready to learn to travel; she's developed faster than I did, either because she's younger or had less fat to start with, and she's a bit shorter than me and weighs less. Apart from having slightly bigger breasts, her body has the same muscular development that I had when we began traversing.'

'Okay, Jane, teach her the safety rules, how to use rope levers, and how to traverse. Keep the rope short, only ten metres to start with. Teach her to weave baskets, use glue nets, collect wood, and light a fire. She must participate once we travel again, as we have three mouths to feed. You can also teach her how to use the mallet I made for her.'

'How will we travel with three?'

'With me in the middle. For the first few days, you anchor for me while I lead, then you'll follow, and then I secure you while you advance. Then Alice will come to me and continue to you, and I'll join you. Once I'm confident, you and Alice can function as one but with two ropes. If you don't stay together, only one may fall; I can support that.'

Secretly, Tarzan was pleased; Jane now liked Alice, and he thought they would work well as Alice settled into a routine and Jane could spend time foraging.

As the fourth week ended, Jane didn't tell Tarzan, but after taking Alice several hundred metres away from their nest to collect fruits, she said. 'Alice, sit here and take off your breast-band.' Alice did, and Jane did as well.

'Why, Jane?'

'Let's find out if there are silipusses around. Don't talk; I'll call.'

Kitty, come, we share.

Ten minutes later, Alice thought no cat would come when a cat appeared from the shadows.

Hello Kitty.

Hello, thing.

Jane imagined a picture of her mother, identified as such, with bare breasts and two young girls playing beside her. Then, she envisioned the children growing to resemble her and Alice.

The cat looked at Alice; Jane thought it showed interest – *Still young.*

Learning.

The cat stepped towards Alice and looked directly at her from two metres away. Alice smiled as she stared into its eyes – *We share.* Surprised, Alice could only think – *We share.*

The cat turned back to Jane – *A lovely kitten.* Then, it silently vanished as only a silipuss can.

'Jane, did it say, "we share" to me?'

'Yes, and then it said, "nice kitten" to me.'

'But I'm not a kitten.'

'No, but we think of the silipusses as cats, and if they *thelt* the feeling of a child, my brain turns that into "kitten."'

'So, I can sort of hear them?'

'Lots of practice, Alice, and you'll become good at communicating, and one day, you'll talk to Tarzan and me like that.'

'Like when you were making love?'

'Exactly.'

'Why did you bring me today?'

'Because in a few days, we're leaving, and now, if you're ever lost, as they now identify you as my sister, I can ask a silipuss where you are.'

'But it won't be that cat.'

'It doesn't matter, Alice. Every cat on Tarik will know you're one of us within a few days. Remember what you felt: "We Share", not "I share". Now you know, the terragon that came to the tree where you were hanging on the first day left because Tarzan told her we're part of this forest, and we share it with them.'

Alice said nothing; she had to think about what she had learnt.

Travelling was slower again, but they adapted to the new traversing routine within a week. When Jane and Alice traversed ahead with Tarzan anchoring, they took different routes, and Tarzan watched. Soon, he could pick the one that would be quickest for him, and the speed grew until it was the same as before they rescued Alice.

Alice was a quick learner, and with Jane and Tarzan describing the forest and the animals, she learnt about them within four months. Jane had forgotten Tarzan's promise to tell her about the worms, but when Alice heard it mentioned, she insisted on a description.

Lying on the nest between the two girls, Tarzan felt happy while he told them.

'My father mentioned them. He told me there had to be giant worms in the forest, and maybe one with a hard shell that could climb trees and has headlights.'

'Whose leg are you pulling, mine or Alice's?'

'Neither; I've seen the smaller hard-shell worm. And it moults when it grows, replacing the old shell that's too small, but it does that at night when buried inside the first level floor, so you can't see an empty shell lying around. They're a secondary danger for us. If we step on a branch supported by a carapace, it can collapse, and your leg drops into a void.'

Jane asked, 'What kind of headlights?'

'Not bright beams but several glowing spots around its mouth, like those insects we call fireflies. The lights flicker.'

'Did your dad propose a reason for the worm's existence?'

'He said the worms eat the rotting vegetation, accelerating the process. It's so calm in the forest that it needs something to stir it up. Worms do an excellent job digesting the vegetation and aerating.'

Jane sounded disappointed, 'I know about those, but they're small. Our colony has a big box for all the waste and masses of worms. My dad said they came with our spaceship, and he had the job of looking after them. The compost they produced fertilized the plant beds. Does your colony have one, too, Alice?'

'Well, it has a box where we must put our food and green waste, but it smells, and I've never dug for worms.'

Tarzan added, 'My dad has a box too, but he adds Tarik vegetation high in iron, and the worms are much bigger. He doesn't know how big they will grow in a thousand years.'

'Why does he use Tarik vegetation?'

'He did it to grow Tarik plants; he said they needed forest compost.'

'Okay, but the worm with a hard shell?'

'He thinks they do the same thing on the upper levels, and when they grow too big, they come down, lose their shells and grow more. So, the ground-level ones can be fifty metres long.'

'That's a monster, but why the headlights?'

'He said they must be nocturnal to avoid the darters, and when there's no moon, a small light can show them what's ahead. Slithering too deep into an upper floor might mean a fifty-metre fall. They aren't powerful lights; several small ones flickering around a huge circular mouth.'

'Why do they have hard shells?'

'To support little legs with hooks so they can climb. I know that the hard-shell worm loves luminous plants. One can strip an area in a night. When I told Dad, he said the luminescent chemicals from the plants must power the worm's headlights. So, when night falls, I check on the glowing plants; if there are none in view, I worry about a worm in the area.'

Alice asked, 'What eats the big ones at ground level?'

'The boars, but only after they die of starvation.'

'How can they starve? There are tons of stuff to eat.'

Tarzan could see the smile on Jane's face. *She can sense my thoughts and knows when I'll tell a story.*

'Once they grow too long, say thirty metres, they risk circling a tree and meeting their tail. If they swallow it, the worm continues around the tree, trying to eat more of the tail moving away, so the loop tightens until the worm is stuck and starves.'

Alice burst into laughter. 'Jane, does he tell such stories often?'

'Oh yes, he's exceptionally good at it, but be careful. Sometimes, he tells the truth!'

29

The forest seemed unchanging for months, but Tarzan announced his estimate for their arrival each month. The routine changed nine months after they rescued Alice.

Before they started that morning, Jane said, 'Tarzan, I have a funny feeling.'

'I've had one for half an hour, Jane. Alice, have you felt anything?'

'I keep thinking of something.'

'What?'

'That terragon you told not to eat us.'

'That confirms what I'm feeling. Jane, you have a strong connection to the cats; tell them we'll wait.'

Twenty minutes later, a silipuss drifted from the shadows. Tarzan and Alice heard the conversation.

Hello, thing.

Hello Kitty. Who comes?

The picture that formed was a male *TerraKid.*

Wait, or travel?

Travel. The puss vanished.

'I'll lead, girls; the pusses will tell us the direction.'

Ten days later, after travelling about a hundred kilometres, Tarzan estimated they were thirty kilometres off the direct line to his home that they had followed before, and a feeling grew that they were near the end of the deviation. Alice had killed a tarizard and Jane a squirrel, and while Tarzan laid branches for a nest beside a tree with a Cascade Creeper, a feeling of anticipation built.

'Tarzan, I feel someone is coming.'

'Me too, Jane. Alice, don't light the fire yet, but we'll shower.'

After showering, Jane washed their clothes and hung them to dry, and then Tarzan felt a *thelt* – *Friend, we share.*

He looked along the level in their direction of travel and saw a male *TerraKid* approaching them unhurriedly. He glanced at its feet. *They can turn almost ninety degrees; I wish we had feet that could grip branches like that.*

The *TerraKid* stopped at five metres, and Tarzan *thelt* – *We share.*

It looked first at Jane, then Alice, then back at Tarzan. Neither of them was conscious of being naked. He thought its eyes were smiling when it replied. To Tarzan, the feeling was unmistakeably masculine and addressed to him – *like us.* Then he sensed – *Come, Show.*

'Dress and rope up; he has something to show us.'

The Terrakid led the way, and a kilometre later, the forest ended at a clearing. The trio looked down on a surrealistic scene from a branch on the last tree. Fifty or more terragons ringed the open space, eating small trees growing near the giants. In the centre of the clearing, a pond of dark red water reflected the setting sun, painting the eastern tree wall with a red glow.

Alice whispered, 'That's a beautiful scene no artist could paint.'

Jane added, 'Or capture the feeling it gives me.'

Equally moved, Tarzan said nothing while he wondered what was wrong. *Else, the TerraKid would not have come. He knows we looked after Happy; does he want help to look after these females?*

He turned to the *Terrakid* to *theel* – *We Help?*

Then, an image of a terragon lying on its side, unmoving, and two human figures carrying weapons that looked like handheld missile launcher tubes formed in his mind. A feeling of horror boiled up in his gut, and he knew that Jane and Alice both felt the same, for Jane exclaimed, 'The bastards, they must be stopped.' And Alice asked, 'How can our people be so cruel and stupid.'

Tarzan knew the answer, said nothing, and created an image of a sunrise and *thelt* – *Tomorrow.* The *TerraKid* led them back to their nest and then left.

After they ate, sitting around the remains of their little fire, Jane asked, 'Tarzan, why would the *Terrakid* come to us?'

'I wish I knew; I can only guess.'

'Then guess, for Alice and me.'

'I believe we'll learn that the dead Terragon was far from here. Every telepathic creature on the planet must have received that incident.'

'Did he bring us that message because we're telepathic too?'

'Partly, Jane, but I think there is another reason. There may be some terragon hunters not far away. If so, that Terrakid has a problem. He doesn't want to start a war between the Tarik citizens and humans. Fundamentally, the Tarik creatures are peaceful and law-abiding. He has learnt we're trustworthy and hopes we can avert a bloody war where thousands may die. You know what humans are like. Once a war starts, it will escalate and will not stop until one side wins. Half a million humans don't have a chance against billions of telepathically linked terragons, megalons, and silipusses. We three might be the only survivors.'

Alice asked, 'So you think he sees us as a police force?'

'Possibly. Stopping wars isn't something I've studied. Can either of you suggest something?'

Alice answered, 'In my admin studies, we touched on the subject; once a war starts, historically, it usually continues until one side wins. Keeping it from starting is far better. One important thing is to ensure no innocents die, only combatants. It can then be labelled a police action, and escalation doesn't happen, for the average citizen doesn't take sides. But we only studied wars between humans, not humans and other races.'

'Okay, girls, we'll find out more tomorrow. I don't know if I want us to be the police force.'

Jane reminded Tarzan, 'You once said, "We have yet to work out what Tarik wants us to do." Tarik may be telling us what we need to do.'

'Okay, Jane, I'll remember that, but the first step is to investigate.'

Alice had the last word, 'You sound like a policeman.'

When morning dawned, Tarzan ordered, 'Eat some fruit; our guide is coming.'

They left when the *TerraKid* appeared, and six hours later, Tarzan saw the *TerraKid* stop beside a tree. Tarzan stopped. 'Shorten to ten metres, girls.'

When he reached the *TerraKid*, it *thelt – come –* while moving slowly around the tree. 'Attach your tails; I'll look.'

When Tarzan followed, the *TerraKid* made an unmistakable gesture, its two clawed hands opening an imaginary curtain. Tarzan stepped along the branch to the foliage at the end, pulled apart the fronds, and saw a dried-up lake. In the middle was an oval palisade fortress with a rectangular prefab building in the centre of the oval. Tarzan bent and attached his tail, pulled the ropes to the girls tight, then thelt – *Girls, come.*

First Jane, then Alice came to join him, then he said, 'Move along a branch, and if you have an unobstructed view, secure your tail and then study what you can see; I want to compare notes.'

Once the two girls could see the fortress, Tarzan asked, 'Jane, what can you see?'

'The barrier, about ten to fifteen metres high. I think it's about a hundred and twenty metres from us. The oval is about a hundred metres long and fifty in width. At the ends of the long axis, some towers look as if they have machinery on the top.'

'It may be further away than one-twenty because of our height, but less than one-fifty. Alice, what do you see?'

'I recognise that machinery; they're missile batteries and carry ten missiles in the tubes. Dad told me about them. We had a missile battery near our house. They're heat-seeking and fire in pairs. I can't see a gate or a door, but there must be one. We must look at the other side. I can also see where they cut down the trees for the fortification; there are hundreds of stumps below us and more around the dry lake. If we had a photographic drone, we could see inside.'

'Alice, you're a gem. Did your dad tell you what range the missiles have?'

'He said they could reach the beach about two kilometres from our house but didn't say that was the maximum.'

'That makes sense; the megalons usually float well above that and would not trigger missile fire. I'll ask a megalon to fly over the installation and tell us what it sees. It might be better than a drone.'

Tarzan turned to the *TerraKid*. The picture he *thelt* was of a megalon floating high over the clearing, followed by an image of what the megalon might see. He was sure the *TerraKid* understood when he heard the reply – *Wait.*

While the *TerraKid* stood looking at nothing, to Tarzan, he was communicating with others; Jane remarked, 'There are at least three men down there. I saw them on the roof of the building. I think it's a new camp – only recently built. There would be piles of rubbish if it were old.'

'We must look for the door.' Tarzan sensed the same image he had created the day before – *Tomorrow.* Then he turned to the *TerraKid*, pointed at the barrier, and gestured to open a door.

Come.

It took two hours of careful traversing forty metres from the lake before they reached the other side, and the *TerraKid* indicated they should look.

'Tarzan, that's a bigger door than a man needs.'

'Yes, I should have expected that. Look at the tracks, Jane; they have one or more forest bikes and attachments for cutting trees. They will have missile carriers for them, too.'

'What's a forest bike?'

'A motorcycle with ribbed tracks instead of wheels, Alice. They can navigate between trees and climb over fallen branches and brushwood.'

Alice remarked, 'They can only carry two people. Three or four men didn't build this. There must have been many.'

Jane replied, 'A GravBus can carry fifty workers on benches

instead of twenty-six passengers in comfort. Many of them armed guards.'

'We don't need to worry about them, girls. Do you have any ideas about how to close this down?'

Jane replied, 'First, let's see the aerial view tomorrow.'

Tarzan faced the *TerraKid*, pointed to the fort, and then raised his hand with five fingers showing – *How many?*

The unhappiness made him fold his little finger, and happiness flooded in. 'Girls, there are four men in there. We're contemplating killing them in one way or another. If we're acting as the police, we should give them a warning and a chance to pack up and leave.'

Jane replied indignantly, 'They're killers; they kill terragons, our people. They deserve nothing else. Trying to talk to them will be dangerous for us.'

'I agree, Jane, but our creed of "We Share" prevents us from attacking anyone who doesn't attack us. The terragons can justifiably kill them, not us.'

Alice retorted, 'In the admin lessons we learnt, there's no point in making laws unless we enforce them. In a pioneer society, the punishment must be drastic. There aren't enough people for police and jails, so death is no more than justice in this case.'

'Let's think about it. Maybe we can allow our friends to destroy the hunters' camp, making them feel proud.'

Tarzan *thelt* once again – *tomorrow*, and the *TerraKid* slipped away.

They returned to where they had first seen the fortress, collecting fruit en route. Then Tarzan said, 'Let's eat, and then we can talk about what to do.'

During their fruit lunch, Jane asked, 'Tarzan, who are these men?'

'Girls, I remember that at my meeting in Colony One with the geneticists, they mentioned criminal activity by men with specialist skills and only labourer's jobs. I guess these men come from that group, from which colony I don't know, and this may not be an isolated case. They're educated and may have organised. I think they will be dangerous. There's no point in talking unless we can do so from a position of strength.'

Jane protested, 'Tarzan, you keep using "Girls": We aren't, but certainly not ladies. Do you have a better word?'

'Wives? Partners? Warriors?'

Alice answered, 'How about Amazons? They were a fabled group of female warriors.'

'I like "Girls", it's sweet and short, you're my partners, but that's too long. Unless you have a suggestion, I'll propose "Sirens". That makes me think of police.'

Jane laughed. 'Alice, we won't reach an agreement with this hunk. "Girls" it is, until we have a better word.'

Alice had the last word; it made them think. 'I fancy "Mothers"; that's how the silipusses think of us.'

'Where will we camp?'

'Beside the Cascade Creeper on that tree behind us. I'll make the nest.'

Jane and Alice left for food, firewood and fruit.

30

The girls returned with a squirrel as Tarzan finished the nest, and then they showered. The showering process, which after the crash had been a sequence where Jane or Tarzan washed followed by the other, and later, after the purple fruit incident, had evolved into a joint exercise, evolved further when Alice, watching them together, decided to join them. She could tell if the hand scrubbing her back belonged to Jane or Tarzan; he was gentler.

They sat around their little fire as they had done hundreds of times, but for once in silent thought until Jane said. 'If a megalon can eat a GravEx and zoom up again, it can carry a huge weight.'

Alice replied, 'I know the physics of that. Low down, a balloon can carry much more than at higher altitudes; too high, it will burst.'

Tarzan asked, 'Jane, what is your idea?'

'Only that we're at a massive disadvantage. Those murderers have missiles, and we have only bow and arrows. Historically, the military had bombs. Could the megalons drop something on them?'

'Drop what? They have only mud, plants and poo.'

Alice chuckled at the thought, then burst out laughing, 'Poo might make their hideout unliveable, but we have trees; we saw the terragons eating them. Let me work out something: Math and physics have always been my favourite subjects. And it's easy to calculate.'

She stood, and using a burnt stick, she scratched a formula on the tree trunk. $1/2MV^2$, then added a line of numbers. Alice then announced after making a quick calculation. 'A one-ton tree from three thousand metres is about thirty kilograms of a high explosive. That's more than a missile!

'Tarzan, ask *TeeKay* if he could organise an experiment. We can return to the terragon clearing; they can provide trees, and megalons can pick them up and drop them on a target.'

'Alice, are those initials?'

'Yes, it suits him, *TeeKay* for *TerraKid*. You call a silipuss *Kitty.*' Then she remarked, 'I feel happiness; I'm enjoying this.'

Jane added, 'I agree, Alice, maybe Tarik is pleased.'

After waking, washing, and eating fruit, Tarzan said, 'While waiting for the aerial images, let's consider what target we need for the experiment.'

Alice proposed a square of logs. Tarzan asked how big, and she replied, 'About the size of what we want to hit. If they hit inside, that's fine; the military doesn't practice with explosive bullets.'

Jane added, 'Wait until we see the aerial picture and choose something. If we form a square, we can lay logs across it diagonally.'

Then *TeeKay* appeared.

We share.

TeeKay stepped forward to Tarzan and looked into his eyes. A picture began to form in Tarzan's mind.

He concentrated.

Two forest bikes are beside the gate, with a mono-wheel trailer for one. Three men erecting what might be drying racks, but there are no skins. - The letter G is a GravBus landing mark on the rectangular box. There's a water tank - a bank of solar panels is at one end next to a missile battery.

Tarzan opened his eyes. *The panel array is about twenty by thirty metres. That's our target.*

We thank our friends.

'Our experiment will be difficult to transmit, Jane.'

'Can we try something other than a simple *theel*? We can make a model megalon and demonstrate dropping a tree.'

'Okay, what do you need?'

Jane *thelt – Wait, sit. TeeKay* sat.

'We could try a milk nut as the megalon's body. Tarzan, can you use one with some vine for the neck and tail?'

'I'll try.'

'Alice, find me sticks to make a small target, a square and a cross. And a bigger one about the size of a tree you imagine our model megalon could carry?'

Alice was quick. Jane then *thelt* an image of the clearing with the terragons, and Alice laid her sticks on the floor to form the target. She did so slowly, and with each rod that she placed, Jane added a tree to her image at the clearing's end so her image had a similar target.

TeeKay, who had observed Alice first in puzzlement, looked up at Jane. She was sure he was still puzzled, but he understood, for his eyes showed admiration.

'Tarzan, are you ready?'

'Yes, Jane. Alice, please stand. I'll move the nut with the hanging stick. Can you pull the fishline end as I take it over your target?'

Jane *thelt* an image of a megalon in the sky with a rod hanging from its mouth. It puzzled *TeeKay* until Tarzan stood and held up his model. Jane saw his eyes light up. When the milk nut passed over the target, and Alice pulled the string, the stick fell and luckily hit the side of the target.

'Girls, he understands; he's excited and likes it. Unless he thinks we're nuts.'

Jane and *TeeKay* stood. He placed a hand on her shoulder. His feelings were unmistakable – *We share. Thank you, tomorrow.*

Jane put a hand on his shoulder and *thelt* – *We Share.*

Then he repeated the gesture with Tarzan and Alice, and they did, too.

When he left, Tarzan said, 'We have enough time to travel; shall we do so?'

Alice replied, 'Yes, we can find food on the way. I want to see the sunset again.'

Seven hours later, they sat entranced, watching the sunset over the clearing with the terragons. Tarzan had made a nest, and once the sun dropped behind the horizon, their practised routine clicked into gear.

As they lay down to sleep, Alice said, 'I can't describe my feelings watching that sunset; there was something special about it.'

Jane replied, 'I think spiritual is the right word. I think Tarik is thanking us for our effort.'

More than ever, Tarzan knew his future; he only said, 'Good night, girls.'

Instead of their customary breakfast, where they sat together and planned the day, this one differed because, taking turns, one was on a branch with a view of the clearing, waiting to see if anything changed.

It was an hour before Alice *thelt* – *I can see TeeKay.*

Tarzan replied – *Return.*

Alice did and said, '*TeeKay* is down there with two terragons; they're walking to the long end of the clearing.'

'Then I'll drop girls; Jane controls my safety. Then you rappel down in turn; I'll manage your safety from below.'

Once safely down, the girls jogged away towards *TeeKay*; Tarzan looped the ropes so they hung above the ground and then ran after the girls. As he caught up, he remained behind to watch both girls' smooth, fluid, effortless rhythm. *They are lovely and run as if they don't touch the ground.*

When they reached *TeeKay* and the terragons, with a profusion of *thelts* conveying – *We share,* Tarzan said, 'Jane, Alice pace out thirty metres from me, then Alice can pace twenty metres at ninety degrees.'

As Alice came to a halt, Tarzan didn't need to tell *TeeKay*; he walked to a position that completed the corners of a rectangle.

The four of them had to repeatedly duck for two hours to avoid the small tree trunks carried to the square by a dozen or more terragons until they had completed the target with a diagonal cross.

'Girls, we can't stay here. We don't know how accurate the megalons will be, and I don't fancy them flattening me with a one-ton tree. Let's run to the opposite side.'

They did, and Tarzan again ran behind them. When they arrived, Jane asked, 'Why were you behind us, Tarzan?'

'I was trying to solve a problem.'

Jane grinned. *A story: I love this man!* 'What problem?'

'Which of you has the most beautiful tail.'

Jane laughed and asked, 'Are you hungry?'

It left Alice puzzled, so she asked, 'What does that have to do with his problem?'

'Because every time he thinks of a girl's bum, he wants to bite it.'

Alice's laughter was catching.

'Where's *TeeKay*?'

Jane replied, 'With the megalon females on the east side and the terragons, they're building a pile of logs. Male megalons are drifting in from the west. But don't change the subject. We want your answer: who has the most beautiful tail?'

'I can't tell you; they both moved similarly.'

'Alice, we'll have to practise a sexy wobble.'

Interested in what was happening, they watched as the megalons came in one after another, then parked their ball for a minute or two to hold them in place while they picked a tree trunk and manoeuvred it into position in their mouths. They then pumped hydrogen until they rose, the tree hanging vertically in line with their neck and head, and as the light breeze caught them, the megalons sailed away as they climbed into the sky.

'Where are they going?' Jane asked.

Tarzan answered, 'They know the winds and breezes better than anyone; winds change direction and strength with altitude, and they'll drift to a position and height where they will cross the target.'

'I hope they'll be high enough to avoid missiles?'

'We'll try to judge, and if we feel they're too low, we'll tell TeeKay.'

...

Then, the first bombardier floated over the clearing and released a tree.

'That was more than a ton, girls; I hope they can't hear that explosion at the hunting camp.'

Jane remarked, 'If they hear anything, it will sound like thunder.'

Eight megalons dropped trees, and then the four returned to see how accurately the megalons had bombed their target.

The impact craters were huge, five inside the target square and three on its edge.

In a puzzled tone, Tarzan asked, 'How can they be so accurate?'

Alice had the answer. 'The log is hanging straight down from their head, and their downward telescope eyes look straight along the outside of the tree, like the sights on a rifle. They release as the edge of the tree reaches the target.'

'We have our bombs, girls; we must return to that camp tomorrow.'

They were on the nest close to the hunters' camp the following night, and *TeeKay* joined them. After discussion, Tarzan said, 'That's decided. Tomorrow afternoon, the megalons will bomb the camp. I don't know what the men will do, but they will be safe if they stay in the centre; the megalons will bomb the missiles and the solar panels.'

Excited about what would happen the next day, they slept poorly, repeatedly waking until daylight crept between the leaves. They stretched their shower time and then breakfast, but the tedious wait and lethargy from a lack of sleep over-whelmed them, and they slept through midday.

'Girls, I need exercise. Let's hunt and find food for tonight.'

They returned two hours later, and Tarzan said, 'The megalons should be assembling now; they will come from the west, out of the setting sun, so let's find a place to watch.'

Tarzan saw two men erecting what he thought were drying racks when Jane said, 'I can see the first megalon if I squint to block out the sun.'

The men didn't look up until the first tree exploded on the forward missile battery. The armed missiles exploded from the shock in a massive explosion that destroyed the forward third of the fortification. It blew the men backwards, and they disap-peared.

The blast also affected the second megalon, blowing it side-ways. It released the tree it carried, which hit the palisade in the centre, knocking out a huge section. The third megalon scored a bullseye in the centre of the solar panel array, which became a mangled mess. Two men who seemed bent on saving their lives ran from the box cabin, mounted the forest bikes, and disappeared into the trees as the fourth megalon narrowly missed the missile battery by the solar panels. Still, the shock blew the assembly out and onto the ground. Ten more mega-lons continued to rain trees on the camp but avoided the box cabin. Then silence fell.

'Tarzan.'

'Yes, Alice.'

'Did you expect that much damage?'

'No, I'm shocked.'

Jane asked. 'Are those first two men alive?'

'We must look tomorrow morning in daylight; it's too dark now.'

'And those two on forest-bikes. Where have they gone?'

'We'll have to ask the silipusses. Those men must be armed, and they have missiles on the bikes. We must warn *TeeKay*. It will be dark in an hour.'

TeeKay, come.

He came and placed his hands on Tarzan's shoulders. Tarzan understood the accentuated meaning of – *WE ALL SHARE.* So, he put his on *TeeKay's* shoulders – *We all share.*

Then Tarzan pictured the forest bikes, and after several thelts, believed he had emphasised they were dangerous.

'Tarzan, what will happen now?'

We'll wait until morning, Jane. I'll ask *TeeKay* for another aerial view before we visit the wreckage.' He did and heard – *Tomorrow.*

'Now, let's sleep.'

31

They woke to find a pile of fruit and two silipusses waiting for them.

Hello Kitty's. We Share

Hello, things.

An image formed in Tarzan's mind of the two bikes with two men sleeping between them, then two hours later, the aerial picture *TeeKay* provided showed the missile battery that collapsed outwards, the blackened equipment strewn on the ground from the missile battery that exploded and destroyed the other end of the fortification. Jagged pieces of the mangled solar panels protruded between logs piled on them. The box cabin was still standing, although they could see timber shards had pierced the walls.

Jane asked, 'Tarzan, what do we do now?'

'If we act as policemen, we must look for evidence. We should split up. There are now three ways into the camp: the gate on the far side that's still open, the zone where the missiles exploded, and on this side where the megalon missed the panels. Alice and *TeeKay* can enter from this side. Stay well apart because we don't know if the two men inside are alive. I'll cross with Jane to the other side, drop, take the exploded end, and Jane the gate. Until we know the men are dead, we must assume they're hiding, alive, armed, and likely to shoot. So be careful.'

'What if they're alive but injured? Do we help them?'

'No help until we know the whereabouts of all four.'

'When we leave our nest, minimum noise, no talking, *theel*. We'll wait for *TeeKay,* then tell him.'

TeeKay disappeared after Tarzan explained the plan and reappeared below five minutes later. Tarzan knew he used a vine to climb down. *TeeKay's* feet and hands ensured he didn't slip. Tarzan controlled Alice's safety line as she rappelled down. He and Jane watched while they separated, crossed to the remaining pieces of the broken barrier, and edged along to the gap.

We'll wait.

'Safety line, Jane, you lead.'

Twenty minutes later, Tarzan stopped, 'We're about opposite the gate, Jane. You drop, then you can control my line. We'll then advance and separate. *Theel* when you reach the gate.'

Five minutes more, and Jane *thelt* – *I'm beside the gate.*

Tarzan replied – *I'm ready this end, Alice, ready?*

Ready.

Slow and Careful...

TeeKay was the first to *thelt* when he found a man crushed under a fallen tree. – *One is dead here.*

Jane sidled around the open gate and along it into the camp, then turned to follow the barrier. The sight of a headless body brought a stifled gasp, and she *thelt* – *One dead here.*

Tarzan replied – *That's both men - everyone to meet me at the cabin door.*

Jane could see the box cabin door was open. She crossed to the cabin and had to duck under a timber shard five metres from the door as she crept forward and waited until Tarzan, *TeeKay,* and Alice joined her.

...

TeeKay - Watch. 'We'll enter, girls. Search for anything that might identify who's behind this operation.'

The cabin was a mess; the exploding missile battery had severely shaken it up, and the shocks had thrown the contents of the shelves to the floor, forced open cupboard doors, and dumped the items in piles. Tarzan and the girls looked around in dismay, wondering how they could find anything in such a mess, but as Tarzan did, he noticed a blinking red light on the end wall. He pushed some items out of the way and climbed over a box until he could read the label on the small box with the blinking light: ELT.

'Girls, out, and back to the forest. The shock must have triggered the emergency beacon. A GravBus could arrive at any time.'

With *TeeKay*, the four returned rapidly to the nest.

Back on the nest, the four sat together to eat. Jane asked, 'Tarzan, what do we do about the GravBus?'

'I haven't worked that out; a bus full of armed guards seems beyond our abilities.'

'Do you remember describing what our pilots did wrong before our crash?'

'Yes, Jane, why?'

'If *TeeKay* can arrange for a megalon to give us aerial photos, I hope he can organise a high megalon to eat the GravBus.'

'Brilliant, Jane, but we would need others to force the

GravBus straight up first. In a circle at least six kilometres in diameter to stay out of missile range.'

Alice replied, 'When will the Gravbus come?'

Tomorrow or the day after, around midday. It must return in daylight.'

'Okay, I'll ask *TeeKay*.'

Tarzan and Jane both followed her thought pictures while she talked telepathically to *TeeKay*. She started with a picture of sunrise to say tomorrow.

TeeKay left them with an image – *Tomorrow. We share.*

'He understood, Jane.'

'He did. All intelligent species should participate. I'm hungry. Tarzan, firewood, Alice, let's collect and prepare food. I'm also tired after last night, so a snooze this afternoon would be great.'

Jane's no longer an unsure girl; she doesn't know it but is now a wife.

The three spent the remainder of the day watching. Before the sunlight faded, the silipusses returned.

We Share.

Jane replied – *Hello, Kitties.*

The silipusses *thelted* image was unmistakable. 'Tarzan, those two men have returned.'

'I understood, Jane; we can't do anything about them. Let's sleep.'

The following day, after a copious breakfast supplied by the silipusses, they took turns watching for the GravBus. Tarzan looked up to the sky several times during the morning; he counted megalons, and the numbers grew. 'Rig the ropes, girls; we'll be dropping soon.'

As the morning ended, the GravBus came. It landed, and Tarzan was surprised at the speed with which the megalons created the threatening tube. *They don't need to wait for the wind; they can sacrifice altitude for distance.* Armed with shoulder-carried missile tubes, the guards did as he had imagined, taking positions around the GravBus while four others with the two remaining men examined the wrecked hunting camp. It appeared from agitated arm waving they were arguing, but then, five minutes later, the GravBus lifted when the door closed on the two men and the last of the guards.

As it passed through seven thousand metres, a megalon, diving vertically, hit the centre with its head, and the pressurised GravBus exploded.

Tarzan remarked, 'They're furious and determined. That megalon had two backups.'

As the GravBus parts hit the ground, Tarzan said, 'I want emergency packs, missiles, and launchers. Let's drop.'

TeeKay joined them. The first thing he did was place both his hands on Tarzan's shoulders – *Friends*. Then, he repeated it with each of the girls. Jane was intrigued when she saw Alice blush.

There were no survivors. Tarzan checked every missile they found, and if armed, he promptly disarmed it. Once *TeeKay* saw Jane carry one, he joined in. Undamaged launch tubes joined their growing pile. Tarzan carried away the emergency bag and a long coil of rope lying beside it. Then, after checking the missile battery, Tarzan gave a sweeping signal, and *TeeKay* took over.

Ten minutes later, Alice said, 'Tarzan, they're further along the evolutionary road than I thought; they can think logically and know what fire is; they might use it for something.'

'How do you know that?'

'*TeeKay* wasn't surprised or afraid of it when I lit the fire, and would you have thought of asking a megalon to dump its ball on the cabin and flatten it?'

'No, but it's damned effective. That *is* logical thought. By tomorrow, there'll be little left here. With fifty terragons at work, the only problem will be what to do with the missiles.'

'What do you want to do?'

'Transport them to the headquarters where the GravBus came from.'

'Why?'

'So, we can destroy it.'

'Then ask *TeeKay*.'

Ask someone, including any intelligent life, when you don't know the answer.

'Did you *theel* that, Alice?'

'No, although I might have thought something similar.'

Jane said, 'Tarzan, we're missing something.'

'What?'

'You said this can't be the only hunting camp. We must tell *TeeKay* to find and destroy all the others. Tell him the megalons must first check if there are women and children in those camps. I don't think there will be, but we don't know.'

Teekay joined them, and after a telepathic conversation,

TeeKay, visibly thrilled and smiling, placed both hands on Tarzan's shoulders – *WE SHARE.* He repeated it with Alice and Jane.

Tarzan wondered if *TeeKay* would understand a map. He took an arrow from his quiver, drew a large oval on the ground, and stepped into it. Then he looked in the direction the GravBus had come from and strode forward, dragging the tip of the arrow to draw a line, turned to *TeeKay* and *thelt* – *Where?*

Jane and Alice watched while *TeeKay* looked at the oval and line, then, after a pause, reached out to take the arrow and drew another oval at the end of the line. But he didn't stop; he held up his free arm and its four-clawed hand, raised the centre claw, and drew a short vertical line. Tarzan received his *thelt*, a sunrise. He then lifted another claw and then a third, marking a vertical each time, and with the fourth claw, he scratched an angled line through them.

Alice said, 'Incredible. He's counting; that's one, two, three, four.'

Under the line between the two ovals, *TeeKay* drew five angle lines, one after the other.

Tarzan said, 'The hunter hideout is twenty days' travel from here, about three hundred kilometres.'

Thank you. Tarzan took back the arrow, pointed to their heap of missiles and launchers, and drew a pile on the ground next to the first oval, moved to the second oval, sketched the same, and then rubbed out the first heap drawing with his foot.

At first, he wondered if *TeeKay* had understood, but the message after a minute was definite – *Wait.*

'Girls, let's sit on the emergency bag and the rope; *TeeKay* has called someone.'

Alice remarked, '*TeeKay's* eyes are the same green as yours, and Jane's eyes *are* green. We're not in foliage now.'

Tarzan looked. 'Jane, she's right,' then turned to look at Alice, 'and yours are turning green, too. It must be what we eat.'

Tarzan examined the rope while Jane sat beside him and watched Alice, who had taken the arrow, begin scratching on the ground, with *TeeKay* watching with interest.

She outlined a hand, then to the right of it a line icon of *TeeKay's* claws, then under the hand a vertical bar, the number one, and the same under the icon.

She continued with a 10 below the hand and 11 below the claw.

'Alice, what are you doing?'

'Finding out if *TeeKay* can understand binary numbers.'

Then she added the following lines, 11 and 111, then 100 and scratched a sloping line through the 111 to make the sign for four that *TeeKay* had used.

She continued with the binaries for five, six, and seven, and then after eight, 1000, with two four groups under the claw, she offered the arrow to *TeeKay*.

'How far are you, Alice?'

'I've written up to eight and asked him to do nine...

'Jane, he's done it; now he's doing ten.'

TeeKay continued to sixteen, 10000, and the four groups of four that represented sixteen in his notation. Then, he handed the arrow to Alice and placed a claw on her shoulder – *Thank you.*

She replied – *We Share.*

Tarzan stood and approached as another *TerraKid* arrived, and *TeeKay* rubbed out Alice's numbers with a dragging foot. Tarzan thought the newcomer was much older and felt respect. The Elder approached him and placed a claw on his shoulder, and Tarzan sensed again – *Friends, we share*, so he reciprocated. Others appeared from the trees as the Elder greeted Jane and Alice. The slow and courteous ceremony seemed interminable until twelve *TerraKids* assembled, and then they squatted, so Tarzan and the girls did, too. He couldn't follow all their thoughts, but he understood when a female terragon came from the forest and sat. The image of a terragon with missiles strapped to it was clear.

As they stood, Alice said, 'For them, this is a new idea; they will experiment. Let's sit on the bag and watch.'

An hour later, Alice said, 'I knew they could do it. They're further along the evolutionary path than we first thought.'

'You're right, Alice, very much further. You gave *TeeKay* some information; he rubbed it out before the others came, and I think he'll use that knowledge to establish his authority. But we must return to our nest and find food.'

They said goodbye, a collective *theel* of – *We share*, then walked to the tree with the hanging ropes carrying the bag and coil of cord. *TeeKay* came with them, used a stick to scratch the binary number for twenty on the ground, and gave them a final image of him touching their shoulders with the *theel* – *We share*. He watched as Alice, then Jane and Tarzan climbed the ropes hand over hand.

Jane took over. 'Well, we don't need to hunt; the *TerraKids* have brought us fruit and a neurotic pig. Tarzan can butcher it and call a kitty for the rest. Alice, if you can do the fire, I can prepare the meat.'

After a splendid meal that Tarzan thought Jane had prepared carefully, spreading the assorted items on thick leaves, they showered and lay down on the nest.

'Well, that was quite a day, girls. What were your highlights?'

Jane answered, 'I was sorry for those men, but we had to stop them, and there was no other way; we had no firepower. I learnt though that meticulous planning and detail attention pays off.'

Alice added, 'I never thought of the men; they had to die for what they've done. Learning how intelligent the terragons are and that we belong has made me feel good.'

'Alice,' Jane asked, 'When *TeeKay* placed his hands on both your shoulders to say thank you, why did you blush.'

Alice hesitated, then said, 'He projected a picture of me giving Tarzan an egg.'

Tarzan laughed joyfully, and Jane asked, 'Are you fertile, Alice?'

'No.'

'I am, so if Tarzan agrees, share with us tonight.'

Jane moved, so Alice was between them.

They began slowly, learning about each other's bodies; they kissed gently, their lips lingering and investigating the taste of each other, eyes locked together, and Alice felt his thoughts:

beautiful, brave, courageous, intelligent, strong; then she closed her eyes. Immediately, her senses heightened as her skin shivered under his caresses and Jane's experienced hands. The fires grew slowly, teasingly, and a glow spread throughout her body until she was unable to support more; she rolled on top of him and accepted his manhood, which brought an explosion of heat and spasms of ecstasy until she felt her mind join with his. They rode to heaven on a chariot of delight that spilt them onto a soft cloud, where Jane enveloped them in her embrace.

Alice whispered without opening her eyes, 'Tarzan, kiss me.' She felt like a shaving of inflammable bark, and his kiss was the spark of a lighter that brought a blaze of fire, 'Please, again.' And she felt him again, massive and throbbing, then convulsions took control, and she felt Jane's ecstasy doubling hers...

The three are now one.

Who said that?

No one; it's a truth that needs no voice.

32

They were late rising, reluctant to do so, and then Tarzan, Jane, and Alice showered and dressed.

'Girls, we have a change in our travelling routine.'

'Why?'

'We hit the jackpot with that emergency kit. It has carabiners for rappelling, and the coil of rope is K-stretch.'

Jane asked, 'I've never heard of it; what's special?'

'There's not much on the planet; the administrators seized most of it on arrival. The same diameter as the cord we've been using, it can support fifteen tons of static load, but the most important thing is that it has a twenty per cent stretch up to twelve tons. Falling with the old rope meant a sudden stop; a body can only survive a ten-metre drop as it stops. With K-stretch, a forty-metre length can stretch to forty-eight, and you slow progressively and harmlessly.'

'How does that change our routine.'

'We tie each other with fifty-metre spacing, then traverse without anchoring if we stay far enough apart so the ropes don't catch. It will double our speed or more. If one of us falls, it doesn't matter how far; the other two can hold who falls between them.

'We'll take it slowly until we're used to it; each is independent and can stop to throw a mallet or collect fruit; just warn the others with a *thelt*.'

Four days later, they travelled fifteen kilometres in a day. Hunting, fruit collecting, and camping took a chunk out of each day. But then they became faster when they received unexpected help. After Tarzan built a nest, young *TerraKid* females often brought them squirrels and fruit.

The first obstacle in their path was another river they came to on the tenth day. Perched in a tree beside it, Jane remarked, 'It's not very wide, perhaps half a rope.'

'Yes, about fifty metres to the opposite tree. It's too far for a swing.'

Alice asked, 'What do you mean?'

'Up to forty metres, I could try to shoot an arrow with a cord and a grappling hook over a branch. I've done it before. Then it's only a swing down and a climb up the rope. Now we're three; I would tie this end, so we have a rope across the river, then cross hanging from the rope, and take the free end to have two. But I doubt I can shoot a grappling hook that far, and I would have to carve one.'

Jane said, 'Before we attempt to find a place upriver, why don't you try?'

'Okay, I'll find a suitable forking branch to carve.'

Three hours later, he was ready; the grapple, made from the heartwood after stripping all the bark and softwood, was half a metre long with a short backwards-facing hook at the rounded end. It was the third he had made; the first Tarzan rejected once he saw a fault in the core wood, and the second broke when he hooked it over a branch and tried to support his weight. The third didn't fail, and after winding and knotting the cord, he threw it over a high branch and climbed. 'This one will do, girls.'

Ten minutes later, after attaching an arrow to the hook with some fishline and coiling the rope carefully so it would feed easily, he said, 'Tie the end in case the arrow flies too far.' Then, once Alice had tied it, he stepped forward, pulled as far as he could and released the arrow. It soared over the river and entered the foliage on the other side. Alice, excited, said, 'Great shot. You can do that distance easily.'

'I suppose I'm much stronger now. Jane, pull the rope.'

It came loose and fell to the riverbank, so they carefully pulled it back, coiling the rope.

The second was more successful, 'Tarzan, it's holding.'

'Let me give it a good yank, Jane.'

He did and staggered backwards when it suddenly came loose.

The third was a repeat of the first, and feeling disappointed, Alice said, 'I can swim across and tie the rope.'

'Never, Alice. Jane knows what's in that water; you wouldn't pass halfway. We'll keep trying.'

The fourth also came loose, but only after another strong pull; they could see it had stuck in the small branches nearest them, for they moved when they pulled together.

The hook fell towards the river but didn't reach the water before a monster rose from the water. Its gaping mouth took the grapple, and the cord whipped out as it swam upriver until the tied-to-branch swung sideways. Tarzan, Jane and Alice had to jump to a safer branch. The tree shook as the cord thrummed and then slackened, and the branch snapped back.

'Now I know what you meant. I'm not swimming in a river, *ever!*'

Tarzan grinned, 'That's a good decision, Alice. Now gather and coil the rope; I'll make a new grapple.'

Jane instructed, 'Then make one with two hooks at ninety degrees; I think it's twisting and one hook slides over the branch. And make it with a curve, so the hook end hangs down a bit.'

Practice makes perfect, and two hours later, on the first try, the new grapple caught. Tarzan untied the line, passed it under a branch, attached it to his tail, snapped it to the bridge rope, and pulled a free loop to tie around the bough. 'Okay, I'll cross. Feed the rope to me, but keep holding in case the bridge cord comes loose and I swing back. Once I'm across, you can release the knot; I'll secure both bridge lines and signal. Snap your tails to both ropes and come across.'

Jane crossed like a neurotic pig hanging upside down, with her legs on the cords. Alice tried crawling on both ropes, then fell and finished the last half swinging free hand to hand.

'Girls, after that, we set up camp and rest.'

The second river, five days later, was double the width. 'Tarzan, that's too far for an arrow; we must try upriver.'

'Yes, it's eighty metres or more. The cats might provide some information.'

Kitty, come, Help.

It took no more than an hour while they lay or sat on comfortable branches and ate the fruit they had collected before two silipusses emerged silently from the forest.

Hello, thing,

Hello, Kitty.

The cats each laid down a squirrel – *We share.*

Thank you. Tarzan pointed to the river and *thelt* – *far.* Then he pointed upriver and downriver – *Where?*

The reply surprised them – *Wait.* The cats did their disappearing trick.

After a prolonged silence, Tarzan asked, 'Do either of you know what for?'

Alice answered, 'Before they *thelt* wait, I had a fuzzy picture of megalons. They might think that megalons can help.'

'There are signs of them on the riverbank, but not fresh. While we wait, we can cook the squirrels. And shower.'

Nothing happened that day. Relaxed, when they lay down to sleep, Jane said, 'Tarzan, let's love.'

Alice knew she was fertile, but she caressed Jane and shared her mind with Tarzan and Jane as all three reached the unimagined heights brought by love.

When they woke, two silipusses sat looking at them; Tarzan thought they were smiling. – *We Share.*

Then, a picture of megalon females and the feeling of – *our friends coming* spurred Tarzan into action. 'Girls, we must prepare everything to drop; the megalons are coming.'

While Jane rigged the rope, with a cat watching what she did, Alice packed gear, and Tarzan strapped on his claws. The cats showed interest in what he did, and then when Alice and Jane didn't strap on claws, one of the cats looked at Jane, and she sensed – *No claws?*

Without thinking, she pictured a neurotic pig – *Too small.*

Alice exclaimed, 'They're coming! I can see them.'

Tarzan replied, 'I sense a picture; they will cross the river before us. We must use them as stepping stones. I'll drop as soon as the first enters the water, then you both rappel down, and I'll pull the cord down.'

The last thing he did as he jumped was to *theel – Thank you. We share.*

Coiling up the rope loosely, he urgently instructed, 'When the first one reaches the other side, run up the tail of one and jump when you can from one to another until you can jump to the riverbank.'

Alice, Jane, and finally, Tarzan jumped from a megalon to the riverbank five minutes later. They dashed away from the bank as the megalons broke it down to a ramp as they climbed out.

'Come, girls, we must climb while the megalons are here.'

They turned to a tree and found a silipuss in front of it. The image they sensed amazed them, but Tarzan stepped forward and proffered the end of the cord. The cat seized it in its mouth, then turned, scampered up the tree using its claws, crossed over a branch and came down the other side backwards. When Tarzan took the cord from its mouth, he sensed – *we share.* Then the cat climbed back up the tree, and Tarzan climbed just behind it using the ropes, hand over hand, and foot claws. Jane and Alice followed, climbing one rope with the other attached to their tails that Tarzan kept tight.

'How do you feel, girls?'

Jane replied, 'That was the most exciting experience I've ever had, lovemaking excepted. When we reach your parents, will they believe we crossed a river using megalons as stepping stones?'

'My parents might, but no one else.'

Alice added, 'I'm now sure I belong here. When cats and megalons help, it brings meaning to "we share", and I'll never abandon the forest and our friends.'

Jane added, 'I feel the same; this is where I belong. How about you, Tarzan?'

'I've felt that for years, but now I want to ensure that humans integrate without harming the planet's intelligent life. Right now, it's a nest and food we need.'

Two days later, after a day of travelling, Tarzan made a nest. The light was fading, and he hadn't finished when Jane said, 'Tarzan, I have an odd feeling. I think a silipuss is trying to tell us something, but they aren't close.'

Tarzan tied a final vine, stood, and gazed unseeing down the terrace. Jane and Alice joined him.

Alice said, 'They've gone.'

'Who?'

'The cats, I can't sense a silipuss.'

'Tarzan, can you see any phosphorescent plants.'

'No, Jane, but we'll only see them well after dark.'

'I didn't see any while I was collecting firewood and fruit. Alice, did you recognise any?'

'I wasn't looking.'

'Tarzan, how do the cats escape one of the armour-plated worms you told me about? Do they leave the area where one is feeding?'

'The worm hides and sleeps in daylight; it's active at night, and if there's enough light to move around, the cats can easily avoid it. They might leave on exceptionally dark nights because, although they can climb, holding on for hours must be exhausting, and travelling in the dark is dangerous for them and us.'

'Then I propose we consider there's one around here. The moons will be down soon. What precautions must we take?'

'It's too late to move now. I'll hammer pegs into our tree sixteen metres above us and hang ropes down. Then we can climb in the dark. Give me your carabiners.'

Tarzan hammered and climbed until…

'Okay, girls, we each have a rope to climb, and we can hook onto the pegs. Snap the carabiners back on your tails. Then, snap them on your belts so the tail is a short loop to hook on with. If anything comes in the night, we climb.'

'Let's take all our gear now and hang it from the spare pegs; the worm will swallow anything, and taking our stuff up in the dark will be risky.'

Tired, after eating the fruit they had collected, they lay down, dressed and with tails. Despite quite bright light from the two moons that shone, they fell asleep quickly.

Tarzan woke, unmoving; he listened and then opened his eyes. The moons had set, and the night was pitch black. *Something woke me.*

Jane awakened and sensed Tarzan was awake yet frozen in silence. Her heartbeat rose as tension spread – *There's something out there.*

What is it?

It may be a worm. Listen.

Alice heard the *thelt* and woke, but she was lying on her left side, facing the middle terrace – *Flickering lights ahead of me.*

Tarzan, followed by Jane, sat up and turned to look in front of Alice. She whispered, 'It must be a worm with a shell.'

'It's still far away; let's watch it, then if it comes too close, we'll climb. It's not looking for us but for the smell of rotting stuff.'

Jane remarked, 'Tarzan, maybe we smell rotten to the worm but not to ourselves.'

Alice chuckled, 'There have been nights when we smelt, but not what I would call rotten.'

'What would you call it?'

'Jane, if I could bottle it and sell it to women, I would call it "EcstaticOhhh".'

'Alice, you have one track mind. Tarzan, are those flickering lights any closer?'

'I'm trying to judge by the size of its maw. The lights define a circle, and the circle is growing. Let's climb. Are you ready?'

...

'I hope we won't need to hang here for hours. I feel like a dress on a hangar in my cupboard.'

'You're lucky, Jane; I have only one peg. I'm a bathrobe on a hook behind the door.'

'It won't be long, girls. It'll bury itself soon; I can see a glimmer of daylight.'

'Tarzan, that thing could swallow one of us whole.'

'I'll better understand its maw size when its lights shine on the tree...

'I guess about a metre. That's the biggest I've seen on the middle terrace. It's about the size the worms reach when they descend to ground level.'

'So how long is it?'

'I can't tell, I reckon about twenty metres.'

'For the sake of science, I'll drop and measure it.'

'Goodbye, Alice. It's nice to have known you.'

'Thanks, Jane. I didn't know you cared.'

'Girls, if it buries itself close by, we must move away as soon as we return to the nest and have breakfast a kilometre away.'

33

Fifteen days after they left the hunters' destroyed camp, they came to another river.

'This one is impossible; it must be three hundred metres at least, and I suspect much deeper. We must think of a solution.'

'Ask the silipusses, Tarzan; I'm sure they're telling me to head upriver.'

'Then we will.'

Two days and thirty kilometres later, Tarzan said, 'The river is spreading, and there's an island ahead.'

After another five kilometres, Jane remarked, 'There's a mass of islands, and the river has split into narrow ones between them. It's like a delta in reverse.'

Alice added, '*TeeKay* is ahead a kilometre from the river. He welcomes us.'

'How do you know Alice?'

'I sense him; maybe a silipuss is relaying the message.'

Alice was right, and forty minutes later, they found *TeeKay* waiting for them. He led them to the riverbank where, from the tree, they saw the terragons with the missile packs on their backs, a dozen males as guards, and a gathering herd of megalons beyond them.

They dropped from the tree.

The greeting ritual, hands and claws on shoulders and the *thelt – We Share* seemed a pleasure to the trio and the *TerraKids*. Then *TeeKay* explained what he had planned with a series of images.

The megalons would cross in two rows, head to tail, to guard the terragon females and their loads; they and the *Terrakids* would ride on the megalons.

Tarzan couldn't think of a better solution, so forty minutes later, two megalons began to cross side by side, with male *TerraKids* on them. Jane and Alice had the next pair that followed so closely that their heads overlapped the tails of those in front. The terragon carriers began to file into the water. Tarzan and *TeeKay* were on the next pair, and the remaining guards followed as the female terragons waded in one by one.

Tarzan observed that the first islands were little more than shallow areas covered in reeds and floating plants that the megalons waded through, churning up mud and plants. He could see a much higher island ahead that blocked the view beyond it. The water seemed too shallow for the river monsters, for it never rose further than the megalons' knees, or the demons feared the megalons. He relaxed and enjoyed the view and the ride; he could see Jane and Alice enjoying it, for they both looked back at him and waved.

The last river section looked calmer and deeper; Tarzan leaned over to watch as the megalon sank deeper until the water reached its belly; he saw Jane do the same.

Catastrophe struck as Jane's megalon took another step. A river monster shot from the water to bite the megalon's neck. The megalon shied, and Jane tumbled into the water.

As Jane sank below the surface, thoughts flashed through her mind; the first was *I can't swim*, followed without a pause with,

I won't drown. A monster will eat me. I wish I had held on. With her eyes shut and her mind whirling, she felt water rushing past as the beast came. *At least Tarzan has Alice.* Then the monster engulfed her, and she *thelt – I love you both.* Then she felt herself rising and air blowing on her face. *It's jumped out of the water.* She couldn't hold her breath any longer, and it exploded from her mouth as she opened her eyes. *No hooked or sharp teeth, but it's vast inside its mouth.* It took almost thirty seconds for her to realise where she was.

Tarzan stood erect an instant after she fell and swung a double rope end around his head to throw to Jane when she surfaced, but he didn't need to. The megalon turned its flexible neck around and picked Jane out of the water using its mouth like a spoon, then straightened and continued to the island; Alice could see Jane spluttering and coughing in the megalon's gaping mouth.

The megalon ignored the monster still locked to its neck, and as the two megalons reached the island, Alice's mount swung its head to bite the beast. The sound of crunching bones was loud, but the monster didn't fall to the ground. Once he could, Tarzan slid down his mount's neck and ran to Jane. She was smiling, bedraggled and mud-covered and said, 'Now I've done something you haven't. Swum in a river and ridden in a megalon's mouth. Beat that!'

Tarzan laughed, 'I never will, Jane. Are you fine?'

'Yes, but my megalon isn't. We must remove that monster from her neck.'

TeeKay slid off his mount and joined them as Tarzan looked at the hanging monster and *thelt – can you lower your neck?*

When the megalon did, he tied one end of the rope around one of the monster's jaws by feeding it between the teeth that he could see had not pierced the skin, only compressed it. Then he tied the rope around Alice's megalon's neck – *Pull.*

The megalons pulled so hard that the jaw tore off the monster, leaving Tarzan with a jawbone packed with vicious hooked and sharp teeth on the rope's end, while Jane's megalon picked up the crushed body and threw it downstream with a contemptuous flick.

The arriving terragon transporters would overcrowd the island, so Tarzan took the rope and jawbone with him when he remounted after asking Jane to remount. *TeeKay* climbed onto his mount behind Jane, and the columns moved again. When they reached the far bank and dismounted, *TeeKay* held up two fingers and pointed.

'He says we have two days to the final meeting point.'

'Thanks, Alice. We must climb and camp.'

After the shoulder-touching ceremony and multiple *We Share* confirmations, the trio found they were at a five-star hotel. The cats took their rope up, and behind the nearby tree with a Cascade Creeper lay three squirrels and a pile of fruit.

A shower, fruit, and squirrels later, they laid on the bed Tarzan had built, and he said, 'Jane, you terrified me today. I had visions that I had lost you.'

Alice added, 'I saw him standing on his megalon whirling a rope around his head to throw to you when your mount scooped you up. What was it like inside a megalon?'

'I wouldn't remember if it had closed its mouth, but its teeth are flat for grinding vegetation, so comfortable, and its mouth is big enough to be a house. That reminds me, Tarzan, what will you do with that jawbone?'

'I'll use the axe to cut eight front teeth from the bone, then clean off the teeth with my knife; I'll see if they will make good claws for my girls.'

'Jane, we must remember to take them off before loving!'

They met the team again two days later, unloaded the carriers, and Tarzan announced. 'I'll ask *TeeKay* for an aerial view.'

TeeKay ate with them, and Tarzan explained what they planned for the next day; then *TeeKay* left, and they slept.

The morning aerial view surprised them. Tarzan immediately remarked, 'Girls, are those women and children I see?'

Jane replied, 'I'm sure they are. They must be part of the support staff for the hunters and their organisation. There's a GravBus there, and the crew and hunters need feeding.'

'Then that makes missiles impossible to use; we can't kill women and children.'

Alice added something more. 'Have a look at the missile installations. There's one by the solar panels, three others in front and beside the building with the GravBus on it at the end opposite the panels. All the little houses are in the centre. The families must live in the centre, the hunters in the big building with the GravBus on top.'

'Do you think it's safe to fire missiles into the batteries around the main building?'

'If you want to keep the GravBus in one piece, only the front missile battery. Taking out the others might damage the GravBus. We don't need to fire our missiles; let the megalons drop trees on the forward and aft batteries and the solar array. Six trees forward and eight aft.'

'Okay, girls, if we don't harm the GravBus, they will have to take off quickly to avoid further damage, hopefully with the boss on board. Then it's up to the megalons, like the last time. Then we wait to see who's left. We'll explain it to *TeeKay...*'

TeeKay confirmed the megalons were ready.

The continuous barrage of noise from exploding tree trunks sounded like an attack from an overwhelming force and caused a rush for the GravBus. Tarzan tried to count the men that piled in and arrived at a surprising fifteen; then he saw a man with a woman and a child escorted by four more men running towards the GravBus. He tried to tell her not to leave – *Ma'am, stay behind with your child.* It seemed the forest wall surrounding the clearing echoed his *thelt* multiple times. He saw the man climb in and turn to the woman, who, it appeared, refused to enter. When a guard tried to grab her, she hit him. The man in the GravBus gestured, the escort climbed in, the door closed, and the GravBus lifted.

The woman lifted the child and ran to the stairs.

The GravBus fell in two parts.

No one moved in the remains of the fort.

'What do we do tomorrow?'

'That depends on what they do.'

They sat on a branch together, like three birds in a row, and ate fruit that Tarzan passed along to them; below, a hundred metres out in the clearing, the shattered remains of two missile emplacements lay scattered between twisted and bent solar panels. Nothing moved inside the area defined by the remaining sections of the palisade wall.

'How many people are there, Tarzan?'

'We know five or six men were loading the GravBus and stayed, as well as the woman and child. But there must be more to support the numbers that climbed into the GravBus.'

'They deserved to die; not only did they kill terragons, but they ran like scared rats and left at least one woman and child behind.'

'I agree, and a man is peeping out of the rubble beside the gate.'

'Where did he come from?'

'There must be houses on the other side of the barrier.'

Seeing no movement, the man stepped into view and raised a handle with something white on the end.

'What's that white?'

Alice answered, 'It looks like a woman's panties.'

'Why would he do that?'

Jane replied, 'Something they mention in the history books, a white flag is a sign of submission. We can't kill him, and he wants to talk.'

'That's a shame.'

'*Alice!* You don't mean that.'

'No, but I want to make history and be the first person to break that rule.'

'Girls, concentrate. Can we make him walk towards us?'

'We'll try.' – *Advance.*

They saw the man take ten hesitant steps forward.

Advance.

As nothing had attacked him, the man advanced further, and after two more instructions, he was twenty metres in front of them. – *Wait.*

He saw a rope drop from the tree and a creature fall from it, slowing to a near halt before jumping to the ground, turning to him, and throwing the tail between its legs over a shoulder.

Tarzan thought the man clutched the white flag in terror as he stepped towards him and stopped at four metres. He gave him half a minute to calm down and asked, 'What is your name.'

Shocked, he replied timidly, 'Wilfred, Wilfred Alawi.'

'Wilfred will do. What is your position here?'

'Cook.'

'You're the leader?' Visibly, a normal conversation helped him to overcome his fear.

'No, he was in the GravBus. Everyone knows the cook; they chose me to come. Who are you?'

'I'm Tarzan, chief of the Tarik police. It's against the law to kill the intelligent species of Tarik. That is murder, so we have acted.'

He thought cooks must have a sense of humour when Wilfred replied. 'I noticed.'

'The humans on Tarik must integrate with life here or die. We don't harm those who don't hurt us, and we care for females and children of all species; we'll not harm your women or their young children.

'How many people remain?'

'Fourteen male workers, twelve women, and ten young children. Oh, and the woman and her child who, for some reason, refused to escape with the GravBus.'

Tarzan's answer staggered him. 'I told her not to leave. You'll pass these instructions to them all.

'If you have a transmitter, send no messages; you'll endanger yourselves and others. You'll carry all missiles, launchers, and explosive weapons here. You may keep knives and axes. Then, you'll open all closed areas and storage for inspection. Check on your water and food supplies and tell me if you have a working transmitter. You need not fear attack if you obey these instructions. I shall arrange a GravBus with safe passage for those who want to leave. Now execute my instructions.'

He watched while Tarzan strode back to the tree; he didn't see him snap his tail to the rope but did see him climb the tree like a cat. He didn't notice the cord rise with him as Alice pulled it up.

Tarzan dropped again when the first missiles arrived and checked or disarmed them.

Four hours later, after what seemed the last of the weapons landed on the pile, Wilfred stayed, unexpectedly, with a woman and a child.

Wilfred had seen Tarzan before; the woman and child stared in amazement.

'Well, Wilfred, who are your companions, and what can you tell me?'

'This is the woman you told not to enter the GravBus. She told us she heard voices telling her not to. She wants to say thank you.'

Tarzan turned to her, 'Ma'am, no thanks are necessary; the intelligent beings on Tarik all protect women and children. You'll be safer with them than your kind.'

'That may be. But thank you.'

'Wilfred?'

'We have five days of food; the rainwater collection system is undamaged. The electricity supply has failed. There's a transmitter, but it's dead with no power.'

'Then you may be here for thirty or more days; you must prepare for that. If you need food, our people will bring what you need, but you may enter the forest without risk. On Tarik, we sleep as the sun sets and rise with it. Electricity is unnecessary; there are ways to light a dark room when the sun is up. Inspection will be tomorrow morning an hour after sunrise.'

He turned and climbed the tree to join Alice and Jane.

'Girls, tomorrow you'll look at everything and meet the women and children. They need reassurance. I shall look at the transmitter. If we can't use it, we must take it away and hide it. I don't want those people sending messages we know nothing about. Unless I can send a message, they're here for a month. I'll call *TeeKay* to store the weapons somewhere.'

TeeKay arrived.

TeeKay, we should recover the missiles in the GravBus.

I have done it; I have watched how you kill the missiles.

Then, TeeKay, please take all the weapons and hide them. We may need them again. Those here can leave; I will call or send a transport. Can you give it safe passage and look after the people until I know more?

We will do so.

TeeKay left to organise the weapons movement.

34

Tarzan asked when they woke the following day, 'Girls, we must organise a GravBus to take these people to a colony. Shall we wait here and leave with them?'

Alice surprised him. 'Not me. I've had one experience of a GravBus breakdown. I'd rather travel in the trees.'

Jane echoed her feelings. 'I agree with Alice. We vote for the forest.'

To the consternation of the people on the ground, three terragon females arrived with ten males to load the weapons. First, Wilfred, with his wife and child and the woman with her child whom Tarzan had saved, approached, curious and hoping for a better look. When the others saw they didn't become breakfast, they came singly or in pairs to join them.

'Okay, girls, let's drop.'

The ropes dropped, and then the audience watched in amazement as Tarzan appeared to free fall before braking; the girls, using leather sleeves, were as fast.

As the three figures strode towards them, several people stepped back.

Tarzan looked them over individually and stopped at a group of three, a man, woman and child at the back – *Jane. Look at the family at the back; they have eaten Tarik food for some time.*

He saw the surprise on the faces of the woman and her son and thelt – *boy; I want to know your name.*

The little boy seemed to struggle, then he replied – *Grunt.*

Good name.

Then he spoke, 'Ma'am, will you and your family come here, please.'

They did, and Tarzan smiled. *Their eyes are green.* 'You have eaten Tarik food for some time. Why?'

'My son cannot speak; for years, we spent all our credits on his treatment, and we had to sell all we could produce. We had nothing for ourselves, so we collected food from the forest. We took this job because the pay was much higher, but we can now hear him, and he can hear us.'

'Those who Tarik adopts speak between minds, with feelings, not words. Now you have begun, continue.' *Jane, Alice, listen.* 'I'm Tarzan. Jane and Alice will bring *TeeKay*, a male terragon who speaks as we do. You and your son will translate for him when we have left.'

As he walked away, he looked back and thought, *I didn't re-alise how much the girls have grown until I could compare; these people must believe we're giants in height and build.*

Jane intercepted the thought and replied. *You too, Tarzan. Alice and I think you're magnificent.*

Tarzan examined the transmitter while the others inspected everything else. He thought the transmitter was undamaged and might work with electricity. However, the aerial fell during the tree assault.

He asked if there were forest bikes, found two and gave instructions; within two hours, a jury-rig aerial leant against a remaining piece of palisade wall, with the forest bike batteries connected to the transmitter. He switched it on. He had no idea if it would transmit a satisfactory message, but tried to compose a message using the microphone and found the software translated his voice badly, presenting a garbled text message. When Wilfred joined him, he said, 'This thing can't understand my voice.'

'There's a keyboard somewhere we use when we want to be private. I'll find it.'

When Jane entered the hut, she found Tarzan trying to type with a hunt and peck. 'Tarzan, let me type; you haven't done so for years. What do you want to write?'

'I must call myself the Chief of Police, Jane. Alice said that police action is acceptable to people. The satellite receiver will add our position, so:

> From: Tarzan of Tarik. Chief of Tarik Police. At the position of this transmitter.
>
> To: Gordon Furnival, Colony Nine.
>
> We have destroyed the terragon hunter's headquarters at this position. The Tarik Police have done so for hunting the intelligent species of Tarik must stop.
>
> The non-combatant humans remaining at the camp are:
>
> Males: 14 – fourteen.
>
> Females: 13 – thirteen.
>
> Children, both sexes: 11 – Eleven.
>
> Please arrange GravBus pickup. Safe passage for unarmed reconnaissance drone and unarmed GravBus guaranteed.

Then Tarzan grinned. 'Jane, add a line.'

> Dad, please believe this. Timothy.

'Wilfred, do you have a watch or clock?'

'Yes.'

'This place, I'm sure, isn't on the communications map; I can only send blind. I'll set the send for a repeat every five minutes for fifteen minutes every two hours. Can you come every six hours and look at the log? It should show you the message received. It should arrive in two or three days. Then you can disconnect the batteries.'

'I will. But if the message doesn't arrive?'

'Then I'll tell them in person in about a month. If Colony Nine receives the message, they will still take days to organise a pickup.'

At their nest that evening, Tarzan asked, 'Girls, did you find anything during your inspection?'

'Nothing except one locked store that Wilfred broke open. It has a dozen or more boxes of what we think are drugs. Alice asked the men, and they don't know what they are.'

'I'll have them burnt. Tomorrow must be our last day. I have something I want to do; what about you?'

'Alice and I will introduce the children to the silipusses and feed the children a roasted squirrel. I'm fascinated by how the people have accepted us as the police. I sense they're glad we came.'

'Most people don't like killing. Introducing the silipusses sounds like a great idea. Let's sleep.'

'Tarzan, I'll be glad to begin travelling again; being with you and Alice in the forest is heaven; there are too many people here.'

I feel the same.

So do I, Alice. Let's sleep.

Tarzan visited the medical cabinet with Wilfred and chose a pair of forceps, then visited the workshop where the day before he had seen a collection of miscellaneous items; he needed a pin three millimetres or less in diameter, and after scratching around, Wilfred found a three-millimetre nail.

'Now, I want a small fire to heat the nail.' From his belt pouch, Tarzan emptied the eight claws onto the bench.

'What are those?'

'The teeth from a river monster. I want to burn five holes along the bottom edge of each.'

'Okay, I'll collect firewood. We have a fireplace for this, but I'll need to blow because the fan won't work.'

It took all morning to make the forty holes. Once the nail was red hot, Tarzan held it in the forceps and positioned it, and the nail burnt through quickly before he dropped it back in the fire. Once they finished, Wilfred said. 'I'm glad I've no more blowing to do. What thread will you use to sew on the claws?'

'I used plaited threads from a GravBus safety belt for a bow-string. Do you have something you can suggest?'

'No, but I know a woman we can ask.'

'Then we must find her.'

Wilfred led the way and talked while they walked, 'This woman's husband is a GravBus pilot; I know he resigned and refused to fly for some reason. Since then, he has cut trees for people. He and his wife have climbing tackle and ropes.'

They found her hanging washing on a line strung between

two poles. 'Rashida, I want to introduce Tarzan to you.'

'I already know who he is, Wilfred, but I'm pleased to meet you, Tarzan. My husband will be back soon, and he'll be thrilled. Why have you come to see us?'

Tarzan showed her one of his titanium claws and then a monster's tooth. 'I need a thread to sew eight claws with holes to megalon's hide. Like the attached one. I was about to strip filaments from a safety belt and plait them, but Wilfred suggested we see you.'

'Come in. We'll look in Zayn's store. When he gave up the GravBus job, he took everything that he had brought with him.'

'Why did he give up flying?'

'You must ask him; he was miserable when he did.'

The store surprised Tarzan with coils of rope and climbing gear, but nothing seemed suitable. He was looking at a loading strap about five metres long when Zayn arrived. Tarzan shook hands with the delighted man, and Rashida explained what Tarzan was looking for. After examining the claws, including the mounted one, Zayn said, 'You have a good eye. That strap is the only thing I can suggest. If I pull one filament, it should work. The strap rating is sixty tons, two tons per filament, and they're slightly less than a millimetre in diameter. I don't mind losing one in the centre. Rashida can dig it out for you. You'll need a sharp skewer to pierce megalon's hide.'

'Wilfred will find me one. Thank you both; you've helped to make our lives safer.

'Can you tell me why you stopped flying the GravBus?'

'When the boss ordered the installation of missiles on the GravBus, I thought it was like asking someone to shoot at me.'

'If you want to fly again, talk to the GravBus pilots that come to collect you.'

All the children were with Alice and Jane; they sat in two rows of five, with Grunt alone in front of the first row. Grunt's mother and two interested women came and stood at the back, then Jane announced.

'Children, I'll call a silipuss to come and meet you. They may look ferocious, but they will never harm you if you don't harm them; they can talk, although you haven't yet learnt how, except Grunt, who knows how.'

'How did he learn, miss?'

'Partly by eating Tarik food, but mostly because although he can't talk, which isn't his fault, he's not stupid, and he found another way to talk with his mother.'

Kitty, come.

Kitty scrambled down the tree and approached Jane, who stood beside Grunt.

Hello, thing.

Jane was surprised when the boy replied – *not thing, Grunt.*

The puss and the boy stared at each other for half a minute, and then the puss *thelt – Grunt, friend.*

Kitty friend.

And she laid down beside Grunt!

Then Jane said, 'Alice and I will help you cook a squirrel. The rule on Tarik that guarantees safety between species is: "We share". You can decide when each pair have roasted a squirrel on a stick. Take your squirrels to Wilfred so he can include them in lunch for everyone, take half a squirrel home to your mother, or eat the squirrel between you. Grunt will give half to Kitty.'

Three silipusses scrambled down the tree, each with two squirrels in their mouths, and laid a squirrel in front of each pair in the row of five and another before Grunt.

The women came forward and helped to clean the squirrels and to light six little fires. No one had noticed the pile of fire-wood sticks and the freshly cut skewers.

They said goodbye before the light faded, returned to their nest for a shower and food, and then laid down as night fell.

'Tarzan, did you finish what you planned to do?'

'Yes, Jane, I have eight claws with holes to tie them on mega-lon's hide strips and cord for tying. How did you do?'

'I feel good. Alice, can you explain?'

'We did the right thing. The kids have lost their fear of the cats, and Grunt has progressed amazingly in two days. The kids still call him Grunt, but it's no longer derision but respect – like he's important.'

Jane added, 'Two years from now, those kids will be forest dwellers like us. I'm not sure they'll leave for Colony Nine. They gave us a sign today.'

'What was that?'

'They all took their squirrels to Wilfred to share with the community after giving the cats a head each.'

'We'll learn if they remain when we reach my home. Sleep: we travel tomorrow.'

Before they left in the morning, *TeeKay* returned. After greeting Alice and Jane with the hands-on shoulders gesture and – *We Share*, he turned to Tarzan and repeated it; then, a picture began to build, and another took its place when it faded. The girls sensed the pictures as well. They were all aerial images of palisade fortresses like Wilfred's one, but with notable differences, and all had piles of logs on solar panels. When the ninth one faded, *TeeKay thelt* – *Thank You. WE ALL SHARE.*

TeeKay then left. 'Girls, if you followed, I'm sure he showed us that all the hunter's fortresses are now incapacitated.'

Alice replied, 'That makes me happy. I hope there are kids like Grunt in them.'

It took eight days for them to achieve maximum travelling speed; each day, they stopped early. The girls hunted, collected fruit and firewood and prepared their food; Tarzan sat with his tools and cut megalon's hide straps to support claws. Once he had adjusted them to suit Jane and Alice's legs and hands, he began tying on the claws.

Jane was the most interested. 'Tarzan, how can you tie the teeth so they stick out? Yours have a flat base.'

'Have a look, Jane.'

'That's smart; it's tight between double folds of the hide, but how can we practice?'

'You can try them out when we find another lake or clearing or reach the sea. Trying to find a way through the forest floor would be dangerous.'

35

Ten days later, when Jane finished her lead traverse, and Tarzan caught up, she remarked, 'Tarzan, the humidity is higher, and the air smells salty. Are we nearing the sea?'

'I think so, and that's a worry.'

'Why?'

'We might have travelled faster than I expected or are a bit south of our course. If so, I hope not too much. We'll have a long trip upriver if we're too far south because there's a mega river southeast of Colony Nine.'

Alice remarked, 'We've solved every problem as we've come to it. Let's look. I want to see the sea. I haven't built sandcastles for years.'

Jane replied, 'I've never built a sandcastle!'

'Okay, ten-metre lines...'

'Saltwater is more slippery than fresh...'

'Jane, the trees end in fifty metres. Slow now.'

'I can see the sea!'

'Further, Alice, there's a narrow beach.'

'Tarzan, are there tides?'

'Confusing ones, Jane.'

'Then tell us without the confusion!'

'I can't; I can tell you what causes them. The most important is the sun and the planet's rotation; it makes a high tide and then a low tide at the eastern and western ends of the sea daily.

In the middle, the tide is zero. Then, our sister planet has an effect, as do the three moons. So, five things are tugging at the seawater in different directions, and the directions are continuously changing. Without a computer, I can't tell you what the tide state will be. Alice, what's the beach like?'

'It's about thirty metres, only tiny waves, and I can see three sunbathing monsters.'

'Secure your tail, Alice. Jane, join her, then I'll follow.'

'Those are slidagons. They don't have the split tail of the fish and river monsters.'

'What do they eat, Tarzan?'

'Something in the sea, Jane. They come out to bask in the sunshine. If you stay more than two metres from them, they don't move. They can twist sideways but only slide on their bellies, so we're safe two metres ahead if they aren't in ten centimetres of water.'

'Can we walk on the beach? Will those flying things attack us as the darters do?'

'There are two species, Jane; one has webbed feet. The closest thing to them in the "Life of the Known Worlds" catalogue is a fruit-eating bat, but that's nocturnal and cannot swim. We have these near Colony Nine. Dad calls them *TeeGulls* with clawed feet and *EssGulls* with webbed feet. He says they must have a common ancestor. They both have hands halfway along their wings, like a squirrel's front paws. Their feet also have the same structure. The *EssGulls* have a beak with a hooked tip and a pouch underneath; they scoop up little fish. The land ones have a mouth that opens wide to catch flying insects and teeth to gnaw fruit. Their acrobatics are marvellous to watch when they're catching insects. They won't attack us. We can walk on the beach but should stay away from the water unless we find a separate pool.'

Jane asked, 'How about walking along the beach to your river?'

'That's physically possible, but not for us. Building enough suntan to permit a two-hour walk without a painful sunburn will take at least two weeks. You said you met Piotr at my Colony; do you remember his tan?'

'Okay, then we build sandcastles and climb back. But first, I've been dying to try the claws for five days.'

'Okay, strap on your claws. I'll hitch a safety line to your tail; then, you can descend halfway and return. Who's first?'

'Jane.'

'No free fall until you know how to use the claws for braking. Only one hand or foot in the air at a time.'

With Tarzan controlling the safety line, if Jane slipped, she would fall a metre or less. She slapped her claws against the tree, scuttled rapidly down, and looked up – *Coming up!*

She came up faster than climbing a rope hand over hand, with a wide grin.

'That was great, Tarzan, but my groin muscles need practice. Can we do that every morning?'

'Yes, Jane. Now it's Alice's turn.'

Tarzan thought there was only a minor difference between the two girls; Alice descended faster, and Jane climbed faster.

'I'll drop with you, and we'll build sandcastles.'

Four minutes later, Tarzan left the rope hanging for their return. 'We'll stay far enough from the trees to have time to react if anything appears, but keep away from the slidagons.

Alice collected shells; Jane, once she found airholes in the sand, fetched a digging stick and dug out some odd creatures. 'Tarzan, what's this thing?'

'I can't help Jane and don't know if it's edible. I haven't done much beach walking, and I'm beginning to learn why. How are your feet?'

'I need the shade of the trees. This dark red sand is heating up.'

'Then we'll move to the shade. The little strip of water ahead looks attractive, but I'll bet it's a slidagon's basking channel. Alice, come with us.'

Tarzan almost flew to the shadows, followed by the girls.

'Alice, our handsome hero has tender feet.'

'Well, we're wearing our megalon's hide soles; he didn't put his ones on when it became damp.'

'Tarzan, it's not just feet. I'm sure we'll have pink skin in an hour. As you said, we're strangers to direct sunlight.'

'We could walk once the sun is lower if we make parasols.'

'Do you know enough about what we might meet as the sun sets so we can walk later?'

'No, Jane, let's climb.'

The routine of survival took over. Jane – convinced the veg they had collected would have loads of salt – took control of the cooking. She tasted it several times while she cooked and added only those herbs low in salt.

'Girls, that squirrel was delicious. Am I right that it had more salt than we're used to?'

Jane answered, 'Not the squirrel, but the garlic herb I used does have more salt despite washing it twice. The vegetables are saltier. I suppose the sea air carries salt everywhere.'

Within two days, the girls took turns zipping down to collect driftwood for a fire. After another week, they could freefall down a fixed rope using a megalon's hide sleeve and then use their claws to brake in the last ten metres.

Two days later, they made a short excursion to check they were still following the coastline. 'This is great,' said Jane, 'The air by the sea is so much fresher, crispier than the atmosphere in the trees. I think the food tastes better as well.'

'That may be,' Alice added, 'we can see much farther out to sea from up here. There's a monster sea snake out there.'

'Where?'

'Straight out from here, moving westwards. It's about a kilometre away, moving fast.'

'Yes, I see it. It has a hump behind the head and neck.'

'Girls, if you sank a megalon female in the water until only her head and some neck came out, she might look like that. I've seen them often from my colony.'

The beast dived, and the tail momentarily appeared behind the head and body.

'That's not a megalon; the tail doesn't have a ball but a horizontal flat flipper.'

They waited for it to reappear. After an hour, Jane said, 'It may be far away, or it may be sitting on the bottom, chuckling at our puzzlement.'

'It could be, girls; if there's any relationship to a megalon, it will have a body so stocked with air that it can float or sink and use its stored air for several hours. Let's continue.'

Five days later, they stared across a vast expanse of muddy water, 'Girls, that's what a mega-river looks like. It must be ten kilometres wide. There's no way we can cross it.'

'Well, that's a problem for later. Let's camp then turn towards the sea tomorrow morning.'

They reached the sea after three hours. 'Tarzan, Alice and I want to try to cook and eat those things I dig from the sand. Tell us what you plan.'

'I'll build a nest, then try calling *TeeKay*, with the silipusses' help, and see if he can persuade a megalon to come here.'

'Why?'

'I'd like to know if the sea megalon can *theel*. Then, if it can, I can ask it to carry us over the river. The land megalon females will float, but they have no flippers, and the river current will carry them out to sea.'

'How would we cross? Just sitting on its back?'

'Either that, or we tie four tree trunks together with a gap in the middle, and the megalon sticks its head through the gap and swims.'

'That would be much safer. Megalons are not easy to sit on. What's the alternative?'

'At least a hundred kilometres upriver and then a hundred and fifty back, all forest travel.'

'Where's Colony Nine?'

'Forty-plus kilometres the other side of this river.'

'Tarzan, it's corny to say, "So near and yet so far." I don't know whether to feel happy or sad.'

'Happy to be near or far, Jane?'

'I don't know; maybe I don't want the trip to end. How about you, Alice?'

'Neither, Jane, reaching Tarzan's home ceased to be an objective months ago; this is just another stop on our life journey. If it were an ending, I would be sad. I suppose we'll all be happy to see our parents again, but I'm sure it's not an ending, and there's much more to come.'

'Together, Alice?' asked Tarzan.

'Of course, have you thought how different we are from the other colonists? Not just what we look like, but how we think, feel, and *thelt*? We can't live in a colony with people who don't share our values and see us as a different species, although I'm sure that with a little help, there will be many like us. We must remain together.'

Jane replied, 'Thanks, Alice, you've straightened my thinking, Tarzan, do you agree?'

'Fully. I'll add that we're a trio; we love each other and must continue because a breakup of our trio would kill me and maybe you both. More than anything, we have a purpose in life; how do you like the idea of being a police force?'

'We adore it. Alice, are you ready?'

'Yes.'

'Then let's drop.'

36

Tarzan collected timber and vines and then built the nest. He did so quickly as he wanted to join the girls on the beach, but before dropping, he sat cross-legged on the nest, slowed his breathing and heartbeat, and concentrated. *TeeKay* was likely far away.

He imagined *TeeKay* in an affectionate theel – *Hello TeeKay, We Share.*

The reply surprised him; it came quickly – *We Share.*

TeeKay must be keeping tabs on us. Tarzan pictured a megalon male at the riverbank, head-to-head with another sunk in the water with its flipper tail in the air and projected it. The feeling of amusement confirmed that *TeeKay* had a sense of humour – *Wait.*

He dropped and joined the women on the beach. Jane asked, 'Did you *theel* to *TeeKay*?'

'Yes, he may be following us closely because he answered immediately. He thinks my idea is amusing.'

'He probably thinks it crazy and has no feeling for that.'

'We'll see; I think it will take two days for a megalon to arrive.'

Two days later, while they sat on the dune with the silipusses, eating a bag of boiled shellfish with wooden skewers, Alice announced, '*TeeKay's* coming, and he has a female terragon and a female megalon following him, with a male megalon floating overhead. He's coming along the side of the river.'

Jane urged two hours later, 'We should walk to the river; they're coming.'

Led by the megalon female, then the terragon and *TeeKay*, they came along the riverbank near the tree line, and high above floated a megalon.

Alice remarked, 'The slidagons have gone, Tarzan.'

'They're no match for a megalon, at least on land. In the water, it might be different.'

They stepped forward to meet the group. The welcome with *TeeKay* was touching, with the hands-on-shoulders gesture and – *Friend, We Share*. With the megalon and terragon, simply a sustained look and – *We Share*. Then the airborne megalon came down, and for a minute, while his gas bag floated and his tail ball anchored him from drifting away, he looked at each of them with the eyes in the top of his head and *thelt* – *We Share*. When he gazed at Tarzan, Tarzan pictured the sea horizon with the head and neck of a megalon looking a bit like a sea snake and *thelt* the question – *Do We Share?*

When fully airborne, a light breeze blew him away across the river, but they saw him descending in a swoop out to sea once he had sufficient height. The rise and swoop continued until the direction, no longer random, drew their eyes to the east, and they could see a snake-like head.

For over an hour, the girls watched the megalon out at sea, and Tarzan had a picture conversation with *TeeKay*, enhanced with maps drawn on the sand.

The megalon flew back and parked his tail ball nearby.

The sadness was unmistakable – *No Memories.*

'Tarzan, that means your idea won't work. Do you have another?'

'Two ideas, Jane. *TeeKay* has told me that about a hundred and forty kilometres upriver, there's a place where megalons can cross like we did the last time. Once across the river, we can travel through the forest. It'll take a month.

'Alternatively, did you see which way the megalon floated once he started climbing? It was across the river. The sea breeze blowing inland is now strengthening. If we make a raft, and he has his ball on the raft, and we cast off when the land breeze dies away, we should sail across the river. Would you like to try it?'

'Alice, I think Tarzan's crazy. How about you?'

'I think he's crazy, too. But another crossing where river monsters attack isn't my idea of a holiday. Tarzan, are there river monsters here, too?'

'Jane knows the river monsters don't like sea water; they can only come a little way as they float on the surface in seawater. The slidagons don't like the freshwater; they sink, so there's a sort of 'no-monsters' land at the junction. In the flood season, the river washes the monsters too far; I've seen them thrashing on the surface. The slidagons come and feast, but now the brackish water band must be at its widest.'

'Tarzan, ask *TeeKay.*'

A long telepathic conversation with *TeeKay* followed.

'We'll try. *TeeKay* likes the idea! He's called for more megalons to break down trees and terragons to pull vines from the trees; we must help with our axes. The first task is to choose a launch site.'

Jane had the answer, 'A crustacean I watched dug a small harbour by pushing sand into the river. Do the same with the megalons. Then, put the tree trunks into the river, tow them into the harbour with a vine, and tie them together. Then launching is unnecessary.'

'Brilliant!'

Five days later, they stood looking at the water-filled harbour with four floating twenty-metre-long tree trunk sections strapped to each other with vines. 'Girls, it's not a pretty raft; after breaking those tree trunks with the mass of a two-hundred-ton megalon, we're lucky they're within two or three metres in length. But they'll keep us dry and away from the river monsters.'

'Tarzan, should we check that the megalon can sail this raft to the other side without risking our lives? Like a trial run?'

'No, Jane, The vines may not last. We should load it up and check how well it floats with the megalon's ball, *TeeKay*, and us on board. I've asked him to send us a megalon and a terragon to wait on the other side.'

'Why?'

'Alice, we don't have a harbour there, can't see how steep the bank is, and we'll look stupid if we're stuck with thirty metres of water between us and the shore. At a minimum, they can lay down a young tree to walk across.'

'Let's do the load test. If that's okay, I'll tell *TeeKay* we must all be on board early tomorrow. The land breeze will blow the raft to the side of the harbour, then when it dies, a megalon can push us away, and we should sail across the river.'

The male megalon drifted slowly down early the following day and dumped his tail ball on the raft while everyone watched. 'Tarzan, I was worried when the megalon dumped his ball onto the raft, but it held. Why didn't you tie it to the raft with a line or vine? He could float above us.'

'Jane, with the mass of that ball, this raft is steady. If any monster comes up from below, it won't rock and throw us off. Now let's load everything, and us, onboard.' – *TeeKay, We Travel.*

The megalon, blown seaward by the light land breeze, held the raft against the seaward side of their harbour, and they waited until the breeze died away. The megalon females took their cue from the male and pushed; moments later, they sailed into the river.

Alarmed, Alice said, 'Tarzan, the river is taking us out to sea.'

'I expected we'd drift out slowly until the sea breeze began to affect our direction, and that would bring us back.'

'I wish you had mentioned that before; what if it doesn't bring us back.'

'Then we take the emergency life raft.'

'What's that?'

'I throw our ropes over the megalon's ball; we tie on and let him fly us to the beach.'

'Like a bunch of dangling fruit?'

'Exactly.'

'Jane, is it okay if I never speak to this madman again?'

'I'll join you, Alice, if we don't reach the other side.'

Jane was the first to notice. 'Tarzan, we aren't moving out to sea anymore.'

'I agree. We've done over two kilometres, and now we're sailing straight across; the breeze has picked up. I'm guessing that we have two more hours before the first sea breeze starts. We should have crossed most of the river, more than eight kilometres, before it blows us back towards the land.'

Almost two hours later, Jane remarked, 'That was a good guess; I can feel the first flutters of the sea breeze, and we can see the waiting megalons. Arrival will be interesting.'

'Yes, everyone must wait until the raft is stationary against the riverbank and our megalon sail is holding it there before we move. I'll tell *TeeKay* our shore crew must keep up with us.'

'Tarzan, there's a fallen tree half in the water upriver of us about a kilometre ahead. If we plough into that, it might stop us, but if it doesn't, it could brush us off the raft.'

'Change of plan girls.' Tarzan *thelt – TeeKay, if we hit the tree, the megalon must lift.*

Tarzan took his claws from his shoulder bag and strapped them on. 'Girls take a rope each. Tie one end to a binding vine and tie it to the tree if we hit it so the river's current doesn't take us out to sea.'

As they closed slowly on the tree, they could see the massive trunk stretched from a vast tangle of roots on the riverbank, and in the water, fifty metres into the river, the collection of branches that had supported the forest floor rose into the air, those underwater had hopefully buried themselves in the riverbed.

'We will collide, Tarzan, but only just.'

'Okay, stay out of the way of the ball and tie your rope onto the tree. I'll take a rope from the far end of the raft, climb the tree trunk, and take it to the roots so the raft swings that way.'

Although the tree was massive, the raft with the megalon's

ball was also an enormous force, although travelling slowly. *'Hold on, everyone!'*

Megalon must start lifting NOW!

The call was just in time. The fallen tree shook and shuddered as the raft ploughed into the end with the branches below and above water; the ball slid forward, the raft's end dipped towards the water, and water almost reached the raft's surface before the megalon had pumped sufficient gas into its bag to raise the ball. It provided an unexpected advantage, for until the ball lifted free, it kept the front of the raft hard against the fallen tree while Jane and Alice tied two ropes to the branches. Tarzan ran from the far end and leapt onto the tree trunk, his claws cut in, and seconds later, he scrambled onto the trunk three metres above the water, ran along the tree to its roots, hauled the rope tight and tied it to a thick root. Then he stood up, looked up at the megalon now rising fifty metres above, and *thelt – Thank you. We Share.*

TeeKay, Come, Jane Alice, Claws. Lives first, gear after.

Two hours later, they camped at the tree line with a Cascade Creeper for water. A megalon sat in front and a terragon behind. The raft had floated out to sea.

TeeKay brought firewood, and Jane and Alice cooked. They ate and slept together.

They felt sad saying goodbye to *TeeKay*, the emotion visible on all four faces as they held each other's shoulders and *thelt – WE SHARE.*

A silipuss carried a safety rope up a tree, then Tarzan ordered, 'Kit up, with claws. Jane, you climb first. Alice and I will follow.'

Within five minutes of their first traverse, the K-stretch line with Jane and Alice at the ends and Tarzan in the middle had extended, and they fell back into the dancing rhythm they had practised for hundreds of days, and the speed built as their muscles warmed up and pleasure flooded their bodies. Sometimes Jane, Alice, Tarzan or both girls were out ahead, not racing, not competing, but joined mentally by the joy of their exercise, the breeze in their hair, the brush of leaves, the spring from the roots they touched on ever so lightly as they skipped, jumped and leapt along the terrace.

Tarzan called a halt after three hours. 'Girls, we should rest.'

Jane replied, 'I could continue all day; I had forgotten how marvellous dancing with you and Alice through the forest feels. She keeps on *thelting* – *Whoopee! Wow! Wheee! Wonderful.*

'I know, Jane, but I caught a couple of rude ones.'

Alice answered, 'I'll own up, I did *theel* – *Oh, shit.* I hit a tarizard with my mallet, but he fell through the floor. I have some fruit. Let's eat.'

They continued for another two hours, and then Tarzan stopped and called them.

'Girls, we've done over thirty kilometres; we'll reach Colony Nine tomorrow early. Look at the mark on this tree. I cut it when I was about thirteen.'

'Then we should prepare to meet your parents. You need a shave, and we must shower and comb our hair.'

'It's cut short, as short as mine. Why do you need to comb it?'

Alice answered, 'Because we do, Tarzan, and yours needs combing too. I'll shave you. It's my turn. Jane can fetch some soap plants, and we can cook up the squirrel she has on her belt. I'll collect firewood, and you make the nest.'

Jane added, 'I'll fetch enough soap plants to wash all our clothes and a *Decaspider* depilatory net. Do you want one, Alice?'

'Please.'

Tarzan could only think, *I'm no longer the boss.*

When they lay down to sleep, their clothing hanging from pegs on the tree, Jane said, 'Tarzan, this is the last night of our journey. When will we travel together again?'

'We have some things to do. You and Alice must meet your parents, and I must report everything we learnt to my father. I want to visit the icecap soon, and if you come with me, we will travel together then.'

'That's another day, Tarzan. Alice and I are not fertile, so we have agreed that tonight, we want to celebrate the end of the trip in style. No more talking.'

Jane, who's first?

Whoever's ready first, you'll know.

What if it's both of you?

Then you have a problem.

It wasn't a problem...

'Tarzan, I don't know how I could imagine a forest glade I've never seen.'

'Was there a small stream of blue water, Jane, and green grass?'

'Yes, we were lying on the grass. Did you see anything, Alice?'

'Of course, I was in your head and Tarzan's. I saw the same picture and the stream running down a white slope to the grassy clearing.'

'Girls, I can't explain it. Maybe we linked with a telepath in that place. We might find it one day; that white slope might be ice.'

Can we go back there? It was marvellous.

Now?

Yes.

Minds locked to minds; they rode together on the same ecstatic journey each time.

37

They set off washed and polished in clean clothes after breakfast, and an hour later, Tarzan, Jane, and Alice peered between the foliage of a giant tree on the edge of the cleared area beside the sea.

Alice asked, 'Is that where you were born?'

'Yes, it's still the same as when I last saw it. I hope my parents are still there.'

'How can we find out?'

'I'll need to ask; let's move around closer to the river on the right. The house was there.'

Five minutes later, from a new vantage point, Jane observed, 'There's at least one person in there, there's smoke. Is it a log cabin?'

'It is, and the roof is small tree trunks and rammed soil. How do we persuade them to show themselves?'

Jane replied, 'I'll throw a branch onto the roof. If one of your parents comes out, you can drop then meet them; we'll stay here until you tell us to come.'

She turned and searched for a suitable projectile; Tarzan tied one end of his rope to his tail, passed it around a branch and gave it to Alice. 'Use the megalon hide slider.'

Jane threw the misshapen branch; it whistled after the fifty-metre drop before it landed with a thump they could hear.

I could never have thrown that far before I met Tarzan.

'That should do it.'

The wait seemed long, although it was only five minutes. Then the rear door opened slowly, and a man peered out.

Tarzan exclaimed, 'That's Dad,' then dropped off the branch, and fifty metres later, after Alice tightened the loop for the last ten metres, stepped lightly onto the ground. His father was searching for the source of the noise, looking in the wrong direction, and only saw Tarzan after he had walked a dozen paces towards him.

Jane and Alice saw Tarzan approaching his father; they couldn't see the puzzlement on the face of the older man, confronted with a two-metre-tall naked mythical creature with a tail and an assortment of items hanging from a belt holding up a loincloth. It was enough to make him turn and run. But the smile and lack of threat kept him in place until he recognised his son's face. Then he broke into a run.

'*Timothy!* I knew you would come.' And the two men embraced.

'It's fantastic to see you again. You've grown, and you're no longer the boy who left here. We've lived for two years believing you would return. Let me give you another hug.

'This is wonderful; I'll call your mother.'

'*Marthaaaa!* Tim's back!'

She ran from the house towards them, 'Where is he?'

Then she recognised her son and ran forward into Tarzan's arms with a joyous cry.

After hugs and kisses galore, she stepped back to look at him. 'You've grown and changed, Timothy.'

'More than you'll ever understand, Mum. There are two women with me that you must meet.'

'Then call them. Today will be a day I'll never forget.'

Jane, Alice, come.

'I have done. Watch that tree.'

His dad asked, 'How did you do that?'

'I'll explain later.'

Then they saw two ropes fall from the tree, and two women dropped at a breathtaking speed to land lightly and walk towards them. Dressed the same way as her son but with a breast band, Martha noted the outstanding physique and the glow of health radiating from them.

'Who are they, Timothy.'

'My wives, Jane and Alice, my name in the forest is Tarzan. Jane has been with me for two years, and Alice one.'

As the two reached them, Tarzan said, 'This is Jane, the tallest, and Alice. Girls, this is my mother, Martha, and my dad, Gordon Furnival.'

Both girls and his parents examined each other closely; Gordon was the first to smile. 'I have a question. Who looks after whom? I first thought it would be Tim who looked after you; now I suspect you ladies look after him.'

'Dad, we're a gestalt trio; we look after each other.'

Martha stopped any further discussion, 'To me, you're both very tall and beautiful, with lovely green eyes. Come into the house and sit. You have a lot to tell us.'

Two separate conversations developed; Jane and Alice told Martha and answered her questions – Timothy alias Tarzan did the same with his father. At first, they were straightforward accounts of their journey, but then Gordon asked, 'There was a message from Tarzan of Tarik. At the bottom, you wrote I must believe it. After almost two years, we began losing faith in your coming. It told us you were. So, are you Tarzan of Tarik?'

'I am, Dad, and before continuing, did a GravBus fetch the remaining people?'

'Yes, and all except one refused to return; his wife was here, and he now wants to return there with her. They said it was safe there, that they had lots to do, with no bosses ruling them, and were all equal. The pilots said they had overgrown cats roaming around and saw what looked like a *TerraKid*. I've proposed that we call it Colony Nine B.'

'I'm delighted to hear they stayed. Call them Village-Ten, for they will never be dependent. The silipusses resemble cats. They and the *TerraKids* are citizens of Tarik.'

'Tim, how did you call your wives from the tree?'

He called them my wives; he's accepted them!

'Dad, there's a lot you don't know about Tarik and the people who live here. I should say intelligent life.

'We have met three species, and they can communicate with each other, and oddly, with the three of us, and at Village-Ten with a ten-year-old boy who cannot speak and with his parents. We communicate in a kind of telepathy, which consists of feelings and pictures, not words. We're alive because they've accepted us as belonging here.'

'What species?'

'The megalons, terragons, *Terrakids*, and the silipusses.'

'My god. If they can think and are united, we'll have to leave.'

'There's no way you can leave, but those who can integrate as we have can live well on Tarik. The others will eventually die.

'You asked how I called my wives. I thought, "Jane, Alice, come", although it was more like projecting a feeling that I wanted them with me.

'A silipuss picked up my message and told the girls. If Jane were a thousand kilometres from here, she would have heard as the message would spread to all silipusses, and the one nearest Jane would tell her.'

'Incredible. Do you know why you can communicate with these creatures?'

'No, I first thought our Tarik food had changed our minds. Then, I thought that was ridiculous, but we might have a genetic ability dating from prehistoric times, and elements in the food stimulate those genes. As the boy and his parents have eaten Tarik food for years and have done hard physical work to survive, that might be it. I think it's more likely that the life we lead of continuous exercise and danger has woken our ability. Take your pick.'

Martha asked, 'Why do you call my son Tarzan?'

Alice answered, 'I didn't know Timothy's name until today, but Tarzan suits him better.'

Jane answered, 'I can tell you; I remembered an ancient story from Old Earth about a man called Tarzan, raised by apes in a jungle, and Tarzan's wife, Jane. I told Tim I thought he was like Tarzan, and he said, "Okay. Me Tarzan, you Jane." Only weeks later, I realised that by doing so, he cut all my fears from what I was before; they stayed with Jessica.'

'So, when you met him, Alice, he introduced himself as Tarzan?'

'No, there were no introductions. The GravEx landed. He ripped the door open, came in, shouted, "Megalon, everyone out!" and then took the emergency bag from a locker. I didn't move; I was terrified and tried to hide in a corner, so he grabbed me, threw me over his shoulder and ran. We reached a tree, he tied a rope to me, said hold on, and Jane, who I didn't know was up in the tree, hauled me up. I was even more terrified when I saw how high I was. I could see him; he had another rope but didn't climb; he just stood there while a megalon swooped and took the GravEx, and then Tarzan told a terragon to push off. He came up and helped lift me, and I heard him call her Jane, and she called him Tarzan, so I followed on. They called me Alice; I was Elisabeth before I met them.'

'I can understand that being terrifying.'

'Yes, but after he told the terragon to leave, I knew I was safe with him. It took months, but one day, I realised I was part of our trio, and we married.'

'Why the name Alice?'

'Jane proposed it, she said that Alice came from an ancient book called Alice in Wonderland and that Alice fell through a hole in a tree into a beautiful world. It explained everything peculiar, including their tails, so I felt happy!'

'What do you mean by, "he told a terragon to push off."'

'What I said. I can't explain how he did it, but now Jane and I can, too. Megalons as well.'

Martha shook her head and decided to ask Gordon.

'Gordon, the girls say they're telepaths.'

Tarzan replied, 'Mum, they are, and so am I. If you think about it, you'll say people have replaced the ability with electronic communication.'

Martha exclaimed, 'Do you mean social media?'

'Yes. You must have studied the phenomenon. Tell Dad.'

'Gordon, don't you remember that on Earth Four, we could send a message to someone, and they would send it to others?

What we called "going viral"?'

'Yes, of course.'

'Well, if Tim and the girls can send a message to each other or terragons, and they send it to others, a telepathic message is the same.'

'That's right, Mum, but with a small difference. The messages are short, and each receiver instantly forwards them to all the others in his vicinity. The receiver doesn't need to decide who to send it to.'

'Doesn't that clutter up everyone's brains?'

'No, there's no social chitchat, only messages that need action, not opinion; the ability exists for survival. Once survival became easy, humanity lost the ability.'

Then Martha asked.

'Do you sleep in one bed?'

The two girls looked at each other and grinned. Jane replied, 'Martha, I've never thought about it; of course, we do. Staying close together all the time is a survival need. And before you ask, we share him equally; it gives me pleasure to see him love Alice, and she says the same when he loves me.'

Then Alice added, 'Tarzan says making love is now safer. There's one of us on danger watch while the other two can lose themselves in each other.'

Martha grinned. 'I approve if you do, but I don't have a bed big enough for three!'

'Don't think of it. We can't sleep in a house, so we'll return to our nest and come again in the morning. I brought a bag of fruit, and Alice has three squirrels. Let's make some food for our men.'

As the women left the room, Tarzan asked, 'Dad, when you gave me my knife eight years ago, you bought three. One for me and one each for you and Mum. Do you use yours?'

'Me, hardly ever. I take a machete with me when I look for samples. Your mother never, she claims it's too big for her. She has one of the stub knives like the one I gave you.'

'Then please, give your knives to Jane and Alice; they're a lifesaver for us.'

'I'll speak to Martha; she'll love the idea.'

38

It was after their meal that Gordon asked the question Tarzan had anticipated.

'Tim, will you stay here, do a doctorate at university, or return to the forest?'

'To the forest, Dad, there's still an enormous amount to learn. I'll come and report it to you when I can. Please think of this suggestion. This colony, beside the sea, is the best place for a university research centre investigating the planet's evolution and biology. Colony One is not. Could you organise it?'

'Tim, I would say no, but I suspect just doing it would work. I'll think about it; it may be a promising idea.'

'Inform Arvak Dirovic, play the expert, Dad; make it big. All the disciplines associated with the planet's origins. Zoology, Botany, Entomology, Biology, land and marine, and others. He'll love the idea of the colony becoming famous. I'll tell him about the intelligent life and emphasise they're harmless to humans.'

Jane asked, 'Can you send a message for me and one for Alice? We want to tell our parents we're alive and invite them to visit us here.'

'Of course, I'll fetch a notebook and pencil; you can write what you want to say. Then I'll take it to comms. If you visit without an introduction, Jonas at comms will have a heart attack.'

'Tarzan, I don't know what to say. Alice, do you?'

'I'll keep it simple, Jane, but ensure they understand I can't visit them.'

> Mum, Dad, I want to see you again. I'm in Colony Nine with my husband after a long trip. I'll never fly again, so please come to see me. Elisabeth.

'That's perfect, Alice. I'll send the same.'

'Thanks, Mum, we'll return to our nest. There's still a lot that I must ask. It can wait until tomorrow.'

On reaching their nest, Tarzan asked, 'Alice, if your parents don't come, will you fly to see them?'

'I'm not leaving you. I'm returning to the forest with you. Although I want to see my parents, especially my mother – we're far more important.'

'How do you know I'm returning?'

'Where else do Tarzan, Jane and I belong?'

'Jane, do you feel the same?'

'Yes, I'll never take a GravBus. I'll keep my feet solidly anchored on a tree branch. The one that you or Alice are standing on. I've had two years of excitement with you; a village or colony has nothing to offer. I agree with Alice; they must come here to see me.'

They dropped the following morning and joined Tarzan's parents. After breakfast, Tarzan asked, 'Dad, can you and I meet with Arvak?'

'I'll arrange it.'

'One other thing, Dad, you must stop the practice of steriliz-ing boys at sixteen. Let Tarik keep the population under con-trol.'

'From things I have heard, it might have stopped already. The families with boys resist strongly.'

Martha objected, 'Although it's not the only cause, it may in-crease the problems society has with rape, gender violence, ex-ploitation of young girls, child pornography and the rest.'

After a pause, Tarzan replied, 'Mum, I can't be sure it won't. For two reasons, I don't think it will. If everyone learns to com-municate telepathically, women will sense such intentions and feelings before the men can practice them. The other reason is that many people will perceive and understand such feelings and desires. They will force such men to live alone, and they will not pass on their DNA. Their urges will no longer remain hidden and ignored; you can't conceal that kind of violence from telepaths or lie to them.'

'Dad, where will we meet with Arvak?'

'He's coming here, Tim; I sent a message. He should be here in an hour.'

Three days later, as the daylight leaked away, the trio returned to their nest, and Tarzan said, 'Girls, we seem to have started something that's now running away from us.'

Alice grinned, 'If you had asked, I would have warned you that my father might take over your research university project.'

'That pleases me, but I'm sure Jane's dad is responsible.'

'Because of the hybrid coffee he brought?'

'Yes.'

'That may be one of my dad's reasons for staying to manage the university, but I think it's because he wants to do something new.'

'The coffee may have a more significant effect than you believe; your father has already arranged with the administrator here for an offer to your parents, your mother will supply boards and paper to the university, and your father will participate in plant research.

'So, girls, we'll end up with parents in Colony Nine. We can return to the forest. How about that trip to the southern icecap?'

Jane replied. 'Tarzan, before you say anything more, Alice and I have decided on a plan.'

Puzzled, he asked, 'What?'

'We *do* want to visit the icecap. Your dad thinks we'll find birds with feathers to keep warm, but we don't want to make the journey right now. Do you remember telling Alice and me that you wanted to ensure that humans integrate and do no harm to the planet's intelligent life?'

'Yes, it seems ages ago.'

'Before I met you, I had no idea what I wanted to do, and Alice says she was the same, but now we both know. We want to make sure that what we've started continues.'

'That may take years. I doubt we can do so on our own.'

'Not on our own, Tarzan. I'm sure that Tarik wants us to do so, whether it's the planet, the forest, or collectively, all the intelligent life. Alice and I agree we can do so with Tarik and our Tarik friends helping. We reckon a year. By then, it should be evident that the momentum has built to a level that makes reversal impossible, but we can intervene if we hear of anything that needs our help.'

'Why a year?'

'Nine months pregnant, plus three months until our babies can play with kittens and travel in a chest pouch and a backpack later. Then we'll visit the icecaps.'

'Have you checked our DNA with the insemination centre?'

'Yes. Alice, you and I are unrelated. But your dad is related.'

'Why did you check his DNA?'

'Because you look like him!'

Tarzan's eyes lit up, 'He's my biological Dad? That's wonderful. I wonder if he knows?'

'Alice says he and your mother must know. They were actively involved with the insemination centre researching the fertility test and would have checked.'

Alice added, 'He's a biologist; I bet he organised it initially. That would fit with the way he insisted on sex before their marriage and what he told you.'

Tarzan's happy smile thrilled them both. 'We'll find out, and I agree with your plan. Do we start tonight?'

'Morning and night for a week, simultaneously. We're fertile. We'll make a joint effort.'

'You'll reduce me to a wreck.'

'You deserve it for ignoring us...'

Sometime later

Tarzan flew with a GravLifter to recover the remains of the crashed GravBus. Megalons guarded his flight every kilometre. He wanted the thrust engine for the first research boat on the sea. The GravLifter lowered the half GravBus hanging below it, covered in clinging vines, onto the open beach where Jane and Alice waited. The first thing Jane did was to collect the two phones.

That night, after the phones had lain on charging plates for two hours, she switched hers on, and when the screen lit up, hopefully, she spoke, 'Hello, Goggles, I'm back.'

'Hello Jane, it's been a long wait.'

About to answer, she paused. 'Tarzan, come here.'

He did, and she said, 'Switch on your phone and say hello.'

'Hello, Puss.'

'Hello Tarzan, how can I help.'

Tarzan and Jane stared at each other for over a minute, and then he said, 'Tarik has secrets we might never uncover, but we'll try.'

The two babies, a boy and a girl born on the same day had green eyes.